PROUD SORROWS

PROUD SORROWS

A Billy Boyle World War II Mystery

James R. Benn

Published by Soho Press, Inc.
227 W 17th Street
New York, NY 10011

Library of Congress Cataloging-in-Publication Data

Names: Benn, James R., author.
Title: Proud sorrows / James R. Benn.
Description: New York, NY : Soho Press, [2023]
Series: A Billy Boyle World War II mystery
Identifiers: LCCN 2023003249

ISBN 978-1-64129-415-7
eISBN 978-1-64129-416-4

Subjects: LCSH: Boyle, Billy (Fictitious character)—Fiction.
World War, 1939-1945—Fiction. | LCGFT: Detective and mystery fiction.
War fiction. | Novels. | Classification: LCC PS3602.E6644 P76 2023
DDC 813/.6—dc23/eng/20230130
LC record available at https://lccn.loc.gov/2023003249

Map: © duncan1890, iStock

Printed in the United States of America

10 9 8 7 6 5 4 3 2 1

Dedicated to my great-granddaughter
Walker Mae Countiss

Three things remain with us from paradise: stars, flowers and children.
—Dante Alighieri

I will instruct my sorrows to be proud,
For grief is proud and makes his owner stoop.

—William Shakespeare, *King John*, act 3, scene 1

PROUD
SORROWS

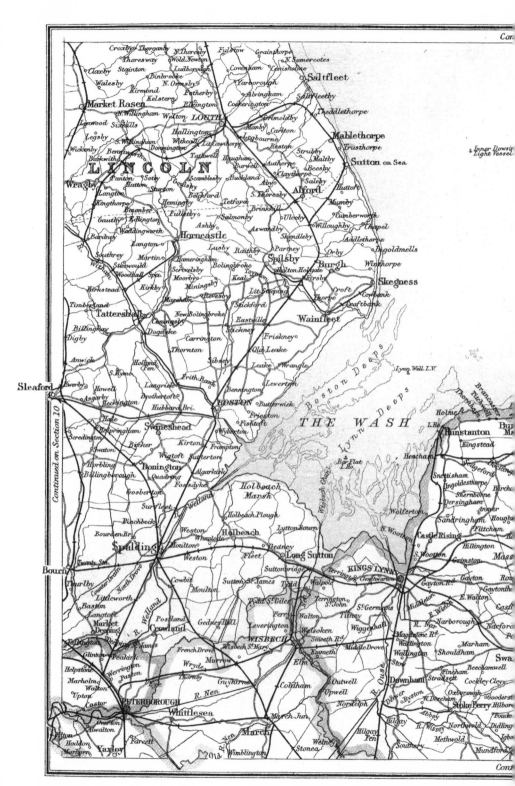

Continued on Section 10

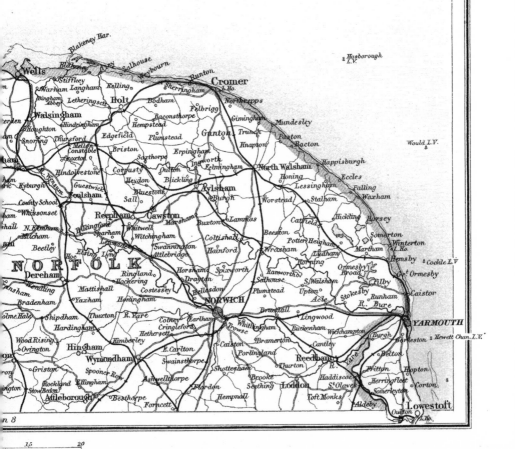

N O R T H   S E A

‡ *Dudgeon*
Light Vessel

‡ *Hasborough L.V.*

Blakeney Har.

‡ Wells Blakeney Salthouse Weybourn Runton Cromer L. Ho.
Stiffkey Kelling Sherringham
‡ Warham Langham Holt Bodham Felbrigg Northrepps
Bingham Letheringsett Baconsthorpe Gimingham Mundesley
Abbey Hempstead
Walsingham Hindringham Edgefield Plumstead Gunton Trunch Paston Would L.V. ‡
Houghton Mellon Briston Erpingham Knapton Bacton
Snoring Thursford Constable Saxthorpe Ingworth Happisburgh
Scoxton Corpusty Oulton Felmingham North Walsham Eccles
Hindolveston Heydon Blickling Honing Lessingham Falling
Ryburgh Guestwick Bluestone Aylsham Burgh Worstead Stalham Waxham
County School Foulsham Sall Hickling Horsey
Whissonset Reepham Cawston Marsham Buxton Lammas Catfield Somerton
N. Elmham Billingford Whitwell Witchingham Coltishall Beeston Potter Heigham Winterton L. Ho.
Mileham Sharham Swannington Hainford Wroxham Ludham Martham Hemsby ‡ Cockle L.V.
Beetley Elsing Lyng Attlebridge Horning Ormesby Gt. Ormesby
NORFOLK Ringland Horsham Spixworth Ranworth S. Walsham Runham Caistor
Dereham Hockering Drayton Salhouse Stokesby R. Bure
Wendling Mattishall Costessey Hellasdon Plumstead Upton Acle YARMOUTH
Bradenham Yaxham Heningham NORWICH Brundall Lingwood Burgh
Holme Hale Shipdham Thuxton R. Yare Colney Earlham Whitlingham Buckenham Wichampton Garleston ‡ Hewett Chan. L.V.
Hardingham Cringleford Bowse Bramerton Cantley Belton
Wood Rising Hingham Hethersett Caiston Portinland Thurton Britton Hopton
Ovington Kimberley E. Carlton Reedham R. Yare Corton
Wymondham Swainsthorpe Shottesham Haddiscoe Herringfleet
Griston Spooner Row Brooke Loddon St Olaves Somerleyton
Rockland Ellingham Ashwellthorpe Flordon Seething Toft Monks Aldeby
Snow Bedon Besthorpe Hempnall LOWESTOFT
Attleborough Forncett Oulton L. Ho.

N 8

15   20

MAY 1942

IT BEGAN AS a glow in the night sky, a faint flicker barely visible in the swirling, low clouds and pelting rain. Stephen Elliot saw it as he shut the door behind him and made for his automobile. Marston Hall sat on a hill, with a commanding view of the valley and the flight path of the aircraft. Elliot shielded his eyes from the spitting rain and watched the flames on their descent, calculating exactly where metal would meet ground.

In his surgery, John Bodkin heard the growl of the engine. Instinctively, he looked up, as if to gauge the distance, but quickly returned to finish stitching a farmer's arm. A nasty cut, but clean enough.

Agnes Day, who had received the message that her assistance was needed, risked a look skyward as she pedaled toward the doctor's surgery. The aircraft was close enough to make out the burning portside engine. German, probably. She shuddered, fearful of a sudden crash, of bombs and death, of Germans in their midst, of torn bodies and shrieking men demanding care.

She'd had enough of that in London.

Sir Richard Seaton had been checking on the horses. As he shut the barn door, he followed the arc of light, little more than an indistinct glimmer from where he stood. Still, he knew it was dangerous. His eyes flitted across Seaton Manor, looking for telltale lines of illumination at the edges of blackout curtains.

Nothing. Though the building was as dark and quiet as the Norfolk countryside, worry gnawed at him.

Inside the aircraft—a Heinkel He 111 bomber—flames shot sporadically into the cockpit as the pilot struggled with the controls. Screams pierced the air, louder even than the roar of the engines. The dorsal gunner was badly wounded. The two other gunners had patched him up as best they could before the pilot ordered them to bail out. The navigator was moaning, his head lolling as he held his belly. Wind whistled through the shattered canopy as the pilot tried to ignore the blood pooling in his boot. All he wanted was to find a patch of ground before it found him. They'd never make it back across the North Sea. A night landing in a storm was their only hope.

On the ground below, there was no hint of the agonies they suffered.

Alfred Bunch held the blackout curtain open for his wife, Mildred, as they left the pub. The wind nearly took his cap, and he pulled it on tight as he cocked his head to find the source of the droning sound growing ever closer. Mildred pointed and asked if the light was a shooting star, but Alfred gauged it as something more sinister. They hurried, watching over their shoulders as the glow dropped lower and seemed to follow them.

Father Noel Tanner, at his evening prayers, heard the crippled aircraft overhead. He sighed, said *amen*, rose, and reached for his boots. The living and the dead might be in need of what comfort he could give.

David Archer huddled at the foot of an oak, his hands pressed over his ears to shut out the blaring noise of death. It haunted him, even in the grove of trees perched on a hilltop overlooking the chalk cliffs and the sea. He came here at night for the quiet, the quiet that had never settled over the blasted ground of no-man's-land in the last war. Now, his silent refuge was shattered; the burning aircraft dropped from the sky and drew his gaze as the space between hurtling metal and hard ground narrowed into nothingness.

Archer pressed his face against the oak, and rubbed his cheek on the rough bark, the warm blood soothing in the darkness.

Throughout the village, eyes turned skyward at the sound. A child asked if she should make a wish, but was shushed and told to get back in bed. The war had come to Slewford, and everyone who eyed the crippled bomber hoped it would keep on going. Out to sea or back to Germany, if need be, but away from here.

Graham Cheatwood stood at his third-floor bedroom window. He watched Stephen Elliot stop and gaze at the sky, then drive away. He searched for what the man had been looking at and spotted it. A voice beckoned him to come back to bed, but he knew that wasn't going to happen.

He picked up the telephone and barked out an order. Then he threw on his uniform and watched the slow descent of the aircraft as it vanished behind a hilltop close to the cliffs above the sea. Then, there was nothing but the motionless reflection of flames in the fog.

CHAPTER ONE

November 1944

ANGELIKA STOOD AT the top of the stairs, her mouth set in a tight-lipped grimace. Dull, gray light filtered in from a large window behind her as slivers of rain beat against the glass. Next to her, Agnes Day placed her hand on Angelika's elbow.

"No," Angelika said in little more than a whisper. "I must do this."

Agnes nodded, took a half step back, and clasped her hands in front of her pale-blue nurse's uniform. She gave Angelika the briefest smile of encouragement.

"This is too soon," Kaz muttered, staring up at his sister. "And there are too many of us. It is bound to make her nervous. Step back, Billy."

"Stop worrying, Piotr," Angelika said. "I like the audience. If I fall, you will all cushion my landing."

"Don't you dare talk of falling, deary," Mrs. Rutledge said, shaking her finger. "Just come down so I can get myself back to work. Dinner won't cook itself, mind you."

Mrs. Rutledge spoke her words sharply, but I saw a quiver in her lips as she finished. She was worried. We all were.

"Very well," Angelika said, holding on to the banister with one hand as she stepped off on her good leg, leaving all her weight on her right leg, where her calf was swathed in bandages. She wavered for a second, and Agnes reached out but caught herself, allowing Angelika to navigate the steep staircase on her own.

Which was how she wanted it.

"This is foolish, Baron," whispered Dr. John Bodkin from behind us. "There's no need."

"Angelika feels she must do it," Kaz said, not looking back at the local MD. "Which is need enough for me."

Angelika brought her injured leg down to meet her good one. She let go of the banister and took a deep breath. One step down, twenty to go.

She put her good foot on the next step, then brought down the other, her hand trailing on the polished wooden banister. It was a slow process, and I wondered if she might give up and retreat to her bedroom, where she'd been recovering from surgeries under the watchful eye of Agnes Day.

Proper surgeries, the kind that healed wounds instead of inflicted them.

Angelika was recovering from a Nazi concentration camp and brutal medical experiments. Recovering from dangerous resistance activities with the Polish Home Army.

Recovering from the loss of her family.

Angelika had survived all that, so I shouldn't have been surprised when she took the next two steps, one after the other, leaving the hesitancy of an invalid behind. Two more, then she rested for a moment, puffed breath from her cheeks, and let go of the banister. She descended the stairs, hands swishing at her sides, ruffling the fabric of the vibrant red dress she'd selected for her debut.

Mrs. Rutledge pressed a handkerchief to her cheeks, wiping away tears. Agnes rushed down the stairs and put her arm across Angelika's shoulder, pulling her close. Angelika beamed and took the left hand offered by Sir Richard Seaton.

"Congratulations, Angelika," Sir Richard said, squeezing her hand and grinning broadly. His right sleeve was pinned up; the arm was a casualty of a naval battle in the last war. He had pure white hair and a neatly trimmed beard—there was something nautical about him even on dry land. "You've done well."

"I owe it to all of you," Angelika said, scanning the assembly. "But especially Mr. Hamilton."

"My pleasure, Miss Kazimierz," Ian Hamilton said, taking her hand in his. His fingers were long and supple, perfect for the delicate handling of a surgeon's blade. He had a hawklike face and graying hair slicked back from a widow's peak. "I had no doubt you would recuperate quickly."

"I only hope you do not move too quickly in this recovery," Dr. Bodkin said, avoiding Hamilton's gaze. "Rest is your friend, not exertion."

"Come, come, Bodkin," Sir Richard said. "You are cautious by nature, I know, but at least admit Hamilton's surgery was the right thing to do." There was an edge to Sir Richard's words, a barely hidden harshness that led me to wonder what grudge there might have been between the two men. Slewford was a small village, and as the only doctor, Bodkin was sure to have crossed paths with Sir Richard and his family.

"Surgery was needed, indeed," Bodkin said, watching as Hamilton spoke softly with Angelika and kneeled to gently check the bandages on her calf. "And I am in your debt, Sir Richard, for taking Agnes on as her nurse."

Bodkin stood straight, arms behind his back and his chin jutting forward, as if acknowledging this debt cost him more than he wished to show.

"Not at all," Sir Richard said, looking relieved at the chance to let the undercurrent of tension fade away. "It worked out well for all. We needed the help, Mrs. Rutledge and I, as well as Angelika."

"It's done wonders for Agnes," Bodkin said as the others headed for the sitting room.

"How so?" I asked. I'd only been at Seaton Manor for two days, and although I'd heard Sir Richard had arranged nursing care for Angelika, I knew next to nothing about Agnes Day, other than that she and Angelika had grown close.

"Agnes is from Slewford," Bodkin said, brushing back his thick gray hair. He stood tall and looked firm, probably from bicycling around Slewford to visit his patients. "She went off to London for her nurse's training at St. Matthew's Hospital in Shoreditch. That was in 1939. Just a child, she was. She worked during the Blitz, saw the worst of it, horrible things. Then she joined the Royal Army Nursing Corps."

"And witnessed the horrors of war in France and Holland," Sir Richard said. "It was time for her to come home."

"She was shattered," Bodkin said. "In spirit." The two men glanced at each other, briefly nodding in agreement, and moved off to join the others. Whatever divided them, they shared similar feelings about Agnes Day.

I stood at the edge of the group, watching Kaz hover over his sister while Bodkin and Hamilton continued to spar over the benefits of rest versus physical activity. I caught Agnes rolling her eyes once, but I couldn't tell which side of the debate she came down on. She didn't say much but kept a careful watch over Angelika while the medical terms flew.

I couldn't imagine what Agnes and other nurses like her had endured. The German bombs falling on London every night overloaded the hospitals, which were often struck themselves. Going from tending injured civilians to treating wounded soldiers was nothing more than trading one level of hell for another.

"Billy, isn't she remarkable?" Kaz asked after he extricated himself from the conversation. "I can't believe she's really here, safe and in such good hands."

"She's a Kazimierz." I placed my hand on Kaz's shoulder. "She's tough."

"And lucky," Kaz said. "If she hadn't been released from that camp, she would likely be dead by now."

Angelika Kazimierz had been a courier with the Polish Underground. She'd been picked up in a sweep and sent to Ravensbrück, a Nazi concentration camp for women, where she was put to work building components for the V-2 rockets that were even now hitting London. Not long after her arrival, she was earmarked for medical experiments. She'd suffered through one horrific surgery on her leg before her release was engineered through the Swedish Red Cross.

Surgery isn't even the right word for what the Nazi doctors had done. It was torture. They'd ripped open her calf and cut out muscle, inserting wood splinters to test reactions to infections. She'd come to us hobbling on her bad leg and in constant pain.

Sir Richard had offered his home for her recuperation, which was why we were all here. Kaz and I had been offered a ten-day leave after our last job, and the peaceful village of Slewford was the perfect spot.

Except for the temporary absence of Diana Seaton, Sir Richard's daughter and Angelika's fellow prisoner in Ravensbrück. Diana was the woman I loved, and the main reason I was spending my leave here. It was a long-overdue leave after back-to-back missions.

Diana had been released, along with Angelika, after a mercifully brief imprisonment of a few weeks in that hellhole. She'd taken some time to recover but was soon back at work with the Special Operations Executive. The SOE was the British spy and sabotage outfit that operated behind enemy lines, but this last mission was a humanitarian venture in liberated areas of France, distributing funds to the families of those *résistants* who had been killed working with SOE agents.

She should have been home on leave by now, but she was stuck in London, accounting for every franc that she'd handed out on that last job. The brass can be cavalier about sending you off to get your brains blown out, but they take their detailed reports about the dispensing of gold coins as seriously as a Boston Brahmin banker.

As if he were reading my mind, Sir Richard appeared at my side.

"I'll make a call to the Admiralty," he said, smiling as he watched Angelika. "See what the holdup is. Damned bureaucrats." Although he was retired from the service, Sir Richard was still involved in government work. Secret stuff, which seemed to run in the family.

"Thanks," I said, knowing he wanted Diana home as much as I did. We were both nervous that she'd find a way back into the war. She'd beaten the odds too many times to risk her life again. Hell, the war was almost over, according to some, so this was no time for heroics. "I'm sure he's very qualified, but if you don't mind my asking, do you have confidence in Dr. Hamilton?"

"It's Mr. Hamilton, Billy. For some reason lost to me, British surgeons are not addressed as doctor. Point of pride or some such," Sir Richard said. "But yes, I have every confidence in Ian Hamilton. Have had ever since he cut off what was left of this arm while my cruiser burned during the Battle of Jutland. Hamilton has a good mind and a steady hand. I'd trust him with my life."

"And Dr. Bodkin?"

"He can set a bone well enough, and helped Agnes when she first came back, which speaks well of him. Gave her what work he could, enough to give her a sense of purpose, but nothing too demanding," Sir Richard said. "Now I'll see if I can get through to London and find out where Diana is. She's done more than her bit, hasn't she?"

Sir Richard didn't wait for an answer. All I had to do was look around at Angelika, Agnes, Kaz, and my own reflection in the window. We'd all done our bit and then some, but there would be more demanded of us, even if the war was over by Christmas. *Out the door in '44* was the saying making the rounds, although *Home alive in '45* was the new, and perhaps more realistic, wish.

Dr. Bodkin laughed at something Agnes said, and Hamilton joined in, their professional disagreement set aside.

He can set a bone well enough.

Talk about damning a man with faint praise. But maybe it was meant well, since a village doctor in the Norfolk countryside would need to know his way around broken bones.

But that wasn't any of my concern. All I wanted was to wait for good news from Diana while sitting by a warm fire with a whiskey. I was on leave, even if it was with three old men, a traumatized nurse, a barely mobile patient, and her doting brother—who did nothing but worry about her or brag about her, depending on his ever-changing mood. Not to mention being in the middle of nowhere with nothing but one cramped, smoky pub for entertainment.

I found the drinks cart in the library and sat myself down with a measure of Sir Richard's good whiskey. The coals in the fireplace were banked, barely keeping the autumn chill out of the room, but I knew I shouldn't complain. I was dry and no one was shooting at me.

I thought about writing a letter home and decided it was a good idea. After all, this was a leave only a mother could love.

CHAPTER TWO

"I SEE YOU are a headquarters man, Captain Boyle," Ian Hamilton said as he helped himself to a whiskey and sat across from me, stretching his legs toward the warmth of the fireplace. "That shoulder patch is General Eisenhower's unit, is it not?"

"Yes. SHAEF," I said. I wore the flaming sword patch of the Supreme Headquarters, Allied Expeditionary Force, and I was proud of it. Did I detect a hint of disdain in Hamilton's voice at the notion of an able-bodied man being deskbound, even in the service of General Eisenhower? There was only so much I could say about the work we did. "I'm with the Office of Special Investigations, along with Kaz." I took another drink and stared at Hamilton over the rim of my glass.

"Yes, I know," he said. "I didn't mean to cast any aspersion, Captain Boyle. I've heard your name often enough from Sir Richard to know he respects you and the baron. I don't know the details, but I can see you two are no paper pushers. Diana certainly wouldn't give you the time of day if you were."

"You've known the family for some years?" I asked.

"Oh, yes. After that business at Jutland, I stayed in touch with Seaton. Not hard, since I'm based in Cambridge, south of here. Knew his wife—who sadly died far too young—and Daphne, of course. Poor dear."

"She was terrific," I said. "She and Kaz took me under their wings when I first arrived in London. I met Diana through them.

Daphne's death was a real shock." I'd never been able to shake
the notion that I was partly responsible for what had happened.
More than two years had passed, but I could still see Daphne
waving to me as she and Kaz headed for her Riley Imp two-
seater.

"It nearly broke Sir Richard," Hamilton said, shaking me out
of the crystal clear memory. "I understand the baron was left
scarred, and I don't mean that wound to his face."

"He was in bad shape for a while," I said. The same explosion
that had killed Daphne had left Kaz with a long scar from the
corner of one eye to his chin. I didn't mention that he'd courted
death a dozen times or so before he turned a corner and decided
to live, or at least not throw his life away. He was a dead shot
with his Webley revolver, but there had been days I wouldn't have
been surprised if he'd turned it on himself. "But now that he has
Angelika, it's a different story. He has hope."

"Well, I'm glad I could help," Hamilton said. "I'll check in on
her again in a week or so to see how she's progressing. Those
bastards did a lot of damage with that one operation. She was
damned lucky to get out when she did."

"What was their purpose?" I asked. "Torture?"

"They'd call it research, the bastards," Hamilton said, his lip
rising in a sneer of disgust. "Creating wounds to simulate battlefield injuries and experiment with different treatments. My first
surgery was simply to clean out the wood splinters they'd inserted
and to deal with the muscle damage."

"So what was this second one about? Kaz said something
about neuromas, but I didn't quite get it," I said.

"Angelika had manifested a traumatic neuroma," Hamilton
said. "A swelling of the nerves as a result of damage during surgery. Neuromas occur at the terminus of injured nerve fibers
when the body attempts to repair itself, but the process goes
wrong and a painful tumor develops, usually at the site of the
original incision, which was the case with Angelika."

"The operation was a success?" I asked.

"Yes, it was straightforward. The important thing now is for Angelika to keep using her calf muscles and regain what strength she can. I don't believe in bed rest in a case like this. It will result only in reduced mobility over time," Hamilton said.

"Dr. Bodkin doesn't agree," I said, finishing off my whiskey.

"He's a fine country doctor." Hamilton turned his gaze to the rain-streaked window. "Quite a blow brewing up, isn't it?"

Hamilton had given me my cue to drop that line of questioning. I guess doctors and surgeons might argue with each other but would still close ranks when it came to outsiders butting in.

A tree branch blew against the window, and I realized he wasn't just making conversation. The storm was freshening, blowing in from the North Sea with nothing much to stop it.

"One more question, Mr. Hamilton," I said as I stood for a better view out the window. "Will Angelika recover?"

"Physically? Yes. Her calf will be scarred for life, and she may never lose a slight limp, but she should be fine if she follows my instructions," Hamilton said. "The threat of infection and other complications has passed. She is young, Captain Boyle. She has a very good nurse, and Sir Richard is dedicated to her care. Bodkin is close by as well. All this argues for a chance at a recovery few girls in that Nazi camp could ever dream of. But she may still throw all that away. Are you aware she desperately wants to join the Special Operations Executive?"

"No, I wasn't." Now it was my turn to shut down the conversation. "It's nearly dinnertime, isn't it?"

I needed time to think this through. If Angelika got mixed up with the SOE, they'd send her to occupied Poland in a heartbeat. If the Gestapo got a hold of her, the black dog of depression would be at Kaz's throat once again.

If he lost her a second time, it would be the last time.

For both of them.

"Yes. Excuse me—I must check on Angelika before she comes down." Hamilton rose from his chair. "Her stitches come out in two days, and I want to be certain the incision is perfectly healed."

"Is that the kind of thing Dr. Bodkin could do for her?" I asked, curious as to how Hamilton would reply.

"Perhaps, but he has departed. Dr. Bodkin does not dine at Seaton Manor," Hamilton said as he left, his voice flat, offering nothing but the bare truth: Dr. John Bodkin was regarded well enough to serve as a backup in terms of basic medical care, but not well enough to sit at Sir Richard's table.

Why? Not that it mattered to me, but curiosity is the curse of any decent cop, and my dad and Uncle Dan, both detectives with the Boston Police Department, had drummed that into my thick Irish skull on many occasions. *Always wonder why things happen*, they'd say. *Figure things out, even little things.* It's good practice for when the real thing comes along. I'd seen plenty of the real deal since my days as a rookie cop before the war, but it was still solid advice. Besides, there was little entertainment to be had in these parts, so I might as well puzzle this one out until Diana was cut loose by the bookkeeper's brigade.

I STOOD IN front of the fire, staring at the coals, until raised voices and the slamming of the front door drew me into the main hallway.

"Oh, my dear, what a night!" exclaimed a woman as she handed Sir Richard an umbrella that had been thoroughly defeated by the wind. "It's beastly."

"I rang you, Charlotte, to ask if you'd rather not come out," Sir Richard said, "but you had already left."

"It would take a heavier gale than this to keep me away," she said as Sir Richard helped her out of her dripping coat. As soon as she was free of it, her eyes drilled into me. "This must be the American lad we've heard so much about."

"Charlotte Mothersole, this is Captain William Boyle," Sir Richard said. "Mrs. Mothersole is a good friend of the family, and I thought Angelika would enjoy some more female company."

"We've heard so much about all of you," Mrs. Mothersole said. "It's wonderful that the poor girl is well enough to meet people, even country mice like us. And you, Captain Boyle! I can see why Diana goes on about you!"

"Don't you believe half of what she says, Mrs. Mothersole. And, please, call me Billy."

"I love Americans, don't you, Sir Richard? So direct and informal. It would take an Englishman ten years to offer up his given name, let alone a diminutive, but here we are! You must call me Charlotte, Billy," she said, linking her arm in mine as we went into the dining room. Charlotte Mothersole was around forty or so, and probably more *or so* than forty. She wore an elegant cream-colored dress with a slim matching jacket, and she didn't look much like a country mouse.

As we moved through the foyer, Hamilton came downstairs and announced that Angelika was doing very well, better than expected, and would be down shortly. Sir Richard introduced Charlotte, and Agnes came down, having changed out of her nursing uniform into a floral-print dress.

"Agnes, darling, so nice to have you back with us," Charlotte said, taking her by the hands. "It's been far too long, and I can't imagine what you went through. But no more of that—let's simply have ourselves a delightful evening, shall we?"

"I hope so," Agnes said. "How have you been, Mrs. Mothersole?"

Charlotte didn't have a chance to answer. Sir Richard gasped, and our heads turned to the top of the stairs. Angelika stood with Kaz at her side, and together they descended. Kaz looked dashing in his tailored British Army uniform, brass buttons gleaming, and the leather belt buffed to a glow.

Angelika wore a dress of deep blue, prewar by the cut of it, with enough ruffles and fabric to make two of the utility dresses allowed these days due to clothes rationing. A sapphire pin and broad smile completed the outfit.

"Shall we?" Sir Richard said, his voice breaking as he gestured for us to go through. He turned away, hiding his face and heaving a great sigh.

"They're Daphne's dress and jewels," Charlotte whispered as we entered the room. "He's a stern man, but Richard Seaton's never gotten over her death. Thank God Diana made it home."

I didn't argue with that. We mingled a bit, waiting for Sir Richard to pull himself together. There must have been many times he'd looked up at that staircase and watched Daphne come down in that very dress. This must have been like seeing a ghost. Kaz had mentioned Mrs. Rutledge going through Daphne's clothes to outfit Angelika, but I hadn't considered the effect of this ensemble on Sir Richard.

Agnes stepped in to introduce Angelika to Mrs. Mothersole, who cooed over her and congratulated her on her excellent English.

"It was my father's wish that we make England our home," Angelika said. "He prepared us well, but the war came sooner than anyone expected." The rest of Kaz's family had been wiped out by the Nazis soon after the invasion. He'd learned only recently that Angelika had survived and gone into hiding before working as a courier with the Polish Home Army. When the war had broken out, Kaz was studying at Oxford. His father had managed to transfer the family fortune out of Poland and into Swiss bank accounts. Whatever the future held, Kaz and Angelika didn't have to worry about where their next meal was coming from.

Kaz kept a suite at the Dorchester Hotel in London, the same room in which his family had gathered on a visit the year before the war. The war that came more suddenly than Kaz's father had ever imagined, trapping him and the rest of the family in defeated Poland.

Sir Richard rejoined us, his face a mask. We sat at the long table, Sir Richard at the head and Kaz and Angelika on either side. Charlotte and Hamilton faced each other, with Agnes and me at the tail end.

"To a full recovery," Sir Richard said, raising his glass. "I know Daphne would've been so happy to share her clothes with you, Angelika."

"I am honored, Sir Richard," Angelika said. "I hope this does not awaken too many unhappy memories."

"The war does that on its own," Sir Richard said. "So we must make our own happy memories."

We readily drank to that.

"Now, you all must forgive me," Mrs. Rutledge said, bustling in from the kitchen. "I sent our two girls home when that wind started up. Didn't want them drenched and blown away on their bicycles."

"A wise precaution," Sir Richard said. "We are in no hurry, Mrs. Rutledge."

The wine was passed around and glasses were topped off as Mrs. Rutledge brought in the dishes one by one. Lamb chops with boiled potatoes, parsnip, and roasted carrots. Root vegetables from the ample garden out back and, judging by the number of sheep I'd seen, a local farmer's chops. Country mice certainly ate better than city mice when it came to rationing.

Mrs. Rutledge served Sir Richard last, and I noticed that the chops on his plate had been perfectly cut into bite-size pieces and reassembled along the bone. The perfect presentation for a one-armed man.

"Some more good news before we begin this delicious meal," Sir Richard said, raising his glass once again. "Diana will be home in the morning. She's finished with the accountants and will be on the night train from London."

"Wonderful!" Angelika said, laughing like a schoolgirl, which was basically what she was. It was infectious, and we all joined in.

"Your assignment, Billy, is to pick her up at the station in King's Lynn, seven o'clock sharp," Sir Richard said, as thunder rumbled and lightning crackled in the sky.

"Maybe I should leave now," I said, and in the merriment, everyone thought that was hilarious as well.

Kaz offered to come along, and Angelika insisted on joining, but I declined both offers. Hamilton agreed and said Angelika should keep her leg dry until the bandages came off. Kaz realized he'd be a third wheel and dropped it. Diana and I had been together for a while in Southern France when our overlapping missions allowed. But this was going to be different. No war, no investigations, at least for a few days. I wanted to make the most of it.

"Billy," Kaz said, getting my attention. My mind had wandered, thinking about Diana. He nodded to Charlotte, who'd been trying to talk to me.

"I said, if you'd like to meet some fellow Americans, you should come to Marston Hall," Charlotte repeated.

"I'm sorry, you have Americans at your home?" I asked.

"Well, the ownership of Marston Hall is somewhat complicated," Charlotte said. "It is owned by my brother. I live on the grounds, in Marston Cottage."

"A very nice cottage," Agnes chimed in.

"Thank you, dear. When my brother, Stephen Elliot, went missing," Charlotte said, waving her hand as if dismissing his disappearance as no more than an annoyance, "the British Army took over Marston Hall and shunted me off to the cottage. They started up with a lot of hush-hush stuff, then brought in the Americans last year. Now it's hush-hush-husher, but I'm sure they'd welcome General Eisenhower's nephew."

"What? I am impressed, Captain Boyle," Hamilton said. "I'd

no idea you were related to the general. He's no Montgomery but seems to be doing a fine job."

"That's true," I said, keeping my thoughts about the British general to myself. "General Eisenhower is a distant relative, on my mother's side. But I don't think that will get me into a top secret establishment." I also had zero interest in whatever was happening at Marston Hall. Secrets are best kept secret.

"Billy and his Uncle Ike are quite close," Kaz said. I caught the corner of his mouth rising in a smirk, and I knew he was having his fun. Ike—okay, Uncle Ike—was a distant cousin as far as I could figure. But since he was a generation older, it was always *Uncle Ike* . . . and only when we were alone. He'd brought me on board when he first came to England in 1942 and wanted a trained detective to investigate various crimes that had to be kept quiet for the sake of the war effort.

Sometimes keeping things quiet got very loud.

Luckily, the conversation turned in a different direction. Hamilton asked, as delicately as he could, where Stephen Elliot had been reported missing.

"Oh, well, it wasn't quite like that," Charlotte said. "It wasn't on a battlefield. One day he was here, still living at Marston Hall, as I was. A small contingent of soldiers was in place already, and the army was about to take the whole place over for the duration. Anyway, the next day, he was simply gone."

"That's terrible," Angelika said. "You've never had word from him?"

"Nothing," Charlotte said. The table went quiet, and I sensed that a lot was not being said.

"Was he in the service?" I asked, just to say something.

"He was—is, I mean—a lieutenant. Royal Corps of Signals. Fought in North Africa," Sir Richard said. "He was home recovering from shrapnel wounds and was nearly ready to report back to his unit. There was never any talk of him shirking his duty, none at all."

"Richard, there's no need." Charlotte set down her glass hard enough for the red wine to slosh over the side. "Really."

"Fine." He held up his hand in surrender. Back to silence.

"What goes on in Marston Hall?" Kaz said after a long ten seconds or so. "You must have some sense, living on the grounds."

"Don't you know?" Charlotte said, looking around the table. "They've Germans up there. Nazis, coming and going all the time. Loads of them."

We were back to silence again, except for thunder in the distance, rumbling like a barrage creeping over the battlefield.

CHAPTER THREE

"I MUST APOLOGIZE for Charlotte," Sir Richard said later that night. "I had no idea she would blurt that out."

"Angelika was shaken," Kaz replied. We were hoisting a nightcap in the library at the invitation of Sir Richard, who obviously felt guilty about the bombshell Charlotte Mothersole had dropped. "Having Germans in such close proximity came as a shock, no matter how securely they're locked up."

"Yes, it was the last thing she would have expected, I know," Sir Richard said. "I planned on telling her when she was ready to leave the house. I saw no reason to bring it up sooner. I wish I had."

"I assume it's an open secret in Slewford?" I asked.

"Just part of the scenery by now," Sir Richard said. "They started bringing high-profile POWs here in early 1942. The villagers were happy enough to know we were capturing Germans at all, so there was little complaining. The arrival of the American contingent caused more of a stir, if truth be told."

"This doesn't sound like a regular POW camp," I said.

"No. Prisoners are brought here for interrogation, then shipped out, mostly to the United States. Marston Hall deals in high-value prisoners," Sir Richard explained. "They are of all ranks. What is important is what's stored in their brains. Technical or economic data. Political information. Military plans. They're sorted out in POW cages and sent on to Marston Hall and some other similar facilities. Then the expert interrogators have a go at them."

"You seem to know a lot about this, Sir Richard," Kaz said, eyeing our host. "How exactly was Marston Hall selected?"

"I know many things, Baron," he said, with a half smile. "Now I will say good night. Billy has an early start. By the way, the weather will begin to clear soon. It should be a fine morning, as many are after a big blow."

As we went upstairs, Kaz reminded me that weather forecasts were not broadcast on the BBC, since they would only help the Germans. That Sir Richard knew the morning forecast with such certainty proved he had the connections to make things happen. Why he'd want a bunch of Nazis on his doorstep, I had no idea. But I was glad the sun would be shining when I met Diana at the train station.

MRS. RUTLEDGE WAS up early and had a plate of warm buttered bread waiting for me. After a quick bite and a cup of Uncle Sam's coffee—I'd brought as much coffee and sugar as I could lay my hands on—I headed out the door and started the jeep.

I had to hand it to Sir Richard—he had the inside track on the weather. The sun was rising into a blue sky, and a light breeze was cascading across the fields. The smell of damp, fertile soil rose from the earth as long shadows stretched across the road, offering the promise of a good day.

There weren't many of those in this war, and I was ready for this one. By the time I pulled in front of the glazed brick railroad station in King's Lynn, it was warm enough to toss my mackinaw in the rear seat. I brushed my trousers and tugged at my Ike jacket, making sure I looked as good as I could in my new pinks and greens, courtesy of Kaz's Savile Row tailor.

"Billy!"

Diana Seaton burst out of the station and ran down the steps, her canvas rucksack swinging from her shoulder. We collided rather than embraced, twirling each other around until we were a mix of laughing khaki madness, drawing smiles from the other departing passengers. Everybody loves a wartime reunion.

We kissed, and for a moment we were a stone in a swift-moving current as people scurried around us, heading for their own special destinations.

Ours was right here, in each other's arms.

"Tell me all the news, Billy," Diana said as she stuffed her pack and trench coat into the back. "How is Angelika?"

"The surgeries went well, at least according to Hamilton," I said. "Angelika is practically skipping down the stairs. But first, tell me what happened. Those bureaucrats didn't suspect you of theft, did they?"

"No, worse than that." Diana laughed as I pulled out onto the road. "Those idiots were worried I'd given gold to communists. Can you believe it?"

"Somebody got a bee in their bonnet over that? Most of the Resistance was Red. Hell, we send boatloads of supplies to the Soviets, and SOE is worried about a few gold pieces?"

"It wasn't SOE. Apparently, some very conservative members of Parliament didn't like the idea of the French Communist Party organizing itself after the war using our gold," she said. "They are probably worried British workers might follow suit."

"They're worried about the gold coins you gave to families? Families who lost people to the Nazis after they helped SOE agents? Crazy," I said.

"Sadly, it makes sense. Some of those politicians were among the appeasers before the war. But let's forget all that for now. I'm here with you, and it's a lovely day," Diana said, stretching as much as was possible in the passenger seat of a US Army jeep and loosening the tie of her FANY uniform.

"Hey, you got a promotion," I said.

"Yes, I'm a captain now, Billy, just like you." Diana tapped the three pips on her shoulder boards. "You no longer outrank me."

"Congratulations. You deserve it," I said. "Does this mean you'll be stationed in London?"

"I didn't ask. Didn't care. I only wanted to get home," she said. I was fine not talking about the SOE, since I didn't know if Diana knew about Angelika's plan to join up. Or what my reaction would be if she did know. "Now, tell me more about Angelika . . . and Father . . . and Mrs. Rutledge."

"Mrs. Rutledge is preparing a breakfast feast for your homecoming. Angelika is in good spirits, and Hamilton says there should be no lasting effects other than the scars and a slight limp," I said. "Kaz hovers over her like a nervous nanny, which she bears with great patience."

"She has an inner strength," Diana said. "Angelika is much like her brother: smart and passionate. Tell me, how is my father bearing up with two more women in the house?"

"He seems genuinely happy to be doing it," I said. I told Diana about his reaction to seeing Angelika in Daphne's dress.

"Yes, I can see how that would be painful and wonderful at the same time," she said. "I've thought about it too—about having another sister. After what we went through together, it's easy to think of Angelika that way. Oh, I wish Daphne could have met her. They're so much alike, you know? Young, determined, quite intelligent. Of course, Daphne shall always be young, even as we grow old. Timeless."

I glanced at Diana. She was blinking back tears, and I knew enough of her steely upper lip resolve to allow her a moment to collect herself.

"Do you think your father might regret taking Angelika in?" I asked as I slowed to take a narrow curve.

"No. He needs company, Billy. Since the war began, he's had little of that. Some youthful energy is what he requires. How is Agnes getting on?"

"She and Angelika appear to get along, and Agnes keeps an eye on her," I said. "She's fairly quiet. I hear she went through a lot during the Blitz and in France."

"She worked in London during the worst of it," Diana said. "She saw more blood and bone in one year than most nurses see in a lifetime. She came back to Slewford for a while but then signed on with the army and worked in field hospitals, first in Malta, then France. Father said she suffered from nervous exhaustion and was invalided out. She seemed fine when I last saw her, but who knows what memories and visions come to her in the night?"

"Well, she has a good job in a comfortable house, although I don't know how long Angelika will need a nurse at this point. Does Agnes have family close by?"

"None that I know of," Diana said. "Her father died before she was born, I think. And her mother in childbirth. She had to go live with an aunt about ten miles distant. She'd often bicycle to Slewford when she was older. She never said, but I got the notion her uncle wasn't happy having another mouth to feed. She stayed close to Dr. Bodkin, as I recall. Perhaps that's why she went to nursing school as soon as she could."

"I've met some other distinguished residents of Slewford," I said, slowing as a truck pulled out in front of us. "Charlotte Mothersole came to dinner last night. She's a lively one."

"Dear Charlotte. Such fun at a party, although I'd hate to be her the morning after. But a charming woman. Father thought she'd help with the female conversation, I'd guess?"

"Close to it," I said. "But Charlotte dropped the bombshell about the Germans at Marston Hall. You never mentioned high-ranking Nazis passing through Slewford, not that I recall anyway."

"No, I must not have," Diana said. "It was drummed into us from the beginning to keep mum about it. They were bringing them in when you first visited Seaton Manor. That was more than two years ago. We had other things on our mind, if you recall, Billy. When I visited you in your room, it wasn't to discuss POWs. Who else have you met?"

"Other than Dr. Bodkin? No one," I said, smiling at the memory.

"John Bodkin was invited to father's house?"

"He was there with Ian Hamilton. Sort of a handoff from the surgeon to the local sawbones," I said. "He wasn't asked to stay for dinner. What's that all about?"

"Ancient history, Billy. God, I am so tired. That was a beastly train ride. I'm going to close my eyes for a bit, and when I open them, I expect to smell the bacon frying in Mrs. Rutledge's skillet."

Diana thought she was smart, distracting me with talk of sizzling bacon, but I knew she didn't want to discuss Bodkin and her father for another second. She had to be exhausted, but it wasn't until I brought up the doctor's name that she'd decided she needed some shut-eye.

Still, I had to admit I did begin to think about that bacon and lost interest in Slewford village gossip.

CHAPTER FOUR

THERE WERE HUGS all around when we arrived at Seaton Manor. Sir Richard beamed as Diana kissed him on the cheek. Mrs. Rutledge fussed over her, excusing herself to finish preparations for breakfast as she wiped away a tear, muttering about how much work there was to do. Agnes went to help her, and Kaz, after gallantly kissing Diana's hand, stepped aside as she and Angelika embraced.

All the other greetings had been joyful and boisterous, but this reunion was silent, almost prayerful. Diana had been gone only a few weeks, but the bond that had grown between the two women during their time in Ravensbrück was palpable as they stood still with their arms wrapped around each other in tender celebration of their unexpected survival.

I had to look away, feeling like I was trespassing on their exposed emotions. Sir Richard caught my eye, and I saw the same discomfort play across his face. In that moment, Diana and Angelika were someplace else. A place of terror and sudden deliverance.

We could never understand, only wait for them to return.

Diana took Kaz and Angelika by the arm and led them into the dining room, smiling and chatting away. They were back.

The much-anticipated bacon was waiting, along with fried eggs, smoked ham, fresh rolls, orange marmalade, coffee, and, of course, tea. Mrs. Rutledge thanked me for the hundredth time for the coffee and sugar I'd brought, courtesy of a souvenir-hungry supply sergeant at Norfolk House in London, where some of the SHAEF offices were still based. It was surprising how much coffee a Nazi dagger bought you.

"I imagine you'll wish to rest after your journey, Diana," Sir Richard said after the plates had been cleared.

"It's tempting, but I can't waste a beautiful day like this, especially after last night's weather," Diana said. "What I'd really like to do is go for a ride. How does that sound, Billy?"

"I'll drive you wherever you want," I said.

"No, Billy, not that kind of ride. This is the English countryside, you know," she said.

"Horses, Billy." Kaz was barely suppressing a grin. "She means horses."

"I ride!" Angelika said. "May I go, please?"

"No, you may not," Agnes said. "Stitches, remember?"

"When you're ready, of course you may," Sir Richard said. "We have a good dozen mounts you can choose from."

That satisfied Angelika, and all eyes went back to me.

"Oh, Billy, do you ride?" Diana asked. "We've never had the time when you were here before."

"Yes, you might be surprised to know I do. I had a friend on the Boston Police Mounted Unit who showed me the ropes," I said. "I went out on a few patrols in the Back Bay Fens along the Muddy River."

"Well, you learned in the right sort of place," Sir Richard said. "We have our fair share of fens around here. Plenty of marshes and wetlands."

"Too dreary," Diana said. "We'll go out to the chalk cliffs and ride up to Tower Hill. It'll be a marvelous view."

"From the tower?" I asked.

"You'd think there'd be one, wouldn't you?" Agnes said. "According to legend, the Romans built a tower there, but no one's ever found it."

"The Romans were active all around here," Sir Richard said. "They built roads and causeways across the wetlands, which we have in abundance. The only trace of a tower is in the name, sad to say. I did some digging up there as a lad and never found a thing. I'll get the horses out. Angelika, will you help? If Agnes allows, that is."

Agnes said that would be fine, and Diana went off to change into riding clothes. I switched out my low-quarter shoes for boots, and we rendezvoused in front of the horse barn. Sir Richard was leading a black mare, and Angelika followed with a chestnut gelding.

"Yours is Dante, the chestnut, Billy," Sir Richard said as one of his hired hands brought out a saddle. "He's very mild-mannered. Diana's favorite is Felicity. She's got a lot of energy."

"A good match, then." I helped cinch the saddle while Angelika did the same with Felicity. "Is there much demand for horses these days?"

"There is. Out in the country, with plenty of grass and hay, well-bred horses are in demand. No petrol rationing, you see," Sir Richard said.

"The perfect pastime for a retired naval officer," Diana said as she joined us, wearing jodhpurs and a riding jacket. "That, and the other business you get up to with the Admiralty."

"I have asked Sir Richard what it is he does," Angelika said, handing me the reins. "But he won't say a thing. Which is clever of him."

Sir Richard bowed his head in acknowledgment of the compliment. As Diana and I mounted our horses, Sir Richard and Angelika walked back to the house, chatting about horseflesh.

"It's done him a world of good to have her here," Diana said. "Now, are you sure you're ready for Dante?"

I almost wasn't. It had been a while since I'd ridden, and I got the idea Dante was feeling frisky. He bucked a bit as we took a path around the barn and into the fields beyond.

"He probably hasn't been exercised much," Diana said. "Ready for a canter?"

I wasn't so sure, but Dante was. He fell into the gait easily and settled down as he warmed up. We rode along a country lane with farmland on either side, then took a route along a narrow river, which was still raging from last night's rains. The sky was an azure blue, and the sun warmed my face as we took a turn that led up a gently rising slope.

"This was a great idea," I said when Diana pulled on the reins and halted at the top of the hill. The view of the fields and the sea beyond was stunning.

"I dreamt of this while I sat in that office going over accounts," she said. "And when you get a sunny day in England at this time of year, you grab at the chance to enjoy it."

"Does your father own all this?" I stretched out my arm to encompass the land around us.

"No, we left his property a while back. These lanes are all rights-of-way. We can take them down to Tower Hill. See that rise with the trees on the top? That's it. Just beyond it is Marston Hall. We'll have a good view from there."

"Great. I can't wait to see more Nazis," I said. "Is that the North Sea we're looking at?" I could see whitecaps out to the horizon, even at this distance.

"It's the Wash," Diana said. "It's a massive bay and estuary. If you've noticed a big indentation in the coastline on maps, that's the Wash. There are several rivers that feed into it, but it's very shallow. Inland from the Wash, the land is quite marshy. Like your fens in Boston, I imagine. Our chalk cliffs are one of the few high points along the shoreline."

"Yeah, it's like a notch on the maps, I remember. Never knew the name."

"Want to gawk at the caged Nazis?" Diana asked. "Then we'll ride to the cliffs."

"Lead on," I said, my curiosity piqued by Marston Hall and

what went on there, despite my desire to ignore the war for as long as I could. Diana led the way along a narrow path that went through a wooded glade and descended to fenced-off fields dotted with woolly black-faced sheep.

"Suffolk sheep," Diana said, looking back at me. "You'll see a lot of them in these parts."

"I think I saw some parts on my plate last night," I said. "Your father doesn't raise them himself, does he?"

"No, he's strictly a horseman. This herd belongs to Alfred Bunch. He and his wife, Mildred, live in that cottage." Diana pointed to a brick-faced house off in the distance with a large barn next to it. "They used to work at Marston Hall, as a matter of fact. When Stephen Elliot disappeared, they lost their positions and had to go into raising sheep."

"Charlotte Mothersole is his sister, right? Couldn't she have kept them on?"

"Not with the government taking over the place for the duration," Diana said. "And with no trace of Elliot, it was impossible for her to inherit. She's lucky to have the cottage."

"Did you know Elliot? I assume he grew up around here."

"He inherited Marston Hall from his aunt when he was barely eighteen years old. Last cousin standing or some such thing. I'm sure Charlotte misses him," Diana said, avoiding any personal references.

"Your father made a point of saying there was no hint of cowardice or desertion," I said. "I'm not too sure Charlotte was pleased that he even brought up the notion."

"Billy, can we please just enjoy this beautiful day?" Diana said, not bothering to look at me. "Stay out of other people's business, will you? And don't interrogate me, it's boring."

With that, she gave Felicity a kick and broke into a gallop. Dante quickly took up the same pace, while I held on and tried not to make a greater fool of myself by falling off.

As we neared Tower Hill, Diana slowed to a trot, and I tried to figure out what to say. I tended to ask too many questions, but I'd only been making conversation. Sometimes I claimed it was a cop's occupational hazard, but I knew it would be no different if I were a ditchdigger. I liked to pry; it was that simple. Though you can't pry things apart if they fit well, and there were flaws in the stories of Sir Richard, Elliot, and Bodkin that invited questions. What did Sir Richard have against Bodkin? Why had Diana reacted the way she did when I'd brought up Elliot, and why had her father defended the man, only to have Charlotte tell him to drop it?

Now, I may've been overly curious, but I wasn't stupid. When I caught up to Diana, I reined in Dante, patted his neck, and told him he was a good horse.

"That's Marston Cottage," Diana said, pointing to a small two-story stone house—built from Norfolk flint—with smoke curling up from the chimney. Charlotte's place was nestled against a pine grove, about a hundred yards from where we were.

"Nice cottage," I said. "I can't wait to see Marston Hall."

"Let's go," Diana said, snapping the reins. I did my best to keep up as we made for the crest. It wasn't much as hills go, but in this flat coastal terrain, it stood out like a mountain. It would have been the perfect place for a watchtower back in the old days.

"There," Diana said, halting in a clearing near the top. "That's Marston Hall."

"Wow, some joint," I said. Four stories of stonework with turrets at the front corners and a wing that jutted out from the side. "Elliot's family must have been loaded."

"Land rich, cash poor, like much of the landed gentry," she said, shielding her eyes from the sunlight as she gazed out over the distant grounds. I did the same, trying to focus on the figures walking around the estate. British and American khaki uniforms mingled with the field-gray Wehrmacht uniforms and the occasional Kriegsmarine blue.

"It looks like a resort, not a POW camp," I said. "They're just wandering around. I can't even see a fence."

"It's there. I saw them installing it when the army first took over. Right at the edge of the woods around the hall. You can't see the main gate from here, but it's well guarded. I don't know what Charlotte told you, but it's an interrogation center, not a real POW camp. Prisoners are brought in and out all the time," Diana said.

"It's made to look nonthreatening," I said. "Soften up the Krauts so they'll spill."

"I think that's the idea," Diana said.

"Sir Richard must have had something to do with setting this up," I said. "Didn't he?"

"Oh my god, Billy, do shut up," Diana said. This time she shook her head and started for the other side of the hill, taking the path down to the cliffs.

Not my business, not my business, I kept repeating to myself. All I had to do was remember that ten minutes from now.

We cleared the woods and came down on the path to the cliffs. The sea—or the Wash—was still churning, as if it hadn't gotten over last night's storm. I came along Diana's side and was about to try for an apology when I saw a man walking toward us. He was maybe fifty, with unkempt gray hair swirling around his hatless head. His coat was worn and dirty, but that was nothing compared to the look in his eyes: wild with fear. His hands were pressed against his skull, as if to keep it from exploding.

"Mr. Archer," Diana said, drawing her mare to a halt. "Are you all right?"

"He's come back," Archer said. "He's come, I tell you. It's the devil's work."

"Oh dear," Diana said, watching as the man stumbled up the hill, disappearing into the woods. "I've never seen him so bad."

"Who is he?" I asked.

"David Archer. He went off to war in 1914 with a company

of local men. He was the only one to come back. He'd been buried in a shell hole, covered by the bodies of his mates. He's had a hard time of it, but something's really gotten to him," she said.

"Jesus. Should we check out the beach?"

"We might as well. Who knows what he saw? Anything can set him off," she said, dismounting. "The cliff edge can be dangerous and crumble beneath your feet, so be careful."

"Maybe that happened, and he saw the body," I said as we got close to the edge.

"My god," Diana said, looking down at the rocky beach.

It was the devil, in the guise of a German bomber. Waves crashed over the metal hulk half encased in sand as the receding tide pulled at it and tried to wrench it free from its underwater grave.

"What the hell is it doing here?" I asked, not expecting a real answer.

"A German bomber crashed here in 1942," Diana said. "People saw it going down, but it was never recovered. The storm, along with the tides and shifting sands, must've dislodged it."

"What should we do?" I asked. For all I cared, the sea could have it back.

"You ride back and tell Father. You can find your way, can't you?" Diana said, not waiting for an answer. "I'm going to Marston Hall. I know the commander. I'll ask him to send some men down to guard the wreck."

"Why? It crashed two years ago."

"You never know what intelligence can still be gathered, Billy. You're not the only one who can't stop thinking about their job." With that, she mounted Felicity and dashed off at a gallop, leaving me to stare at the black swastika on the tail fin, wondering if these dead Nazis were still capable of causing harm in the peaceful village of Slewford.

David Archer certainly thought so.

CHAPTER FIVE

"UNBELIEVABLE," SIR RICHARD said, hanging up the telephone in his office. "I saw it going down myself back in '42. Raced out to find it, same as half the village. Found nothing but a gouge in the earth leading right to the cliff edge. Maybe they were trying to ditch in the ocean or crash-land, but they had the worst of both. I figured they skidded along until the ground dropped out from under them. Impossible to see clearly in the dark, and it was raining buckets that night. The next morning, there was no sign of the aircraft."

"What now?" I asked.

"We get some recovery gear in place," Sir Richard said. "Graham is organizing rope and whatever else he can get his hands on to secure the aircraft. We don't want it to be pulled back by the tides now that it's come unstuck."

"Graham?" I asked.

"Colonel Cheatwood. Commanding officer at Marston Hall. Meanwhile, I've called Alex Drake. He dredges, keeps the rivers and canals from filling up with vegetation. He's got a flat-bottomed barge with a crane and a winch. He can help raise the damn thing. Did you make out what sort of bomber?"

"Yes, sir. Heinkel He 111. Twin engine. But I don't understand, Sir Richard. Why is this so urgent? It's been in the drink more than two years."

"Could be nothing, but we may still find something. There

was a bit of a flap when it came down, in late May of that year, I think," Sir Richard said, pushing back from his desk and reaching for his coat. "The War Office put the contingent at Marston Hall on alert and brought in the Home Guard to search the entire area."

"All that for a few Fritzes in a bomber crew?" I asked.

"Does Sandringham House mean anything to you?"

"No, I can't say it does," I answered, watching as Sir Richard expertly thrust his damaged arm into the sleeve and then shrugged the coat onto his other shoulder, buttoning it deftly.

"Sandringham House is a royal estate, just up the coast from us. Massive place—King George is quite attached to it," Sir Richard said. "Any enemy activity in the area is naturally viewed with great suspicion. Officially, the estate is closed for the duration, except for staff to look after it. But the king has made several visits with family, staying in the outlying guest cottages in the greatest of secrecy."

"Was the king there when the bomber came down?" I asked.

"What I told you is in confidence, Billy. Officially, Sandringham House is shuttered. Now, will you drive? Drake should be there shortly. He had a crew out dredging the Thirty Foot Drain, which isn't far. Shall we?"

Sir Richard explained that Kaz had driven Agnes and Angelika to the village to do some shopping and that he didn't wish to wait for their return. It seemed to be his way of saying he preferred not to drive one handed, so I readily agreed.

I still had a lot of questions, not the least of which was about a thirty-foot drain. But Sir Richard was in a hurry, so I waited until we were on the road to ask that one.

"It's a connection between two canals," he explained. "An artificial drainage system, part of a network of sluices and floodgates. This area is prone to flooding, especially during storms at high tide. We're lucky to have a bit of high ground at hand, but for others, keeping the waterways open is vital."

"Okay, that makes sense," I said. "But I do have to wonder what you're going to find in that wreck."

"I've always been concerned about Sandringham House as a possible target," Sir Richard said. "The Germans don't know it's been closed, and they could attempt a raid, especially if they get word of an unannounced visit. I simply want to satisfy myself that this bomber is nothing more than a normal Luftwaffe aircraft."

"So you're looking for evidence of commandos," I guessed. "Arms, maps, anything that would suggest they were part of a special mission."

"Exactly. There won't be much left after two years underwater, but we should be able to draw some conclusions. German paratrooper helmets, for instance. Or British uniforms, for that matter. As for maps, I doubt they would have lasted."

"I assume there was an actual air raid at the time," I said.

"Of course. Perfect cover for an airdrop," Sir Richard said. "They bombed Norwich. Chances are this pilot was trying to get his crippled aircraft back out over the North Sea, but then something went wrong and he attempted a crash landing. I saw the thing at a distance, and it looked to me as if an engine was on fire."

"Probably all it was," I said. "Lucky that you've got soldiers close by at Marston Hall. Or was that deliberate?"

"Because of Sandringham, you mean? More of a beneficial coincidence," Sir Richard said. "The guard force there does regular patrols up and down the beaches in the direction of Sandringham, watching for any evidence of an approach. They could be there in fifteen minutes by lorry if need be."

"Along with other reinforcements?"

"I've said too much already, Boyle. Now be quiet and drive. That's a good lad," Sir Richard said. It was delivered a bit more nicely than Diana's similar request, but it amounted to the same thing.

I zipped it and drove.

At the cliffs, I pulled over next to an old Morris dropside lorry. A British Army staff car and lorry were also parked a respectful distance from the cliff edge, next to a few bicycles. A clutch of onlookers hovered near the cliff, and I could hear instructions being shouted from down below.

"Looks like word traveled quickly, Sir Richard," I said as we drew closer.

"Always does in a small village," he said, waving to a couple. "Alfred, Mrs. Bunch, mind where you step now."

"Isn't this something, Sir Richard?" Mrs. Bunch said. She wore Wellingtons and sturdy clothes fit for outdoor work. Dark hair flecked with gray blew about her face as she looked down to the Wash. "After all this time."

"Doesn't look so threatening now, does it?" Alfred said. A bitter laugh escaped his lips, and a few of the crowd joined in.

"Just how I like them," Sir Richard said, giving Alfred a polite smile as he steered me to a path leading down to the beach. "We get our lambs from Alfred and Mildred. Hard workers, those two."

The path was guarded by a British soldier, who stepped aside smartly as Sir Richard passed. On our descent, I spotted Diana standing near a British officer. Soldiers, their uniforms soaked, were securing ropes and cables to the rocks along the shore, having wrapped them around the wings and tail section of the aircraft.

"Ah, here comes Drake," Sir Richard said when we were halfway down. I heard an engine and spotted the barge coming around the bend to the left, hugging the shore. It had a backhoe dredger on the bow and a winch at the stern. It wasn't much to look at, but when it came to hauling wrecks out of shallow water, it was tailor-made.

"Colonel Cheatwood, this is Captain Boyle," Sir Richard said as he stepped over the ropes strung along the rocky shore.

"Pleased to meet you, Captain Boyle." Cheatwood returned my salute. "Miss Seaton has been telling me about you. Sorry to interrupt your leave with all this, but I am glad you two spotted it. This high tide might have covered it up otherwise."

"We probably would have seen it anyway, but credit goes to David Archer," Diana said. "He alerted us to it."

"Poor Archer," Cheatwood said. "Part of him is still in those damned trenches. Now, Sir Richard, as soon as Drake maneuvers himself into place, I think we can bring this safely ashore."

Cheatwood pointed to a cable tied to the aircraft's tail section and wound around a large boulder behind us. The cable on Drake's winch would be connected to that and to stout ropes tied around the wings. Drake would then use his gas-powered winch to pull the bomber onto the beach. The nose appeared to be stuck in the sand, so he would lift it gently with his backhoe bucket, digging under the sand to protect the cockpit.

"Do you think it will work?" I asked, eyeing the arrangement of cables.

"We know about shallow-water salvage around here," Colonel Cheatwood said. "I must say, when I saw this aircraft losing altitude, I never expected to be raising her two and a half years later. This is going to be a bit tricky, though. I suggest once the cables are in place, we clear the beach. If one snaps under pressure, it could take off a leg."

"Or an arm, and where would that leave me?" Sir Richard said. He and Cheatwood had a laugh over that, and I saw enough sense in the joke to head for the high ground with Diana.

"Cheatwood sounds like a local man," I said, once we reached the top.

"He is. Joined the army before the war and went to France in 1940 as a captain," Diana said. "He was evacuated out of Dunkirk on one of the small boats." Diana had been there as well, serving as a switchboard operator at British headquarters. She'd joined the First Aid Nursing Yeomanry to do her bit in the war effort, never suspecting that the rear-area HQ would be in the front lines so quickly. She was taken out on a destroyer, which was bombed and sank in the channel, sending far too many wounded men on stretchers to the bottom. She'd been picked up by a small boat, one of the hundreds of private ships that had answered Churchill's call to rescue the soldiers trapped on the beaches of Dunkirk. I knew the memory still haunted her and that she would be forever doing her bit as penance for surviving it.

"He was badly wounded when his boat was strafed," Diana continued. "After he was discharged from hospital, they gave him this posting. Helps that he knew the area and speaks German. A decent enough fellow."

"I take it he knows how close Sandringham House is." I watched Drake fight the tide as he moved his barge into position.

"Father has his pet theory about Germans targeting it. Commandos disguised as British soldiers, that sort of thing. I'm not surprised he brought it up. He did, didn't he?" Diana said, apparently worried she'd spilled the beans.

"Yes, he did, but only after I pressed him on why this salvage operation was so important. Does Cheatwood think there's anything to it?"

"I haven't asked. I'd guess that it's simply an interesting diversion from questioning Germans all day," Diana said. "Look, they've connected the cables!"

"I hope we haven't missed anything," Kaz said from behind us.

"Half the village is here," Agnes said, holding out her arm for Angelika. "Careful."

"Do not worry," Angelika said, eyeing the soldiers coming up from the beach. "I did not come this far to tumble into the sea. But I would not mind chatting with these boys."

"We brought Dr. Bodkin along." Kaz raised an eyebrow in his sister's direction. "We had room and thought to save him the petrol."

"Doctor, I think the crewmen are far beyond needing your services," I said.

"True enough, Captain, but there are accidents and injuries to be had. Sharp serrated metal being hauled out of the water is cause enough for concern," Bodkin said, peering over the edge.

I didn't doubt it, and I didn't doubt that this was an exciting event, even in a village that counted Nazi prisoners among its population.

It didn't take long for the young soldiers from the beach to gather around Agnes and Angelika and start asking them questions. Diana moved closer, an older sister guarding the younger girls. But they were enjoying themselves, more intent on life and laughter than on the raising of the steel coffin below.

The sharp whine of the winch drew everyone's attention. Drake's bucket dipped into the water and vanished below the surface. The tail rose slightly as the winch pulled the cable around the rock and hauled the aircraft slowly toward the shore. Waves rocked the barge and broke over the rising wreckage as the winch began to hiss and smoke.

"The tail is going to snap off," Kaz said. At that moment, the thick ropes wrapped around the wings went taut, and the cable from the barge began to lift the entire fuselage. Even after this amount of time in the water, the damage to the fire-blackened port engine was clear to see. Drake raised the backhoe bucket, and the nose of the aircraft appeared as it was plucked from the sandy bottom.

"No, it's holding," Diana said, and she was right. The entire aircraft began to move above the waterline, the tail assembly up high with the nose supported by the bucket. It wasn't exactly graceful, and maybe not the way Cheatwood had planned it, but the He 111 was rising from its watery grave.

A rope on the starboard wing snapped and whipped around, sending stones flying and proving the wisdom of moving people off the shingle. The airplane tilted to the side, but the main cable held and the other wing dug into the rocky shore, propping the bomber ass-end up as the tail fin fell against the chalk cliff face.

The winch powered down, and everyone went silent, waiting for the plane to fall back into the water. Instead, it gave out a *creak* and a *clank* of metal, then settled into place.

A cheer went up. Drake waved to the crowd, taking the bow that was his due for that delicate work.

"She seemed heavier than I expected," Sir Richard said. "I can't imagine they'd still have bombs aboard, though. The pilot would have dropped them once he got into trouble."

"It's mud." Cheatwood pointed to the open canopy. "The thing is filled with it."

Streaks of sandy mud were oozing out of the port windows and from the top gunner's position where the sliding canopy was open. The He 111 had a fully glazed nose cone, which gave the pilot and bombardier excellent visibility, but this one was cracked, possibly from flak or the impact. The escape hatch above the pilot's position was wide open, and muddy water sluiced out from it.

"It's going to be a right mess going through this, Sir Richard," Colonel Cheatwood said. "Have to take the damn thing apart right here."

It was another engineering problem for these men to solve, but as I walked closer, I realized there was still the matter of human remains to deal with. Kaz had realized it too.

"The mud will have preserved the bodies to a certain extent," he said. "Better than if they had been in open water."

"You'd have nothing more than skeletons then," Diana said. "But the mud may have protected them from sea creatures. Gruesome."

"It might have preserved intelligence data as well," Kaz said. "It is a stroke of good luck."

I was hardly listening. I walked closer to the cockpit, my eyes on the escape hatch. Given the angle of the bomber as it rested against the cliff, the open hatch was just above my head, close enough to make out the shape of an arm, or what once had been an arm, dripping mud from the skeletal fingertips.

I looked at it again, more closely.

"Kaz, come over here, please," I said.

"Oh, you found one of the poor bastards already," he said.

I didn't reply. I grabbed his sleeve and studied it, then let go and brushed away what filth I could from the sodden wool dangling above me.

"This isn't a Luftwaffe uniform. It's British Army," I said.

CHAPTER SIX

"FATHER, YOU WERE right!" Diana said, taking Sir Richard by the arm and leading him closer to the cockpit. "It's a British uniform."

"What? Really?" Sir Richard looked astonished as he stepped over a jumble of rocks to get a closer look. "By god, it might be."

"I believe it is," Kaz said. "Luftwaffe flight suits are tan or a light brown. This sleeve, what we can see of it, is a match for my own wool serge."

"Well, this is a nice bit of luck," Sir Richard said, still stunned at his prediction coming true. "Graham, we must keep this quiet, don't you agree?"

"Absolutely," Colonel Cheatwood said. "I suggest we inform our audience that there is unexploded ordnance aboard and we need to clear the area. I'll radio for some acetylene torches and take this thing apart. There's no telling what else we may find inside."

"Excellent. We shall depart. Give the warning to those above and clear them out," Sir Richard said. "I'll contact the War Office while you organize the rest. Of course, you can trust in the discretion of my guests."

"Undoubtably," Cheatwood said. "It may take some time to get the equipment here, but we'll work into the night and pry this beast open. Then we'll see what we have."

"All right, Diana, please lead the way back up, and look suitably frightened, will you?" Sir Richard said.

"A mysterious corpse is just the thing in case you were finding leave in Slewford boring, Billy," Kaz said as we clambered back up the path.

"After this little performance, I plan on staying far away from corpses for a while," I said. "Boredom would suit me right now."

"We need to leave the area," Diana announced to those gathering at the top. "There are live bombs below."

"Oh my goodness," Mildred Bunch said, her hand going to her mouth, her eyes darting about. "Alfred . . ."

"Yes, my dear, let's go," he said, taking her by the elbow. "Wouldn't do to get blown up now, eh?"

"Come, everyone, clear out," Sir Richard said. "Let's leave it to the army."

"Perhaps I should stay," Dr. Bodkin said. "In case of injuries."

"Don't be a fool, Bodkin. If one of those bombs goes off, there won't be enough left to slap a bandage on," Sir Richard said.

Bodkin's face went dark, but he turned on his heel and left before he could reply.

"A bit harsh," I whispered to Kaz.

"But effective," he said. "Everyone is leaving quickly. Shall we?"

"Billy, can you run me up to Marston Hall? I had to leave Felicity there," Diana said.

"Go on," Sir Richard said. "I'll ride back with the baron."

"They'll let us in?" I asked as Diana got into the jeep.

"I'm expected, Billy. Graham told the sentry he might have to stay with the aircraft."

"Not the kind of security I'd expect at a top secret interrogation center," I said, backing out and waiting for the Bunches' truck to leave. For the first time, I noticed a furrow in the ground that was running alongside the road and leading straight to the cliff edge.

"Is that where the bomber went down?" I asked, nodding in the direction of the overgrown rut.

"Oh, yes, that's it. Two years ago, it was a terrible scar, but the ground has settled since then, and the grasses have filled in." She looked toward the cliff and sighed. "Even though they were the enemy, I have to feel sorry for them. Thinking they'd survived a crash landing, only to find themselves flying off that cliff. At least it must have been quick."

"It had to be a shock." I shifted into first and followed Alfred and Mildred. I could see her looking at the furrowed ground herself. When war comes to a small, remote village, it leaves a scar of memory as well as of land.

We trailed Alfred until he turned off on a side road marked by a sign for RINGSTEAD SHEEP FARM.

"That's their farm," Diana said. "They bought it from old Mr. Ringstead when they were let go after Elliot's disappearance. Mr. Ringstead didn't have much left of his flock, but Alfred and Mildred have worked hard. They had to."

"Do I have it right that Colonel Cheatwood was already here when the bomber went down? As was Elliot?" I said, moving along the two-lane road with Tower Hill on our left.

"Yes. Cheatwood had been sent to organize and staff the facility before the first POWs were brought in. Lieutenant Elliot had been discharged from the hospital and was awaiting orders. He and his sister, Charlotte, were still in residence, along with Alfred and Mildred as staff. But they all knew their time at Marston Hall was limited. Elliot's disappearance only accelerated things."

"Whose decision was it to let them go?" I asked.

"The government's. The army's. How would I know?" Diana asked.

"There's something about Elliot you and your father are holding back, isn't there?"

"Yes. He was a pompous idiot who asked too many questions," Diana said. "Take this right."

"At the sign that says NO UNAUTHORIZED PERSONNEL, ENTRY PROHIBITED?" I asked, ignoring the sarcasm. Or maybe she wasn't talking about me? No, better not to chance it.

"I am authorized, Billy. But I might leave you here since you enjoy interrogations so much."

When I pulled up to the gate, the sentry gave Diana a smile and me the once-over. When he finally decided I wasn't a German commando, he flashed me one of those open-palm salutes the Brits like so much. I tossed the Yank version back and drove on.

Diana directed me around to the back of Marston Hall, which took some time since it was a massive pile of that distinctive Norfolk flint. Brick bordered all the doors and windows. Turrets on each corner extended above the roofline. It was big and impressive, but nothing about it was pleasing to the eye.

Especially not the Germans strolling around the grounds in their neatly pressed uniforms. Some of them wore an impressive array of medals, which the Krauts really seemed to go for.

"Do these guys get regular deliveries from their tailor in Berlin?" I asked.

"Some of them dress in their finest to surrender, I hear," Diana said. "Others get uniforms sent via the Red Cross. But remember, everything about this place is geared to getting the prisoners to speak freely, without realizing they're being interrogated."

"Yeah, but I think they should use the Gestapo treatment first, so they can really appreciate this kid-glove stuff," I said, watching two Fritzes walk along a garden path, puffing on cigars.

"Billy . . ."

"I know, I should shut up."

"Yes, that too, but also pull over on the right. There's Felicity."

I parked on the grass and spotted Felicity near a garage tucked away behind the big house. I guessed it was a garage, but my house in South Boston could have easily fit inside. Felicity was tied to a fence post and was being brushed down by a German officer in shiny black boots. An American sergeant lounged against the garage, enjoying a smoke break.

"Get away from my horse," Diana said.

"*Es tut mir leid,*" the officer said, taking a step away from Felicity and standing at attention. "I am sorry."

"He is a cavalry officer, ma'am," the sergeant said as he gave me a quick salute. "He could not help himself. The former owners kept horses. He found a brush and got to work." The Yank's accent was unmistakably German.

"I mean no harm," the officer said. "She is a fine animal."

"I don't need you to tell me that," Diana said, turning to the sergeant. "Please escort this man elsewhere."

"As you wish," the sergeant said. "*Kommen Sie mit,* Oberst Hansen."

"Sergeant, did you graduate from POW to GI? That's some accent," I said.

"Sergeant Hank Klein, at your service, Captain. Formerly Henrich. Formerly of Berlin, until my parents sent me to America in 1935. I am an American citizen, just like you," Klein said. He jutted out his square jaw, a subtle gesture of defiance that told me he was fed up with explaining himself.

"I get it, Sergeant. You *sprechen* the lingo pretty well. Did your parents get out before the war?"

"It was not easy for Jews to get out of Germany, Captain. The Nazis made it difficult, and not many countries would accept Jewish refugees. I had an uncle in Chicago who agreed to sponsor me. But there was only one visa to be had. My parents and sister were waiting for theirs right up until they were sent to the east. For resettlement, the Nazis claim."

"I hope you can find them after the war, Sergeant," I said, knowing how slim those chances were.

"Thanks, Captain. Now I'll take Colonel Hansen back to his room. *Ja,* Oberst?"

"*Ja. Es tut mir leid,*" the colonel said one last time to Diana, who ignored him.

"I bet he says that a lot," I said, watching the two of them walk back to the main house.

"I don't know how Sergeant Klein does it." Diana shook her head as she leaned against her horse. "I know why it must be done, but when that man laid his hands on Felicity, I saw red. Just like—oh, never mind."

"Memories of Ravensbrück?" I asked quietly.

"No, no, not that. Memories of this place in 1940, before I left for France." Diana sighed, her face wilting as she looked at the house. "The grounds were beginning to show signs of neglect. We should have taken notice. Stephen Elliot gave an afternoon party, and he played the role of viscount to the hilt."

"Is that a big deal over here?" I asked, never having gotten the hang of all the titles British aristocrats threw around.

"To some, yes." Diana laughed. "His uncle was the Earl of Marston, and Elliot inherited the title of viscount with the estate. It's a minor title, although a step up from Father's knighthood."

"Which he earned in battle," I said. "While Elliot received his by being the last living relative, as you said. Bit of a difference."

"Yes, but not a difference recognized by people like Stephen Elliot. I don't know what he was like before he came here, but once he settled in, he showed little interest in the village or much else."

"When was this, exactly?"

"I'm not sure. He was older than I. After the Great Influenza epidemic, I think, so early 1920s? He came from Cambridge, where he studied medieval history, which seemed to be the only thing he cared about, other than women. Girls, rather."

"Did he try and pull anything with you?"

"I knew of his reputation and steered clear of him. But I did go to the party, thinking I might not see some of these people again," Diana said, stroking Felicity's neck. "Father went as well. Daphne was in London at the time, probably carrying on with Piotr." A faint smile of memory rose from her face, then vanished. "Anyway, I saw him follow a maid into the kitchen. Knowing his reputation, I went in after them. There he was, pushing her into a corner, grabbing at her, telling her to be quiet." Her voice dropped as she revisited the scene.

"You stopped it," I said.

"Not before he struck her—a hard slap to show who was in control. That's when I tried to pull him off her. He was enraged, his face contorted in anger. Stephen Elliot didn't like it when people refused him. He went to hit me—with his fist, not a slap—but I backed up, and he tripped, fell flat on the floor. He was likely drunk."

"Was that it?"

"No. I hadn't realized it at the time, but Father had the same suspicions and followed me. He saw everything and called Elliot a coward to his face. There were more words, and, unfortunately, Charlotte was among those who witnessed it. She was terribly embarrassed, but she had the sense to take the maid away and saw to her."

"What was it about the Kraut that reminded you of that?" I asked.

"The nonchalant arrogance. He wanted to get close to Felicity, so he did. No thought of asking permission, nothing but a whiny, childish apology when he was confronted. Just like Elliot, only Elliot didn't even bother with the apology."

"Was that the end of it?" I said.

"Well, that put an end to the party. Father told Elliot if he ever raised his hand to a woman again, he'd regret it. Elliot called him a washed-up, one-armed blowhard. Father threatened to throttle Elliot, and I had to hold him back for fear he might actually do it."

"I imagine Elliot went into the army soon after," I said.

"Right. Ended up in North Africa. Royal Signals, then back here. After that, who knows what happened? A jealous husband, maybe?"

"Let's get back," I said. "I wasn't crazy about the Nazis here, and now I'm not crazy about the former occupant either."

CHAPTER SEVEN

DIANA RODE FELICITY through the gate at Marston Hall, and as I followed, I hoped it was the last time we visited that monstrosity. Since she'd said she was going to take a bath and a nap before dinner, I decided to swing by the cliffs and see what progress Cheatwood had made.

There were lorries with equipment being unloaded and soldiers carrying shovels to the beach. I watched from the top of the cliff, not wanting to get in the way or be drawn into this military drama. The whole notion of a failed German commando raid on Sandringham House seemed a stretch, but it could be true. Or there had been a single agent dressed as a British officer who was to be parachuted in under cover of the air raid, for purposes unknown. That was far more likely, but Sir Richard was quite invested in his pet theory. I didn't care much either way.

A sharp pinpoint of white light sparked from the shingle. They had one acetylene torch going, and another was being brought down. Sometime tonight they'd crack open the fuselage and see what was under all that silt.

Have at it, boys, I thought as I headed back. *I'm on leave.*

At Seaton Manor, I cleaned the mud off my boots and changed into fresh khakis. I settled into an armchair by the fire and read the war news in the local paper. American troops had taken the German border city of Aachen. MacArthur had landed back in the Philippines and informed the world he had returned, demonstrating the difference between Uncle Ike and him. You'd never see General Eisenhower hogging the limelight while troops under his command were fighting and dying for an objective. As the hall clock chimed five, I stopped reading and headed for the drinks cart.

I told it I had returned.

Kaz came in, excited about news he'd received of a Polish fighter squadron at a nearby Royal Air Force base east of Norwich. He'd been informed that a friend he hadn't seen since before the war was assigned there. He was taking Angelika, with Agnes as well, to visit the air base at Coltishall and look for his pal. After an overnight in Norwich, they'd head to Cambridge for Angelika's appointment with Ian Hamilton to have her stitches removed.

I told him it sounded like more fun than could be had in Slewford in a week of Sundays and wished him and Angelika luck.

Diana made it down for dinner but didn't last long, being exhausted from her overnight rail journey and the day's events. Agnes took Angelika upstairs after the meal to pack a few belongings and rest up.

"Quite the day, eh, gentlemen?" Sir Richard said, draining his wineglass.

"Slewford is full of surprises," I said. "I never expected Nazis or waterlogged bombers."

"I daresay we have nothing else up our collective sleeves, Billy," Sir Richard said, grinning. "At least I hope not."

"You may find more of the unexpected inside that aircraft," Kaz said.

"Or maybe we discover that it isn't even a British uniform. Perhaps it's one of those Brownshirts or even an Italian. Not impossible, I grant you, but my money is still on an Abwehr operation. German intelligence would like nothing better than to strike at the royal family," Sir Richard said. The Abwehr was the German Army's intelligence outfit. They'd pulled off several successful operations, so it wasn't beyond their capabilities.

"It would be interesting to track the route of the Luftwaffe bomber formation that attacked Norwich that night," Kaz said. "To see if their return leg would have brought them near here."

"Nobody saw any other aircraft," Sir Richard said. "He must have dropped out of formation while attention was focused on the Norwich attack. But that is a worthwhile idea, Baron. I shall make some calls."

"I couldn't make out any bullet holes," I said. "It looked like flak damage to me."

"We'll know more tomorrow," Sir Richard said. "Graham will have everything of value taken to Marston Hall, including the body we discovered and any others they might find. Bodkin will attempt an autopsy, which will tell us how they died—bullets, shrapnel, impact, or drowning. He should be able to handle that."

"Diana was telling me about a party at Marston Hall," I said, ignoring Sir Richard's cutting remark about Dr. Bodkin. "Back before Dunkirk. It sounded like Stephen Elliot behaved rather poorly."

"That affair with the serving girl? Yes, and the fact that he was drunk had little bearing," Sir Richard said. "That was his personality. Probably was like that before, but when he inherited Marston Hall, it went to his head and brought out the worst in him. Thought he was the great lord and could do no wrong. Made a fool out of himself that day."

"It must have been hard for Charlotte to witness that," I said.

"Indeed. I think she likely talked him into signing up after that," Sir Richard said. "Smart to get him into uniform and away. Although I'm sure Elliot would have rather stayed holed up in his library. Fancied himself a historian. Claimed to be writing a book but would never say about what. Ah, well, after he disappeared, there weren't many tears shed, I'll tell you that. I wouldn't put it past him to have made improper advances to a young lady, again, and gotten his brains bashed in for his troubles. He could very well be rotting a yard deep in some farmer's field."

"Has Charlotte ever offered her suspicions as to what happened?" Kaz asked.

"No, other than to say he must have had his reasons," Sir Richard said. "She was certain enough he would return that she talked Graham into storing all his belongings, papers, and books in a locked room."

"So he can finish writing his book upon his return," Kaz said, sitting back in his chair. "His sister has faith that he is alive."

"What else is there, in the face of nothingness, Baron?" Sir Richard asked. "You've met Charlotte. Despair doesn't suit her."

THE NEXT MORNING, Kaz, Angelika, and Agnes breakfasted early and set off for RAF Coltishall. Kaz carried their bags out to Sir Richard's Vauxhall Ten Saloon.

"Don't let Angelika do too much," Sir Richard said, walking Agnes outside. "I don't want her showing up at Hamilton's worse than when he saw her last."

"Don't worry, Sir Richard," Agnes said, holding the door for Angelika. "I won't let those Polish pilots sweep her off her feet."

"I will be so careful," Angelika promised, her breath frosted in the cold morning air. "Piotr has already lectured me, but this is so exciting. You have no idea what it will mean to see our boys in uniform striking back."

"Have fun," Diana said. "I hope you find your friend. Or at least a good-looking lad."

"Do not encourage her," Kaz shouted from the driver's seat.

We all waved goodbye as Kaz drove away.

"Will you help me feed the horses, Billy?" Diana asked as we turned to walk inside.

"Telephone, Sir Richard," Mrs. Rutledge announced from the doorway. "Colonel Cheatwood. It's urgent."

CHAPTER EIGHT

I ENDED UP chauffeuring Sir Richard again, leaving Diana to deliver hay and alfalfa to the horses, which suited her fine. Several bodies had been removed from the bomber and brought to Marston Hall—the wine cellar serving as a temporary morgue. Colonel Cheatwood wouldn't explain on the telephone, but he'd said Sir Richard should come immediately.

It must have been too early or too chilly for POWs to be sauntering around the grounds, so I was spared the sight of them. But as we headed down stone steps past an armed guard on our way to a grim makeshift morgue, I could only take so much solace from that thought.

At the bottom of the stairs, another guard opened a stout wooden door. We entered a long room with wine racks on either side, sadly empty except for cobwebs. The damp stone walls held in the chill, which was good for corpses as well as wine.

"Sir Richard, Captain Boyle," Cheatwood said, striding toward us and leaving Dr. Bodkin in conversation with an American officer. "This is most remarkable."

"For heaven's sake, Graham, what is?" Sir Richard demanded. Cheatwood looked more troubled than elated, and I looked to Dr. Bodkin for a clue. He was grim faced, as was the Yank. Behind them were three tables with the unmistakable shapes of the shrouded dead. Other tables were set along the far wall, where clothing in various stages of decay was laid out.

"We'll get to that," Cheatwood said. "Captain Boyle, this is Major Thomas Hudson, the commander of our American contingent."

"Major, I'm only along for the ride," I said. "Don't mean to get in the way here."

"Don't worry, Captain Boyle. We've checked you out—you're okay," Major Hudson said.

"We?" I asked.

"Military Intelligence Service, Section Y," he said. "It's our job."

"Now let's get on with *this* job," Sir Richard said. "What the blazes have you found?"

"Doctor?" Colonel Cheatwood said, giving Bodkin the floor. I could almost feel Sir Richard tense up in frustration at having to listen to Dr. Bodkin.

"As you can see, three bodies were recovered." Dr. Bodkin walked to the first table. As we approached, the smell became stronger. Not the stink of putrefaction, but the more indistinct odor of damp decay. "Based on the location, it seems likely this fellow was a gunner."

Bodkin pulled the sheet off, revealing carefully laid out bones. Bits and pieces of sinew dangled from a few discolored joints, but mainly it was a skeleton.

"No hands," I said.

"Correct," Bodkin said. "When a body has been submerged, hands and feet are the first to go. The small bones in the wrist and ankle give way easily, especially to predators. This man was in the rear of the fuselage, which had little silt."

"But his feet are here," Sir Richard said, gesturing to the detached bones and the end of the tibia and fibula, as if catching Bodkin in an error.

"They were collected from his footwear," Bodkin said, pointing to a pair of sodden leather boots. "Here, you can see where shrapnel cut into his rib cage, especially in the back. There are matching tears in his flight suit."

The thick cotton flight suit was laid out to show where flak had sent shrapnel slicing into the gunner's back. It didn't look pretty.

"Anything else in the rear compartment?" Sir Richard asked.

"Nothing you wouldn't expect," Cheatwood said. "Dr. Bodkin, please show us the next body."

"The bombardier," Bodkin said. "Who, I understand, also serves as the navigator." He replaced the sheet over the bones of the gunner and moved to the next table, folding back the sheet carefully so as not to disturb the remains. "This man was covered in silt, which preserved him from the worst of the marine depredation."

There wasn't much left in the way of flesh and organ, but leathery shreds of skin and muscle were drawn tight along the bones. His head must have been above the mud, a fact which I was grateful for, as the skull was well cleaned. The smell was worse than the previous body, and I stepped back as it hit my nostrils.

"How do you know this is the bombardier?" Sir Richard asked, his eyes darting to the next table with the final corpse.

"He was strapped into the bombardier's seat," Major Hudson said.

"We found maps in the large pocket of his flying suit." Cheatwood gestured to a thick, wet pile of folded maps on the table alongside what was left of the man's clothing.

"He was badly wounded," Bodkin said, pointing to the shattered sternum. "Perhaps already dead when the aircraft crashed."

"That means it was the pilot in the British uniform?" Sir Richard furrowed his forehead in confusion. "If an agent was being parachuted in, he wouldn't also be the pilot. It doesn't make sense."

"No, that would not make sense," Bodkin said, replacing the shroud. Cheatwood looked away and coughed, as if to avoid any comment.

"Where are the third man's clothes?" Sir Richard asked, motioning to the empty space on the table. "Were you unable to remove them?"

"I chose not to," Dr. Bodkin said. "The police prefer evidence to be kept intact."

"What the bloody hell are you talking about, man? What do the police care about dead Germans?" Sir Richard said, his voice rising with every word. "Show us what you've found!"

Dr. Bodkin held Sir Richard's gaze for a moment as something unspoken passed between them. Dr. Bodkin said nothing but grasped the sheet and pulled it off the corpse.

It hadn't been cleaned like the others. Gritty sand still caked the clothing, bone, and what bits of skin were left. The only part of the uniform that had been scrubbed clean was the upper arm on the left side. Sewed onto the brown wool was a shoulder flash, the deep blue color still clear. As was the stitching that read ROYAL SIGNALS.

"May I present the late viscount, Lieutenant Stephen Elliot, as found in the cockpit of the German bomber, which crashed in May of 1942, the same night he vanished," Dr. Bodkin said, obviously enjoying the revelation and the look on Sir Richard's face.

"Impossible," Sir Richard managed, croaking out the words. "Impossible."

"So it would seem," Colonel Cheatwood said. "But there he is. Or there he was, when we opened the aircraft nose."

"You're sure it's Elliot?" I asked, trying to take in what I was seeing. It looked like the uniform sleeve I'd seen yesterday, but the shoulder flash hadn't been visible through the mud. How could this be? There was still skin, or muscle, pulled taut across the cheekbones and jaw, but I doubt anyone could have identified him. He looked like something out of a nightmare.

"There are no identity discs," Cheatwood said. "Or wallet. We did check for those."

"But the body is of the correct stature, and, of course, there's the shoulder flash," Dr. Bodkin said. "We know Elliot was with the Royal Signal Corps. I've seen him wear that very shoulder flash, as have you, Sir Richard."

"Yes, yes, but how can this be?" Sir Richard managed.

"All I know is that I caught a glimpse of Elliot getting into his automobile that night," Cheatwood said. "I never saw him at the crash site, which surprised me at the time. Later, I assumed he'd deserted."

No one had an answer. My mind raced to make sense of what I was seeing. How *could* this be?

"I don't have an answer about Elliot," I said. "But I do have a question. Who landed the plane?"

"Someone did," Colonel Cheatwood said. "I saw it descend myself. It was hardly an uncontrolled crash."

"Maybe this is the pilot," I said, trying to work through the possibilities. "Elliot arrives at the crash site and the pilot attacks him, takes his uniform."

"And then Elliot goes off in a Luftwaffe uniform, leaving a German pilot to get back into his aircraft, which is already in the water?" Cheatwood said. "Hardly plausible."

"The police ..." Sir Richard tapped his finger against his chin. "You mentioned contacting the police. Why?"

"This is why, Sir Richard," Bodkin said, carefully turning the skull to one side. "This man was killed with a blunt object, resulting in a depressed fracture. Pieces of bone would have been driven into his brain."

The fracture was clear to see; the bone was crushed and splintered.

Whether this was the body of Stephen Elliot or someone else, he'd been murdered from behind. By whom? And what the hell was he doing in a German bomber?

This isn't your business, Billy, I told myself. *You're on leave. The only reason you're here is because you gave Diana's father a lift. Don't ask any questions. Don't offer any ideas.*

"Perhaps we should go, Sir Richard," I said, congratulating myself on my restraint. "And leave these men to their work."

"I think Sir Richard should stay and speak with the police," Colonel Cheatwood said. "They will be here shortly."

Sir Richard looked at Cheatwood but said nothing. He turned to Bodkin, who was covering the victim. He started to speak, but then held back. Whatever history these two men had, it was simmering right below the surface.

"I'd like to speak with you privately, Captain Boyle," Major Hudson said. "Upstairs, while we wait."

"Sure," I said, unable to come up with a reason to turn on my heel and walk away from an officer who outranked me. On the plus side, I'd be able to get the stink of the dead out of my nostrils.

CHAPTER NINE

"CAPTAIN WILLIAM BOYLE," Major Hudson intoned, reading from a file at his desk. "Graduated from Officer Candidate School in 1942. Rock bottom in your class of one hundred and seventy. That's some accomplishment, Captain."

"School was never my strong point, Major," I said, shifting to get comfortable in the wooden chair opposite Hudson. "Listen, sir, I don't really know what I'm doing here. I understand why the police want to talk to Sir Richard, since he knew the deceased—the presumed deceased—but that's got nothing to do with me."

"Boyle, I don't care about Sir Richard or this Elliot fellow or a bomber that crashed here two years ago." Hudson turned in his chair to stare out the window. From the second story, he had a swell view of the grounds and the Fritzes walking around in their overcoats, with the occasional GI keeping a close eye. Through the open door, I could hear someone pecking away at a typewriter. "I care about the security of this facility."

"Totally understandable and commendable, Major. However, right now, I'm on leave, and I've got a lady waiting for me. Maybe you guys can give Sir Richard a lift when the cops are done with him?" I pushed back my chair, ready to get up at the slightest suggestion of a dismissal.

"Yes, Diana Seaton, of the Special Operations Executive. Sir Richard's daughter," Hudson said, returning to the file. He was a tall guy with dark hair and a high forehead. A little on the gaunt side, like he spent all day with files in a dreary stone mansion. "But let's get back to you. You were a detective with the Boston Police Department before the war."

"Yeah, but only because my Uncle Dan was on the promotions board, so don't start thinking I'm Dick Tracy, okay, Major?"

"Immediately after OCS, you were sent to England, assigned to SHAEF," Hudson continued, his thin finger tracing the lines typed on the report. He arched an eyebrow and looked at me. "You came via air transport, top priority. General Eisenhower must've wanted you over here toot sweet."

"I'm a joy to have around." I drummed my fingers on the armrest. Maybe I could irritate him into throwing me out.

"And then, nothing." Hudson held up a sheet of paper with the word *Classified* at the top. "Nothing except for your promotions. First lieutenant, then captain. If you're still employed at SHAEF, this colonel you work for must think you're good at something." He stopped to consult another page. "Colonel Samuel Harding. West Point. Veteran of the last war. Sounds like a no-nonsense kind of guy."

"That's right," I said. "He's the colonel who gave me my leave papers, and he won't be happy about a major keeping me from it. Sir."

"What's the SHAEF Office of Special Investigations all about?" Hudson said, doing a good job of ignoring me and not taking the bait.

"What's Section Y all about?" I countered.

"How long have you known Sir Richard Seaton?" Hudson asked, tossing the file on his desk.

"Doesn't it tell you in there?" I pointed to the folder with my name on it.

"It's a simple question, Captain," Hudson said. "Let's just chat, okay?" He pushed his chair back, crossed his legs, and got comfortable.

"June of '42," I said, easing up on the guy a bit. "I came here with his daughter Daphne. That's when I met Diana."

"Do you know him well?" Hudson tossed the question off casually, as if it didn't matter. With the police on the way, I knew it did.

"I've gotten to know him since then," I said. "I only stayed one night at Seaton Manor that first time. He's a stand-up guy. How long have you known Graham Cheatwood?"

"I was assigned here in January 1943," Hudson said. "Colonel Cheatwood was here, had been since the year before—but he isn't the issue here, is he?"

"Hey, I don't know what the issue is." I crossed my legs and sat back, adopting Hudson's posture. It was an interrogation trick my dad had taught me. If you want to put a guy at ease, mimic his gestures. If you're not too obvious about it, it can loosen him up. "All I know is that you're keeping Sir Richard on ice for the cops, and it seems Cheatwood gets a free pass. They were both here when Elliot went missing. And when that bomber went down."

"Very good point." Hudson's eyes flickered, and a smile escaped his lips as he unfolded his legs and drew his chair closer to the desk. "I see you have some experience questioning people."

"Okay, you got me there," I said. "You're the professional interrogator, after all. But level with me, Major. What do you want?"

"I want you to investigate this matter on behalf of the US Army," he said.

"Call in the MPs. Call in the Criminal Investigation Division. They've got plenty of people," I said. A bit heavy handed and short on investigative skills, but I kept that to myself.

"That won't work," Hudson said. "For security purposes, I need someone who is connected at the highest levels, someone who can be discreet. You proved you have that quality when you kept quiet about your job at SHAEF. I need *you*, Boyle."

"Talk to my boss," I said, standing. "In the meantime, I'll wait outside."

"I already have. He agreed, and he's cutting your new orders now," Hudson said. "They'll be here tomorrow morning. Sorry, Boyle."

I sat down. I could tell he wasn't kidding. If the fix was in, there was no point stalling.

"You got any coffee around here, Major?"

"Oskar! Hustle up some coffee, willya?" Hudson shouted.

The typing stopped, and a few seconds later, Oskar popped his head in, asking in a thick German accent if the major wanted anything else. Hudson said strong coffee, and I began to warm to the guy.

"This place is thick with Jerries, isn't it?" I said as the sergeant left.

"Be careful, Boyle," Hudson said. "Sergeant Goldstein and the others are American citizens and American soldiers. They've had a tough time of it all around. Some had to leave families behind in Germany. You know what that means."

"I understand. Sorry," I said. "I talked to Hank Klein yesterday. He told me he was the only one in his family to get out. I have to get used to the accent, that's all."

"I'm a bit sensitive on the subject," Hudson said. "When I went looking for native German speakers for this assignment, I found a platoon of men who had been born in Germany isolated at one camp. They'd been given tents and were fenced in on a parade ground, all because their commanding officer didn't trust them. They were kept there a full year, doing nothing. A complete waste. Oskar was one of them."

All I could do was shake my head. The army was filled with as many idiots as in civilian life. The only problem was the military idiots had rank and the MPs on their side.

"Well, I'm glad the army finally smartened up and put him where he's useful," I said. It wasn't always the case. "I understand you're concerned about security, Major, but it seems like everyone in the village already knows about this place."

"Coffee, Major Hudson," Oskar said, entering with a serving tray. I could hear the hard *K* when he said coffee. It was odd to hear, coming from a US Army noncom, but I could see the benefit when interrogating German POWs.

"Thanks," I said as Oskar set down the tray on Hudson's desk. It held a silver coffee pot and bone china cups. Oskar smiled and left us. Hudson poured himself a cup. I did the same, feeling the heft of the silver pot and giving the major a questioning glance.

"No reason not to use the furnishings," Hudson said, blowing on the hot joe. "The British government took over the entire place. And the former owner is in no shape to complain."

"*If* that's Stephen Elliot downstairs," I said. "That's yet to be proven beyond a doubt. Let's get back to why you're so concerned about security when the entire village of Slewford seems to know what's going on here."

"They don't know everything, Captain Boyle. There's a lot that goes on here, and much closer to the front lines, that must be kept secret. I'll brief you once I have your orders in hand."

Fair answer. No reason for Hudson to fill me in if he didn't have me on a short leash. I drank my coffee, emitting a contented sigh. I appreciated Mrs. Rutledge's coffee, but she didn't have the knack for brewing up the strong stuff. It didn't come naturally to most Brits.

"What's the story about you and Colonel Cheatwood?" I asked. "Who does what?"

"The colonel was in charge when this was an exclusively British operation," Hudson said. "It was a traditional POW interrogation center, charged with assessing which prisoners were to be sent on for further treatment."

"Treatment?" I asked.

"The London Cage, a special interrogation center. Purely a British operation. Assessments were done here, then prisoners were sent to London or, if they were lucky, Canada," Hudson said. "Our approach is different, that's all I'll say for now."

"You haven't answered my question. What's Cheatwood's role here?"

"He's the commanding officer. I'm in charge of the interrogation process, but he runs the place. For instance, he decides which prisoners should go to the London Cage once we're done with them. He's also in charge of the building and grounds and security detachment."

"The guys who patrol the beach up to Sandringham House?" I asked.

"That's right. If you know that, you've picked up a few things on your own already," Hudson said. "Gives me confidence in your detective skills."

I had a lot more questions, but I didn't want to ask them right then. I needed time to think, about what was going on between Dr. Bodkin and Sir Richard, and if that had any part to play in the dark cloud of suspicion that was gathering over Diana's father. Bodkin had made a point of surprising Sir Richard with the identity of the third corpse. Was he really suggesting Sir Richard was a suspect, or was it the result of some long-simmering animosity?

Also, how could a one-armed man overpower a younger, able-bodied man and get him inside a German bomber? Was that even possible, much less plausible?

Perhaps the most important question—how would Diana react to my investigating her father?

CHAPTER TEN

"I'LL NOT STAND for any Americans hanging about," Chief Inspector Roland Gwynne declared, pointing at Major Hudson and me.

We'd spotted his car pulling into the drive and had gone out to greet him along with Colonel Cheatwood. A constable had jumped out from the driver's seat and held open the rear door. The inspector unfolded himself and stood tall, his eyes roaming the grounds before lighting on any of us. He was thickset with a long, drooping face, sort of like a basset hound sitting atop a barrel. Cheatwood made the introductions, to which Gwynne grunted. He rocked back and forth on his heels, hands clasped behind his back, as he announced his general dislike of Yanks.

"Inspector," Cheatwood said. "Major Hudson and I—"

"Chief Inspector," Gwynne interjected. "I don't expect you'd appreciate being called by a lesser rank, Colonel?"

"No, Chief Inspector, not at all," Cheatwood stammered. "I am merely pointing out that Major Hudson and I command this establishment jointly."

"Nevertheless, we seem to have a British body on British property, reported to me by a British officer, at the urging of a British doctor," Gwynne said. "And I am here as a representative of the Norfolk Constabulary, a British territorial police force. If I need to speak with any American during my investigation, I shall communicate that to you, Colonel. Now, take me to this corpse of yours."

Cheatwood led Chief Inspector Gwynne inside, leaving his constable behind.

"He makes a nice first impression," I said to the constable, who was staring at the Germans walking not ten yards away.

"Best not to disparage the chief inspector," the constable said. "He'd take it poorly, especially coming from an American."

"Still sore about losing the colonies, is that it?" I asked.

"He wouldn't like it from any foreigner, not one bit. Don't let that put you off, though," the constable said. "He's smart, and he doesn't let up once he's got the bit in his mouth."

"Thanks for the advice," I said, and headed to the cellar. Time to crash this party.

"Captain Boyle, where are you going?" Hudson said, following me to the basement door.

"To talk to Inspector Gwynne about the concept of Allied unity," I said. Maybe the guy was a good detective, but I didn't like his attitude one damn bit. As a bonus, Hudson may have second thoughts about taking me on for this job, and I could get myself fired before I even started.

"Chief Inspector," Hudson reminded me as I opened the door.

"I have no interest in dead Germans," Gwynne was saying, waving his hand in irritation. "Move on, Dr. Bodkin." Bodkin moved to the next table and lifted the shroud just as Gwynne spotted me.

"Your presence here is a distraction, sir," Gwynne said. "Please leave."

"Captain Boyle is a former police officer, Chief Inspector. Major Hudson, my American counterpart, has asked him to help investigate this . . . this situation," Cheatwood said, struggling with what to call the array of dead bodies.

"I need no assistance," Gwynne said, focusing on the body. "A physical match to Stephen Elliot, you say?"

"Yes," Bodkin said, turning the dead man's head. "You can see where the blow landed."

"A killing strike," Gwynne said, squinting as he got closer. So far, the guy seemed to know his way around a corpse. He certainly wasn't squeamish, which made me wonder how many putrefying bodies he'd run across.

"We checked for identity discs or a wallet, but found nothing," Cheatwood said.

"Wish you hadn't," Gwynne said. "The less interference the better. How many people have touched this man?"

"Dr. Bodkin," Cheatwood said. "And the two lads who pulled him out of the aircraft. No one else."

"I brushed the sand from his sleeve when I first saw the body," I said, trying to be helpful.

"Are you still here? By god, get out from underfoot," Gwynne said, without even looking at me. "Well, at least you didn't remove the uniform, there's that. The morgue is sending a van to take him away within the hour. We'll have a full autopsy done by morning. Open his mouth, will you, Doctor?"

Dr. Bodkin complied, and Gwynne took another squinty-eyed gander. He announced that some of the dental work was recent, and he'd have dental records checked.

"Who would know his dentist?" Gwynne asked, looking at Bodkin and Cheatwood while ignoring me.

"His sister, I am sure," Bodkin said. "He has no other relatives."

"She lives just outside the main gate, in a small cottage," Cheatwood said. "We haven't yet informed her. She wasn't at the cliffs yesterday, so she doesn't know."

"Doesn't know what, precisely, Colonel?" Gwynne said.

Cheatwood gave him a rundown on the aircraft's salvaging and the crowd it had attracted. Now that I thought about it, I hadn't seen Charlotte Mothersole among the other gawkers.

"I'm surprised you didn't sell tickets," Gwynne said. "Dr. Bodkin, please remain here until the morgue comes for the body.

Colonel Cheatwood, take me to this aircraft, and then we'll see the sister. That should do for now."

"What about the rest of them?" I asked. "There are three other men in a Heinkel 111 crew. They haven't been found."

"What?" Gwynne said. "You haven't accounted for the other Germans?" He did a good job of covering up the fact that he hadn't thought of it by jumping all over Cheatwood.

"We haven't found their bodies," Cheatwood answered, neglecting to mention he hadn't searched for them.

"They could have bailed out," I said. "We know these two were badly wounded. The others could have jumped. It would be useful to find out where downed crewmen were found the night of the attack. If any of these crewmen are alive and in a POW camp, it would be good to interview them."

"I'll order an inquiry right away," Cheatwood said. "I'm sure the War Office has records."

"Do that, Colonel," Gwynne said, staring at me. "Then we go to the cliffs."

"Chief Inspector, don't you wish to speak with Sir Richard?" Bodkin said.

"The one-armed fellow who had some argument with Elliot, you mean?" Gwynne said, facing Bodkin. "Plenty of time to talk to everyone who had words with Stephen Elliot once we confirm this is him. One thing at a time, Doctor. Unless you have other evidence you have not shared?"

"No, I just thought it important," Bodkin said.

"I won't mix in your profession, Dr. Bodkin. Please grant me the same courtesy. Colonel, I will be outside. We leave in five minutes," Gwynne announced. This was my chance to skip out and pray that my orders were delayed tomorrow. I knew I ought to get back to Diana, but I thought it was important to be there when Gwynne knocked on Charlotte's door.

"I'll give you a lift," I told Cheatwood, figuring Gwynne might not blow his stack at a Yank driver. I found Sergeant Goldstein and asked where they'd stashed Sir Richard. They had him in the library, where I gave him the news that he wasn't about to get the thumbscrew treatment.

Sir Richard was ready to leave, but I told him to wait and that I'd explain when I got back. I needed to tell him that I'd been dragooned into this affair, but right now I didn't want to miss the visit with Charlotte. There was a lot to be said for seeing a close relation's reaction to bad news. People have a way of revealing secrets when they try to cover them up by acting shocked. Shocked is hard to pull off. When you see the real thing, you know it, and it takes a practiced liar to fake it.

So I left Sir Richard confused but relieved, and he settled into an armchair with a book. *The History of King John.* Wasn't he the bad guy in the Robin Hood stories? Or was that Claude Rains? *Never mind*, I told myself. I'll ask Diana tonight, if she's still speaking to me.

I had the jeep idling and ready when Cheatwood came out. I drove around Gwynne's motorcar and waved to the constable at the wheel, who looked surprised. But he must've gotten the high sign from Gwynne since he pulled out and followed dutifully.

"I've contacted the War Office," Cheatwood said. "The POW section of the Intelligence Corps is assembling a list of captured fliers from the night of the raid on Norwich. We should have the list by the end of the day."

"I hope they're still in England," I said.

"Even if they've been shipped to Canada, we'll get them back," Cheatwood said. "It's well within our purview."

"Good. I'd like to hear from an eyewitness," I said.

"Why?" Cheatwood asked as I took a sharp turn around Tower Hill.

"Just professional curiosity." I realized he might not know of Hudson's move to officially assign me to investigate. Which led me to wonder why Hudson was keeping that to himself. The last thing I needed right now was more secrets.

CHAPTER ELEVEN

CHIEF INSPECTOR GWYNNE stared at the furrow in the ground leading to the cliff. He walked to the edge, hunching his shoulders against the surging wind coming off the water. Below, the incoming tide lapped at the bomber. The nose had been completely cut away. A section of the rear fuselage sat on the stones, and the tail was still resting against the cliff face. A detail working with acetylene torches was busy cutting away one of the wide wings with its black-and-white iron cross.

"We've gone through it for everything of military value," Cheatwood said. "A barge is coming tomorrow to haul away the wreckage for scrap metal."

"I am sure an ironmonger would be fascinated," Gwynne said. "The aircraft landed in the night and then went off the cliff before it could halt itself, I presume?" The inspector eyed Cheatwood as he tested the ground close to the edge with one foot. A crumble of sod broke loose, sending dirt and stone tumbling to the beach.

"Yes, that's the presumption," Cheatwood said. "The momentum might have carried it some distance before it hit water, which would explain why we found no trace of the aircraft the next morning."

"It would explain that." Gwynne stepped back from the edge. "And little else."

"Well, certainly not the matter of Stephen Elliot," Cheatwood said.

"Did you know him?" Gwynne said to Cheatwood as he jutted his chin at him.

"I did. He was still in residence at Marston Hall when I arrived."

"Did you like him?" Gwynne demanded.

Colonel Cheatwood looked out at the lapping waves bringing in the tide. "No."

"Who did?" Gwynne asked, keeping his gaze fixed on Cheatwood.

"His sister, Charlotte," Cheatwood said. "She adored him."

"No school chums about? Old pals or lady friends?" Gwynne asked.

"Elliot didn't attend school around here," Cheatwood said. "Came to Slewford as a young man and kept to himself."

"A monk then, was he?" Gwynne asked, the hint of a smile playing across his face. He jumped at the simple notion of a love interest being involved. "Come, take me to the sister. Then we'll look into his history with the opposite sex. An approach that often pays dividends. Perhaps your Yank driver has even heard of it out amongst the cowboys."

I had to admit, Gwynne had a point. It was a smart place to start this investigation. Unless you were Sir Richard Seaton, who'd threatened to throttle Stephen Elliot after he assaulted a maid and took a swing at Diana. Given what little I knew of Elliot, it was likely there were similar encounters and no shortage of angry men and women. Not a happy thought, but at least it might serve to divert attention from Sir Richard.

Because he was innocent. He had to be. If only for purely physical reasons, he couldn't have done it. For that matter, I couldn't see how anyone had managed it. I had to believe that no matter what the inspector or I came up with, Sir Richard was not involved with murder.

Until now, I'd viewed Sir Richard as a kind older gentleman. I saw him through Diana's worshipping eyes and the pain he'd endured losing Daphne, not to mention his wife. He was a father, and that formed my vision of him. But there was more to the man than that. He was a fighting sailor, had been grievously wounded in the last war, and was playing some sort of shadowy role in this one. There were also his interactions with Dr. Bodkin, which hinted at secrets long buried. Had they risen along with the aircraft?

"Why did he bother coming out here?" Cheatwood muttered as we walked to the jeep. I'd been lost in my thoughts and hardly noticed Gwynne stalking off from the cliff edge. "He barely spent a minute."

"Gwynne had to see the place for himself," I said as I started the jeep. "To make it real, would be my guess, since nothing about the body or the aircraft makes sense. It's not like there are any clues lying around."

"I wish the damn thing had never turned up," Cheatwood said. "Although Charlotte may find some comfort in finally putting her brother to rest. Small recompense, I must say, for all the attention this affair is drawing."

"I'd bet the inspector will steer clear of Marston Hall," I said. "At least of the current occupants."

"I hope you're right, Captain." Cheatwood glanced back at Gwynne's motorcar.

I knew I was. I could see it in Gwynne's reaction at the crash site. It perplexed him, and he moved swiftly into more certain territory: sex, love, passion, jealousy. These commonplace motivators of murder were threads he could start to unravel by digging into Elliot's life and relationships. The more impossible or improbable the circumstances of the corpse ending up in the bomber, the more Chief Inspector Gwynne would pursue the possible and the understandable. He'd ignore what he couldn't explain and make an arrest based on what he could.

How could I be so sure?

I knew how the bosses in police departments worked. It was no different for the cowboys or at Scotland Yard. Close the case. Don't leave embarrassing facts hanging. Marston Hall was an uncomfortable detail, not for what went on there but because it was a secret facility. Officials who let secrets see the light of day were apt to lose their jobs. I knew there'd be pressure applied to the Norfolk Constabulary, and that pressure would roll downhill from the chief constable right onto the shoulders of the chief inspector.

Close the case, quickly. Not spoken in so many words, but the message would be unmistakable. Protect the secrets, protect the powers that be, protect your boss. My money was on a visit to Seaton Manor tomorrow, just for a chat. Then, if nothing else caught Gwynne's attention, the next day would see an official interview at the station. After that, all bets were off. It was my job to find something tantalizing to distract the chief inspector with.

Because Sir Richard *was* innocent, I kept telling myself.

I took a sharp turn, heading back around Tower Hill, and caught a glimpse of that Archer fellow. David Archer, dressed in the same worn jacket he'd had on yesterday, vanishing up a trail into the woods.

"Archer," I said to Cheatwood, crooking my thumb in the direction of the hilltop. "You know much about him?"

"Shell shock. Never got over it, poor soul," Cheatwood said. "I've heard stories about him being buried under a mound of corpses after his trench took a direct hit. Most villages have one or two like him, some worse than others. He seems harmless, and I take it that people look out for him, bring him food on occasion."

"Diana and I saw him at the cliffs," I said. "He was the first to spot the bomber in the surf."

"He prefers the outdoors, so I understand. Feels less like being buried alive, I suppose. He's at the edge of the fence now and then, eyeing the Germans," Cheatwood said. "Can't be pleasant for him."

The British had been in the trenches a lot longer than the Yanks, so I didn't doubt that most villages over here would have a troubled veteran or two. We had a guy like that back in my neighborhood in South Boston. He'd been a merchant seaman with the Red Star Line, and his steamer had been torpedoed by a German U-Boat in 1916. He was one of the lucky ones from below decks who'd made it out before the ship went down. He'd climbed a steel ladder, going straight up, hand over hand, until he reached an open hatch. The seawater slammed it shut just as he cleared it, dooming the men behind him.

He'd made it back to Boston, but he was never the same. He'd walk around the neighborhood, raising his legs high with every step, as if he were still going up that ladder, rung by rung. He never spoke, not that I knew of, anyway. We kids were scared of him, not because of anything he did or said, but for what he signified: the reality and finality of war's crippling possibilities.

I pulled over in front of Charlotte Mothersole's cottage, which was built with the familiar Norfolk flint with brickwork framing the windows and doors. A curtain on the second floor opened, and I spotted Charlotte eyeing us. As we got out, Cheatwood waved to her and attempted a smile. Gwynne and his driver parked behind us.

"Oh my," Charlotte said when she answered the door. "This cannot be good."

"Mrs. Mothersole," Cheatwood said. "This is Chief Inspector Roland Gwynne. I believe you know Captain Boyle."

"Yes, yes, come in. Do sit down," she said as she led us into a sitting room. She took a chair by the fireplace, and we arranged ourselves facing her. "What news have you?"

"It's about the body in the aircraft," Gwynne said. "I am sorry to bring you this news, and we don't yet have positive identification, but there is a chance we've found the remains of your brother, Stephen."

"What ever are you talking about?" Charlotte said. "What aircraft? What body, for that matter?" She looked confused, as if Gwynne were speaking to her in a foreign language.

"You don't know about the German bomber?" Gwynne asked. "The tides and currents surfaced it yesterday, after the storm. Right where it went down."

"Yesterday? No, I've not left the house since returning from Sir Richard's the night before. I feared I caught a chill in that wind and rain, so I kept to my bed." She dabbed at her nose with a lace handkerchief. "But what does this have to do with my brother? I don't understand."

"There were three bodies recovered from the wreck," Cheatwood said, leaning forward and speaking gently. "One was wearing a British Army uniform. A Signals officer."

"But how?" Charlotte gasped. "You're talking about that bomber that went down in 1942? How could Stephen possibly be on it? Or in it, I guess. Either way, it's simply not possible. Is this a joke?"

"Not at all, Mrs. Mothersole," Gwynne said. "I agree that it makes little sense. But the fact remains, we have a body. Once dental tests are complete, we can confirm whether it is your brother. Can you tell us where Stephen had his dental work done?"

"We both use Dr. Victor Farthing, on Purfleet Street in King's Lynn," Charlotte said, her eyes darting among the three of us, as if someone might tell her not to worry. Then it dawned on her. "Oh. Dental records. I see."

"Mrs. Mothersole, we must put aside the strange circumstances that led to the discovery of this body and focus on who might have wanted to harm your brother," Gwynne said. "Do you have any idea who would wish him ill?"

"Wait, wait." Charlotte held up a hand as if to ward off the words. "Are you now saying he was murdered? You don't even know if it's Stephen—you said so yourself. This is simply too fantastical. I'd like you to leave, all of you. I wish you luck in identifying this mysterious body. If it turns out to be Stephen, beyond any doubt, I will answer all your questions. But not until then."

"Very well, Mrs. Mothersole." Gwynne pushed himself off his chair with a grunt. "I thought you should be warned of the possibility, and I am sorry if I upset you." He nodded in her direction and clomped toward the door.

"I'm sorry for the intrusion," I said, watching her eyes. They flitted to Cheatwood and then back to me.

"Thank you," she said in a quiet voice, her head bowed in sadness.

I followed Gwynne to the door, glancing back at Charlotte. Cheatwood patted her arm and told her he'd be in touch.

The look in her eyes told me she wouldn't mind a bit of comfort.

CHAPTER TWELVE

"COLONEL CHEATWOOD, I will have the findings from the dental records by the end of the day," Gwynne said, grinding to a halt on the path outside. "You'll be informed of the results tomorrow. It may be necessary to interview Mrs. Mothersole again and to search Elliot's possessions. Are they still at Marston Hall?"

"Yes. Charlotte was insistent that we store everything in his private library on the second floor. She's always been certain he would return," Cheatwood said.

"A loyal sister." Gwynne nodded his approval. "That will be a help. As for you, Captain, your services as a chauffeur are no longer required."

"Are you speaking to me, Inspector? I'm startled by the attention," I said.

"Chief Inspector," Gwynne muttered and climbed into the back seat. His constable shut the door and gave me a wink.

"So, where do you think this is all going?" I asked Cheatwood as we drove through the gate at Marston Hall.

"It makes no sense at all." He heaved out a sigh. "Elliot certainly had more enemies than friends, but how that ended him up where we found him, God knows. I expect you'll be glad to get on with your leave, Boyle."

"I would be," I said, parking the jeep and avoiding any mention of the orders I expected in the morning. "But until then, maybe we should take a look through Elliot's room?"

"No, I think not," Cheatwood said. "Best to wait until we are sure it is him. I did promise Charlotte I would keep his belongings secure, and I'd rather not go back on that. Thank you for the ride, Captain. I shall do my best to handle Gwynne by myself tomorrow."

I wished him luck with that and went off to find Sir Richard, thinking about the smile Cheatwood had sent up to Charlotte's second-story window and the gentle touch to her arm as we departed. They had something going on. Good for them. Cheatwood was keeping it on the QT, which wasn't any of my concern, but it did make me want to get back to Diana as soon as possible. We were supposed to be enjoying ourselves, and so far, the highlight of this leave was a horseback ride topped off with three corpses.

"What the devil is going on?" Sir Richard barked as soon as I entered the library. He snapped his book closed, glancing behind me to see who might be listening. "Am I under suspicion?"

"Chief Inspector Gwynne will want to talk to you," I said. "For now, you're not a prime suspect."

"Why would I be at any time?" Sir Richard growled.

"Because someone told Gwynne about the altercation you had with Stephen Elliot. I believe you threatened to throttle him," I said.

"As any decent man would've! Elliot's behavior was repellent," he said.

"Yes. His behavior toward your own daughter, which angered you."

"Of course it did! Ah, well, I see your point. It would be logical for the police to speak with anyone who got into an argument with the man," Sir Richard said. "It won't be a short list—I can promise you that."

I gave Sir Richard my assessment of the chief inspector—that being unable to explain the appearance of Elliot's body in the aircraft, he'd focus on more traditional motives and likely give up on explaining the unexplainable. And that threats of throttling were as traditional as steak and kidney pie.

"That's why I'm sure he'll come calling, and soon," I said. "The only thing that might stall him is finding out about someone else who actually followed through on a threat against Elliot. You have any ideas?"

"Nothing specific, no. My threat might have had some impact on Elliot," Sir Richard said. "I didn't hear of any further incidents after that party."

"Would you have?"

"News travels in a small village," Sir Richard said. "You tell one person, and the next morning the milkman is delivering the gossip. Anyway, Elliot joined the service not too long after that. Sobered him up, perhaps. Whatever happened, I know who informed on me to Gwynne. It had to be Bodkin."

"What's the bad blood between you two all about, anyway?" I asked.

"Never mind. None of your business," Sir Richard snapped as he stood. "Let's get back, shall we?"

"Wait a minute," I said. "There's something else." I took a seat, and Sir Richard returned to his chair.

"I apologize, Billy. I'm a bit short-tempered today. Now, what is it?"

"Major Hudson wants me to investigate what happened to Elliot," I said. "He's apparently contacted Colonel Harding, and I'm being officially assigned to this case."

"Yes." Sir Richard drummed his fingers on the arm of the chair. "I can see his logic. Keep the local police from bumbling about, and the findings can be kept quiet."

"Right. Keeping the lid tamped down on Marston Hall would be important. For all concerned," I said. "Plus, there's the embarrassment of a British officer turning up in that aircraft. It has all the makings of a scandal, and the men behind the scenes hate that sort of thing."

"Oh, yes, Billy. Those men do hate publicity," Sir Richard said. "I daresay there are officials at the War Office who are looking for a scapegoat as we speak. Someone they can sacrifice to save their precious careers."

"Someone like you," I said.

"I am the perfect candidate," he said. "I've threatened Elliot. I am not currently connected with Marston Hall, but I was involved in the selection of the estate for the interrogation program. There could be allusions to his anger at the Hall being taken over at my suggestion. All sorts of possibilities. Which is why I am glad you've been selected to investigate this. Not for your sake, or Diana's, especially, but for my own. I know you'll do a fine job."

"Thank you, Sir Richard. I'll do my best."

"I trust you will, but there's something else you must do."

"Name it," I said.

"Move out of Seaton Manor. Tonight," he said. "It won't do to have an investigator enjoying the hospitality of a potential suspect."

"Is that necessary?" I asked, knowing it was.

"Yes. I'm thinking of your credibility. And of Diana's as well. If this goes badly for me, I don't want her name connected with the slightest hint of undue influence. I'm sure you understand, Billy," Sir Richard said. "The Rose and Crown in the village has decent rooms. There'll be one waiting for you."

"This isn't the way I expected my visit to go," I said. "But you're right. In case I go head-to-head with Gwynne, I don't want him accusing me of favoritism. I'll take you home and pack my stuff."

"That's settled, then." Sir Richard's relief was evident on his face. "Stay and dine with us, though."

"No, I think I'd do better to eat at the Rose and Crown," I said. "I can try to pick up any local gossip. I'm sure tongues are wagging."

"They always are in a small village, and this is an irresistible story," Sir Richard said, carrying the book about King John with him as we left the library.

"Before we leave," I said, "do you know where Elliot's private library is?"

"Yes, on the second floor. He showed me his collection once. Called himself a historian. I must admit, he had books enough to lay the claim," Sir Richard said. "Why?"

"Let's take a look," I said. "Before anyone else does."

We took a back staircase, avoiding the British and American soldiers moving through the house who were sometimes in the company of Germans. Sir Richard led me to a door at the end of the hallway on the second floor. I glanced around, making sure we were alone.

"It's probably locked," Sir Richard said.

As I grasped the handle, I was sure I heard footsteps from within. I raised my finger to my lips and leaned closer to the polished wooden door. Soft murmurs of snatched conversation between two people who were intent on keeping things quiet were all I could make out. I pressed the latch. It was unlocked. I swung the door open.

"Mildred!" Sir Richard said at the sight of Mrs. Bunch standing not six feet away with a khaki-brown British Army uniform draped across her arm. Trousers, jacket, leather belt, shirt, and all. "What are you doing here?"

"Oh, Sir Richard, you startled me," she said in a high-pitched voice. "My goodness. We're here fetching a decent set of clothes for Mr. Elliot. I can't imagine what state his clothing is in now. The poor dear, he was so particular about his appearance."

She laid the uniform across the back of the chair in the small sitting room. Twin leather armchairs faced a fireplace overseen by portraits of dour ancestors from the last century. Behind Mildred, Alfred stood under arched double doors that led into the library.

"How did you get in here?" I asked.

"We let ourselves in, Captain," Alfred said. "We'd just delivered seventy pounds of lamb to the kitchen, and Mildred here wanted to be sure Mr. Elliot was put into the ground proper like. That was the uniform he'd had tailored for himself. Don't know what he was wearing when he left here last, but he'd like to meet his maker wearing his best."

"Shouldn't Mrs. Mothersole be the one to decide that?" I said, holding back mention of Elliot having met his maker long before now.

"She'll be in a right state for a while," Mildred said. "Them bein' so close. I'm sure this has shattered her."

"As Sir Richard knows, we worked at Marston Hall for years," Alfred said. "Mr. Elliot was very good to us, and we wanted to do him this good turn. As well as save Mrs. Mothersole the unfortunate business of visiting the undertaker."

"Copping and Sons, I expect," Sir Richard said. "Over in Castle Rising."

"Aye, they're the closest, and fair at their trade," Alfred said, eyeing me as I wandered into the library. It was a long, narrow room. The shelves were filled with books, some newer, but many old and tattered. A large chest and several crates held what must have been Elliot's personal effects. These were stacked next to an open armoire at the far end of the room, displaying a selection of fine suits. Beyond that, a narrow door to a closet stood open. A ten-foot wooden table was strewn with papers. Old, dusty magazines, maps, and yellowed documents spilled from folders. Next to an equally messy desk at one end of the room, situated beneath a large south-facing window, was a framed map.

"The Wash, isn't it?" I asked, seeing that Alfred had followed me closely.

"As it was nearly two hundred years ago," he said. "The coastline has shifted, and land has been filled in where there once were rivers and marshes. A treacherous place, it was."

"Come, Alfred, we must go," Mildred said, buttoning her coat. "There's still work to do."

"Always," Alfred said, gesturing for me to walk ahead as we exited the library. "Sir Richard, what brought you here?"

"Captain Boyle is interested in medieval British history," Sir Richard said. "We came hoping the rooms would be open so I could show him Elliot's collection. He was quite an expert, wasn't he?"

"That he was. Spent a lot of his time up here," Alfred said. "For now, we must go. I need to lock up, otherwise Mrs. Mothersole will be upset with us."

"We're no longer the caretakers, but we do care." Mildred smiled as she picked up the uniform and brushed it with one hand. "We spent so many years here, it still feels like home, even though now Mr. Elliot will never return."

Alfred nodded sadly as he locked the door.

Outside, I started the jeep and watched as they drove off in their van.

"There was something strange about that," I said.

"You mean the key? I wondered about that myself," Sir Richard said. "Perhaps I'll ask Charlotte about it, once things settle down."

"Good idea," I said. But I didn't mention what really bothered me. There was a decent layer of dust over the papers on the library table. Enough of it to notice that documents had been moved.

What was Alfred looking for?

The more I thought about it, the more it seemed like Mildred had been standing guard, in case anyone walked in on them. She'd had the uniform in hand. If that's what they were there for, why had Alfred been poking around in the library?

CHAPTER THIRTEEN

"YOU MUST BE joking," Diana said. "You have leave? Colonel Harding signed the papers? What happened to the time we were to have together?"

Diana had a pitchfork in one hand. I'd found her in the barn mucking out the stalls, and I probably should have thought about waiting until she wasn't armed with a sharp implement before delivering the news.

"It's out of my hands, Diana. Major Hudson got in touch with Harding before I knew what was going on," I said. "According to Hudson, the orders are due to arrive in the morning."

"But you didn't have to spend the whole day snooping around, did you? You could have driven Father and left him at Marston Hall," she said, sticking the pitchfork into a bale of hay with some serious enthusiasm. "What have you been doing?"

I gave her the rundown. Viewing the bodies. Talking with Hudson. Going to the cliffs and then visiting Charlotte. Finding Alfred and Mildred in the library.

"All you had to do was get a whiff of those orders, and you were off and running." Diana advanced on me with her hands on her hips and shit on her boots. "No thought of coming back here and being with me. You and Father just pranced off together to find out how Stephen got into that bomber?"

"No, no, not really. I left Sir Richard in the library," I said, suddenly realizing that sounded even worse. "I thought the chief inspector would want to talk to him, but he didn't. Not today, anyway."

"So you could have come back, but you didn't. You couldn't leave the tantalizing mystery alone, could you? Not the great detective. Not Billy Boyle!"

"Diana, it wasn't like that," I said.

"All I know is you prefer the company of policemen and dead bodies to me," Diana said. "Perhaps it was a mistake for you to come here. Perhaps domestic life is too boring for you."

"I couldn't help it," I protested, sitting on the bale of hay with the pitchfork for company. I wanted to explain myself, which was hard because there was a hefty grain of truth in what she'd said. Not that I preferred cops and corpses to her, but that the draw of this case was strong. It was a tantalizing mystery, and her father's involvement made it personal. "Your father is a suspect."

"You said he wasn't."

"No, Gwynne just didn't want to talk to him today. He'll get around to it, believe me. He's already heard about the threats Sir Richard made to Elliot," I said. "There's going to be a lot of pressure for him to make an arrest and keep Marston Hall out of the limelight. I had to make sure I know whatever Gwynne knows. To protect Sir Richard."

"Oh dear. Does Father know?"

"Yes. He agrees he'd be the perfect scapegoat. Apparently, he was the one who recommended Marston Hall to the War Office," I said. "That and the threats will be enough to point Gwynne in his direction."

"Threat. It was singular," Diana said. "One throttle."

"Noted." I figured silence was my best next step.

"I'm sorry." Diana waved her hand in front of her face as if brushing away a bad memory. "I've waited so long to have you here, to have you to myself, and then today it was like the war wouldn't leave us alone, even in peaceful little Slewford."

"I know. Me too. Which makes the next bit of news even

harder to say. Sir Richard told me to leave tonight. I can't stay here and investigate a crime in which he's a suspect."

"God. The man knows how to manage a crisis, I'll give him that," Diana said as she settled on a stool opposite me. We sat quietly, the only sounds coming from the horses snuffling in their stalls. "The Rose and Crown?"

"Yes. Maybe you could come and visit me," I said.

"Scandalous, Billy! How dare you," Diana said, standing and walking over to a ladder that led to the hayloft. She pulled off her Wellingtons and climbed up, tossing me a smile over her shoulder.

I unlaced my boots in record time and followed.

A FEW HOURS later, I'd checked into my room at the Rose and Crown. It was clean, spacious enough, and upstairs at the back of the building, away from the road and the noise downstairs. I was drinking an ale and tucking into poacher's pie, which Dorothy had recommended. She and her husband, Brian, owned the place. She'd advised me that any dish made from game meat, rabbit in this case, and root vegetables, such as carrots and potatoes, was a good bet, what with all the rationing. They had a fine garden, and the marshes were full of rabbits.

I savored the warm, crusty pie, pausing every now and then to discreetly dig wisps of hay out of places you'd never expect them to be. I nodded a greeting to Alfred and Mildred as they entered. Mrs. Bunch went into the snug—a lounge off to the side for women and couples—as her husband was greeted by a clutch of men at the bar. The snug was where the ladies drank their half pints and sherries, serious drinking by women being frowned upon. Brian took Mildred's order through a sliding glass window between the two rooms.

The barroom was a male domain, and I wondered how long it would be until Diana and I would sit together in the snug. I knew she wouldn't sashay through the door and join me anytime soon. We'd agreed it was best to keep our distance, at least publicly, until Sir Richard was in the clear.

My seat was in the corner by the fireplace, on a bench built into the wall. One lonely chair was across from me, but I'd been left to myself so far. Four American sergeants were at a table in the back of the room, but they were smart enough to ignore an officer. Alfred was waiting for Brian to pull his pint, and I spotted him glancing toward me and whispering. Another guy leaned in to listen and then whispered to the guy next to him in a perfect demonstration of the village gossip machine.

"You liked the pie, Captain?" Dorothy asked as she cleared away my plate. Behind her, two more Americans walked in.

"Terrific," I said, ordering another ale. "Only GIs in here tonight? No British soldiers?"

"Most are on one of their patrols along the beach," she said. "Colonel Cheatwood likes to keep his boys fit. The rest have duty at Marston Hall. The Yanks make up for it, don't they? Overpaid and all, as they say."

As Dorothy left, Dr. Bodkin walked in and glanced around, finally noticing me.

"Good evening, Boyle," he said, shrugging off his coat. "Any news from the chief inspector?"

"I doubt I'd be the first to hear," I said. "Would you like to join me?"

"Thank you, but I need to chat with one of the lads. Next time, eh?"

I didn't especially want company, but I was beginning to feel like an outcast. I walked over to the corner where the other Yanks were gathered. A game of darts was underway.

"Captain," Hank Klein said, raising his glass in greeting. Oskar Goldstein threw his final dart and turned away from the board, his expression telling me he'd lost. Sergeant Goldstein introduced me, telling his pals I was an officer but that I seemed okay. They laughed, all but one doing it with a German accent. It felt nice to be around guys who were friendly.

"Scuttlebutt is you are some kind of detective," Oskar said, draining his beer. "Is it true?"

"Some kind, yeah," I said. "But what kind, that's the question. What do you guys hear about the body in the Brit uniform?"

"Everybody's got a theory," Hank said. "Nazi spy. The bomber landed on top of Elliot. He tried to retrieve secret documents and got pulled under."

"I like that last one," Oskar said, eyeing his empty glass.

"Hey, guys, this round's on me," I said. There were only six of them, and I might need some friends among the noncommissioned ranks at Marston Hall. They commented on what a natural leader of men I was, then I went to the bar to order.

"Coming up," Brian said. "We'll have chops for dinner tomorrow, Captain. Alfred's just brought his delivery."

"Sounds good," I said, turning to Alfred. "Busy day today?"

"Aye. Slaughtered in the early hours, then delivered fresh to my customers," Alfred said. "Nigel here's my cousin and come down to help. Mildred isn't much for butchery. Too messy for her."

"A right mess it is, too, if things go bad," Nigel said. "Bad enough even doin' it proper."

Nigel looked to be older than Alfred, with more gray in his hair and a weathered face. The back of his neck and his hands were scarred. By the look of it, and from what Dad and Uncle Dan had told me, it was the result of mustard gas. If it settled on skin, it produced blistering burns.

"Gassed," Nigel said, catching me looking at his hands.

"Sorry, I didn't mean to stare," I said, looking straight ahead.

"Not the first one," he said with a harsh laugh. "I'm lucky I got my mask on in time. Plenty of lads didn't."

"Lucky, since your face is ugly enough as it is!" Alfred said, and they both chuckled, like people do over a well-worn yet still welcome joke.

"Alfred tells me you're the fella looking into who killed his old lord and master," Nigel said, draining his pint.

"That would be Chief Inspector Gwynne," I said.

"Old Glum Gwynnie?" Nigel said. "There's one suckled on sour milk."

"You know the fella?" Alfred asked his cousin.

"Sure. He came to look around the estate a few times," Nigel said. "We had two break-ins last month, and the police needed to put on a big show about it."

"What estate?" I asked.

"Sandringham House," Nigel said. "It's a royal residence. It belongs to whoever wears the crown."

"Don't let him get wound up, Captain," Alfred said. "Next, he'll tell you he's in line for the throne!"

"It's true, in a sense," Nigel said. "I'm in charge of the plumbing, don't you see!"

Nigel could barely contain himself over the joke but calmed down enough to describe his duties with an evident sense of pride. Sandringham House boasted fifty-two bedrooms for the royals and their guests, one hundred and eighty-eight for staff, and seventy-eight bathrooms. That was the main house and didn't count the numerous guest cottages on the grounds.

"That's a lot of pipe," Nigel said. "Everything's got to be in working order, especially now that it's not being used on account of the war. The smallest leak could be a disaster if it's not caught quick and put right. It's not just the bathrooms; it's the kitchens and water heaters to boot."

"You have any royal visitors lately?" I asked.

"I haven't kept me job over the last twelve years by tellin' tales of the high and mighty," he said. "Glum Gwynnie had a lot of questions, too, and I told him the same."

"Did he ever catch anyone?"

"Nah. Probably just kids actin' on a dare," Nigel said. "We all take turns standin' watch, but it's a huge place."

"You got your Home Guard out there too," Alfred said.

"True, but there're fewer of us these days. No one's worried about Jerry invading like they were in 1940," Nigel said. "But Colonel Cheatwood still marches his boys up our way now and then."

"Aye, there was a platoon patrolling along the beach today, or at least that's what the cooks told me," Alfred said. "Cheatwood didn't go with them this time. Usually does. Likes a good walk, that one."

"You sell to the royals?" I asked Alfred.

"No, only to the staff," Alfred said. "I give them a nice discount on account of Nigel bein' my cousin. They order nice and regular, not like His Highness, who comes and goes on a whim. Good business, it is. Don't hurt none to say I sell to the royal estate, though."

"Keeps him flush." Nigel slapped his hand down on the bar.

I saw my seat by the fire was still free, excused myself after a decent laugh, and sat down to finish my ale. The door opened with a rush of cool air as Major Hudson walked in along with a lieutenant. He told me to drop by at 0800 to review my orders. I raised my glass to him and said nothing, hoping that the army might forget the whole thing.

Behind Hudson, David Archer entered the pub. He did so warily, taking a few steps along the wall and surveying the room. His eyes flitted from one person to the other as he drew his shoulders in to make himself smaller.

Less of a target.

A few people noticed him and quickly looked away. Cheatwood had said the villagers looked out for Archer, but that didn't mean they wanted his company.

"Archer," I said, then repeated myself. "David Archer?"

"Who are you?" He took three quick steps and put his back against the wall next to me. "Do I know you?"

"I saw you at the cliffs yesterday," I said. "I was out riding with Miss Seaton. My name's Billy."

"You saw it then? It came out of the sea, didn't it, Billy?"

"That it did. Have a seat. Can I buy you a pint?"

"Wouldn't mind it," Archer said. "But I can't sit there. Switch seats?"

"Sure," I said. My bench was against the wall, while the chair had its back to the room. He wouldn't like that, so I got up. He took off his coat, threw it on the bench, and slid in. I signaled to Dorothy for two pints.

"Miss Seaton's a nice girl," Archer said. "Always been kind."

"She is. It must have been a shock to see that bomber come out of the surf."

"And the sea gave up the dead which were in it; and death and hell delivered up the dead which were in them; and they were judged every man according to their works," Archer answered. "That's in the Bible. Book of Revelation. It was time for Stephen Elliot to be judged, don't you think?"

"I'm not certain it was him," I said.

"Ha!" Archer spat out a laugh, finding this less than believable. "Who then?"

"We may know soon, one way or the other," I said, noticing Colonel Cheatwood making his way to the bar. He caught my eye but then turned to talk with Brian.

"I know right now," Archer said. "I know what goes on in Marston Hall as well."

"With the prisoners? Hardly a well-kept secret," I said. Again, the laugh.

"Here you go, boys," Dorothy said, setting down the pints. "How are you tonight, Mr. Archer?"

"Fair enough, Miss Dorothy," he said as he kept watch on anyone who drew near. A wary man. "Beautiful night. Clear skies."

"You'll catch your death out there, Mr. Archer," Dorothy said. "Get to your bed sometime tonight, will you?" She gave Archer a wink as she returned to her work.

"Cheers," I said as we raised our glasses. "What did she mean by that?"

"Oh, I like the outdoors," he said. "Don't much like being between walls. Especially at night. How about you? Billy, is it?"

"Yeah. Billy Boyle. I like the outdoors myself, but I like a soft bed too."

It took the rest of the pint, but David Archer laid it out in bits and pieces. Without ever mentioning the war, he made it clear that being inside at night was absolutely frightening and that he needed the open dome of the sky to feel safe. Dawn was what he longed for since it meant he'd survived another day. Another day in the trenches, which is where part of him had never left.

I didn't ask about being buried alive under the bodies of his comrades.

I didn't have to.

As Archer talked, I began to understand why people avoided him. Yes, he was a little strange, but he was also the only man from his unit to come back alive. These people were the relatives of his fellow soldiers, all killed in those muddy, bloodied trenches. He was a reminder of how the war would have ground them down had they survived.

At times he was hard to follow, but I realized he'd come back to the bomber.

"It was loud," he said. "I tried to block it out, but I couldn't." He massaged a faint scar on his cheek, and he began to fidget in his seat. "I wished I hadn't seen it." He moaned. "But I did."

"A lot of people saw it that night," I said. "Half the village, from what people say."

"You don't understand."

"Outside, quick!" someone shouted from the open door. Excited voices sounded from the street as the figure darted back outside, leaving the door wide open. Archer scurried out, and I followed as others pushed forward to see what the uproar was all about.

"Look!" Alfred shouted, pointing to the northern sky.

Pinpoints of pulsing light streamed across it, far above us. There were ten—no, twelve—streams of light accompanied by a very distinctive sound, like a car with a defective exhaust. It was a loud, rapid, sputtering that I'd heard before.

A V-1 rocket. I'd never seen so many at once.

"Oh my god!" Mildred shrieked, and others joined in with their own terrors, the small crowd jostling one another for a better view or to find their friends.

"They've never come this far north," Sergeant Goldstein said.

"They don't have the range," another man said.

Off to my side, Archer gasped at the sight that must have reminded him of the bomber on fire hurtling toward the ground.

It's a new rocket; *it's gas*; *it's an invasion* . . . All sorts of crazy notions swept through the gathering crowd. I knew it was the V-1, but I also knew they'd never been seen in these numbers and certainly not this far north of London.

We watched the rocket engines fly west until they were lost in the darkness. Everyone watched the sky in silence, awed at what we had witnessed.

"Oi, what's this?" Nigel shouted as he tripped near the door to the pub.

Mildred screamed again, this time not into the night sky but toward the ground.

Where David Archer lay dead.

CHAPTER FOURTEEN

DAVID ARCHER HAD survived the trenches of the last war. He'd managed, in his own way, to live with the demons that had haunted him when he came home, wounded in spirit, to live in a village filled with the ghosts of his comrades. He'd kept to himself, better suited to the dark night sky than the warmth and comfort of any four walls.

But his crafty wariness had not saved him when all eyes were focused on the buzz of bombs overhead. That gasp I'd heard hadn't been one of awe or surprise at the sight of the V-1 rockets. It had been his last breath escaping after a blade had pierced his heart.

The crowd pressed in after Nigel tripped over Archer's body, the shock of the rockets replaced by the shock of death even closer at hand. It was only then that I spotted Sir Richard standing behind Alfred. He was comforting his wife, who was in tears.

I pressed my fingers to Archer's still-warm throat, but there was no blood coursing through his veins. He'd fallen on his side, his back hardly bloodied where he'd been stabbed.

Brian called for the nearest constable, who was in Heacham, five miles away. It took a while to get through, since the lines were clogged with people calling in reports of the V-1s, but Constable Parker finally showed up on his bicycle, ordering the crowd into the pub to wait for the chief inspector, who would arrive shortly. Parker remained outside and stood guard over the body.

Sir Richard told me he and Diana had argued, and he'd decided a visit to the pub was in order before things got out of hand. He'd left his bicycle around the side and entered through the rear door. I didn't ask what the argument was about, figuring it had to be about Stephen Elliot's death, but what could she blame him for? Kicking me out of the house? She'd agreed that had been necessary. Before I could decide whether I even wanted to ask, Sir Richard left to chat with the men at the bar.

Now everyone wanted to be my friend. I was peppered with questions about what Archer and I had been talking about and who I thought had killed him. Since the pub had emptied out in the excitement over the rocket's red glare, everyone was a potential suspect. Tongues were wagging and fingers pointing. The unwritten rule about a woman's place being in the snug had gone by the boards, given the fright the murder in the night had put into everyone. Charlotte Mothersole was there, calming one of the other ladies, who was sobbing in her arms. Sir Richard was soon by their side.

Brian and Cheatwood joined forces to keep everyone calm as well as in place. A British colonel and the resident publican were the two highest ranks in the room, so I sat with my whiskey and tried to think things through.

You don't understand.

Those had been Archer's last words to me. I hadn't even understood what it was that I didn't understand. Somebody else had, though. Someone who knew that Archer was finally going to say something about that night. I strolled around, glancing at sleeves and cuffs, looking for any telltale signs of blood. I chatted with the Yank contingent, huddled in a corner with Major Hudson.

Dr. Bodkin was with another knot of customers, explaining how the death was likely instantaneous, given the lack of blood.

When he stated that the killer knew something of anatomy, one man edged away from him.

A clump of men stood around Nigel and Alfred, their conversation veering from disbelief about Archer's death to the sudden appearance of what now had grown into a vast armada of V-1s.

"Billy, would you take this cuppa out to Constable Parker? He won't have a drink on duty, but some tea will do him good," Dorothy said, handing me a steaming mug. "It's fixed just the way he likes it." She gave a wink as she went back to the bar.

I gave the tea a sniff and approved. Laced with whiskey was just the way I liked it too.

"Cold night, Constable," I said by way of greeting. "Dorothy asked me to bring you this."

"You're right about that, Captain, and thank you. How are they getting on in there?" Parker sipped the tea and gave an approving smile.

"Still in shock," I said. "The V-1s were enough of a surprise, but Archer put them over the edge. I suspect they'll be clamoring to go home as soon as they settle down."

"Well, that may be, but the fact is that someone put a knife to poor Archer here, and they're probably in that pub. Or even out here bringing me tea, if you don't mind the honest truth," he said.

"I find that refreshing, Constable. No one else out and wandering the village?"

"No, all quiet," he said, returning to his tea. "I hope the chief inspector shows up soon, or I'll have my hands full."

I could see the church down the lane and a few shops across the way. Faint light filtered through several windows, but nothing that would violate the new blackout rules. Dim light, no brighter than a full moon, was now allowed. It wouldn't have been enough to see who had been moving toward Archer in that crowd, especially with everyone coming out of a well-lit room and looking to the heavens. It had been the perfect moment for an unplanned murder. Which told me this killer was not afraid to act on impulse.

"No sign of a weapon?" I asked.

"No, but there hasn't been a proper search," Parker said. "Best you go inside, sir, before Chief Inspector Gwynne arrives."

I took his advice, stopping at Archer's body to pay him a moment of respect.

"Constable, just one question. You must have known David Archer. What did you think of him?"

"He kept himself to himself, more than most. But if the stories about what happened to him are even half-true, more's the wonder that he managed as well as he did," Parker said. "People were wary of him. He frightened some, with his habit of wandering around all night, but that's understandable. Folks in their beds don't like thinking about a half-mad ex-soldier outside their windows. What he did with himself all night, I'll never know. Anyway, he never gave anyone trouble, not that I know of. What do you think? Is this because of that bomber?"

"I think Archer was the first to see it. But why do you say that?"

"Why wouldn't I? A downed German bomber suddenly reappears. A local man is found inside it. That's two mysterious things. Then someone kills David Archer, but for no reason I can see. That makes three strange occurrences. We haven't had three such mysteries in these parts since I joined the force. They have to be connected, in my mind at least."

"Solid thinking, Constable," I said, and headed back inside. I knew what I had to do next, as soon as it was light. I needed to walk the ground, just like David Archer.

"Oh, Billy, when will they let us leave?" Charlotte said once I entered. She was drying her eyes, seated on the bench by the fire. "This is all too terrible."

"It's best for everyone to stay," I said. "Otherwise, the police might not be able to find out who did it. It's one of those times it's best to set an example for others." I figured an appeal to her status as the possible heir to Marston Hall might work.

"Yes, of course. I hope that the chief inspector gets here soon and is quick about it. He's a bit much, isn't he? No bedside manner at all. But that's for doctors, not policemen, isn't it? What do policemen have, Billy?"

"A suspicious disposition, mostly. Occupational hazard," I said. "Don't take it personally, though; he's only doing his job."

"I've seen Archer near my cottage many times," Charlotte said. "He never bothered me. He spent a lot of time watching the Germans behind the fence at Marston Hall. And hiking up to Tower Hill."

"You saw him there often?" I asked.

"Yes. Should I mention that to the inspector?"

I told her she should, not that I thought he'd pay any attention to it. But I would.

Half an hour of increasing restlessness followed before the door banged open, announcing the arrival of Chief Inspector Gwynne.

"May I have your attention," he shouted, flanked by two constables. "We shall be taking statements from you all. When we are done, you may leave. But not until all statements are taken. Do not attempt to leave without permission. Now, let's get to it."

There was a chorus of protests and a litany of reasons why people needed to leave as soon as possible. Sick children and bedridden grandparents were so prominent that I wondered how the citizens of Slewford could ever have left so many of their relatives alone for even a quick drink. Gwynne was unmoved, and he was right. Conflicting statements had to be checked, and it would save him time to do it tonight.

"Why am I not surprised to find you here, Captain Boyle?" Gwynne said, settling into a chair with a heavy grunt.

"It's the only pub in town," I said.

"And you were the last to speak with Archer, I understand," he said.

"Unless his killer said something to him, yes."

"Leave off with that. Just tell me what you were talking about," Gwynne said.

"The last war. His nocturnal roaming. Things he saw," I said.

"Who else talked with him?"

"Dorothy said hello to him when he came in and sat with me. I bought him a beer and we talked. Someone yelled to come outside, and we all did. It was a mad stampede," I said.

"You went out with Archer?"

"Yes," I said. "Then there were a lot of exclamations, as you might expect, when we saw the rockets. I heard Archer gasp, but I thought it was in surprise, not from a knife in the back."

"It's a thin cut for a knife," Gwynne said, his voice low as he shared that tidbit. "We'll know more once the coroner looks him over."

"I think he was trying to tell me something about the bomber," I said. "He said he saw something. And that he knew what goes on at Marston Hall."

"Everybody knows what goes on there," Gwynne said. "The man was unwell, you know." He tapped his temple to make his point.

You don't understand, I wanted to say. But neither did I, so I said nothing.

When the coroner's wagon showed up to take the body away—how quickly it went from *David Archer* to *the body*—Constable Parker was brought in to search for the weapon while Gwynne and his two men worked through the statements.

Parker rummaged through trash, checked coat pockets, and even asked the ladies to move back into the snug where he had them empty their purses. He came up with nothing. The bar was next, and he went over each shelf, moving bottles and glasses.

"Anyone go into the cellar?" Parker asked Brian. There was a trapdoor on the floor behind the bar—just below the window to the snug—where the kegs were kept in the cellar.

"No, that case of Burton's has been on the trapdoor all night," Brian said, giving the box a push with his foot. He glanced at the shelf underneath the sliding glass window, now open to the snug. Then he looked underneath the bar, his search increasingly frantic.

"What is it, man?" Parker demanded.

"My ice pick is missing."

I'd seen it earlier myself and hadn't noticed it was gone. A long, narrow, sharp-tipped blade with a worn wooden handle. Great for breaking up chunks of block ice. And a favored weapon of Murder, Incorporated—the New York gang that provided assassination services for the Italian and Jewish mobs. Through the ear was the standard method, but the route between the shoulder blades and into the heart was just as fatal.

CHAPTER FIFTEEN

"ALMOST DONE WITH the statements, Captain," Gwynne said after a short but fruitless search for the ice pick. "We just have those Germans left." He stood with his hands behind his back, rocking on his heels as he scanned the pub.

"They're Americans," I said. "You must have noticed the uniform."

"I know who they are," he said, his eyes narrowing. "A German is a German, and a Jew a Jew."

"That upsets you?" I asked. "That men who suffered under the Nazis want to fight back?"

"What upsets me is all the foreigners who'll want to stay here once the war is over," Gwynne said at high volume. "You Yanks will go back home, but we'll be saddled with every Pole, Czech, Jew, and who knows what else, who wants to remain in England, you mark my words."

"They're marked," I said, keeping my thoughts about my Irish background to myself. I knew Gwynne's type, and right now giving him lip would only make things harder for Sir Richard. That's how things worked with men like Gwynne, especially when they had the power of the law behind them.

"You're staying in the pub now, I understand," the chief inspector said. "No longer with Sir Richard and his daughter?"

"Looks like I picked the wrong night to change lodgings." I

got up from my seat. "I'll leave you to it. I'm sure folks want to get home to their beds."

"And I'm sure I want to find the murder weapon," he said. "I may keep everyone here until I do."

"Here's an idea," I said, not because I was feeling charitable, but because I wanted to get to sleep. "Check the ground near the body. If I wanted to get rid of an ice pick, I'd stick it in the ground and step down on it. That thin spike and handle would vanish into the dirt."

Gwynne grunted and moved off to where his constable was starting to question the American contingent. My bet was that he'd quietly order the search. The nature of the weapon and where it was used suggested a simple way to dispose of it. For all I knew, the killer had slipped it into his boot, but that would make for an unintelligent murderer, and whoever did this was a quick thinker.

I watched as Sir Richard ordered another whiskey at last call. He nearly spilled it as he turned away to avoid Dr. Bodkin, then disappeared into the snug. How snug was he with Charlotte Mothersole in there, and what did Colonel Cheatwood think of that? An idle mind is a suspicious thing, so I decided to do something useful. I asked Brian if I could use the telephone and rang up Seaton Manor. I told Diana what had happened and that since her father had downed several whiskeys, she might want to drive over and fetch him. A tipsy one-armed man on two wheels could easily end up in a ditch.

By the time Gwynne wrapped up taking statements, things had gotten testy. It was well past closing time, and without drinks, the pub felt like a prison. When everyone was finally cleared to leave, I walked outside with Sir Richard to where Diana was waiting. Archer's body was gone, but we skirted the grass where he'd lain.

"A bad end for a man who'd suffered more than his share," Sir Richard said as Diana took his hand, her face softening in the scant light. Whatever their argument had been, there was no trace of it now. "It was foolish of me to come here."

"Let's go home, Father," Diana said, leaning in to give me a kiss. "Be careful, Billy."

I said I would be. After all, I was on leave in a peaceful English village, wasn't I? I promised I'd bring the bicycle back to Seaton Manor tomorrow, which provided a good excuse to visit.

Up in my room, I pushed back the curtain to look outside. I could hear murmured voices and see shielded lights as Gwynne and his men searched the ground. I smiled as I thought about telling him that idea had come from an Irishman.

AFTER A FEW hours of sleep and a solid breakfast, I set out to trace the journeys of David Archer. I knew Major Hudson would be waiting for me with my orders, but he could cool his heels a while longer. My gut told me that understanding Archer was the key to understanding this whole case. The killer certainly agreed with me, so now was the time to follow in Archer's footsteps.

I walked to the side of the pub where Sir Richard had left his bike. I wheeled it out to the road to toss in the back of my jeep just as Chief Inspector Gwynne arrived, his police sedan grinding to a halt in front of me.

"Stop right there," he said, vaulting out of the back seat and snapping his fingers for his driver. "Constable, search that bag."

"What's this all about?" I asked as the constable pulled the bicycle out of my grasp.

"Searching for evidence," Gwynne said. "Evidence you were about to take away, Captain."

The constable opened the leather bag under the handlebars. He removed a folded cloth and carefully unwrapped it, revealing a thin-handled ice pick. Bloodstains had soaked the fabric.

"The murder weapon, Chief Inspector," the constable announced.

"You tried to throw us off the scent by suggesting the killer buried it," Gwynne said, stepping in close. "But all along you knew where it was. Now you're trying to get rid of it, aren't you?"

"Chief Inspector, if I had known about it and had wanted to get rid of it, I would have done it last night, before someone tipped you off about it, wouldn't I?"

"Who says anybody tipped us off?" Gwynne said.

"The way you pulled up," I said. "You knew what you were after. Since you didn't bother to look last night, someone must've dropped a nickel on me."

"Dropped a what?" Gwynne asked.

"It's an American coin, Chief Inspector," the constable said. "What they use to make telephone calls. I heard the phrase in a gangster film."

"Hush!" Gwynne said, clearly irritated at my logic and the constable's helpfulness. "I'm taking this machine as evidence, and I'll be questioning Sir Richard Seaton very carefully about it. You keep quiet about this, Captain Boyle, or else I'll haul you in."

"It makes sense to question Sir Richard, Chief Inspector," I said. "As well as me. Along with the other twenty-odd people in the pub last night. Anybody could have slipped the ice pick in this bag at any point. What time did the call come in?"

"None of your business," Gwynne said, and ordered the constable to get the bicycle into the boot.

As Gwynne shoved his bulk into the rear seat, the constable caught my eye, looked at his wristwatch, and whispered, "Thirty minutes ago."

The call could have come from anywhere. Not every home had a telephone, not by a long shot. But there were public telephones in those bright red boxes, and Marston Hall had wires strung in the hallways.

I needed to telephone Diana, but there was no reason to let

Brian or Dorothy know I was tipping off anyone at Seaton Manor. A few doors down the street, I spotted a phone box across from Dr. Bodkin's office. I trotted over, dropped a penny in the coin slot, and dialed the number for Seaton Manor. Diana answered, and I filled her in on the discovery of the ice pick.

"Don't let Gwynne know I called," I said. "But tell your father he's coming so he won't be caught off guard."

"Father is never off guard, more's the pity," she said. "Except when it comes to women, apparently."

"Is that what you argued about?"

"Yes, but I've got to go. It won't take long for Gwynne to get to Seaton Manor, and I need to give Father time to calm down."

I wished her luck and got in my jeep. I didn't get the sense an arrest was imminent, since even a bigoted blockhead like Gwynne could see that anyone could have planted that ice pick. Whether he was bright enough to realize that it had been the killer who'd called in the tip was another matter.

I drove past Charlotte Mothersole as she entered a bakery, and Dr. Bodkin on a bicycle, his black bag strapped to the fender. Folks were out on the street, going about their business as if nothing had happened. The church at the end of the lane looked out over the village, its squat Norman tower a solid, flinty gray under the growing clouds.

Buttoning my jacket, I drove to Tower Hill, turning off the main road that led to Marston Hall. A narrow lane took me to the base of the hill, where I parked and found the track I'd seen Archer take. It was well trodden, probably made by generations of walkers searching for the Roman tower or taking in a view of the Wash.

I walked slowly, focusing on each step and the sights and smells around me. The rotting leaves of fall, the tangy scent of pine, the thick, moist smell of damp earth. Gray stones, rough oak bark, and the *whoosh* of branches in the breeze. All these were part of David Archer and how he'd seen the world. A world I needed to grasp and understand. The trail took me to a ledge overlooking the Wash. It was a gloomy day, and it must have been low tide, since all I could see were mud flats and marshland.

I found a few cigarette butts and the casual leavings of picnicking hikers. Nothing that spoke to me of David Archer and his need to be out under the open sky at all hours. I decided this path was not for him. It was too common, too everyday. The ledge had a nice view, but it wasn't the highest point, and it was fully exposed. I pushed aside low pine branches and moved higher, off the path, scrambling over a jumble of rocks and a fallen tree.

It was well hidden.

Beyond the tree trunk, behind a low, flat stone, was a foxhole. David Archer wouldn't have called it that. It was a trench, or his personal section of a trench, six feet long and four feet deep, lined with rocks covered by tree limbs. A small shovel was wrapped in oilskin and hidden in the crook of a tree. This was where David Archer felt safe. On top of the highest hill within miles, the night sky above. Dug in, away from prying and pitying eyes. Alone, but still connected to that war that had defined his life and haunted his nights.

Maybe he'd felt the presence of his friends here. Maybe he'd mourned them, but I had no desire to ever understand that depth of suffering.

One thing I did understand was the commanding view this emplacement had afforded Archer. To the left was the road that led to the cliffs, parallel to the still-visible gouge the bomber had made going in. At the right side of the trench, I could see directly down to the cliff edge, right where the airplane had gone over.

David Archer had seen it all.

He's come back, he'd said. *It's the devil's work.*

Those weren't the ravings of a madman. Archer had been

talking about Stephen Elliot. If he knew Elliot had come back, he must have known how Elliot had gotten inside the bomber. He had witnessed everything.

You don't understand.

He was right. I hadn't understood because I wasn't listening.

CHAPTER SIXTEEN

I STOOD AT the cliff edge, the surging updraft embracing me even as the sandy soil began to crumble at my feet. It would have been so easy to fall into the empty air to the rocks below. I took a step back and looked up at Tower Hill, from where Archer had had a ringside seat to a frightening tragedy.

Plenty of people had seen the bomber come down, but Archer had been very close. Close enough to see whoever came to the scene. I needed to confirm the timeline for everyone who had come out here that night, but Elliot had to have been the first, or damn near it.

I didn't know why Elliot had been killed, but his body in the aircraft? That was starting to make more sense to me. I hadn't been certain it was him, but now logic seemed to demand it. Especially in light of what we'd learned examining the other bodies, neither of whom was the pilot. Armed with that information, it was time to enlist the aid of Sherlock Holmes and something he'd said in several of the stories.

If you eliminate the impossible, whatever remains, however improbable, must be the truth.

Therefore, the pilot had left the aircraft, and Stephen Elliot had taken his place.

Otherwise, how could one man have left the plane and the other have gotten in?

Which led to another conclusion.

The bomber had not gone straight off the cliff.

It couldn't have, because if it had, the pilot would not have escaped, and Elliot would not have been put in his place. But he was.

I moved back to the edge of the cliff and scuffed at the chalky, sandy ground. It gave way as a blast of cold air hit me, and I had to steady myself to keep from staggering over the side. I worked at imagining myself on this spot, having brought my burning aircraft to a slamming halt right before going over. Dead or dying crewmen inside, flames licking at the engine, and heavy winds buffeting me as I opened the forward hatch and dropped to the ground.

Maybe the pilot went right over. Or maybe he stumbled along the edge or ran from the sound of approaching vehicles and fell farther down the cliff face. Either way, he likely went in and was taken by the tides out into the Wash.

I was so deep in thought that I hardly noticed the wind whipping up and heavy drops of rain splattering against me. I squeezed my eyes shut and tried to visualize what might have happened next.

I couldn't figure it.

All I knew for sure was that the pilot had to have walked away, and Elliot had to have been put in the bomber. By whom and why, that was beyond me. The fact was, the bomber must have settled right on the cliff edge and stayed there long enough for Elliot to be stuffed inside.

At that point, the engine would still have been on fire.

It was a good way to dispose of the body, to let the flames spread and incinerate everyone aboard. I kicked at a stone and dislodged it along with a clump of dirt, sending them cascading down the cliff. It had been a good idea, but the ten-ton aircraft hadn't cooperated; it had slid into the swirling storm waters, extinguishing the fire and burying the bomber in thick silt until it was retrieved by the tides.

Which had put the fear of God into the killer.

Still, we weren't entirely certain the body was Stephen Elliot, so I might have been getting ahead of myself. I had to remember to ask Gwynne about the dental records the next time I saw him. Not that he'd been in the mood to share information this morning.

I made it to Marston Hall as lightning crackled through the sky and heavy rains lashed against the windows. Major Hudson had had the same late night I did and didn't seem upset that I'd taken my time getting here. He called for coffee and handed me an envelope.

"Your orders, Captain," Hudson said. "You are authorized by SHAEF to investigate all matters concerning security at Marston Hall. Signed by your Colonel Harding and countersigned by me."

"What about Colonel Cheatwood, sir?" I said as I scanned the single sheet filled with army jargon, which amounted to exactly what Hudson had said, plus the usual warning about the penalties for revealing top secret information.

"Not his call," Hudson said. "I'm Military Intelligence Service, Section Y. I run the interrogation operations here. The colonel oversees the facility and security. Marston Hall was originally all British. When we arrived, he was kept on due to the proximity to Sandringham House and his familiarity with the area."

"I understand he was wounded badly at Dunkirk," I said, glancing at the rain spitting against the window.

"Yes, shot through the lungs. He was almost mustered out when he was released from the hospital. He heard about Marston Hall being used as a POW center and went after the assignment," Hudson said. "I think your friend Sir Richard pulled some strings for him, and I'm glad he did. It's a good arrangement and lets me concentrate on what's critical."

Coffee was brought in, and as I took the first sip, I was reminded of what Cheatwood had promised to do yesterday.

"Any word on the two crewmen who bailed out?" I asked. "The colonel was going to check with the War Office."

"Yes. Word came in early this morning," Hudson said, setting his cup down. "Two German airmen were picked up near Castle Acre, twelve miles away, the morning after the raid on Norwich. They're being transported here today. Lucky for us, they weren't sent to the States or Canada."

"I don't know what we can learn from them, but we should follow up. As soon as Gwynne gets an identification through dental records and we are assured it's Stephen Elliot. Until then, we must consider the possibility of an enemy agent," I said. It was highly doubtful, but it wasn't the kind of thing to overlook. Besides, one of them might have seen something, or someone, that would help.

"Far-fetched, but I agree," Hudson said. "Although the uniform matches Elliot, down to rank and unit patch."

"Information that could have been supplied by an enemy agent. Remember, Elliot was about to receive his orders. Signals people are at the center of things, and a substitute fitting his description could have taken his place," I said. It wasn't a theory I held much stock in, but I figured it was better to be found wrong about it than wanting.

"I also asked Colonel Cheatwood to look for any reports of the pilot's body," Hudson said. "It could have washed up anywhere or been borne out into the North Sea. He said he'd have the records checked for a week after the crash."

"Good idea," I said, finishing my coffee. "And now that you've got me assigned to this job officially, why don't you tell me what's really at stake here? I understand Marston Hall isn't a normal POW camp, but what's so special about this outfit?"

"Oskar!" Hudson yelled. Sergeant Goldstein appeared at the door, and the major told him to take a seat. Goldstein sat, stifling a yawn.

"Late night, Sarge, wasn't it?" I asked.

"I didn't mind the late hour, but that police inspector reminded me too much of home," Oskar said. "Berlin, that is."

"He's a fool," I said. "Unfortunately, whoever killed Archer isn't. Now, what's the secret of Marston Hall?"

"This isn't just about Marston Hall," Hudson said. "We're part of a much larger enterprise. MIS, Section Y operates interrogation facilities in the States, Great Britain, and on the Continent."

"We have teams attached to divisions on the front lines," Oskar said. "Our guys interrogate POWs while the lead is still flying."

"Okay, I get that using native German speakers makes for an easier interrogation," I said. "That's common sense. But why so hush-hush?"

"There are over fifteen thousand Ritchie Boys working for MIS," Hudson said. "And it's not only interrogations. We develop reports on German military organizations, economics, and politics. Aerial photo interpretation as well. Everything necessary to create a complete picture of the enemy."

"Wait, what's a Ritchie Boy?" I asked.

"We were trained at Camp Ritchie in Maryland," Oskar said. "Guys from all over—Italy, Greece, France, and plenty other places. About one in five of us are German or Austrian Jews."

"All right, so you have a full-service intelligence outfit," I said. "But there are others. The OSS, SOE, and probably more of the alphabet than I know. What makes you so special?"

"Everything we do is designed to elicit the information we want from a prisoner," Hudson said. "We have guys who know the composition of a panzer division better than any of its own officers. We have dossiers on German commanders, accurate right down to the latest gossip about their wives. We've put together a detailed order of battle for all German forces. We can dazzle a prisoner with what we know about his commanding officer and then show him an aerial photograph of where he was encamped before he was captured."

"Then we pick the right interrogator," Oskar said. "Me, I get all the Berliners. I know the same streets they know. I speak with the same accent. Then when I lay out all I know about their unit, they can't believe it. They're shocked. A lot of them open up right then and there."

"The Germans who are sent here have strategic information locked up in their heads," Hudson said. "We take our time with them. Closer to the front lines, it's different. But the process is the same."

"So, what sounds like a friendly chat is really a way to break down their defenses." I was beginning to see the larger picture. "You don't want your modus operandi to get out, and you want to protect your frontline guys. The Nazis probably wouldn't treat captured German Jews like POWs."

"We've already taken losses," Oskar said.

"And damn right we don't want our operation to become known," Hudson said. "The prisoners here think they're the luckiest POWs in Europe. They have no clue they're the most loose lipped."

"We have six basic principles in our work," Oskar said, and went on to describe each one.

"The first is not to touch the prisoner. No violence. It's counterproductive and fear inhibits the subject.

"Exhibit superior knowledge. The first question you ask is one you already know the answer to. When the prisoner declines to answer, you reveal you had the information all along, demonstrating you have the upper hand.

"When a POW starts talking, the interrogator acts as a friend. Privileges such as candy or cigarettes are doled out, and the interrogator shows interest in the prisoner as a person.

"Interrogators work to find a subject of common interest with the prisoner. Books, films, sports, it doesn't matter. What's important is to create a human bond.

"POWs are encouraged to speak on their own area of interest.

Nothing political, but anything else is fair game to delve into. Talk begets talk. Keep their tongues loose.

"Finally, play on the POW's sense of anxiety. Many are worried about the safety of their families, especially given the advances of the Russians. German POWs know there will be revenge taken when Russian forces cross into Germany. The message is that the sooner the war is over, the safer their loved ones will be, and they can help make that happen."

"That's impressive," I said. "The Germans don't know about the scope of this operation, I take it?"

"They know we interrogate POWs," Hudson said. "Everyone does. But they don't know the full depth of our approach."

"The way we work things, a prisoner hardly realizes what he's told us until it's done," Oskar said. "That's why we don't take notes in their presence. We just have nice, long chats in their native language."

"I can't imagine every Nazi is too pleased to be talking to a Jew who fled Germany," I said.

"No, which is why we have a few other tricks up our sleeves," Oskar said. "We don't strike prisoners, but that doesn't mean we don't scare them to death."

"Commissar Krukov is a very effective member of our team," Hudson said, lighting up a smoke as he grinned.

"You have a Soviet officer here?" I asked.

"Commissar Krukov is whoever is in a bad mood that day and can fit into the uniform we had made," Oskar said. "We know enough Russian for a script that calls for Krukov to angrily demand a prisoner be released into his custody for transport to the Soviet Union. That gets even the most hard-core SS man quaking in his boots. They can't talk fast enough if it means they don't have to go with the commissar."

"Sometimes all it takes is for us to move a prisoner to a room in the basement and put a tag around his neck with the letter *R* on it. Then we ask him to fill out a form detailing his next of kin," Hudson said.

"You've got all the bases covered," I said. "I like your approach, but I'm still not clear what kind of threat you see from the discovery of Elliot's body."

"Captain, I don't know if I've made myself clear," Hudson said. "We are one small part of a much larger operation involving thousands of men and a well-devised system. What we do here produces high-quality intelligence, of both tactical and strategic importance."

"The enemy doesn't even realize it," Oskar said. "The wool is over their eyes. That is a saying, yes?"

"It is," I said.

"We must keep it that way." Hudson slammed his palm on the desk. "Fully sixty percent of intelligence provided to frontline commanders is from MIS-Y. Not many people know that, Captain, and you need make sure it stays that way."

"Ritchie Boys, Captain Boyle," Oskar said. "You must protect the secret of what we do and who we are. It is how we strike back. If the Nazis find out how we fool them, it would be a simple matter to order all troops, in case of capture, to say nothing at all. As it is now, most see no harm in talking with a little runaway Jew. *Little* do they know."

"Get to work, Boyle," Hudson said, grinding out his smoke. "I'll sleep better if I know Elliot's death had nothing to do with us. Then we can go back to being a dull backwater base for processing POWs. What's your gut tell you so far?"

"It's a singular affair," I said. "Ever read Sherlock Holmes?" Hudson hadn't, but Oskar was enthusiastic.

"Yes, I have read Arthur Conan Doyle in both English and German," he said.

"I've always remembered something Holmes said in the 'Boscombe Valley Mystery,'" I said, closing my eyes to bring the words into focus. "'Singularity is almost invariably a clue.

The more featureless and commonplace a crime is, the more difficult it is to bring it home.'"

"*Ja*," Oskar said. "If the body had been found in the road, it would have been so ordinary. An accident, perhaps, or a fit of passion."

"Right. But putting the body into the aircraft, that had meaning. All I need to do is understand why that was important to someone," I said.

"I'm more of a *Terry and the Pirates* man myself," Hudson said. "I don't care what theory you have as long as it proves no one is coming after us. And don't you dare draw attention to this unit, Captain."

I knew my cue to leave when I heard it.

CHAPTER SEVENTEEN

COLONEL CHEATWOOD WAS next. A courtesy call was in order since he was the ranking officer, but I also wanted to start building a picture of what happened the night the bomber crashed. Who was at the site and when?

I took the stairs to the second floor and found Cheatwood's office at the end of a hallway on the opposite side of the building from Elliot's private library. This wing was the domain of the British contingent, with Tommies at typewriters, probably producing the same paperwork as their GI counterparts downstairs.

I rapped lightly on the open door. "Do you have a moment, Colonel?"

"Ah, Boyle, do come in," Cheatwood said, slapping a file shut. "I understand you are with us in an official capacity now." He gestured for me to sit in the chair opposite his desk. Behind him were two large windows overlooking the grounds.

"Not for too long, I hope," I said. "Nice vantage point you have up here."

"It pays to keep an eye on our guests," Cheatwood said, swiveling in his chair to survey the lawns. The rain had lessened, and a few prisoners had taken to the paths, collars turned up against the wind. "We don't like arguments breaking out between the recalcitrant and talkative types. The Hun likes things orderly and well organized. They tend to go quiet when there's trouble brewing within their ranks."

"They probably learned that at home, with the Gestapo keeping tabs on things," I said. "David Archer used to watch them as well, I understand."

"Poor blighter. Yes, he liked to see them caged up, I expect. Can't blame him, not after what he went through in the last war," Cheatwood said, turning to look at me. "Now, tell me how I can help you."

"I'd like to take a closer look at Elliot's private library," I said. "I only had time to take a glance the other day when I found Alfred and Mildred Bunch in there. You have a key, I assume?"

"Certainly. What do you expect to find?" Cheatwood asked as he rummaged through a desk drawer.

"I have no idea." I took the key he slid across the desk. It was solid cast iron with ornate Victorian decorations. "Something that points to why Elliot was targeted. Evidence of a grudge against him, or why he'd be more valuable dead than alive."

"No shortage of grudges in his case. Good luck sorting that out, Captain," Cheatwood said. "Major Hudson told you we found the two Luftwaffe aircrew, I assume?"

"Yes, thanks for tracking them down," I said. "You also put out word about the pilot's body?"

"I have, but it will take some time and luck to come up with anything," Cheatwood said. "Who knows where the tides could have carried him? He could have been washed out to the North Sea or buried under the silt in the Wash."

"It's a long shot, and I'm not even sure what we'd learn if we did find where he washed up. Still, it must be followed up on. When the two crewmen get here, I'd like to sit in on their interrogation," I said.

"Be my guest," Cheatwood said. "Or rather, Major Hudson's. He'll be the one organizing those sessions. I'll make sure you are notified. Staying at the Rose and Crown, are you?" Cheatwood raised an eyebrow, his way of inquiring about my status at Seaton Manor.

"Yes, for as long as this investigation takes. I didn't want to put Sir Richard in an awkward position," I said.

"Or yourself, I daresay. I suppose you must consider him a suspect, Captain, even with his record. He and Elliot weren't on the best of terms, as you must know."

"I do, and I agree that no one should be beyond suspicion, Colonel," I said. "Sir Richard is one of a number of people I need to speak with. Tell me, were you the first to arrive on the scene when the bomber crashed?"

"No, Captain, I was not," he said, swiveling in his chair again. He seemed to enjoy surveying his domain. Or not looking me in the eye. "And I take your point. I have no reason to suspect Sir Richard, and I can say with certainty that Stephen Elliot could be quite disagreeable."

"The night the bomber crashed?" I asked, bringing him back to my question.

"Yes, yes. I caught sight of it from my bedroom on the top floor. I could see Elliot already getting into his automobile and racing off. First, I put my men on alert, then I called the fire service, dressed, and went out to look for myself."

"Did you actually see the aircraft crash-land?"

"No, you can't see the cliffs from here. Tower Hill blocks that view. I thought it was headed out to the Wash for certain, but either way, I had to get men organized for a search. At the time, we had no idea if the crew bailed out close by or if there were other parachutists involved."

"Targeting Sandringham House?"

"It's my job to consider the possibility," Cheatwood said. "In hindsight, there was no risk. But in the moment, it had to be taken seriously."

"Who was at the crash site when you arrived?"

"Not Elliot, as far as I knew at the time. I saw Alfred Bunch's van driving away from the cliffs as I was making the turn onto the main road," Cheatwood said. "Dr. Bodkin and Agnes Day were both there. He'd driven out in case there were any injuries, but there was nothing except that great smoking gouge to be seen."

"No trace of the bomber in the water?" I asked.

"Not the way the Wash was that night," he said. "High tide and fierce winds, a bad combination. That's a lot of water churning against those cliffs, not to mention the riptide. No one saw the aircraft hit, so we have no idea how far the momentum carried it off the cliff."

I didn't bother with the flaw in his thinking. I wondered how much he'd actually thought it through. Elliot would have had a hard time jumping into the cockpit of an airplane flying off the cliff.

"It was only the three of you, then?" I said.

"The fire service pulled up, four men in their pump truck," Cheatwood said. "Not much work for them that night, thank God. Sir Richard followed them, then a few lads from the village who'd bicycled out to see what they could. Father Tanner, too, but he left as soon as he saw there were no dead who needed his prayers."

"No one else?"

"Well, David Archer, I believe," Cheatwood said, picking up a pair of binoculars from a side table. "I saw a man keeping to the shadows and then going up Tower Hill. Must have been Archer, but I can't say for certain. You must understand, we were all glad the bomber had come down and no one in the village was hurt. The weather was simply awful, and everyone wanted to get back to their beds."

"Did you send out patrols?" I asked.

"Yes. I called Sandringham House and told them to be on the alert, then sent a squad their way to stand watch until dawn," Cheatwood said, somewhat distracted as he focused the binoculars. "Patrolled our perimeter as well, just to be sure."

"Who are you so interested in?" I asked.

"Colonel Hansen," he said. "He's engaged in what seems to be friendly conversation with Major Schmidt. That's a good sign. Schmidt is one of the talkative ones. Likes his brandy and cigars, which we supply in direct correlation to his chats with us."

"Do you think Schmidt will tell him to talk?" I said.

"No, that's not how it works," Cheatwood said. "But we pay attention to who our prisoners are friendly with. The hardcases stick together and reinforce a rigid discipline. A chap like Schmidt probably brags about how easy it is to get favors from us with no harm done. As I said, a good sign, that's all."

I stood and moved to the window. Colonel Hansen was the calvary officer Diana had given hell to for brushing her horse. He had seemed homesick. Maybe he'd go for a chat with one of the Ritchie Boys.

"How well do you know Dr. Bodkin, Colonel?" I asked as Schmidt and Hansen disappeared from view.

"I've been to see him a few times," Cheatwood said. "Aches and pains, you know."

"Dunkirk, I heard."

"Yes. I thought I was safe on that boat, but Jerry had other ideas. We were machine-gunned by a Stuka." Cheatwood sat down heavily, as if the burden of memory had thrown him into the chair. "I was in hospital for far too long. I don't want the army putting me back in one."

"Which is why you see the local doctor instead of an army physician," I said.

"He's much closer, Captain Boyle, and he's happy to come see me here. Let's leave it at that," Cheatwood said. "I'm fit enough for this post, and I can keep pace with much younger men on patrol. Some of our jaunts to Sandringham House are in double time, mind you."

"You don't have to convince me, Colonel." Although I could tell he was working at it. Or perhaps convincing himself. "I know you're a local man and a perfect choice for this posting. You're from around here, aren't you?"

"Yes, from Flitcham, a small village east of here," Cheatwood said. "I grew up on a pig farm. I still like rashers on my plate, but I'll be glad to never see a damned pig again." He smiled, but it was a grim smile hiding an even grimmer memory. I began to understand why he fought to stay in the army.

"Since you're from these parts, I was curious what you might be able to tell me about Dr. Bodkin and Sir Richard. Seems to be a feud between them."

"Between them? I'm not so sure about that," Cheatwood said. "A one-sided affair, from what little I know. Unless this has a bearing on the investigation, I suggest you discuss it directly with Sir Richard. Village gossip holds little interest for me."

"Right, I was just curious," I said. "I'll leave you to your work, Colonel. Thanks for your time."

"I didn't mean to be so curt, Boyle. I do feel an obligation to Marston Hall, having been here since the beginning. I'm glad not to have been mustered out. Don't know how I'd manage it with the war on," he said, gathering the files on his desk. "Anyway, I wish I could have been more helpful."

"Well, there is one thing that would help," I said. "Would you mind calling Chief Inspector Gwynne? He should have had the dental records checked by now. I'd like to know for certain that it was Stephen Elliot in that plane."

"Ah, you read the man well," Cheatwood said with a brief smile. "He'll respond much better to my accent than yours." The colonel put through the call and asked for the chief inspector. It took a few minutes, but he finally came on the line. Judging by how far Cheatwood held the telephone from his ear, Gwynne wasn't happy, proper English accent or not.

"It's confirmed," Cheatwood said, setting the phone in its cradle. "The dental records do match Stephen Elliot's. Gwynne said he'd be here later today. Charlotte will be quite distraught.

I think I'd better pop over before she hears it from someone else."

"Good idea," I said as we walked out of the office together. I didn't know Charlotte well, but she didn't come off as the delicate fainting type. But Cheatwood could hope, couldn't he? "Is there a local vicar to call?"

"There's Father Tanner at St. Paul's, the only church in the village," Cheatwood said hurriedly. "A kindly old gentleman. Spent time looking after David Archer when he could find him, now that I think of it. A bit musty for the likes of Charlotte, if you know what I mean."

I told him I did, then watched him hotfoot it to his vehicle. There was comforting to be done, and Graham Cheatwood had no intention of an elderly vicar beating him to it. Especially when the person being comforted was the heir to Marston Hall.

CHAPTER EIGHTEEN

I SCANNED THE pathways for Hansen. I was asking everyone
a lot of questions and getting nowhere, so why not give the
enemy the satisfaction of being unhelpful as well? The wind
was still gusting, but the rain had stopped, and more Germans
were taking their morning exercise. Some alone, some in
groups, and others with their interrogators. It reminded me
of Harvard Yard back in Cambridge, except everyone had
better posture.

I spotted Hansen coming around the corner of the building,
his hands stuffed in his greatcoat pockets. I headed for him and
stopped to salute, hoping he wouldn't respond with a Hitler
stiff arm.

He didn't. He snapped off a traditional salute and smiled. A
new face in a POW camp was probably a real occasion.

"Captain, we meet before, yes? With the horse and the lady
who was so angry with me?"

"Boyle," I said. "Yes. She's touchy about her horses."

"Touchy?"

"Particular."

"Ah, I understand. I, too, am particular about my horses. I
should have left the mare alone. Please convey my apologies to
the lady," Hansen said, studying me for some clue as to what I
wanted.

"Mind if I walk with you?" I said.

"It is a free country," Hansen said, falling into step with me. "This is a joke, yes? The Americans here say it all the time."

"Yeah, it's a joke," I said, wondering how that went over with a guy from Hitler's Germany.

"Because we are prisoners," Hansen said, "it is only a little funny to me. Do you speak German, Captain Boyle?"

I told him I didn't.

"Then what is your business here, and what do you want with me?"

"You heard about the bomber they pulled out of the water? I'm investigating that," I said.

Hansen nodded in acknowledgment. "I heard that one of our airplanes crashed here, early in the war. Now there are many rumors. That the man who owned this place was found inside the wreckage. Is that true?"

"How could that be?" I replied, deciding there was no reason to share my suspicions with an enemy officer.

"Rumors and soldiers are probably the same everywhere. It gives us something to talk about." Hansen tossed off a shrug. "But today I heard another rumor. That a man was killed in the village."

"Who said that?"

"It is all the Tommies and Amis talk about this morning," Hansen said. "Was it really Herr Archer?"

"It was," I said as we passed another German and his Yank pal on the path. "How do you know his name?"

"We spoke," Hansen said, as if it were the obvious answer. "Many times. He would come to the fence. At first, I thought he was looking at us. That he might mean some harm."

"What did he want?"

"He did not say. He spent time watching the house, not the prisoners. But we did talk. He suffered greatly in the last war," Hansen said. "As did my father. He came home with no legs. Very sad."

"Wait a minute." I stopped in my tracks. "I knew Archer spent time at the fence, but you say he wasn't there to look at the prisoners? To taunt them, perhaps?"

"No, not at all. He told me some people must be watched," Hansen said, lowering his voice. "The man who delivers lamb. He and his wife used to work here. Herr Archer said they were looking for something. Whenever he saw the truck, he would watch for how long they stayed."

"Alfred Bunch's truck?" I asked. Hansen nodded. "Anyone else?"

"The woman who used to live here, Frau Mothersole," he said, his voice a whisper as he watched for anyone listening. "Also, the Herr Doktor Bodkin, who provides medical care. No one else. Now, I must go—this is dangerous." With that, he turned on his heel and retreated into Marston Hall. No matter what he said, there was someone else Archer had been keeping an eye on, and that someone made Hansen very nervous.

I headed for Elliot's library. The last time I was in there, I'd discovered Alfred and Mildred making a big show of picking up a uniform for the undertaker. Was that a coincidence, or one of the visits Archer would've watched for?

I fingered the library key in my pocket, considering what to do next. If Archer had been convinced there was something going on at Marston Hall, maybe he'd left some evidence at his home. Notes, letters, or a diary, perhaps. It was worth a look, but first I thought I might as well check out Elliot's library more thoroughly.

This time the library door was locked. The key worked with a satisfying clunk, and I pushed it open, entering the sitting room. The curtains were drawn, and the air was still. It felt different to me now that I knew for certain that Stephen Elliot would never again set foot in here. The personal items scattered about the room—a stack of books, pens, pictures, a cut glass decanter—all seemed shorn of any importance. Whatever life their owner's touch had given them was gone. They were no longer Elliot's possessions. They were simply empty things.

I pulled back the curtains, letting the gray light into the library. It didn't exactly cheer up the place. I walked along the bookshelves. Elliot's collection was heavy on English history. Not a Conan Doyle or Rex Stout in sight. There were a lot of books about King John, and I recalled Sir Richard taking one with him from the downstairs library. In addition to the wall map of the Wash, there were rolled-up maps in a wicker basket and several more laid out on a table. Beside them were meteorological bulletins, tide tables for the Wash, and folded maps of hiking paths along the Norfolk shore.

Some of the maps of the Wash were old, the paper brittle and yellowed. The Wash was different in those, much larger than the present-day maps. Ironic that after making a study of that body of water, Elliot would end up in it.

In a glass display case, old coins lay next to corroded nails and other objects I couldn't identify. I went through the drawers in his desk, which yielded nothing but dated correspondence, bills, and pencil stubs. I pawed through the clothes hanging in the armoire and came up with nothing. The narrow closet was deep, filled with boxes and overstuffed cartons that looked ready to topple over. If I started with that stuff, I'd be here all night.

A wooden file cabinet stood along the wall. It wasn't locked, and I opened it to find reams of reports and what looked like college research papers. Typewritten sheets and handwritten pages were crammed into file folders in no discernible order. Someone said Elliot had been writing a book. Was the manuscript somewhere in these files? Did it hold a secret worth killing for?

I shut the drawer, knowing there was too much to go through today. And I was not the guy for the job. Kaz would be back from his jaunt with Angelika and Agnes in the morning. He'd love to spend the day in here. I needed to get out.

I locked up and descended the stairs, bumping into Major

Hudson outside his office. He told me that the mystery of the fleet of V-1 rockets had been solved. The Germans had modified He 111 bombers to carry a V-1 under the fuselage. They'd flown in close to the coast from over the North Sea and launched dozens of the rockets against Manchester. We'd witnessed some of those going overhead. Reportedly enough bombers had been shot down that chances were slim they'd try again.

One question answered. But I had plenty more.

Maybe Father Tanner could help with some heavenly insights. Right now, however, my empty stomach demanded its earthly reward, so I followed the signs for the mess hall. They led me to one of the temporary wooden structures behind the main building. It held all the smells of a rear-area mess, from coffee to cabbage, with the mingled aromas rising from the steam table.

I grabbed a cup of joe and a bacon sandwich. I spotted Hank Klein and Oskar Goldstein at one of the tables and asked if they minded company. Sometimes it paid to let noncoms relax without an officer around, or at least to let them know I gave it a second thought. They waved me to a chair.

"Captain, don't you know about the fancy officers' mess in the British section?" Hank asked, tucking into his pea soup.

"Hey, nothing wrong with good coffee and a bacon sandwich," I said. "But what am I missing?"

"The choicest lamb cutlets. Rack of lamb," Oskar said, digging into his corned beef hash. "Alfred Bunch keeps Colonel Cheatwood well supplied."

"Cheatwood likes good food," Hank said. "He's from around here, so he knows where to go to supplement officer rations. If you ask me, he needs all the help he can get. My mother was a terrible cook, but British cooking is twice as bad as hers."

"Ah, there's more to it than that, I think." Oskar wagged his fork to make his point. "Bunch keeps poking his nose in around here, bringing the colonel delicacies. I think he wants his old job back. Chasing sheep all day must be exhausting."

"How could the colonel help with that?" I asked.

"Maybe hire Alfred to be the caretaker and Mildred as a cook?" Hank offered.

"No, he's got his men to do that. Foolish idea," Oskar said. "But after the war, who will take up residence here? The dear Charlotte Mothersole? I've only spoken to her a few times, but she seems to be very vivacious."

"Where did you meet her? At the pub?" I asked.

"Enough of tales out of school, Captain," Oskar said, finishing up with his mound of hash. "Excuse me, there is much to do. We must prepare for our new guests. Your Luftwaffe friends."

"I'll be sitting in, if that's okay," I said.

"Sure," Hank said. "As long as you keep quiet and look threatening. Welcome to show business."

"Just one quick question. How often does Dr. Bodkin show up here?"

"At least once a week, Captain," Oskar said. "We have a medic, but we need the doctor for anything serious. He checks in on Colonel Cheatwood too. Poor man was wounded early in the war."

I thanked them and went back to munching bacon, thinking about Cheatwood's background. Oskar hadn't spun much of a tale, but it was enough, along with what I'd already observed. The colonel and Charlotte Mothersole were definitely an item. She seemed interested in him, but as far as I could figure, he was the one who had the most to gain.

The biggest joint for miles around, Marston Hall made Seaton Manor look like a ramshackle farm, and Cheatwood already looked damn comfortable in it.

That was one big step up from a pig farm.

Big enough to kill for?

CHAPTER NINETEEN

ALFRED BUNCH SHOULD have been next on my list, but I was curious as to what Father Tanner might tell me about David Archer. If he was one of Tanner's flock, he might have let the vicar in on what his suspicions were.

But first I drove back to the cliffs and watched the waters of the Wash. Standing at the edge, I could feel the misty droplets blowing against my skin. Most of the wreckage below had been cleared away, the only traces a few shards of twisted metal. The tide looked to be moving out, fast. A sandbar was already visible about a hundred yards distant. If the tide came in as quickly during a heavy storm, the waters would be more treacherous than anything I'd ever seen in Quincy Bay. If Elliot had been killed on this cliff, why not simply toss him into the water? He might never have been found, or he might have washed up after days in the water. Why was stuffing his body into that cockpit so important?

The answer to that question was the key to understanding what happened back in 1942 and if there was any real danger to the Ritchie Boys and their operation today.

I knocked on the rectory door and was greeted by a gray-haired woman busily wiping her hands on her apron. She told me not to take too much of the vicar's time, as he was working on his sermon, and pointed me toward his study.

I didn't doubt that he had a lot of work to do, but when I

entered the study, I found Father Tanner snoring lightly as he sat in a comfortable leather chair. A notepad and pen sat on the table next to him. I saw he'd made some progress, but the urge for an after-lunch nap had been too strong. I backed up into the hall and let my boots fall heavily as I took those last few steps again.

"Yes? Can I help you?" Father Tanner said, adjusting his spectacles as he blinked himself awake. His thin, graying hair was splayed across his brow. He brushed it back, revealing a knotted line of scar tissue high on his forehead. He had a prominent nose, a lean frame, and a bit of lunch on the sweater he wore over his clerical collar.

I introduced myself and told him about my investigation. He invited me to sit down, and as I did so, I pantomimed wiping crumbs from my shirt. He smiled his thanks as he brushed off the food, then leaned forward and folded his hands, one of which was missing two fingers.

"How can I help you?"

"I believe you knew David Archer," I said. "Was he one of your parishioners?"

"David was always welcome here, and I in his house," Tanner said. "But he was not the type to come to Sunday services. Too much stonework over his head, you understand."

"I know what happened to him," I said. "I found his dugout up on Tower Hill."

"Ah, then you know he wasn't one who liked being cooped up. David told me about his secret spot on the hill. Never invited me there, not that I would've had an easy time getting to it."

"It was well hidden," I said. "It would have been a good observation post."

"He must have felt safe on that high ground. He had his burdens to bear, poor soul. He was a decent man," Tanner said. "He frightened some, going about at night when everyone else pulls the shades and gets under the covers. I can't blame them. It isn't natural, and David knew it. It's why he tried to stay out of sight. People mistook that."

"You were friends," I said. I left it at that. I had a feeling Father Tanner knew more about David Archer than anyone else in the village. They were roughly the same age, and if his scars were any indication, he'd served in the last war as well.

"We were. It was easier, really, David not being a member of the congregation. I wasn't his vicar, not officially, at least. I could relax with him. Outdoors, that is," Tanner said with a fleeting smile. "But soon I will act as a man of God and bury my friend, when the police release his body."

"Do you have any idea who would've wanted to kill him?" I asked.

"I am not the police, Captain Boyle," Tanner said, sidestepping the question.

"But you were his friend. You must have some idea about who might have had a serious enough grudge to settle it with a knife," I said.

"Have you determined whether the body in the aircraft was Stephen Elliot beyond any doubt?"

"It was confirmed by dental records," I said. "Does that make a difference?"

"If I were the police, I'd be interested in issues of inheritance," Tanner said, steepling his eight fingers. "Was there a will?"

"That's pretty standard stuff in any investigation," I said.

"Of course. I've read enough Agatha Christie to know that," Tanner said. "But ask yourself whose interests would be served by Elliot's vanishing instead of his body being found."

"You were there, the night the bomber went down," I said. "What did you think?"

"I saw the gouges in the earth," he said. "A trail of destruction. Everyone thought the bomber went off that cliff at high speed. I didn't see it that way, but it hardly mattered at the time. I must confess, when I saw I was not needed, I came straight back here. The weather was filthy."

"So who benefited by Elliot not being found?"

"I have no idea, Captain. Fortunately, that's your patch," Tanner said. "Mine is my flock."

"One of whom may be a killer," I said. "Did Archer ever mention watching Marston Hall? One of the prisoners said he basically had the place under surveillance."

"He did," Tanner said. "Rather than tell you what little he shared with me, why don't we go to his house? It's not far."

"Now you're talking, Padre," I said.

Tanner stood, a bit shaky on his feet, just as his housekeeper bustled in.

"Where are you going, Father?" she asked, giving me the eye.

"To David Archer's," he said. "We won't be long."

"You be careful," she said. "Let me get your cane."

"No bother, I'll fetch it. Left it in the sitting room," Tanner said. "Don't mind Mrs. Prentice, Captain. She worries too much."

"And you too little, Father," she called out to him as he left.

"Take care with him, Captain," Mrs. Prentice whispered, taking hold of my arm. "His leg has shrapnel in it still. Stiffens up something terrible."

"I figured he was in the trenches," I said. "That scar looks like a shrapnel wound."

"No, that's from barbed wire. He got hung up dragging a wounded lad back in from no-man's-land. Then the shrapnel came. He got a medal for that, but he won't show it to anyone. Says that's what chaplains are for," Mrs. Prentice said, her voice nearly a whisper.

"Let's go, Captain," Tanner said from the doorway, tapping his cane on the wood floor. "I've never ridden in a jeep. Looks like great fun, especially if you drive like the devil."

"Father!" Mrs. Prentice said, and stalked off, shaking her head.

"We drive each other mad," Tanner said as we stepped outside. "Helps pass the time."

I knew better than to offer the vicar a hand when we got to the jeep. He climbed into the passenger seat with a grunt and settled in.

"Hold on to your hat," I said, and gunned the engine. He told me to take the first left after the pub, which we passed in respectful silence. I drove down the narrow lane, passing two houses built from the familiar Norfolk flint. The next was Archer's, a small one-story cottage set back from the road. The yard was neat and the garden well tended. The roof had a slight bow, and the stonework looked like it had settled into the ground over the years. Off to the side, two wrought iron chairs faced away from the house with a clear view of the fields beyond.

"I've spent many hours sitting there with David," Tanner said. "Looking at the stars late into the night. I hope he's at peace, finally."

"Do you have a key?" I asked as the vicar stabbed his cane into the ground and swiveled out of the jeep.

"David never locked it," he said, advancing on the front door. "He wasn't one for keys." He opened the door, and I followed him through, stooping to not hit my head on the lintel.

Father Tanner stopped. Somebody had beaten us to it.

The place had been ransacked. A table set next to a window was strewn with papers. Cushions had been tossed from the couch, and the drawers of a small desk had been emptied onto the floor. Books had been pulled from shelves and tossed every-where.

"Oh dear," Tanner said. "I should have come sooner. I didn't think . . ."

"Sit down, Father," I said, grabbing a straight-backed chair and shoving books out of the way with my foot. "I'll check the rest of the house."

There were two rooms in the back, a bedroom and the kitchen.

It was the same: everything dumped out and pawed through. In the bedroom, even the linens had been unfolded and thrown on the overturned mattress. The carpet was rolled up, and picture frames broken. Glass scrunched underfoot.

I made my way back to the pastor. "Let's go outside," I said. Tanner sighed, looking at the debris of David Archer's life, and agreed.

Outdoors, we settled into the chairs, our eyes on the fields and woods behind the house.

"Such a desecration," Tanner said. "Everything that was important to him tossed about like garbage."

"I have a feeling not everything, Vicar," I said. "When a house has been gone through so thoroughly, it's usually because the object in question wasn't found. Every square inch of each room had been searched."

"I see," he said. "Chances are they'd find what they were looking for and then leave, you mean?"

"Right. It's unlikely, but if they found what they wanted in the last place searched, it would look just like this mess. It tells me they found nothing and gave up. Now, what were you going to show me?"

"A notebook," Tanner said. "David was suspicious of something at Marston Hall. As you've probably heard, he spent time outside the fence."

"I know. At first, I thought he may have been fixated on the Germans, but a POW said their chats had been friendly. He confirmed Archer had said some people needed watching, but he wouldn't say who. He got real nervous and clammed up," I said. "What's in the notebook?"

"All I know is that he said he kept careful records of persons who needed watching," Tanner said. "And dates and times. Other than that, he wouldn't share a thing. He said it was better if I didn't know details."

"Did you see the notebook? Can you describe it?"

"It had a black cover. About a half-inch thick, maybe six by eight inches," Tanner said. "Well-worn."

I told him I'd look around for it and went back inside. There was plenty of loose paper but nothing that looked like pages from a notebook. I didn't expect to find it. It had to be what the searchers were after, and they'd done an expert job of turning the place over.

When had it happened? During the night? In the early morning hours, or thirty minutes ago?

It didn't matter. All that mattered was that they hadn't found the notebook. I scanned the ruined furnishings, trying to spot any place they'd missed.

Then it hit me.

I knew right where to look.

CHAPTER TWENTY

WHEN I'D ASKED Father Tanner about Archer's dugout on Tower Hill, he'd called it his secret place. Which meant no one else knew about it, I hoped. Maybe the shovel I'd seen there was for more than digging a trench.

"I'm sorry you had to see that, Father," I said as I pulled up in front of the vicarage.

"It's quite sad, but it is one of the ways in which I must witness for my friend," Tanner said as he slowly climbed out of the jeep. "Please let me know what you find, will you?"

I promised him I would. Soon I was climbing Tower Hill once again and felt the chill coming in on the wind. No one else was in sight, and knowing where I was going, I got to the dugout quickly.

But too late.

The shovel lay next to the trench. Gobs of muddy soil had been tossed out, leaving a deep hole at one end. Knotted twine and an oilskin cloth lay discarded at the bottom of the pit. The person who'd dug up the notebook couldn't wait to be sure they'd had their hands on it.

I smoothed out the mess and put the shovel back where it had been wedged between tree branches. No reason not to leave Archer's wooded sanctuary squared away.

Back at the vicarage, Mrs. Prentice gave me a brush to clean my boots before she'd let me in the front door.

"I'll bring you tea," she said, more of an order than an offer. "You see to Father Tanner now. Seeing the house like that was quite a shock for him, not that he'll admit it."

"I was too late," I said, settling into a chair in the vicar's study. I told him about finding the twine and oilskin.

"It's not your fault, Captain," Tanner said. "I should have told the police about David's notebook. Or gone to look for it myself."

"I'm glad you didn't. You might have run into the killer," I said. "Do you have any idea who else might have known about his spot on Tower Hill?"

"No. David was very secretive, but anyone who noticed him going up the hill on more than one occasion could've become curious. People did keep an eye on him, whether out of compassion, curiosity, or worry. Perhaps he was followed?"

"Maybe," I said. "I noticed him going up Tower Hill a couple of times myself. Once I thought it through, it wasn't that hard to find his spot."

Mrs. Prentice came in with the tea. Piping hot, it was just the thing after being out in the cold coming off the Wash.

"I wonder which came first?" Father Tanner said, sipping his tea. "It stands to reason that the house was searched and then they moved on to the dugout. But it might have been the other way around. They could have been looking for more than what they found buried."

"That's a good question, Father, but what I need right now are answers. Can you tell me anything more about this notebook? There must be something else."

"Nothing more than it was a list of names and times," Tanner said. "He refused to elaborate, I'm sorry to say."

"Father, I have to ask this. Was David Archer in his right mind? Could he have been seeing things that weren't there?"

"Captain, given what he saw and experienced in the war, how could he be in his right mind? I doubt my own sanity some days, and all I have are physical scars," he said, brushing his fingertips across the rippled skin on his forehead. "David's ran much deeper. I'm not sure anyone can understand what his mind was like. But I will tell you this much—he knew what beauty was. He loved the night sky. He grew flowers in his garden. He listened to music, sometimes on the wireless and sometimes standing outside the church as the choir sang. He knew all those things were real. I believe he knew something was wrong at Marston Hall. As to what, I cannot say. Now I wish I had pressed him."

"All right. I had to ask," I said. I did suspect David Archer had stumbled onto something, but had he understood what he'd seen? He was a man who saw life through the lens of his horrific experiences in the last war. But how wrong could he have been? He'd gotten killed for what he'd witnessed.

"I understand," Tanner said. "Just so you know, I called Chief Inspector Gwynne and left a message about what I found at David's. I kept your name out of it. Tower Hill as well."

"I take it you've had dealings with Gwynne?" I asked.

"Captain Boyle, I render unto Caesar the things that are Caesar's. Therefore, let Caesar sort it all out."

AS I LEFT the vicarage, the sun was low in the clouding sky. I had no interest in going back to the Rose and Crown yet. There was something I had to clear up with Sir Richard, and the way I saw it, if it happened to be around suppertime, there was nothing wrong with accepting an invitation. If one was offered.

I was preparing myself for what Diana might have to say, so I wasn't ready for the sight of a police car in front of Seaton Manor. I pulled in next to it, hoping that this was no more than the pleasant interview stage of the chief inspector's investigation. Or what passed for pleasant when it came to Gwynne.

I saw a curtain pulled back, and in seconds, Diana opened the door. She looked tense.

"Billy, they've been in Father's study for half an hour," she said, grabbing my sleeve and pulling me inside. Before I answered, I did a quick calculation and concluded Gwynne must have left before he could have received Father Tanner's message about Archer's place being tossed.

"Don't worry," I said as she shut the door. "Taking a statement isn't quick. You have to talk things through and then write it all out."

"Are you sure? Mrs. Rutledge is about to storm the study with a meat cleaver," Diana said. Knowing how protective Mrs. Rutledge was when it came to Sir Richard, I didn't half doubt it.

"I've taken enough statements to know." I left out the part about how some ended in the suspect being taken away in handcuffs. "Listen, let's sit down and wait. Tell me what you've been doing all day?"

"Helping with the horses," Diana said as we went into the sitting room. "Father usually has a boy from the village bicycle in each day to help with the feeding and mucking out the stalls, but the lad's down with the influenza. Dr. Bodkin says he's quite ill."

"Sorry to hear that," I said, but what I was really after were her father's whereabouts today. I'd feel a lot better about seeing Gwynne if I knew that Sir Richard hadn't left the premises. "That must've kept your father busy as well."

"It's a lot of work," Diana said. "Father was lucky to be able to get out for a ride after lunch when the rain let up."

"Is it hard for him, with one arm, I mean? How far does he go by himself?"

"One-armed is the only way he's ever ridden. He took up riding just after the last war," Diana said, her eyebrows knitted. "Why are you so interested, Billy? What's happened?"

"Somebody searched David Archer's cottage," I said. "They tore the place apart looking for something, possibly a notebook."

"And you think it was my father?" She folded her arms across her chest. Not a good sign.

"I have no reason to," I said. "But if he hadn't left the house today, it would have cleared him, which would help keep Gwynne at bay."

"Well, I could have done it." Diana avoided my eyes. "Aren't you going to ask me where *I* was?"

"The body in the aircraft has been positively identified as Stephen Elliot," I said, ignoring the sarcasm.

"The chief inspector didn't mention that," she said.

"No, he'd wait to surprise Sir Richard, watching for his reaction. But Gwynne doesn't know about Archer's place. The vicar was about to call him when I left, but Gwynne must've been on his way here," I said.

"Do you need to tell him?" Diana asked.

"If I don't, he might just come right back. And wonder why I'd kept that information from him."

"Well, we should tell him." Diana tapped her foot nervously as she unfolded her arms. She was struggling with her desire to protect her father while coming to grips with how the case would look to the police.

As I was. But it was intensely personal with Diana, and I could tell it was wearing on her.

"It would be best," I said.

A door opened, and I heard Gwynne's booming voice.

"Leave it to me," whispered Diana, vaulting from her chair and intercepting the inspector in the foyer. A constable trailed Sir Richard, but it didn't look like an arrest. There were no angry protests from Sir Richard, simply a weary resignation to this intrusion.

"I hope Father was a help, Chief Inspector," Diana said, beaming a smile his way.

"I'm glad of all the help I can get, young lady," Gwynne said. "What are you doing here, Boyle?"

"Billy dropped by to give us the news," Diana said. "Isn't it terrible?"

"Isn't what terrible?" Sir Richard asked.

"Never mind, sir," Gwynne said, then repeated the same question.

"How someone ransacked David Archer's cottage, of course," she said. "Haven't you heard? Billy said the vicar called you."

"What's the vicar got to do with this?" Gwynne asked, his eyes darting between me, Diana, and Sir Richard.

"He took me there earlier today," I said, picking up on Diana's idea to sow confusion and anger to keep Gwynne off balance. "He thought there would be something at Archer's place that would aid in the investigation."

"I am conducting this investigation, Boyle!" Gwynne thundered. "What in blazes are you doing bringing the vicar into it? You have no standing here. You're no longer even a guest of Sir Richard, blast it!"

"At the moment, he is," Sir Richard said evenly. "I hope you can join us for dinner, Captain Boyle."

"My pleasure," I said. "As for the investigation, Chief Inspector, I am conducting it as well, authorized by a higher authority than the Norfolk Constabulary." I showed him my orders and watched his face turn red.

"Don't let us keep you, Chief Inspector," Diana said, stepping out of his way. "I am sure you must visit the scene of the crime."

"Of course," he said, thrusting the orders back at me. "Captain Boyle, from this point forward, I hope you will keep me informed of your progress."

"Same here," I said. "Good luck. It was a notebook, by the way."

"What was, man?"

"It was a notebook they were searching for. David Archer kept track of people coming and going at Marston Hall. Other places, too, for all I know. It's missing." I saw no reason to mention Archer's dugout. There was nothing there but the memory of him, and I didn't want policemen's boots trampling over it.

"This came from the vicar, eh?" Gwynne asked.

"He was quite friendly with Archer," Sir Richard said. "Good evening, Chief Inspector."

"Yes, yes," Gwynne mumbled. "One more thing. How do I find this cottage?"

Sir Richard gave directions to the constable just as a car pulled up outside. Slamming doors and excited chatter announced the early return of Kaz, along with Angelika and Agnes.

The three of them stormed into the foyer, creating a tangle of people and suitcases until they noticed the constable and Gwynne.

"Are we to be arrested?" Kaz asked, taking in the situation in his usual bantering manner.

"Poland?" Gwynne said, his mouth turning into a sneer as he read the shoulder flash on Kaz's uniform. "You have foreigners as house guests, Sir Richard? Who are they? What is this all about?"

"That is unbearably rude, Chief Inspector," Agnes said. "These are our friends and allies."

"*Our* friends, you say? Whose friends exactly?"

"I mean friends and allies of our nation. And of all decent Englishmen." Agnes jutted out her chin in defiance.

"Foreigners are everywhere, Miss, and you'd do best to watch out for them," Gwynne said, moving past her. "They're not to be trusted, in my experience."

"That's odd," Agnes said. "We just came from RAF Coltishall, where dozens of them are based and flying against the Nazis. I'd trust them with my life."

Chief Inspector Gwynne snorted and left without another word. He never thought to ask where Sir Richard was today.

Hell, I'd nearly forgotten about it myself.

CHAPTER TWENTY-ONE

I'D WANTED TO talk to Sir Richard about the interview and where he'd gotten himself to this afternoon, but there'd been too much chatter and swirling questions in the hallway after Gwynne's departure. Angelika gave us a quick update on her visit to Hamilton's surgery. The stitches were out, and the decision about the need for another operation would wait until she was fully healed. Agnes promised to be a hard taskmaster when it came to the exercises Hamilton had prescribed, while Angelika did a small dance step to show how well she was doing and how happy she was about the stitches being removed.

Sir Richard went off to talk to Mrs. Rutledge about dinner, telling me he'd give me a rundown later. Diana took Angelika and Agnes upstairs and was already busy giving them the news they'd missed. I gave Kaz a nod in the direction of the door. Soon we were outside, walking along the path past the horse barn.

"Agnes cut that bastard off at the knees quite nicely, didn't she?" Kaz said.

"She's been pretty quiet around the house," I said. "She should get out more often."

"She and Jerzy got along well," Kaz said. That was the friend Kaz had gone to look up. "If we hadn't had the appointment with Hamilton, I think Agnes would have lobbied for a longer stay. I believe seeing those boys and their fighter planes had an effect on her."

"I thought she'd seen a lot of the war already," I said. London during the Blitz was no picnic.

"Yes, but only on the receiving end. She was quite brave, by all reports. But seeing those who have been through so much striking back enlivened her. Gwynne ran into her at the wrong time. I thought it best not to say anything myself and let her have the floor."

"Well, for right now, she's the perfect person for Angelika. Do you know if another surgery will be needed?"

"Hamilton said it all depended on how well the muscles healed and if Angelika kept them limber," Kaz said. "That is what the exercises are for." We stopped on a small rise, watching as the sun dipped low in the sky and the wind rippled the grassy field.

"It's beautiful here. A fine place for Angelika to heal," I said. The talk of Hamilton had reminded me of what he'd said about Angelika wanting to return to the fight. I had no idea if Kaz knew, and I was uncertain if I should be the one to tell him. "Perhaps even stay on, until the war's over."

"I don't see Angelika rusticating in the English countryside, no matter how beautiful," Kaz said. "Just like those fighter pilots, she wants to strike back."

"You know? That she wants to volunteer with SOE?"

"We are Poles, Billy. Between the Nazis and the Communists, our nation has been ground down to almost nothing. But not quite to nothing. We still have ourselves. I cannot retire from the struggle now, nor can Angelika. She could not live with herself if she did. This I know. It is more important than life." Kaz ran his fingers along his scar, his voice choked with emotion.

"Any work they give her would be insanely dangerous," I said.

"Yes," Kaz said. "And I have no desire to see her throw her life away for nothing. I am also not a fool, and I know her injury may prevent her from jumping out of airplanes and that sort of thing. At the very least, though, I hope she can wear this uniform with the patch the chief inspector so adamantly despises. There are many ways to serve."

"What's his problem, anyway?"

"You weren't in Great Britain before the war," Kaz explained. "There was a lot of right-wing activity. The British Union of Fascists was on the rise with fifty thousand members. Gwynne might have been one. His attitude fits. They are still here, Billy, those fifty thousand and their sympathizers. There is no place for eastern Europeans in their vision of English society. Don't underestimate him simply because he acts the bully. He must be intelligent to have made it to chief inspector."

"Or he has supporters in higher ranks, which could mean trouble as well," I said.

"Does he seriously consider Sir Richard a suspect?" Kaz asked, looking at me as we stopped to admire the view.

"Sir Richard and Stephen Elliot had words at a Marston Hall party back in 1940," I said. "Elliot forced himself on a serving girl and Sir Richard intervened, threatening to thrash him if he tried that again. Plus, he was out for a ride today and could have been the one who searched David Archer's cottage."

"Wait, slow down," Kaz said. "Tell me what I've missed, in chronological order, please."

I took a deep breath, ordered my thoughts, and focused on the green rolling hills as I recited the events. I started with Dr. Bodkin's analysis of the bodies from the aircraft, including the update from Gwynne about Elliot's dental records. My suspicions about Colonel Cheatwood and Charlotte Mothersole, even though that seemed little more than gossip. Alfred and Mildred Bunch poking around in Elliot's private library. David Archer and his dugout. His cryptic comments to me at the pub, and then his murder outside the Rose and Crown as the V-1s screeched overhead. His notebook and tossed cottage. Major Hudson dragooning me into this investigation, and the orders Harding had delivered. The Ritchie Boys and their interrogation system, along with the news that the two Luftwaffe aircrew were on their way.

"There are Ritchie Boys at Marston Hall?" Kaz exclaimed. "Very interesting group. I'll be glad to talk with them."

"How do you know about the Ritchie Boys? They're supposed to be top secret."

"Billy, we receive many top secret reports and briefings at SHAEF. You should try reading them sometime," Kaz said. We weren't at headquarters that often, but Kaz always made time to catch up on his reading. Me, I preferred to sleep in when I could.

"Speaking of reading, you're going to love this next bit," I said. "Assuming you want to be in on this job. Your name isn't on the orders."

"It depends on how onerous the task," Kaz said, turning to head back to the house.

"It involves going through materials in Stephen Elliot's library," I said. "At Marston Hall, where the Ritchie Boys are and where the officers' mess is supposed to be excellent."

"Well, I suppose I could take a look," Kaz said with a smile. "Angelika is doing well enough on her own, don't you think?"

"She is, my friend." I clapped Kaz on the shoulder as we walked back to the house. All the while I was wishing for some minor setback that would keep her under a doctor's care for a bit longer.

We found Sir Richard in the library, reading the book about King John he'd taken from Marston Hall.

"Mrs. Rutledge is working at stretching the rabbit stew she's been simmering all afternoon," Sir Richard said, shutting his book. "The ladies will be down shortly, and we'll have drinks to buy her more time."

"How was the interview?" I asked. "Or was it more of an interrogation?"

"Gathering all the pertinent facts was how the chief inspector described it," Sir Richard said. "He was most interested in the confrontation I'd had with Elliot four years ago. Seems like ancient history now, I must say."

"But it is a motive," Kaz said. "Although it sounds like the man could have used a good throttle."

"As I told Gwynne. Elliot was unlikable enough that half a dozen men would have stood in line to have a go at him," Sir Richard said.

"It took only one," I said.

"I reckon when Gwynne calms down it will occur to him to ask me my whereabouts. Sadly, my only witness is four legged. Tell me, Baron, was the news from Hamilton really so positive?" Sir Richard rose and walked to the drinks table. Three whiskeys, each with a splash of soda water from a siphon, were soon in our hands. I had to admit, the man was adept at accomplishing things one handed.

"It was," Kaz said, raising his glass and taking a sip. "He was adamant about physiotherapy, though. Exercises and massage. He said without it, all her progress may be undone."

"In that case, I'm happy to keep Agnes here for as long as necessary," Sir Richard said. "She really tore into Gwynne, didn't she? Never saw her so animated. Quite eloquent."

"Agnes grew up here, didn't she? Are her parents still alive?" I asked. I already knew, but I wanted to learn more about Dr. Bodkin. I knew Sir Richard wouldn't talk about him, but discussing Agnes might reveal something.

"No," Sir Richard said. "She was orphaned when her mother died in childbirth. Bodkin knew of a widow—there were many after the last war, as you can imagine—who desperately wanted a child. She took Agnes in and raised her."

"I thought it was an aunt," I said.

"I don't know the details, but there was no aunt or other relative. That's just the story that was told. It's the way things are often handled in the country," Sir Richard said. "Best all around.

The widow died several years ago and left a small cottage to Agnes. At least she has that."

"Decent of Dr. Bodkin to arrange it," I said. Sir Richard nodded, ever so slightly, giving Bodkin his silent due, but no more. Footsteps announced the arrival of Diana, followed by Angelika and Agnes.

"Piotr, come with us," Angelika ordered. "We must help Mrs. Rutledge, since we are a surprise for dinner. Come, come."

"I look forward to the library, Billy," Kaz said, following the two girls.

"Nice work with the inspector, dear," Sir Richard said to Diana as she poured herself a whiskey, no soda. My kind of woman.

"Try to stay indoors, Father. You never know when there might be another murder," she said, flopping into a chair. "Or have you solved the case already, Billy?"

"Which one? Who killed Elliot in 1942 or who killed Archer last night?" I said, raising my glass in her direction.

"Take your pick. Bound to be the same person, don't you think?" Diana said.

"Related, certainly," I said.

"I agree," Sir Richard said. "No shortage of candidates for the first murder. But I can't see why anyone felt the need to kill David Archer."

"Because he knew something about the first murder," Diana said. "That's obvious."

"Of course," Sir Richard said, finishing his drink. "But why wait over two years? Archer's been here all along."

The connection was Elliot's body in the aircraft. Archer didn't matter to the killer until the body reappeared. But there was no reason to bring that up with Sir Richard right now. I was the investigator, and he was still a suspect, at least as far as the law was concerned. Besides, I could smell hot food.

We dined on ample portions of rabbit stew, roasted onion, and fried pumpkin. All local produce, and a masterpiece of off-ration cooking. Sir Richard thanked Mrs. Rutledge for accommodating the unexpected guests.

"There will be better fare tomorrow, don't you worry," she said. "Mr. Bunch is making his delivery and there will be a nice rack of lamb."

"Apparently Colonel Cheatwood has a taste for the finer things," I said. "Someone at Marston Hall told me he's a good customer of Bunch's."

"Sounds like a smart chap," Kaz said, taking a drink of wine. "Army cooking being what it is."

"Oh, well, I suspect Alfred and Mildred love going back inside the Hall," Mrs. Rutledge said. "They were right disappointed when they were let go. Hoped to stay on, they did. We were all surprised when Mr. Elliot turned them out. Now, I'll get the baked apple custard."

That sounded great to me, but this was a twist on the tale of the Bunches that I hadn't heard before.

"Did Elliot turn them out? I thought they were let go when the military took over Marston Hall," I said, looking to Diana and Sir Richard.

"I recall there being some gossip," Sir Richard said. "Didn't pay much attention at the time."

"I heard it was rather abrupt," Diana offered. "But I expect Elliot didn't see the purpose in keeping them on, what with him about to be posted and the Hall being taken over. At Father's suggestion."

"They can't blame me," Sir Richard said. "Somebody would have taken note of that huge building being unused sooner or later. We could have ended up with an artillery range or some such bothersome affair. Instead, we have a nice, quiet operation. Hardly noticeable day-to-day."

"Did Stephen Elliot have an opinion about that?" I asked.

"Not that he shared with me," Sir Richard said. "Although I never willingly associated with him after his dreadful performance at that party."

"Who did associate with him?" Kaz asked. "Did he have any friends?"

"Not that I knew of," Diana said. "He was too self-important to befriend anyone he considered beneath him, which was most people. I'd say Charlotte was the only person to voluntarily spend time with him."

Then came the baked apple custard, and we stopped speaking of unpleasantries.

Later, as full as I could be, I walked into the kitchen to see Mrs. Rutledge. Since I was one of the spare guests, I offered to help clean up. She wasted no time in handing me a towel.

"Keep up with me, Billy, or we'll be here all night," she said, scrubbing a pot. "And thank you. I was worried Sir Richard might want to help. One arm or two, the man's a disaster in the kitchen."

"I don't mind," I said. "It reminds me of home, helping my mom."

"Sorry you had to leave and stay at the pub," she said. "It's not right, but I understand how things might look."

"This sure isn't how I expected my leave to go," I said, stacking plates in the cupboard. "What did you think of Stephen Elliot? Did you have much to do with him?"

"Not a thing, I'm glad to report. The best thing I can say about the man is that he mostly kept himself to himself," she said, going to work on a cast-iron skillet. "Didn't even bother to attend services, not ever. That's a way to tell a small village you don't care."

"I would have thought he'd enjoy playing lord of the manor. Wouldn't he be given a place in the first pew?"

"It would have been his, and the respect that goes along with it," Mrs. Rutledge said. "But he preferred his books and his research. He was mad about King John, from what I've heard. Now dry that skillet well, mind you."

"Who would have known him best?" I asked, applying elbow grease to wipe off every speck of moisture.

"Hmm. Other than his sister, you mean? I'd have to say Dr.

Bodkin. He attended to both. He never gossiped or had a bad word to say. Charlotte alluded to that once. She said her brother was difficult at times but that Dr. Bodkin was always fair and even-tempered with him. Not many can make that claim, as you've heard."

"Forgive me for asking, Mrs. Rutledge," I said, hanging the skillet on a hook near the stove. "But what's between Sir Richard and Dr. Bodkin? From what little I observed, it's pretty one-sided."

"Oh dear." She leaned on the edge of the sink.

"I'm sorry, I shouldn't have asked."

"No, it's all right. She was so lovely, that's all. The sweetest girl in Norfolk."

"Who?"

"Eveline. Diana's mother. Sir Richard's wife."

"Dr. Bodkin came between them?" I asked.

"No, no. Nothing like that. I'll explain, but I must sit down. And you need to pour me a brandy," she said.

I poured us each a small glass and sat across from her at the kitchen table.

As young men, Richard Seaton and John Bodkin had been friends. One had gone off to medical school and the other into the Royal Navy. Both had courted Eveline Allyn, who showed her preference for the dashing naval lieutenant but urged both men to remain friends, which they did. But when Eveline and Richard were married, shortly before the Great War broke out, Dr. Bodkin declined his invitation. While he did nothing to stand in their way, he was too heartbroken to watch Eveline marry someone else. Even after that, the men remained friends, although, as Mrs. Rutledge said, that had been much easier for her employer.

The war came, and so did children for the Seatons, while Bodkin remained single, working as the only doctor for miles around. Eveline, out of respect for his feelings, had a midwife attend to her births. Still, on the few occasions her husband came home on leave, Bodkin had always been invited.

Then Sir Richard—not yet a *sir*—lost his arm. When he was released from the hospital, Bodkin stood by him and helped him recover. After a period of depression and self-doubt, Sir Richard bounced back. He took up horseback riding and challenged himself to make the best out of surviving, even with the loss of an arm. Eveline had been magnificent, encouraging him every step of the way.

Then came the Great Influenza epidemic. It first hit in 1918, but another wave struck Britain in 1919. That was when Sir Richard came down with it, but it was a mild case.

Not so with Eveline. It hung on, never loosening its deadly grip.

Dr. Bodkin attended to the sick and dying, everyone marveling at how he never sickened himself. As things worsened with Eveline, Bodkin told Sir Richard she might not survive. Sir Richard refused to accept it and lapsed back into the dark depression he'd suffered through when he was first released from the hospital.

He'd stand in Eveline's doorway and tell her she'd be fine, but he couldn't sit with her. Despite encouragement from Mrs. Rutledge and Dr. Bodkin, he refused, saying he must not chance infecting the children. He never moved past the doorway.

But Bodkin did. He'd stop at the end of his day, no matter the time, and sit with Eveline. At first, Sir Richard was glad. Then he became resentful, issuing cutting comments as Bodkin would take his leave. Still, Richard allowed the doctor to visit since Eveline enjoyed his company. Perhaps Eveline and Richard saw what might have been had she chosen differently.

Dr. Bodkin was by Eveline's side when she died.

Sir Richard was in the barn with the horses.

When Bodkin broke the news, Sir Richard calmly told him to leave and never return. Except for medical necessity, once for

Mrs. Rutledge herself and recently for Angelika, he did not set foot again in Seaton Manor.

"It broke his spirit, poor man," Mrs. Rutledge said. "Her dying, but also the fact that he couldn't face it. The children, God bless them, never came down with the influenza, and Sir Richard doted on them every day after that. As if he were trying to make up for how he'd abandoned their mother."

I heard a sob from over my shoulder. Diana stood in the doorway, a hand covering her mouth. She wiped her eyes and, like a true, steely-spined Seaton, walked in and grabbed a dish towel. Mrs. Rutledge returned to the sink, and we all worked in silence, putting the kitchen back in order, as if that might somehow heal the lingering pain that clung to the house from such terrible suffering of body and soul.

CHAPTER TWENTY-TWO

I FELT LIKE a heel thinking about leaving Diana for the night, but the feeling didn't last long. My jeep had been stolen. Or misplaced, by Kaz most likely. I could've searched for it, but that would have meant stumbling around in the dark and looking behind the barn. Diana was smiling as I turned around from the open door. I shut it and embraced her, feeling the warmth of her tears against my cheek.

I was her willing prisoner.

In her bed, wrapped up against the chill, Diana told me she'd known since she was a child about Sir Richard's behavior when her mother died. He'd admitted it himself, but in a condensed version. He hadn't been proud of it and promised he'd be a better father than that. Which he was.

"True to the stiff-upper-lip stereotype, we never talked about it again," Diana said. "Daphne was the youngest and didn't really remember Mother. Peter and I did, but we kept the family secret to ourselves." Peter, Diana's brother, was in the British Army. I'd last seen him in North Africa, but these days he was attached to Field Marshal Montgomery's headquarters in France.

"I'm sorry. I wished I hadn't asked Mrs. Rutledge," I said.

"Don't be." She leaned on her elbow and looked at me. "I know it's how these things work. You need to pull all those loose threads, don't you?"

"Yeah, but it isn't always the decent thing to do," I said.

"Especially when those threads end up having nothing to do with the case, and cause pain to boot."

"So now you know the story, and you can move on. I'm glad I heard Mrs. Rutledge's side of things. I always knew she thought well of my mother, but I never saw it as her loss as well. I shall talk with her tomorrow."

"No more stiff upper lip?"

"Well, let's not go too far. There will be no heart-to-heart with Father. He'd die of embarrassment," she said, laughing in a way I hadn't heard this evening. "God, Billy, when will it all be over?"

"The war? Who knows," I said.

"The war, the hatred, the lack of compassion, the blind willingness to kill, all of it," she said. "I'm so tired of it."

"We've been at it long enough. It almost seems normal," I said.

"God help us, then."

All I could do was hold her.

I WAS KICKED out before dawn. The idea was that no one should be put in the position of lying if Gwynne were to ask about my whereabouts overnight. Other than Diana, of course. As a genuine spy, she was a professional liar, so that didn't count. I got to the Rose and Crown with the milkman and grabbed some shut-eye while waiting for the noise in the kitchen below to announce breakfast.

I was barely awake but working diligently on my eggs and sausage when Chief Inspector Gwynne darkened the door.

"I thought you might have taken up residence with one of my suspects again," Gwynne said, hanging his hat on a peg and settling into the chair opposite me.

"Please join me, why don't you?" My sarcasm was too subtle for him to take note.

"Cup of tea, love," he said, glancing at Dorothy as she passed.

"Now, Boyle, I came by to tell you we found nothing at Archer's place. Nothing but a mess."

"So they got what they wanted?" I said around a mouthful of sausage.

"Seems so. What I want to know is, did Archer say anything to you about it? This notebook," Gwynne said.

"Nothing. His last words to me were 'I wished I hadn't seen it, but I did.' When I mentioned that a lot of people saw the bomber come down, he told me I didn't understand."

"Not much help, are you?" Gwynne said as Dorothy set down a tray with tea, milk, and sugar.

"I do understand now, Chief Inspector," I said. "All we have to do is find out why Elliot's killer stuffed his body into that aircraft. It was the recovery of Elliot's remains that marked Archer as the next target."

"But how the devil did anyone manage that? The bomber was in the water. Use your head, man," Gwynne said, stirring his tea.

"It ended up in the water. You've felt the cliff edge crumble under your feet," I said, dabbing my lips with the napkin. "I say it crash-landed and went right to the edge. Elliot shows up along with the killer. The deed is done, and his body is put in the burning plane to be consumed. Then it tips over the edge and is taken by the rough sea and tides. The killer thinks they're safe. Until the plane returns and David Archer has to die."

"If that's the case, then someone is lying about what they saw at the cliffs," Gwynne said.

"Oh, yes. I think there's a fair amount of lying going on in Slewford. Lying by solid, upstanding Englishmen, I'd say. Now, I'm on my way to interview the Luftwaffe aircrew from that bomber. I'll let you know if anything comes of it," I said.

Gwynne looked confused, thrown off by my promise of assistance.

"Be sure you do," he said, then softened his approach. "Archer's body has been released. It's on the way to Copping and Sons."

"Thanks," I said.

"Go tell the vicar, why don't you, seeing as how you spent so much time with the man."

"I will." I kept my voice calm, which took some effort. The man didn't take to softening for long.

First, I swung back to Seaton Manor to pick up Kaz. The morning was still cold despite the sun rising into a blue sky. Winter was coming with its longer, darker days. Just as Diana had last night, I wondered when it would be over. The idea of fighting through a frigid season on our way to Berlin wasn't a pleasant one. I shook off the thought, but the cold still clung to my bones.

"Billy, you found your jeep," Angelika said, greeting me with a grin. She was dressed in old slacks and a heavy sweater.

"It was easy. The thief was pretty lazy," I said. "Right, Kaz?"

"Indolence is an art form," he said, descending the stairs. "I knew exactly how far to go. Just out of your sight, and it worked perfectly."

"Are you stretching, Angelika?" Agnes shouted from upstairs.

"Yes. Right now." Angelika raised her right foot to rest on a stair, then leaned forward to touch it. "She is so brutal for such a nice person. They could use Agnes on the worst prisoners at Marston Hall."

"I heard that," Agnes said, coming down with a clipboard in hand. "Better stretching than traction, remember."

"Hamilton said he might have to put Angelika into traction if she doesn't stretch out the muscles," Kaz explained. "Then surgery if that fails."

"All right, I am stretching!" Angelika groaned, reaching to grab her foot and bending forward.

Diana and Sir Richard were in the barn, but I decided not to visit. I wanted Mrs. Prentice to appreciate my nice clean boots. On the drive over I told Kaz about Tanner and his service as a chaplain in the last war.

"I can see why Archer was drawn to him as a friend," Kaz said. "A man who endured what he did might doubt the existence of God while finding comfort with a man of God as a friend."

I needn't have worried about tracking mud over Mrs. Prentice's carpets. We found the vicar in the churchyard sweeping leaves from the walkway.

"Padre, the police have released David Archer's body," I told him, after I'd introduced Kaz. "Copping and Sons in Castle Rising."

"I shall telephone them," Tanner said. "I've already picked out a nice spot for David, near the stained-glass window. He liked to listen to the choir from there. I'll show you." The vicar took us around to the south side of the church, where the sunlight bathed the stonework and cast shadows across the green lawn from a magnificent yew tree.

"A very peaceful resting place, Padre," Kaz said.

"Yes. Although I must admit, I chose it as much for myself as for David," he said. "A nice place to visit and remember, don't you think? A small sin on my part, perhaps, but I hope to be forgiven. God will, I'm sure, but some of my parishioners may feel otherwise."

"Because they were frightened of David?" I asked.

"No. Because he wasn't a member of the congregation, and this is valued real estate," Tanner said, a quick laugh escaping his lips. "Thank you for bringing me the news, Captain. I'll have the grave dug. Services will be the day after tomorrow if Copping has everything ready in time."

"Did Archer have family in the area?" I asked as we walked back along the path.

"No one. Perhaps you can attend, Captain?"

"We both shall," Kaz said, placing his hand on the vicar's stooped shoulder. "He deserves that much. If I may, I wish to contribute to the costs of the funeral."

While Tanner and Kaz stopped to talk it over, I strolled on, looking at the names and dates on the tombstones. Some were centuries old, others more recent. Many were dated after the last war, probably from the influenza epidemic. The war dead were there as well, or at least their markers. So many men were missing or buried in France, but it stood to reason families would want a place to leave flowers.

A name caught my eye. Virginia Day Sallow. A relation of Agnes's, or perhaps her mother who had remarried? I walked over to the grave. She'd died in 1920, only eighteen years old. I searched for another stone with that last name, but this was the only one. No one named Day was buried here either.

"Virginia was so young," the vicar said. "One of my first burials when I came here. Hard to forget. I baptized Agnes and laid her mother to rest a day apart."

"Her husband is buried elsewhere?" I asked, thinking France, perhaps, but the dates didn't work.

"No," Tanner said, heaving a sigh. "There was no husband. Agnes has her mother's name." He stood quietly at Virginia's grave, his eyes closed and hands folded in prayer.

"Does Agnes know her father?" Kaz asked after Tanner had finished.

"I think she knows who he was, but perhaps you should ask Dr. Bodkin about it," Tanner said. "When Agnes was older and returned to Slewford, she called herself Day instead of Sallow. She once told me she didn't want people thinking of her only in terms of her birth outside of wedlock. She's a private lass, and I know she wouldn't like her life to be picked over."

"Vicar, if this has anything to do with these killings, it would be helpful if you told us what you know," I said. "Unless you came by the information in confession." I wasn't sure that there was any connection, but in any small town or village, everyone is connected sooner or later.

"Virginia came here from King's Lynn during the war. A bad home life, as I understand. She wanted to make a new start for herself, and she obtained work at Marston Hall," he said. "Just in time for Stephen Elliot to come on the scene."

"What? Are you saying Elliot was the father?" I asked, working out the implications.

"Elliot was quite young when he came into possession of Marston Hall," Tanner said. "Not of an age to have served in the war. When I arrived here after I was mustered out, I started to hear stories. One of my congregation made his daughter quit her employment at Marston Hall, that's how bad it was."

"But you are not certain Elliot was the father?" Kaz asked.

"Virginia Day came to services here every Sunday," he said. "She was a shy girl, and so many of the young men were off to war and never returned home. She had no suitors that I knew of. When she began to show with child, she was turned out from Marston Hall. She came to me to ask forgiveness, but I told her she was not the one who needed forgiving."

"You knew," I said.

"By then, I had the measure of the man. And his sister. Charlotte Mothersole was the one who fired Virginia and told everyone who would listen that she couldn't bear to have a fallen woman about. Charlotte is a regular churchgoer, you see. There's more gossip bantered about in the churchyard after services than I'm comfortable with," Tanner said, his eyes still on Virginia's marker.

"Why didn't you tell me before?" I asked.

"And why should I have? It will only awaken a painful past," the vicar said. "Now you'll need to ask more questions, as if Agnes had any role in this entire affair. It's preposterous."

"No, Padre, I don't think she did. Unless she's the greatest actress in the world, I don't see her as a killer. But if she's Elliot's daughter, I am worried about her being the next victim."

CHAPTER TWENTY-THREE

"ARE YOU GOING to ask her?" Kaz said as I stepped on it and took the jeep too damn fast down the narrow road. One hand was on his hat and the other clenched the metal frame. "Or are you going to kill us?"

"I'm not sure," I said, downshifting for a curve. "About Agnes. As for living, I'm all for it. Sorry."

"I wonder who else knows. Or suspected," he said. I'd slowed enough so Kaz's service cap didn't need any help to stay on, but he still had a white-knuckle grip on the jeep.

"Obviously Charlotte Mothersole," he said. "I didn't take her for the heartless type, but she must have been quite young back then. Pressured by her brother to get rid of Virginia, possibly. Or she simply thought it was expected of her."

"I'm thinking Dr. Bodkin as well," I said, turning onto the dirt road leading to Marston Hall. "I wonder if he hushed it up and placed Agnes with that widow out of guilt. Virginia did die under his care, after all."

"Diana would have told you if she knew, of course," Kaz said.

"Yeah, but I do have to wonder about Sir Richard. If he knew, it might be another grudge he'd hold against Elliot," I said. "I can see him keeping mum for Agnes's sake."

"We must not forget Mildred and Alfred," Kaz said as we pulled up to the gate. "We should find out when they started working here."

I showed the guard my orders, and we were waved through.

"Colonel Cheatwood should be on our list too," I said. "He was living here when Elliot disappeared."

"Perhaps the library should wait," Kaz said. "There are a lot of people to speak to, and if you think Agnes may be in danger, we should act quickly."

"Let's see if those Germans are here yet, then decide," I said, parking the jeep. "I'd like you to listen in and give me your impressions."

Kaz was right about how much we had to do. But I had the feeling there was something in that library that would unlock the mystery behind all this. I hoped it was still there.

I found Major Hudson and introduced Kaz, telling him we'd like to sit in on the aircrew interrogation. He said they were in a holding cell getting nice and nervous, and called for Sergeant Goldstein.

"Oskar, Captain Boyle wants to sit in. Lieutenant Kazimierz, too, if that's okay with you," Hudson said.

"*Ach*, a Pole. Could be handy, Major," Oskar said.

Kaz said something to him in German, and the two of them began jabbering like old pals. I followed them to the end of the hall where a British soldier stood sentry.

"We have our first guest ready to be brought in," Oskar said as he opened the door. Two chairs had been set against one wall, and a table and three chairs were in the middle of the room. A pitcher of water and glasses were set on it. Sunlight streamed in through the window.

"Pleasant," I said.

"We want our friends at ease," Oskar said, smiling. "Please, sit in the chairs by the wall. Say nothing, just watch. We don't want to interrupt the flow. Now, tell me what you need from these men."

"Was there anything special about their mission, or was it a normal bombing run?" I said. "I want to know if they had any passengers on board. An agent, perhaps."

"Have they heard anything about their pilot?" Kaz suggested. "He may have been captured elsewhere."

"They don't know yet about the two bodies found in the bomber," Oskar said. "May I mention that?"

"No reason not to. Anything you can get out of them might help," I said. Probably not, but I kept that to myself. If this had been a secret mission, they weren't likely to blab.

"All set?" Hank Klein asked as he entered. I told him about Kaz. Hank and Oskar exchanged glances.

"If either of these two don't want to cooperate," Oskar said, "how about we tell them the Poles are setting up their own POW camp and we need to send some of ours there?"

"That would be an unpleasant prospect for any German," Kaz said. "American captors are one thing, but to be held by Poles is quite another. There are debts which beg to be paid. As you men must know."

"They will be shaking in their shiny boots," Oskar proclaimed.

Hank said he'd take the lead on the first POW, who was from outside Stuttgart, which wasn't far from Hank's town. His name was Hans Bauer, twenty-three years old. After a final reminder to keep our lips zipped, Bauer was brought in.

He was a thin kid with sandy blond hair and darting eyes. His blue Luftwaffe tunic was faded and worn, and he straightened it as he came to attention.

Hank walked over to him, all smiles, waving his hand. I imagined him saying something like, *Forget that nonsense, we're all enlisted men here.* Bauer sat in the single chair across from Oskar and Hank. Oskar said nothing but smiled politely. Hank shook out smokes from his pack of Camels and the three men lit up, blowing blue smoke toward the ceiling. Bauer seemed to savor the American tobacco, and I wondered what they got to smoke in British POW camps.

Hank spoke Bauer's name, and I could pick out a bunch of numbers. Probably detailing his Luftwaffe unit. Bauer didn't say much but nodded. After two years behind the wire, it hardly mattered that they knew his squadron number.

They gabbed for a couple of minutes. Bauer became more relaxed, even though he kept an eye on us. Hank said something about *Offiziere*, and they all laughed, demonstrating the universal antipathy soldiers hold for the higher ranks.

Then the conversation turned more serious. I heard the word *bomber*, or something close to it, as Hank pointed toward the window. Bauer looked shocked.

"*Hier?*" he gasped.

Yes, Hank told him, the bomber had landed here. He held up two fingers and uttered a mournful phrase. The two dead crewmen, Bauer's pals. Hank's face softened, and in a low voice he asked Bauer a few more questions. Bauer seemed to brighten. After a few more minutes, I noticed Oskar and Hank exchange nods. Bauer was sent off with a handshake and the rest of the Camels.

Oskar said they'd give us the lowdown after they finished with the next guy, Franz Dahl. He was brought in, and Oskar and Hank went through the same routine. Dahl was a small, wiry guy, a good fit for the cramped fuselage of a He 111. He sat erect in his seat and kept up a grim look until another pack of Camels appeared. The routine was pretty much the same, except Dahl wasn't much for small talk. Oskar was having a hard time drawing him out, even after he told him about the crash.

They ended on the same high note as with Bauer. Something they'd said brightened Franz's day. He left with the smokes and an almost friendly *danke*.

"Nothing of value, I'm afraid," Hank said after the door shut. "Their bomber was hit by flak, as you thought. The pilot, Ober-leutnant Werner Brandt, ordered them to bail out, saying he would put the aircraft down because the other two men aboard were too badly wounded. They both thought highly of their pilot and were pleased at the thought he might still be alive in another POW camp."

"Bauer asked if we could find out for him where Brandt was," Oskar said. "I told him it was not allowed. They both thought the question about an agent on board was ludicrous. Dahl said they'd had enough on their hands with the bombing mission. It was a long route."

"I did not sense they were holding anything back," Kaz said.

"They weren't," Hank said. "In this business, you can tell right away. Bauer was happy to have a change of scenery, and Dahl still had a bit of military discipline left in him."

"Still, if we needed anything further, a carton of Camels likely would have gotten it out of them," Oskar said. "Sorry we didn't get to use you in our routine, Lieutenant. It would save one of us dressing up in a Russian uniform."

"If you need me, I shall be working in the library upstairs," Kaz said. "I'd be glad to assist."

"You are looking for the treasure too?" Oskar said.

"Treasure?" I asked.

"Oh, yes," Oskar said. "There's supposedly a treasure in the library. Or the attic—I am not sure."

"Who said this?" I asked.

"I heard Mrs. Mothersole raising her voice yesterday, in Colonel Cheatwood's office," Oskar said. "She said something about a treasure her brother left behind."

"That's a very solid door, Oskar," Hank said. "How could you hear so clearly?"

"Well, my ear may have been close to the door. Quite close, actually," he said. "We are meant to listen to conversations, aren't we?"

"Nazis, Oskar, we're supposed to listen to Nazis," Hank said. "Not nice English ladies."

"If I find the crown jewels in the library, I shall let you know," Kaz said as we left. "This was most enlightening."

"Let's go see Cheatwood," I said. "Then I'll show you the library."

"Are you going to ask him where the map marked with an X is hidden?"

"Hell, I might as well give it a try," I said. "I might get a straight answer, you never know."

We found Colonel Cheatwood in his office and gave him a report on the two Luftwaffe men.

"Too bad, but best to leave no stone unturned," Cheatwood said, gesturing for us to sit. "What's next, Captain?"

"Lieutenant Kazimierz will review the papers in Elliot's library," I said. "I haven't had time to make a thorough search yet. I'll be speaking with Dr. Bodkin soon. He seems to be one of the few people in the village who got along with Elliot."

"Except for his sister, of course," Kaz said. Cheatwood nodded, offering no comment.

"How is she doing, by the way?" I asked. "Holding up all right?"

"As best as can be expected," Cheatwood said. "It wasn't a complete surprise, but still, it was a shock for her."

"It must have been devastating," I said. "Have you seen her since you broke the news?"

"I appreciate your inquiry on behalf of Charlotte, but how often and when I see her hardly seems to be your business, Captain. Unless your remit extends to generating fuel for the village gossips."

"Sorry, Colonel," I said. "I know I ask too many questions."

"He does, Colonel Cheatwood," Kaz offered. "But sometimes they are needed. As in why Mrs. Mothersole was in your office speaking of treasure at Marston Hall, on the same day you delivered the shattering news about her brother."

"Oh my goodness, is this how you run an investigation, Captain Boyle?" Cheatwood said, laughing as he looked from me to Kaz. "Yes, Charlotte came here later in the day. She said she wanted to spend time in Stephen's library, among his possessions. And she did speak of treasure—quite movingly, too—about how

Stephen left it for her. The treasure is Marston Hall, which will become hers now that her brother is officially deceased."

"Well, that's a perfectly satisfactory explanation, isn't it, Billy?" Kaz said, slapping his hands on his knees as he stood.

"Makes all the sense in the world," I said. "Now we can move on and leave all thoughts of treasure behind." Something told me that Cheatwood wasn't being entirely truthful. Kaz knew it too, and my gut told me not to press him until we had a better sense of why he was holding back.

"Yes, please do move on," Cheatwood said, shuffling through papers on his desk. "And I have just the place for you to go. A report came back about a body that may be our German pilot. Found by the Home Guard near Sandringham House back in '42. A contact is attached. The fellow who found the body works there. Oh, by the way, Mrs. Mothersole was back in the library this morning. She wanted to collect a few things. I could hardly deny her since she will soon be in possession."

"No other male heirs around to take precedence?" I asked.

"I am too busy to conjecture," Cheatwood said. "Please treat her with decency. Dismissed."

We left.

"Is this report of any use?" Kaz asked. "A body found two and a half years ago may not tell us much."

"Or it may," I said. "Did either of those Germans mention anything about their pilot being wounded?"

"Bauer said very clearly Werner Brandt was unscathed," Kaz said. "Bauer spoke of how lucky he was compared to the navigator."

"Hmm," I said, scanning the report and the name of the guy listed as our contact. I flicked the page with my finger. "Nigel."

"Who?"

"Nigel Fernsby found the body. He works at Sandringham House and is with the Home Guard. I don't know his last name, but I met a Nigel fitting that description at the Rose and Crown the night Archer was killed. That Nigel is Alfred Bunch's cousin."

"Sometimes a coincidence is just a coincidence, Billy," Kaz said. "What possible connection could there be?"

"My dad taught me not to believe in coincidences," I said. "At least not when it comes to murder. He says *coincidence* is a word people use when they can't see who's pulling the strings."

CHAPTER TWENTY-FOUR

"BEFORE WE GREET the distraught Mrs. Mothersole, we should talk about Agnes," Kaz said, stopping on the second-floor landing. "Do you think she is in danger?"

"If she really is Stephen Elliot's daughter, then she could be," I whispered. "I can't see how this adds up to a crime about inheritance, but that doesn't mean she's safe." I leaned against the wall by a large window, gazing out at the Germans doing their promenade.

"Mrs. Mothersole hardly sounds like an assassin," Kaz said. "Perhaps if we alert Diana and Angelika, they can keep watch over Agnes. Or should we ask for Big Mike?" First Sergeant Mike Miecznikowski was part of our Office of Special Investigations, and he was currently busy with whatever Colonel Harding needed doing back at SHAEF. Big Mike was a former Detroit cop and large enough to give anyone even thinking of doing harm second thoughts. Diana adored him, and I was sure he'd be welcome at Seaton Manor. The only problem was that Diana, as a trained SOE agent, would probably be the best bet as a bodyguard. And not as noticeable.

"Let's hold that in reserve," I said. "Now let's pay our respects."

"And keep mum about Agnes," Kaz reminded me.

The door to the library was locked. I unlocked it to find Charlotte Mothersole in the sitting room, with several framed photographs in her lap.

"Oh, you surprised me!" she said, her hand going over her heart. "Graham told me you might drop by. Lovely to see you again, Baron and Billy." She made it sound as if we were visiting her home for tea. How gracious.

"Thank you," Kaz said with a slight bow. "We are so sorry about your brother."

"Yes, it did hit me hard," she said. "I should have been prepared after all this time, but how can you be, really?" Unleashing a heavy sigh, she went back to looking at the photographs.

"Looking for a memento?" I asked, seeing the pictures were mainly of Elliot.

"Yes. I'm thinking of holding a memorial service, now that we have his body, although that inspector won't tell me when he will release Stephen's remains," she said. "You are still searching for something, Captain? If you tell me what you are after, perhaps I can help."

"I wish I knew, Mrs. Mothersole," I said. "We won't make a mess of things, I promise."

"There is probably nothing to find," Kaz said. "But you know the military. Everything must be done by the book."

"Very well," she said, rising from her seat. "But how this will help find out who attacked Stephen is beyond me." She smoothed out her skirt and knelt to pick up a stack of photographs.

"Mrs. Mothersole, can you leave those for now? Major Hudson has ordered that nothing be taken from this room until we're done with our search," I said. It was always convenient to blame the brass for bad news.

"Pictures? How ridiculous." She tightened her grasp. "Why, I heard Alfred and Mildred were in here carrying off clothing the other day."

"That was before I got my orders, I'm afraid. I know it's silly, but I must insist," I said. "I'll deliver these to you myself once we're done."

"Oh, all right." She thrust the framed photographs at me. "Be sure that you do."

"Will you be taking on the Bunches again, once you move back in?" Kaz asked, escorting her to the door.

"I'm sure they're doing quite well with their sheep," Charlotte said. "Stephen wasn't entirely satisfied with them for some reason. I don't know what it was, but I shan't second-guess him. It's a long time off, anyway. Good day."

"She seems to be holding up under the burden of grief," Kaz said, looking at the furnishings in the sitting room. "This is a nice spot for a gentleman scholar." I set the photographs on the gentleman's chair and looked through them. Elliot in his uniform, Elliot and Charlotte, both looking younger and standing in front of Marston Hall. Prewar, maybe. A faded photograph of an older couple, parents most likely. The usual sort of collection found on mantels or tables covered with doilies.

"Treasured memories?" I said, leaving the pictures behind. Kaz shot me an eye roll and went into the library proper. I could see he was impressed.

"Where to begin?" he said, gesturing at the shelves of books.

"Try to get a sense of what he was researching," I said. "Everybody says he was working on a book, but I don't know if he'd started writing anything or was still gathering information. He was obviously interested in the Wash, but why, I don't know. The file cabinet is full of papers, some typed and some handwritten. His? What are they about, and why did he save them?" I pointed out the coins and the corroded mystery objects in the display case, as well as the closet filled with boxes, but noticed Kaz pushing aside maps on the desk.

"Charlotte forgot a picture," he said, picking up a silver-framed photograph of Elliot. A professional shot, shoulders up, in his dress uniform. There was an empty space on the shelf behind the desk, a thin layer of dust marking the clean outline of where the photo had stood. He set the frame facedown on the desk, next to an open penknife, and the back came right off.

"She's searching for something," Kaz said. "A treasure thin enough to fit within a frame."

"Maybe we should take the idea of a treasure map more seriously," I said. "Do you think she's taken all these frames apart?"

"We can't know, and it would be useless to ask," he said. "So it must be done. It would go faster if I had help."

"I'll help as soon as I get back from Sandringham," I said.

"I was thinking about Oskar or Hank," he said. "They do know how to keep secrets."

A few minutes later, Major Hudson agreed and said Kaz could have their help for a couple of hours. Plenty of time to take apart and reassemble every frame in those rooms. Shake out a few books as well.

ARMED WITH DIRECTIONS, I took off alone for Sandringham House, my mackinaw buttoned up tight against the cold breeze. Leaving Slewford, the terrain was flat and marshy and interspersed with cultivated fields and streams draining into the Wash. I began to think about Nigel and cousins.

There's something about cousins that's different from brothers and sisters. Even if you're close to your own siblings, it's possible to be too close to be pals. Cousins are different. You're connected, but not close enough to get in each other's hair. My cousin Marty and I had a blast whenever we got together, and got into a bit of trouble as well.

I'd do anything for Marty, and I knew I could count on him to do the same. I wondered if it was like that between Nigel and Alfred. Nigel was the older one. Might he feel protective of Alfred? I couldn't figure where that would get me in terms of the investigation, but I needed to be on alert for any signs of defensiveness. Had they gotten in a cousins' heap of trouble when Stephen Elliot kicked the Bunches out? Had it gone too far?

The flat fields turned into thick woods as the road curved away from the small town of Castle Rising, where David Archer was being prepared for burial. I didn't have to ask how much Kaz had given the vicar for the funeral. The look on Tanner's face had said it was more than enough for a dignified send-off.

I glanced at the rough map I'd drawn and spotted the turnoff ahead. Unmarked, of course. No reason to point out a royal estate to German commandos. It was a long, straight stretch under arching trees, but I had to slow down as an armored car parked across the road came into focus.

"What is your business here, sir?" asked a British sergeant after I'd stopped. He had a clipboard in one hand, the other rested on his holster. Two men stood by the armored car, Sten guns slung casually from their shoulders.

"I'm looking for Nigel Fernsby," I said, handing over my orders. "He works at Sandringham House. He's in the Home Guard as well."

"Lieutenant!" shouted the sergeant after one glance at my orders from SHAEF. A tall officer unfolded himself from the armored car and gave me the once-over before saluting. He snatched up the paperwork and scanned them before returning his attention to me.

"Captain Boyle, what brings you to Sandringham? These orders relate to Marston Hall in Slewford."

"What's your name, Lieutenant?" I asked, going for a snide superior-officer tone.

"Lieutenant Andrew Witherspoon, at your service," he said with a hint of a smile beneath his neatly trimmed mustache. "Now, to my question, why are you here? This is a secure area."

"To see a guy who works at Sandringham House," I said. "Nigel Fernsby. He's also in the Home Guard."

"No Home Guard on duty today, I'm afraid," Witherspoon said, glancing at his sergeant as he checked his paperwork.

The noncom's finger stopped at what must have been proof of Nigel's existence. "Fernsby is on staff, Lieutenant," the sergeant said. "I've seen him before. Did his bit in the last war. Seems all right."

"I'll be the judge of that, Sergeant. You are in need of a plumber, Captain?" Witherspoon asked, his eyes narrowing as he read the entry.

"A potential witness, relating to a death at Marston Hall. You know of the place? Colonel Cheatwood is the CO."

"Of course I know of it; that's my job. A POW facility on the coast, south of us. Don't know your colonel, though. You still haven't said what that has to do with anyone here," Witherspoon said.

"In 1942 the body of a German pilot washed up on the beach near here," I said, wondering how long it had been since Cheatwood had been here if this fellow didn't recall him. "Nigel Fernsby discovered it. I have a few questions."

"A dead Jerry from two years ago? What could you possibly want to know about that?" Witherspoon said.

"It doesn't matter what I want, Lieutenant. What matters is I'm authorized to ask whatever questions I want of whomever I wish. If you intend to obstruct a SHAEF investigation, let's get to a telephone and straighten this out," I said.

"I answer to Buckingham Palace, not SHAEF, Captain," he said. "But your papers seem to be in order. Sergeant Bromley will be your escort. He'll take you to your plumber and get you back here quickly. Right, Sergeant?"

"Aye, Lieutenant," Bromley said, sliding into the passenger's seat as the armored car reversed to let us by.

"Buckingham Palace?" I said as Bromley directed me at the next turn.

"We're the Royal Horse Guards, sir. Part of the Household Cavalry, dedicated to protecting the royals," he said.

"I thought the royal family isn't using the estate," I said.

"Never said they were, sir," Bromley said. "Not that I'd know. I just arrived from Holland. That's where most of the unit is. We've been fighting since North Africa, but they rotate us back for protection duties. This is my second time here."

"So you're telling me the Home Guard has the day off and you guys are here, but no king or queen?"

"Absolutely, Captain," he said as we drove out from the woodlands and into a wide-open space. Stretching out in front of me was a long expanse of brickwork, four stories high, with bright limestone around the windows and doors.

"That must be Sandringham House," I said.

"In all its glory," Bromley said with a touch of possessive pride. "You should see the lawns and gardens. All given over now to vegetables and such. They're digging up a late crop of potatoes today."

We drove by a half dozen people working pitchforks into the loose soil and filling bushel baskets with potatoes. A girl— maybe sixteen or so, her dark, wavy hair blown by the breeze—stopped to watch us drive by and gave a wave. Next to her, a younger girl who might have been her sister carried a full bushel to a cart.

As I slowed to wave back, I realized she looked familiar.

"Hey, isn't that . . ."

"No, Captain, that's not Princess Elizabeth and Princess Margaret digging potatoes," Bromley said, shooting me a wink. "And you remember that, sir."

"Remember what?" I said, knowing I had something to write my mother about. Even in a Boston Irish family, a wave to an English princess or two was still worth a mention.

"Well said, sir, and tomorrow it'll be the truth. They're back to London, and we're off duty for a while," the sergeant said.

We pulled around back and parked by a rear entrance. I didn't expect an Irish Yank to be announced at the front door, but it would have been a nice thing to add to the letter. Instead, we ended up in a shabby hallway leading to a cramped office where a man in a dark suit sat hunched over a ledger at a desk. Bromley asked about the whereabouts of Fernsby and was told he could be found in the staff kitchen having a cup of tea.

Bromley led me through a warren of passageways until we came to the kitchen. Windows faced a rear garden, casting light along a well-worn wooden table where Nigel sat, his hands clasping a mug. He looked at me, showing no surprise.

What he did show was a black eye and a nasty-colored bruise on his cheekbone. He looked weary. His formerly ruddy complexion was now pale beneath unkempt graying hair.

"Nigel, what happened?" I asked. Bromley moved off to the stove where the kettle was, intent on fixing his own cuppa while keeping one eye on us.

"It was nothing," Nigel said, raising the mug to his lips. "What do you want?"

"You don't seem surprised to see me," I said.

"Think the world revolves around you, Yank? There was no surprise seeing you at the pub, and there's no surprise seeing you here," he said. "Now what do you want with me?"

"I want to ask you about a body you found washed up on the shore," I said, sitting across from Nigel and checking out his shiner. The eye was half swollen shut.

"What body?"

"How many have you found at Sandringham?"

"All right, then," he said, setting down the mug. "Back in '42. German pilot from the bomber that crashed in Slewford. I was on patrol down to the beach, and there he was."

"Anything unusual?"

"No. I've seen plenty of rotted German corpses. The only difference was this one had a life vest on."

"So what did you do?" I asked.

"Well, he weren't in no shape to cause anyone harm, so I

walked back here and reported it," Nigel said. "Police came and took the body away. Nothing more to it."

"You didn't search the body for documents? Didn't notice anything at all unusual?"

"He had no eyes," Nigel said. "I found that unusual enough and let the rest of him be. Now, I've got work to do, if you've finished wasting my time."

"Have you seen Alfred lately?"

"I see Alfred often. He's family," Nigel said.

"Last night? Is that how you got your face rearranged?"

"We had a bit of a tussle, me and Alfred. It happens," Nigel said, looking away.

"Did he serve in the Great War?" I asked, trying to keep the conversation about Alfred going. "He looks younger than you, but not too young to have joined up."

"He could have," Nigel granted, nodding. "If he hadn't been in prison. Two years for grievous bodily harm. He beat a man he'd had a disagreement with. Nearly killed him."

Nigel rose and turned to walk out, squinting at me through his swollen black eye. I'd seen that look before. Fear. The fear of grievous bodily harm.

CHAPTER TWENTY-FIVE

"THAT WAS A man with a story bottled up inside," Bromley said as we drove back, "and too afraid to tell it. Who is this Cousin Alfred, anyway?"

"A sheep farmer from Slewford," I said. "And a man quick to use his fists. He's not physically stronger than Nigel, but he sure got the drop on him."

"In a fight, be first to strike," Bromley said. "It's what I tell my lads, but that's to stay alive in battle, not to beat your mates senseless. Seems Nigel's cousin has a short fuse."

"Maybe," I said, thinking that rather than going off half-cocked, Alfred had done precisely what he'd intended with that blow. "Tell me, who would have taken charge of the body after Nigel reported it?"

"The local constable to start," Bromley said. "Then the coroner, perhaps? Not sure, but there is a small German military cemetery outside of Norwich. A dozen or so airmen, I think. He probably would've been sent straight there once the paperwork was done."

"Thanks," I said as I dropped the sergeant back at the checkpoint. I didn't know what I'd find, but I did know Alfred wanted Nigel to keep his mouth zipped. That made me curious. I asked where I might find the constable who had responded to the call. Lieutenant Witherspoon gave me directions to the police station in Dersingham, about two miles away. It was the closest to Sandringham House and had responsibility for this area.

In Dersingham, I asked the constable at the desk, but he had no recollection of the body being found and couldn't say who had been on duty at the time. Instead, he directed me to the surgery of Dr. Llewellyn Goose, who had been the coroner ever since the constable could remember.

The doctor was out, but his receptionist said he could be found at the Gamekeeper's Lodge, just a short walk away, having his lunch. I was already hungry, so I said I'd look for him there. Armed with the description of a gray-haired man in a wool three-piece suit, I entered the pub to spot three such gentlemen matching that description. I asked for Dr. Goose and spotted him immediately by the frown on his face, the signature look of a doctor about to have his meal interrupted by an emergency.

"Nothing urgent, Doctor. Do you mind if I join you?" I asked, introducing myself. "I won't take much of your time."

"Please do," Dr. Goose said, his expression softening. "I am curious as to what the American army would want with me." He gave me a good-natured smile, which came easily to his round-cheeked face. He wore a bushy white mustache and tortoiseshell glasses that kept slipping down his nose.

"Just some information, sir," I said, leaning back as the waitress delivered a steaming bowl of dumplings and a half pint to the doctor.

"Norfolk dumplings in a vegetable stew, Captain Boyle," Dr. Goose said. "A local specialty."

I said I'd have the same. "This may seem strange," I began as he wasted no time tucking into his meal. "But do you recall a body being washed up on the beach near Sandringham House? It would have been in the spring of 1942. A German pilot."

"Of course I do," Goose said, nodding as he slurped a spoonful of stew. "We've had a few bodies come ashore from crashed aircraft, but one near the king's residence is bound to be memorable."

"Do you remember anything unusual?"

"Let's see." Goose took a sip of beer. He closed his eyes for a moment, letting the memories flow. "His life jacket had not been inflated. By the condition of the body, he'd drifted on the tides for some time. I think there was a nonlethal cut on his forehead. Eyes gone . . . fingers too. Marine predation, you know."

"Yes, I know." I'd seen it along the Boston waterfront. Fish like to nibble on the soft parts. "Did you search the body?"

"The constable helped with that," he said. "As did an RAF officer who came to take charge of the body. I don't recall anything useful being found. No identification papers or maps. A photograph of a girl was found in his breast pocket—I remember that."

"What killed him?" Before Goose could answer, my meal was delivered, and I set to it. Watching him, I could see that he was thinking about the cause of death, and that it wasn't going to be an easy answer.

"I am not certain, Captain," he said. "He could have drowned. Or it could have been due to a blow to the skull. I was curious at the time, but that was all it was."

"You didn't perform an autopsy?"

"No, there was no call to. His death was not a crime, was it? And drowning is very difficult to prove, even in a proper autopsy. My job was to simply record the death and sign over the corpse to the military. They maintain a cemetery for German war dead not far from here," Goose said, reaching again for his beer. "But it did strike me as odd."

"What exactly was odd?"

"The blow to the head didn't seem like a shrapnel or bullet wound. He'd been struck by something, definitely, but what? It could have been a loose object within the aircraft as it crashed. It may have rendered him unconscious and unable to inflate his life vest. Which might have kept him alive."

"His bomber went down in Slewford," I said. "Near the cliffs."

"Ah, I see. If he were injured in the crash, he could have fallen into the Wash, especially if he was concussed. I've seen those cliffs. Most of our coastline in Norfolk rises gently from the beach, but the cliffs near Tower Hill can be treacherous."

"If it had been an object inside the bomber that rendered him unconscious, he couldn't have exited under his own power, could he?"

"By Jove, you're right enough about that," Goose said, his eyes momentarily wide. "Well, there's any number of reasons for someone bashing him over his head. Perhaps he tried to escape. Resisted arrest. Is that why you're bringing all this up? To arrest some farmer for being too enthusiastic about apprehending a Nazi flier?"

"Not at all," I said. "You see, his bomber recently resurfaced, thanks to the wind and tides. It was hoisted out of the water, and we found a British officer inside. I'm trying to figure out how and why."

"Dear me. The Wash has been known to behave oddly. I've heard of all manner of things coming up from the mud," Goose said. "If I understand you correctly, your German pilot may have witnessed something and been killed for it."

"You're right, Doctor. And even in wartime, that would be murder," I said, returning to my dumplings. Until he'd told me about the injury to the skull, I hadn't seen it that way. But things were beginning to make sense. Not a lot of sense, but some. I'd thought the pilot had been unlucky and fallen off the cliff. Now I knew that by rights, he should still be alive.

"I wish you luck, Captain," Goose said, finishing his meal. "Now I must get back to work. I hope this has been helpful."

"It has ... And his name was Werner Brandt," I said as Goose stood to leave.

"Poor lad. I can't say I have much sympathy, what with my boy serving in the Royal Navy. Even so, Werner should have been taken prisoner properly, not killed like that. I hope you find who's responsible."

"So do I, Doctor."

I finished my stew alone, thinking through what might have happened.

Dazed from the crash landing, Werner Brandt opens the hatch, blood from the cut on his head nearly blinding him. He wants to help his wounded crewmen. What does he do? Call out for help? Try to pull his navigator out the front hatch?

Who does he see? Stephen Elliot? Graham Cheatwood? Alfred or Mildred Bunch? Dr. Bodkin? Agnes? What about Sir Richard? Although I was sure he'd come by too late to be seen. Fairly sure.

Had Werner held his hands in the air and called out *Kamerad*, expecting mercy and assistance? Is that when he witnessed the killing?

What about David Archer? Had he seen the attack on Elliot and Werner and tried to help? Or could he have been part of that? I doubted it.

What I did know with certainty was that Werner Brandt was the third murder victim in this sad, pathetic story. I'd heard stories of Allied aircrew being beaten and abused by German civilians enraged by fleets of bombers attacking them day and night. That was what the Nazis did.

Not us. Whoever did this was as cold-blooded as they come.

I left coins on the table and hustled to the jeep. I felt unnerved by the increased body count and wondered if I'd made a mistake not bringing in Big Mike as an additional bodyguard. I floored it and made for Seaton Manor, praying that I'd find everyone in one piece, and determined to call Harding for help. Diana might be trained in the deadly arts, but she had to sleep. No reason not to double-team Agnes's protection and do it under the guise of a friendly visit.

I made good time, even though I was cursed out by a farmer

when I swerved around his donkey cart. It was overflowing with potatoes, so I guess the royal kids weren't the only ones digging up a late crop.

I turned off the main road, ready to breathe a sigh of relief as I neared Seaton Manor. Then I saw it, and my stomach dropped.

Alfred Bunch's delivery van was parked alongside the manor.

CHAPTER TWENTY-SIX

I DROVE UP next to Bunch's van and parked. I listened for anything that sounded out of place in the midafternoon air. Nothing. I got out, wishing I'd worn my shoulder holster and .38 Police Special revolver. I decided to enter by the rear kitchen door, figuring there was no reason to telegraph my arrival in case Bunch hadn't heard the jeep.

I passed a window and saw a figure moving about inside. I grasped the latch and pushed open the door as quietly as I could. Facing me from across the kitchen table was Alfred Bunch, butcher knife in hand, with Mrs. Rutledge close by.

"Careful now, Mrs. Rutledge, this blade is terrible sharp," Alfred said.

"Oh, Captain Boyle," Mrs. Rutledge said, catching sight of me, "I didn't see you come in! Alfred is helping me with trimming this rack of lamb."

"My husband's quite deft with a knife," Mildred said, coming in from the pantry. "He'll have that done in minutes."

"It's called frenching the bones, Captain," Alfred said, cutting into a layer of fat. "You take the meat off the rib bone so it's easy to handle. Guess the Frogs invented it, eh?"

"Tonight's dinner," I said to Mrs. Rutledge, remembering that she'd mentioned a delivery for today. Now I was relieved I didn't have my revolver on me.

"Yes, will you be staying, Captain?" she asked.

"I'll be here," I said, not sure if I would but wanting Alfred to think I'd be. "I'd like to talk with you, Alfred, once you're finished."

"No time." Alfred kept his eye on the knife as he cut a precise length up each bone. "I spent hours with Chief Inspector Gwynne today and answered every question he put to me. I'll talk to an English policeman as I'm meant to, but I don't need to talk to you, Boyle. I'm not in your army."

"You never were in any army, were you? Although I understand you did wear a uniform," I said.

"The thing is, you need a steady hand and a focused mind to do this cutting," Alfred said. "So I'll just think on what you said when I have the time to spare." He completed the last cut and pulled meat and fat from between the bones. "Perhaps I'll get back to you."

"I'll be waiting," I said.

"That's enough, Billy," Mrs. Rutledge said. "No bad manners in my kitchen."

"He don't know any better, Mrs. Rutledge," Alfred said. "Being half-Yank and half-Irish, he's at a disadvantage, I'd say. Now, let me wash my knife, and I'll scrape the bones with a lesser blade. You keep the sharpest edge for the hardest work in my trade."

"Here's your smoked mutton, dear." Mildred handed a hefty package wrapped in burlap to Mrs. Rutledge, ignoring the tenseness in the air along with the sound of steel against bone. "Almost as good as bacon, I wager. You know what they call this at the Ministry of Food? *Macon*. Mutton and bacon, you see? Them bureaucrats think they dreamt up something special, but we've been having smoked mutton with our eggs for years! Good English country cooking, it is."

"Done!" Alfred proclaimed, the protruding bones as white and clean as if they'd been boiled. "Captain, feel free to ask Gwynne anything you want. If things aren't clear, come see me and I'll straighten it all out. Now, Mildred, leave the bill and I'll clean up. Enjoy, Mrs. Rutledge."

"I'm sure I will," Mrs. Rutledge said, taking the invoice from Mildred. "Although next time I'll do the frenching myself, I think."

"Save me a trip and just tell me when you showed up the night the bomber crashed," I said, standing by the door. "Was Colonel Cheatwood there? Anyone else?"

"What? I hardly remember that far back," Alfred said. "Gwynne's looking for who killed Archer, isn't he? That's what we spoke of, not ancient history! Now step aside—we've got trips of our own. Plenty of deliveries still to make thanks to the inspector wasting my time."

"Who do you think killed Archer?" I said, graciously opening the door for him, mainly to avoid getting bowled over by the departing Bunches.

"Count your Germans—maybe one of them got loose," Alfred said. "The Jewish variety too."

I watched them leave, knowing this was not the time and place to get into it with Alfred. Besides that, I also knew I had to keep my wits about me. Was Alfred trying to goad me into an action that would discredit my investigation? Or perhaps he was ready to fly off the handle at any hint of trouble. I couldn't let my growing dislike of him interfere with getting to the truth. He could be a bully, a horrible cousin, and anti-Semitic while still being innocent.

"Did you think something was amiss, coming through the kitchen door?" Mrs. Rutledge asked. She stood by the window, watching the van back up and leave.

"I forgot you mentioned they were coming by," I said. "I'd just heard about Alfred serving a prison sentence when he was a kid."

"Who said that?" she asked, busying herself with the meats.

"His cousin Nigel," I said. "Alfred left him with a black eye last night."

"Oh, well then, he'd not have much good to say about Alfred, would he?"

"That's true," I said, not wanting to draw her into a conversation about Alfred's penchant for violence. "Mildred sure can talk up a storm, can't she?"

"She's good at putting an end to whatever rubbish Alfred can go on about," she said. "Good trait in a wife with a man like that. He's a good provider, far as I can tell, but he does seem to take everything to heart. Not the most even-tempered man. Now go on, let me get to my work."

I make it a rule not to distract great cooks, especially when I've been invited for dinner, so I left to find Diana. Angelika and Agnes were in the sitting room, but neither was sitting. Agnes was standing over Angelika, who was on the floor doing leg lifts.

"Make her stop, Billy," Angelika said through gritted teeth, her right leg elevated and trembling.

"Don't be a baby," Agnes said. "Now release. Then the other leg."

"I'm not getting in the middle." I held up my hands and backed up.

"Don't listen to her; she's making progress," Agnes said.

"Keep it up, Angelika. It's better than traction," I said. "Hospital food would run a poor second to Mrs. Rutledge's cooking. Rack of lamb is on the menu tonight."

"That is highly motivating," Angelika said.

"Release. Sit up and stretch," Agnes told her. "Think about hospital gruel."

I waited a moment for their bantering and laughter to die down, then asked Agnes about Alfred. "You've lived here all your life—how does he impress you?"

"Rather a gruff man," she said. "I've never had much to do with him."

"Was he that way when he worked at Marston Hall, or did he turn sour after getting fired?" I asked.

"I wouldn't know," she said. "Come, Angelika, time for the stairs." Angelika groaned but rose from the floor with more flexibility than I'd seen before.

"You weren't at any of Elliot's famous parties?" I said, thinking that the man certainly would have invited every pretty young girl in the village.

"I did go to one," Agnes said. "With a friend. I saw no reason to go back."

"Why?"

"Because I didn't like what people were saying," she said, her mouth set in a firm line as her eyes avoided mine. "There are too many gossips in this village."

"Who were they gossiping about?" I asked.

"Stop with the ridiculous questions! Please, leave me alone, will you?" Agnes said, rushing out of the room and choking on a sob.

"What did I say to upset her?" I whispered to Angelika.

"You can be such a *plotkarz*, Billy. You know that, don't you?" Angelika said, brushing past me.

I knew Kaz could translate that for me, but I wasn't sure I wanted to know.

"What's wrong with Agnes?" Diana asked, descending the stairs. Angelika pointed in my direction as she passed her going up.

"I'm a *plotkarz* because I asked Agnes if she'd ever gone to Marston Hall," I said.

"I'm sure that doesn't sound any more pleasant in English," Diana said. "But you obviously upset the poor girl."

"I didn't mean to," I said. "But I did have a reason for asking."

"I'll check with her in a while," Diana said. "Now, other than upsetting people with your questions, what are you here for?"

"First, let me ask you something," I said. "Would you mind inviting Big Mike here? As a houseguest of yours?"

"Why?"

"I spoke with the vicar," I said, lowering my voice and retreating farther into the sitting room. "It's his opinion that Stephen Elliot was Agnes's father."

"Oh god. Does he have any proof?"

"No, but a strong suspicion, and one that sounds logical to me. Did you know Agnes's mother, Virginia, worked at Marston Hall?" I said.

"No, I never did," Diana said. "I heard Agnes was born out of wedlock, but that's not so uncommon. It's the kind of thing country people take in their stride, and I always thought it was none of my business."

"It may be now," I said. "If it's true, she might be a target."

"Because she might inherit? Really, Billy, do you see Charlotte as a murderess?"

"I'm not accusing her. We don't even know the terms of Elliot's will, or if there was one. But I'd feel better with Big Mike here to back you up," I said. "One of you could always stick by Agnes."

"Yes, that makes sense," Diana said. "I'll ask Father to call Colonel Harding. You do realize this qualifies as the worst leave ever in military history?"

I couldn't argue with that one. We agreed that we shouldn't mention Agnes's possible relationship with Elliot to Sir Richard, simply to limit the circle of people who knew about it. The more in on the secret, the quicker it would become common knowledge. Our story was that I wanted backup close at hand in case it was needed, but that otherwise Big Mike would be here for a few days of peace and quiet.

We found Sir Richard in his study. "I'll be glad to have Big Mike here. Charming fellow, even though he eats enough for three. I'll give Sam Harding a call." Sir Richard had his own connections at SHAEF, and my boss was one of them, which meant Big Mike would be packing his bags within hours.

"There's one more thing," I said. "Is it possible to find out if

Chief Inspector Gwynne and Alfred Bunch were members of the British Union of Fascists?"

"There are such lists," Sir Richard said. "When the party was banned at the start of the war, Scotland Yard secured the membership rolls. I'll make some calls, but it may take a while. Given Gwynne's position, I need to make sure the right person handles this in confidence. Is it important?"

"I'd just like to know if Gwynne might be going easy on Bunch as a fellow party member," I said. "They both seem to share the same prejudices."

"I shall have to have Gwynne investigated more thoroughly," Sir Richard said. "After this affair is settled, of course."

I hoped this affair could be settled, and soon.

AS I DROVE toward Marston Hall, I realized I wasn't even sure if Agnes knew who her father was. Tanner had been evasive on the subject, and if she didn't know, I didn't want to be the one to spill that can of beans. I needed to think it through some more, but right now I had something else to attend to. A little breaking and entering at the Bunches' property.

It sounded like Alfred and Mildred were running behind schedule on their deliveries for the day, thanks to the chief inspector. Finally, he was being helpful. So, this was the time to look around and see what there was to find. David Archer's notebook, perhaps?

Their sheep farm was on the other side of the village from Seaton Manor, nestled within a series of rolling hills with fenced-off fields. The place was quiet except for the bleating of sheep, which is to say it was damn noisy. There was no sign of the van or any workers as I parked near the barn, which was stone and timber, both parts ready to collapse into each other. The slate roof was thick with moss, and nothing about the building spoke of a thriving business.

I glanced into the gloomy barn. The scent of blood and slaughter assaulted my nostrils. At least the rack of lamb would be fresh. Woolly sheep watched me from the fence as I trotted over to the house and knocked politely at the door, just in case Alfred had dropped Mildred off.

Nothing.

I tried the knob. Locked. I hustled around back and got the same result. I spotted a window open a few inches, and that was enough to get me into the kitchen. Mildred had everything clean and in order, so much so that I figured Alfred wouldn't hide anything here for fear of its being tidied up.

The kitchen, along with a pantry off to the side, took up most of the rear of the house. Down the hallway was a small room that served as an office, with a desk, two chairs, and a wooden chest. That seemed the best place to start. I flipped through a ledger, a stacks of bills, letters, and the usual debris of a couple's finances. I opened the chest, revealing even older ledgers and tax forms. At the bottom, a small wooden box was wrapped in a cloth.

That looked promising. I carefully opened it, making sure I could put it back exactly as I'd found it. It held family photographs that looked like they came from the last century. Cheap, tarnished frames and scowling countenances. Below those were a few brooches and necklaces, all the worse for wear. Family heirlooms, but not nice enough to wear on a Sunday. Nothing looked valuable, except for one piece, a small emerald maybe, in a gold setting. The prongs were broken and bent. It might have been part of a larger piece, but now this was all that was left, crammed into the bottom of a box of mementos. As I put it back, a small enamel pin fell from a worn envelope. It was blue with a white lightning bolt set within a red circle. I wasn't sure, but I'd bet that was the symbol of the British Union of Fascists and had once been worn proudly on Alfred's lapel. A second pin was in the envelope—this one featured an eagle with its claws on a snake and the initials PJ emblazoned on it.

I put everything back and continued the search, finding nothing that looked like David Archer's notebook.

The other rooms were easier. I looked under the cushions, through drawers, lifted the mattress in the bedroom upstairs, rummaged through the linen closet, and generally violated the privacy of the two people who made this house their home. I didn't mind it, at least not in terms of Alfred, but Mildred was another story. There wasn't much in the way of fancy furnishings, but she kept it all nicely squared away. Maybe it had taken all their savings to buy this place, with nothing left over to spiffy it up. As a matter of fact, there wasn't much to show for their years of service at Marston Hall, not one piece in a prominent place of pride.

The property reeked of failure.

The last place I searched was the coat closet by the front door. Well-worn work coats and Wellington boots. Umbrellas and scarves, along with Stephen Elliot's dress uniform, the one they'd removed from his rooms at Marston Hall. Maybe it was taken as a prop, or perhaps the undertaker had declined to stuff those bones into a suit. Or was Mildred eyeing the expensive cloth for a sewing project?

Well, it hardly mattered to Stephen Elliot.

I glanced at my watch and decided it was time to skedaddle. If Alfred caught me going through his long johns, it wouldn't end well. I slipped out the window, then yanked it down to right where I'd found it. I looked around, making sure I'd left no sign of my presence, and left the dreary place in the rearview mirror.

I hadn't found anything, but I'd learned something.

If I were Alfred or Mildred, I'd kill to leave that life behind.

CHAPTER TWENTY-SEVEN

BACK AT MARSTON Hall, I hustled up the steps to the library, thinking Kaz would be either knee-deep in papers or waiting impatiently for me to drive him back to Seaton Manor.

He was neither. I found him in the sitting room, a nicely banked coal fire warming his feet as he sat in one of the leather armchairs, a whiskey and a book close at hand.

"Don't tell me," I said, shrugging off my coat and flopping down in the other chair. "You've solved the case."

"No, but I have learned a few things." He gestured with his glass to a decanter on a side table. I helped myself. "First, there is nothing hidden in any picture frame or between the pages of any book in this library. You owe Oskar and Hank several rounds at the pub, by the way."

"Of course," I said. "What else?"

"The officers' mess is very good, as you suggested," Kaz said. "Lamb medallions with greens and rice. Delightful. And an ample liquor cabinet as well."

"The library, Kaz." I crooked my thumb in the direction of the other room. "Anything specific about the library?"

"No. The search took longer than expected, given that we put everything back as we'd found it. I thought it important to keep track of what had been gone through," he said. "I'd barely started on the filing cabinet when I had a visitor. A most interesting chap."

"Okay, spill," I said, knowing Kaz had something up his sleeve.

"Before I get to him, tell me what you found at Sandringham House."

"I found a couple of princesses digging potatoes," I said.

"Billy, you don't have to try to best me." Kaz took a sip of his whiskey. "Just stick with the facts."

"They go by the names Margaret and Elizabeth," I said. "I really did see them when I was escorted onto the premises. Apparently, some of the royals are staying in the cottages on the grounds."

"How interesting," Kaz said. "Did you find Nigel?"

I gave Kaz the rundown on Nigel, his rearranged face and his revelation about Alfred's criminal past and penchant for violence.

"It sounds as if Alfred has issued a warning," Kaz said.

"And not a subtle one," I said, describing Alfred's blade-on-bone performance at Seaton Manor. "If what he said can be trusted, Gwynne questioned him only on Archer's murder. Nothing about Elliot."

"Of course not." Kaz stood. "The man is incapable of holding two thoughts in his mind at the same time. Anything else?"

"I took a look at Alfred's place while they were out," I said. "Nothing much of interest except a British Union of Fascists pin and a scattering of old family jewelry. Oh, and they still have Elliot's dress uniform."

"The faithful family retainers," Kaz said. "Wishing their departed master to go out in style. Hardly suspicious."

"Elliot is just a pile of bones at this point. He wouldn't wear it well," I said. "Odds are Mildred will turn it into civilian duds. With rationing, that cloth would be worth something. The place was depressing. Quite a comedown from Marston Hall."

"I find it fascinating that we have so many people who want very much to return to Marston Hall. Cheatwood, who hopes to be in possession after the war, and the Bunch couple, who were thrown out but cannot stay away," Kaz said. "Charlotte

Mothersole, of course. Even Dr. Bodkin turned up today. He was treating one of the prisoners and paid me a visit. He'd heard I was looking through the library and was curious as to what I was after."

"The good doctor as well? What's one more in this scavenger hunt. There's something here, Kaz, something they all want."

"We must think upon that. Now, let me fetch my new friend, and we'll listen to what he has to say."

A few minutes later, Kaz ushered in a British officer and said, "Billy, pour Lieutenant Haycock a drink, will you?" I'd glimpsed Haycock a few times in the hallways. Dark haired, a bit short, with an attempted mustache.

"Thank you, Captain," Haycock said, taking the drink from me and settling into a chair. "Everybody's talking about your investigation. It's the most excitement we've had in ages."

"Cheers," I said, clinking glasses. "I would have thought all these high-value German POWs would be fairly exciting, or at least interesting."

"Yes, for the Americans," Haycock said. "Ever since Major Hudson and his men arrived, they do the interrogations. They're very good at it, and their results are excellent."

"But?" I asked Haycock.

"But it doesn't leave much for us to do," he said. "The British section is half of what it used to be. Our time is spent guarding the place, and there isn't much call for that. The Germans are treated very well here, so well that they hate leaving. They'd be fools to try and escape. Basically, we're glorified house staff."

"I can see that would be boring," I said, glancing at Kaz and wondering where this was going. "How long have you been here?"

"Two years now," Haycock said. "All because I speak German. But I'm not needed for that anymore, am I? There's plenty of Yanks who do it better, and we could bring in the Home Guard to help with sentry duties."

"What exactly are you saying?" I asked.

"Lieutenant Haycock wishes a transfer," Kaz said. "He doesn't want to tell his grandchildren that he sat the war out at Marston Hall."

"Then ask Colonel Cheatwood," I said. "He's your commanding officer."

"I've tried," Haycock said. "He's denied it several times. He doesn't want to diminish the British participation here and thinks approving the transfer of one of his officers would reflect badly on Marston Hall."

"He's also got Sandringham House to think about, doesn't he?" I asked. "The American contingent isn't going to provide security for the royals."

"You mean those jaunts along the beach? Cheatwood issues those orders himself," Haycock said. "He acts as if he were under orders to provide added security for the royal estate, but I've never seen anything from headquarters about it, and I handle communications."

"Listen, Lieutenant," I said, setting down my drink. "You're flirting with insubordination here. A more by-the-book officer might say you're married to it. Are you sure you want to keep on talking?"

"I'm sure I don't want to stay here," Haycock said. "All I know is that Colonel Cheatwood has done everything he can to ensure he stays in charge. He has a monthly checkup at an army hospital for his wounded leg, and he always brings his cane. When he's here, he hikes along the beach like a madman. Both things are done to keep this post. But he can't have it both ways, can he? He's a near cripple for the doctors but marches like a commando to Sandringham House."

"An officer fit only for desk duty who knows the local area is a perfect match for this job," Kaz offered. "And on the other hand, seeming to provide additional security for Sandringham House demonstrates his value."

"I don't know about the American army, but in mine, the left hand often doesn't know what the right hand is up to," Haycock said. "Cheatwood's doctors may think him a near cripple, and his superiors may think the king's life depends on him."

"Do you know when members of the royal family are in residence at Sandringham?" I asked.

"No. If the colonel was ever notified, it must have been by telephone."

"Tell Billy the rest," Kaz said, adding a splash of whiskey to Haycock's glass.

"There's more?"

"It's about the colonel and Mrs. Mothersole," Haycock said.

"We know they're an item," I said.

"Everybody knows that," Haycock said.

There's nothing like common knowledge for making an outsider look stupid. Most people assume if it's common knowledge, everybody must know it.

"But I'd wager you don't know that they've been searching Marston Hall. Quite thoroughly."

"For what?" I asked, figuring it might be more common knowledge.

"No idea. All I know is that it started about a year ago," Haycock said. "I think they had been seeing each other already, but the colonel may have wanted to keep it a secret to protect her reputation. He'd bring her in here to get a personal item or some such thing, but they'd stay behind locked doors for quite a while. We all had a laugh, thinking they didn't care much about reputations anymore."

"What changed your mind?" I asked.

"When they started going into the attic. At night. There are more belongings from Elliot up there," Haycock said. "Hardly the place for a tryst, is it?"

"Did you ask Colonel Cheatwood about it?" Kaz said.

"I approached the subject," Haycock said. "I asked if we should expect regular visits from Mrs. Mothersole. I was told to mind my own business." He rose and went to the window, his hands clenched behind his back. It was a minute before he turned around. "Listen, I am telling you this only because I have no one else to speak to. I can't go over the colonel's head, certainly not without concrete proof of anything. Perhaps you can look into it as part of your case, pull a few strings at SHAEF to send me to a unit in the field."

"I can't make any promises," I said, "but this is valuable information. Tell me, what do you hear about Stephen Elliot? I know that was before your time, but what are people saying?"

"Colonel Cheatwood is the only one who was here when Elliot disappeared," Haycock said. "I've heard comments that he's after Mrs. Mothersole to marry him so he can stay on after the war. But that's just soldier's gossip. As for Elliot, all I know is what I hear in the village. He was a bastard."

"Have you seen anyone else snooping around?" I asked.

"Alfred Bunch and his wife still think they have the run of the place," Haycock said. "I also once saw Dr. Bodkin leaving one of the staff rooms on the top floor. Between the prisoners, us, the Yanks, and Colonel Cheatwood, the doctor covers the entire Hall when he comes. I thought he'd had a patient, but when I checked a few minutes later, no one was there."

"Thank you, Lieutenant. You can rely on our discretion." Kaz led our visitor to the door. "If you learn of anything else, please let me know."

"Your day was much more productive than mine," I told Kaz. "You think Haycock is on the level?"

"I do. He was quite sincere, and as you alluded to, he is close to insubordination. We must be careful not to let Cheatwood know we've spoken to him."

"That reminds me," I said. "When I talked to an officer with the Royal Horse Guards at Sandringham, he knew of Marston Hall, but he didn't recognize Cheatwood's name."

"Which he would have, if the colonel were officially involved in security arrangements," Kaz said. "Perhaps we should ask Cheatwood if the royal family is in residence."

"I don't want him to think we're looking too closely at him," I said. "From what Haycock said, and from what Oskar overheard, I'm beginning to think there is a real treasure hidden in Marston Hall." I found it hard to believe I was saying that out loud. Hidden treasure? All we needed now was a map with X marking the spot.

"I have a feeling we will find nothing in the library," Kaz said, gesturing toward the next room. "At least not the treasure. Certainly, Cheatwood and Mrs. Mothersole have had ample opportunity to search it, not to mention Alfred and Mildred. Still, I may find a clue among those papers tomorrow."

"Maybe we should let it drop that you're finished in the library," I said. "And that we're going to start in the attic tomorrow."

"To spur them on and catch them in the act?" Kaz asked.

"No, they wouldn't be breaking any laws," I said. "I'm more curious what I might overhear."

"You are going to hide in the attic?" Kaz asked. "For the night?"

"For a while," I said. "Let's go."

We found Cheatwood in his office sorting through files. I wondered what kind of work it took him to keep Marston Hall running. I tried to catch a glimpse of what the paperwork was all about, but he was too fast for me—the files were shut and stacked in seconds.

"Gentlemen, how can I help you now?" he asked, a mechanical smile turning up his lips.

"We've searched the library and came up with nothing," I said. "We'd like to go through the attic tomorrow. Do you have a key?"

"I have keys to every room, Captain," Cheatwood said. "What do you want with the attic?"

"To look through Elliot's belongings," I said. "Or have I been misinformed?"

"Oh, yes, I do believe there are some items stored upstairs." Cheatwood knew he couldn't deny it, so he feigned a sudden remembrance. "Furnishings mostly, I think. We also have supplies stored there—blankets, cots, emergency rations, that sort of thing. There was a time when this was a less luxurious establishment, you know."

"When you were first in charge?" Kaz asked. "And Stephen Elliot still lived?"

"Exactly," Cheatwood said. "He was none too happy about the place being overrun by common German soldiers. I think he'd be pleased to know we cater to a more exclusive clientele these days."

"The key, Colonel? We'll be starting early in the morning," I said.

"There are funeral services for David Archer in the morning," Kaz said. "We'd like to be done before paying our respects."

"I am an early riser," Cheatwood said. "See me at seven in the morning for the key. Good day."

Out in the hallway, Kaz said, "Well, we have let him know about our plans to search the attic. Too bad you won't be in it."

"Don't be too sure," I said, fingering the iron library key in my pocket. "Let's check it out."

We went up to the top floor, which consisted of a narrow hallway with rooms for staff on either side. At the far end, a single door faced us, and I figured it led to the attic. I tried the library key, wriggling it around to engage the lever. These old skeleton keys were built to push up the lever at the same time they opened the dead bolt. In a big house with many locks, I was betting on the fact that they weren't all that different. It took some maneuvering, but in a few minutes, I was able to slide the dead bolt back and open the door. A flight of steep steps led to a darkened room above.

"Your second crime today," Kaz said. "We must be making progress. What now?"

"I'll run you back to Seaton Manor," I said. "Then come back here, grab some grub, and find a spot to hide. My sense is Cheatwood and Charlotte won't wait too long."

"Are you sure you don't want me to stay with you?" Kaz asked.

"It's rack of lamb tonight," I said. "Alfred kind of ruined it for me with his knife work, but no reason you shouldn't enjoy."

"I must say, the rations on this case are excellent," Kaz said. "I'll be sure to eat your share."

"That reminds me," I said as we descended the staircase. "Big Mike is coming. Sir Richard said he'd call Sam and set it up."

"Not before dinner, I hope?"

"Doubtful. Unless Sir Richard told him what was on the menu," I said.

On the main floor, we ran into Major Duncan and Oskar engaged in conversation with a British captain. Long and lanky, he sported a shock of brushed-back blond hair and a look of bemusement on his boyish face.

"Ah, here he is, just the man we need," Oskar said, beckoning us to join them. Kaz, specifically.

Major Duncan introduced us to Captain Ian Carmichael of the 30th Armoured Brigade. Duncan said Carmichael was here to observe the interrogation of a German major who had knowledge of minefields in the Netherlands where 30th Armoured was operating.

"But our Russian uniform is out to be cleaned," Oskar said. "And the interrogation must take place tomorrow. Will you join us, Lieutenant? As a Polish officer about to take charge of this POW?"

"I would be happy to," Kaz said. "Although we must be at a funeral tomorrow morning."

"Dashed lot of 'em these days," Carmichael said. "But I think we are scheduled for after lunch, if that works for you, Lieutenant Kazimierz? You as well, Captain Boyle?"

We agreed, and Duncan went off with Oskar to plan for tomorrow.

"You came all the way from the Netherlands for this?" I asked. "Must be important."

"It is. My unit operates those flail tanks, if you're familiar with them," Carmichael said. "Heavy chains, fixed to a rotor forward of the tank, and they spin like mad, detonating buried mines. Makes it a good deal easier for the infantry, as you can imagine. So it's important all right, especially if you're one of our lads on foot and you like the idea of staying in one piece."

"I've heard of flails," I said. "Hobart's Funnies, right?"

"That's us," Carmichael said, with more than a little pride. "Sir Percy Hobart is our CO. He's the fellow who dreamt up all sorts of specialized tanks. Duplex drive amphibious Shermans. Bridge layers that can span thirty feet. Fascine carriers that lay huge bundles of sticks to fill in shell holes. Even flame-throwing tanks. The man's a genius, but we call him Hobo. When he's not around, of course."

"If your unit is equipped with the flail tanks, I assume this prisoner has knowledge of minefields you are concerned with?" Kaz said.

"Yes, I'm with the 22nd Dragoons. We have Sherman flail tanks, absolute beasts as far as the Germans are concerned. But there's far too few of us to cover the entire approach. We need to know exactly where the damned minefields are so we can lead the way through them."

"This German knows where the mines are?" Kaz asked.

"He was in charge of laying 'em," Carmichael said. "The blighter took a wrong turn and ran into one of our reconnaissance units. Shot up his vehicle. He survived, luckily for us, but not before he consigned his maps and plans to the fire. Just happened two days ago. Our intelligence lads recommended Marston Hall for best results, so here we are. I get a few days in the refreshing English countryside and go back with the gen for the next leg of our Low Countries vacation."

"We will be here midday," Kaz said. "Do you need anything else, Captain?"

"Yes, actually," Carmichael said. "You wouldn't know of a place called Seaton Manor, would you?"

"Are you looking for Sir Richard Seaton?" I guessed, thinking it might have something to do with intelligence matters.

"Oh no, not Sir Richard. Gruff old chap." Carmichael waved his hand as if to ward off the notion. "It's his daughter, Diana Seaton. She's the one I'm after."

CHAPTER TWENTY-EIGHT

"AFTER, CAPTAIN? YOU are after the young lady for what purpose?" Kaz asked as we walked outside, steering Carmichael away from passersby in the busy hallway. "Do you know her?"

"Yes, of course I do," Carmichael said, coming to a quick halt as two German officers, swathed in their greatcoats, strolled by. "Goodness. The last time I saw two such blighters, one was dead and the other was close to it. Unnerving to see 'em ambling about, I must say. Now, will you tell me how to get to Seaton Manor?"

"I am headed there myself, Captain," Kaz said. "If you drive me, it will save Billy a trip. He has business to conclude here."

"Glad to," Carmichael said. "Captain, shall we see you there later?"

"Probably not, unless you're planning on staying long," I said. "Like more than an hour or two?"

"I certainly hope so," Carmichael said with a laugh. "I've been invited for two nights. Diana and I are old friends. Do you know her as well?"

"Captain, Billy and Diana Seaton are of long acquaintance," Kaz said, barely suppressing a grin.

"Oh. Oh! I see, said the blind man. No worries there. I've not come to steal your girl, Captain Boyle. Diana and I have known each other since my days at the Royal Academy of Dramatic Art. She had a pal there whom I was seeing for a while, and we've all stayed in touch. I harbor no ulterior motives, I promise you.

Happily married since last year." Carmichael held up his hand, displaying a wedding ring on one finger and another missing its tip. "Anyway, our mutual friend Maggie is in King's Lynn with her theater group, and I'm hoping we can get together tomorrow. Haven't seen either of them in ages."

"Hey, I wasn't worried at all," I said, selling it a bit too enthusiastically. Carmichael and I both looked at Kaz, who was enjoying this exchange immensely.

"Apologies," Kaz said. "But it was terribly amusing to watch Billy's face."

"Well, Lieutenant, I hope we have as much fun tomorrow with our Jerry as you've had with Captain Boyle just now," Carmichael said.

"I think we shall," Kaz said. "I've been impressed with how these fellows conduct their interrogations. Their methods are very effective, and not without a sense of theater."

"I shall look forward to treading the boards with you, Lieutenant. You will join us, Captain?"

"Yes, and call me Billy," I told him. "Everybody does."

"I shall, and I'll be Ian to your Billy. Piotr, let's be off."

"Kaz, could you drop by the vicar's and ask what time the funeral is? You should probably fill in Ian on what he's stepped into the middle of," I said, walking with them to Carmichael's staff car.

"If I do, he might never return," Kaz said.

"Now I'm quite interested," Ian said, opening the door. "Do tell, old boy."

I LEFT THE two of them to it and hustled over to the American mess. I wouldn't admit it to Kaz—and definitely not to Diana— but I did feel a spark of jealousy at a handsome British officer asking about her. Ian seemed to be a good sort, and I didn't hold anything against him. The explanation about being school chums

was logical, but my reaction said something about the relationship between Diana and me. We were different, as different as
two English-speaking people could be. I was working stiff Irish
Catholic, and she hailed from the English upper crust. It would
have been natural for her to fall for a good-looking guy with a
background similar to her own. Easier all around if she had, I
sometimes thought. All either of them would have to do would
be to survive the war, then start a life together, building on
common ground.

Hey, I'm not complaining. I know I'm lucky to have Diana in
my life. Although how long would luck keep us together once
the war was over and life returned to normal? Not that normal
would ever be the same again, but whatever emerged from the
rubble was going to be a challenge for us. I didn't see Diana settling down in Southie any more than I could imagine taking up
residence in Slewford. What other place in the world was there
for us? We were each a part of where we came from, and I
struggled to see how we could create a future for ourselves, especially in the face of what another life for Diana might look like.

As for Slewford, I was getting my fill of this village, and I'd
be happy to not revisit it for some time to come. I wouldn't mind
a vacation with Diana. Just the two of us, far away from deathly
secrets, uniforms, and the churning waters of the Wash.

As I headed to the mess, I realized that seemed a lot to ask.

Maybe someday. Maybe never.

Thankfully, I didn't see Hank, Oskar, or any of my new pals
at the tables. I didn't much feel like talking, and it would be
best if no one noticed I was still hanging around. That's why I
didn't check out the British mess. Better grub wasn't worth
bumping into Colonel Cheatwood and having him wonder
what I was up to.

I topped off on meat-and-vegetable stew washed down with
a cup of coffee. I hadn't gotten much sleep last night, and I
needed that jolt of joe to stay awake. The last thing I wanted to

do was fall asleep and spend all night in that attic. I finished up and hoofed it over to the Hall, sucking in deep breaths of cold air to shock my brain cells into action. There were fewer people in the corridors, the pace of the day slowing down as the sky darkened.

I took the stairs two at a time and stopped at the landing on the fourth floor, listening for any sounds of life from the rooms down the long hallway. Nothing. It was too early for the Yanks or Brits to take to their rooms. They'd be headed to town or settling down for drinks or cards downstairs. I walked to the attic door like I owned the place and put my hand on the latch.

I heard footsteps and voices. One came unmistakably from Charlotte Mothersole, a high-pitched whisper that carried like a shouted command down the echoing wooden hallway. I opened the door and shut it quietly, closing the bolt and feeling my way up the stairs.

I blinked, trying to adjust to the darkness, until I could make out shapes and forms in the crowded space. I managed not to stumble and send piles of boxes crashing to the floor. I found a corner to hide in just as I heard a key rattling in the lock. The door opened, and flashlight beams shone on the rafters as footsteps landed softly on the stairs.

"Graham, do be quiet," Charlotte whispered.

"Sound advice, my dear, but the chaps who live on this floor will be busy in the library drinking Stephen's brandy down to the last drop," Cheatwood said. "I called them in for a well-done speech and left them to it."

"My brandy, you mean," Charlotte said. "Was all this necessary, Graham? We've been through everything in this horrid attic."

"Yes, dear, it is. We've put this off for too long already," Cheatwood said. "We agreed we needed to return for a more thorough search, which is what Boyle undoubtedly has planned for tomorrow."

"I know we have, but I still find it insufferable," Charlotte said.

"Lurking about in my own house, searching for what? We don't even know what we're looking for. Jewels? A map? A key?"

"Treasure," Graham said. "We know that much. Here, I'll start with this chest, you go through that bureau, all right?"

"Yes, yes," Charlotte muttered, and the two of them got to work opening drawers and rummaging through the contents. Nothing sounded much like a tinkling trove of jewels.

"Here's a stack of papers," Cheatwood announced. "Bound in twine and hidden underneath these sweaters. We missed it before."

"Well, take it with you, then. We can't go through them up here," Charlotte said, sliding another drawer open. "Oh, damn! Mice. They've gotten into everything. Disgusting creatures."

"We shall need to have this cleaned out," Cheatwood said. "I'll organize it when we've finished searching."

"You can do what you want with this army property whenever you wish," Charlotte said. "But I'll decide when Stephen's belongings go. No one else."

"Of course," Cheatwood said. "I meant nothing different." I could tell by his tone that he wasn't happy at not calling the shots. But Charlotte had him over a barrel, and that barrel was four stories high and twice as long. They kept up their scavenging for an hour or so, their exchanges betraying a simmering irritation.

"Old newspapers! Whatever was Stephen thinking?" Charlotte said, slamming a stack down on top of the crate I was hiding behind. A page slipped from the pile and floated down to where I knelt, bits of brittle paper and dust filling the air. My nose began to itch. I rubbed it, hoping to distract myself from a growing need to sneeze. It passed for the moment, but I kept my hands cupped over my mouth and nose.

"Maybe they're important," Cheatwood said. "He must have been saving these clippings for some purpose."

"The fool boy saved *everything*," Charlotte said. "It's impossible to tell what might be important."

"I can't believe he never said anything about leaving a will," Cheatwood said. "Most chaps going off to war wish to leave their affairs in order."

"I told you before, Stephen was too self-centered to consider he'd be killed," Charlotte said. "Or to make any provision for his sister. But he alluded to this treasure, whatever it was, often enough. It must be real, and it must be here somewhere."

"Well, he should have done more than allude to it," Cheatwood said. "It wasn't fair to you."

"He enjoyed it," Charlotte said. "He enjoyed holding things over people. Too much so, for any decent man."

"Some days I regret it wasn't me who killed him," Cheatwood said. "Knowing how much pain he caused you."

"You are such a dear boy, Graham," Charlotte said softly, amidst the tune of rustling fabric and a sigh. Apparently, Cheatwood fantasizing about killing her brother was the way to Charlotte's heart. Or wherever his hands were roaming. He might have just eliminated himself as a suspect, although hearing their movements and murmurs was a high price to pay for that information. If I'd had an extra pair of hands, I would have clapped them over my ears.

"Oh, no more, not here," Charlotte said, a gasping moan escaping her lips. "It's too horrid. We're done, aren't we?"

"Yes, that's everything, I think. You go downstairs, my dear, and clean up. I'll put these things back." His voice oozed with affection.

Charlotte descended the stairs and departed. Cheatwood let loose an exasperated sigh and began to work, his flashlight beam dancing in the darkness. He stepped closer to me, picking up the newspapers above my head and showering me with more dust as I squeezed my eyes shut.

"Stupid cow," he muttered as he slammed a chest shut and took to the stairs. "Bloody stupid cow."

I held on as the sneeze built up, waited for him to descend the steps and lock the door behind him, and then released my hands from my face, letting three healthy sneezes clear my nostrils.

"Gesundheit," I told myself, as I thought about Cheatwood's parting comment.

Maybe he hadn't cleared his name after all.

Maybe Charlotte should find a different lover, someone who wouldn't bump her off once they were married.

CHAPTER TWENTY-NINE

As I DROVE to Seaton Manor, I went over what I'd learned from listening to Charlotte and Cheatwood bickering. That he despised her and was only in it for the money—in the form of treasure or property—was certainly obvious. As was her desire to maintain the upper hand in their relationship. She must see something in the man, or maybe she enjoyed the attention and was letting the wool be pulled over her eyes. Not to mention whatever else she was wearing.

The most important thing I picked up from my eavesdropping was what they *didn't* say. There was no mention of Agnes Day. That told me Charlotte was unaware of Agnes as a threat to her inheritance. Or she was unwilling to let her gallant suitor know there was a much younger woman potentially in line to become the mistress of Marston Hall.

Perhaps Charlotte knew, and she was confident Agnes could never make a claim without proof. As I turned onto the long drive leading to the manor, it occurred to me to look into what legal claim Agnes might be able to make as an illegitimate daughter. Maybe she could make a case. Or maybe she wouldn't want to dredge up the shame of her mother giving birth out of wedlock. Far as I could tell, the shame belonged squarely on Stephen Elliot's rotted shoulders, but the villagers might not see it that way. Interesting question. Would Agnes care?

"That was fast," Kaz said by way of greeting at the front door.

"They didn't waste much time. Except mine, that is." I gave Kaz a quick rundown on what I'd heard and what hadn't been said.

"Interesting that Agnes did not come up," Kaz whispered, tapping his finger against his lips. That was his way of filing something away to think about. If Kaz thought that was interesting, it was definitely worth following up on.

"Ian is here, I assume?" I said, trying to sound nonchalant.

"Yes. He and Diana are catching up at the kitchen table," Kaz said. "But you should speak with Sir Richard. Chief Inspector Gwynne has been back." We walked down the hall, passing the sitting room where Agnes and Angelika had pulled up chairs close to the radio.

"It's almost time for the War Report," Angelika said as Agnes fiddled with the dial on the lacquered wood console. The BBC war news came on after the regular nine o'clock news broadcast. "Tell Sir Richard, will you?"

"She can't get enough of the news," Kaz said. "After occupied Poland and Ravensbrück, she's starved for it. Oh, by the way, Big Mike will be here tomorrow morning."

"I'll breathe easier once he is," I said as we entered the library.

"Well, I haven't been taken away in chains," Sir Richard said from his desk as he closed his book. He was still reading about King John. "But that might be next."

"That bad?" I asked, taking a seat. It had been a long day.

"He asked a lot about Stephen Elliot at first," Sir Richard said, leaning back in his chair. "But then he started in on how well I do with one arm: riding a bicycle, saddling a horse, and handling cutlery."

"For Gwynne, that would pass as subtlety," Kaz said.

"He's suggesting you knifed David Archer," I said.

"To be precise, he suggested I was capable of it," Sir Richard said. "I told him I was and that I could do it much more easily than saddling a horse, which does still present difficulties. Then

I told him to get out unless he had some evidence that would point to me in either man's death."

"What did he say to that?" I asked, sensing that Sir Richard had let his anger get the best of him.

"All in due time," he said. "Which is meaningless. He can't prove anything, because there's nothing to prove. About me, anyway. Don't you agree?"

"I do, sir," I told him. "But you must be careful. By now, plenty of people know you're a suspect. Gwynne is probably broadcasting it far and wide. The real killer might decide to help things along."

"Evidence can also be manufactured," Kaz said, glancing at his watch. "We must be on guard against that. Now, we have only a few minutes until the War Report. Angelika will not abide an interruption."

Sir Richard asked me to fetch Diana and Ian from the kitchen, commenting on what a nice chap Ian Carmichael was. Of course. In the hallway, I passed Mrs. Rutledge coming from her room, and she said much the same thing. I was beginning to wish the 22nd Dragoons had sent a more disreputable officer on this assignment.

I walked into the kitchen and stopped dead in my tracks. Diana and Carmichael were sitting across from each other, teacups between them, as Diana cradled his hand in her own.

"Billy!" Diana said, releasing Carmichael's hand. "I didn't know you were here."

"I could tell," I said, not moving from the spot.

"Listen, old chap," Carmichael said, "by the look on your face, I'd say you've got the wrong end of things."

"Billy, you're not jealous, are you?" Diana demanded. "Are you mad?"

"You're holding hands, for crying out loud! What do you think it looks like?" I said, searching their faces for any trace of guilt.

"It looks like what it is," Carmichael said, holding up his left hand with fingers splayed. "Diana was looking at my decapitated finger and recommending I have Agnes look at it, since it healed improperly. It's a proper nuisance."

"Ian is an actor, Billy," Diana said, pushing her chair back as she stood. "I was just giving him some advice on getting that taken care of so people's eyes won't be drawn to it. I thought Agnes might know if it can be smoothed out or something. I'm sorry if that offended you."

"No, I just didn't know," I said, but then remembered that I did know. I'd seen Ian's shortened digit earlier today. "I'm sorry."

"You should be," Diana said.

"How did it happen?" I asked, trying to steer the conversation into safer waters.

"A tank hatch took me by surprise," Ian said. "One of our own, so I can't even blame Jerry. The thing slammed shut during a heavy windstorm and clipped the top bit off rather nicely. Nicer than the job the sawbones did fixing it up. Looks rather like a gnarled wooden branch, and it would be distracting for those who paid to sit in the front row, eh?"

"Let's listen to the BBC," Diana said, brushing past me.

"Listen, Billy," Ian said, laying a hand on my arm to hold me back. "Diana has been singing your praises all evening, telling me what a smart and decent chap you are. Don't go proving her wrong. We've never been an item, but she's a friend, and I do care about her."

"Thanks. Sorry we got off on the wrong foot," I said. "I've got a lot on my mind."

"So the baron told me," Ian said as we left the kitchen. "Well, I've got just what you need to take your mind off things and seal the breach with our lovely Diana. I've secured four tickets to a play tomorrow night. Maggie, the charming woman who really was my gal, is touring the hinterlands with the Royal Shakespeare Company. The baron is interested, and, of course, Diana wants to go. You'll complete the party, and we'll have a delightful time, won't we?"

"That sounds fine," I said. "It's good to clear the mind once in a while. What's the play?"

"*King John*," Ian said. "He's fairly popular in these parts, although I can't say why. The theater is in King's Lynn, where he died."

"So, as Shakespeare said, 'We shall go and tell sad stories of the death of kings,'" I said, showing off one of the lines I remembered from Sister Edith's English class. Which led Ian to declaim:

"How some have been deposed; some slain in war,
Some haunted by the ghosts they have deposed;
Some poison'd by their wives: some sleeping kill'd;
All murder'd . . ."

"Oh, dear me," he said, interrupting himself. "That's hardly taking your mind off murder, is it? Let's go listen to the War Report and hope for the best, shall we?"

We joined the crowd in the sitting room, where Diana scooched over on the couch in what I took as a sign of forgiveness. She kept her arms crossed, though, which put things closer to forbearance. Angelika made a shushing sound as she gave the dial a final adjustment and the *bongs* from Big Ben filled the room.

The announcer rattled off a series of reports. The French 1st Armored Division had reached the banks of the Rhine. Patrols from the US Third Army had crossed the German border. A German V-2 rocket had struck London's East End, killing twenty-five people. British, Polish, and Canadian forces were teaming up in the Netherlands to clear the Scheldt Estuary and open the port of Antwerp to supply Allied forces.

"That's my lot!" Ian said, then hushed up after a glare from Angelika. But as soon as the program concluded, she peppered him with questions about the Polish troops.

"By all accounts, they're terribly keen," Ian said. "Terrific fighters. But I didn't even know they were involved in our action.

They don't tell you much near the front. I learn more from the BBC than I do from our own intelligence lads."

"You'll return after you're done here?" Diana asked.

"Yes. The day after tomorrow, bright and early," Ian said. "I am looking forward to this interrogation. I will feel like I'm back on stage. Of course, Piotr will have the leading role; I'm no more than a spear carrier."

"Did Ian tell you about the play, Billy?" Diana asked, making a show of studying her fingernails.

"Yes. Wouldn't miss it," I said. "Happy to meet another old friend of yours." She smiled at that, which I considered the best part of my day.

"Tomorrow's service is at ten o'clock," Kaz said, reminding me of the funeral. "The vicar said it will be outdoors, which is what David Archer would have preferred."

"I shall attend with you, if that's all right," Ian said, and everyone else agreed to go as well.

"But for now, clear out unless you're going to listen to the next program," Angelika said.

"*Appointment with Fear*," Agnes said. "It's a mystery. Rather frightening stuff, but fun."

"We'll leave you to it, then," Sir Richard said, offering a nightcap to anyone interested. Mrs. Rutledge stayed to listen to the radio while the rest of us trooped into the library.

"As long as Big Mike arrives during the day, there should be no problem with the four of you going into King's Lynn tomorrow night," Sir Richard said, pouring whiskey from a cut glass decanter. "We'll stay close to Agnes at the funeral. I have no idea if she'll be in danger, but it will be out in the open."

"From what Piotr told me, it seems that your culprit, or culprits, owe more to stealth than a frontal attack," Ian said. "If we keep close to Agnes, she should be fine."

"But, Ian, Stephen Elliot was hit over the head," Diana said, accepting a glass from her father. "It might have been a rear assault, but it was hardly stealthy."

"Oh no, I didn't mean the method by which he was done away with," Ian said. "It was the disposal of the body. That was clever. But what do I know? I've read an Agatha Christie or two, but I know far more about stagecraft than murder."

"Don't sell yourself short," Sir Richard said, settling in his chair. "Putting Elliot in that bomber was some fine stagecraft. Murder victim: exit stage right."

"Fair point." Ian laughed.

"Sir Richard, what's your opinion of Charlotte Mothersole?" I asked, smiling at the image. "What was her relationship with her brother?"

"She was very protective," he said. "She wouldn't hear a bad word about him, but I always thought it was to protect herself as much as Stephen."

"So she wouldn't have to face up to what he was like," Kaz said.

"Yes. She was frustrated with him at times," Sir Richard said. "As a matter of fact, she came to me about securing Marston Cottage for herself when the government took over the Hall. They let Stephen stay on since he was in the military, but they wanted everyone else out."

"Stephen didn't arrange that?" Diana asked. "I never knew."

"You were away at one of your finishing schools," her father said. I noticed Ian raise an eyebrow in Diana's direction, but she didn't respond. He evidently didn't know of her work with SOE, and I took a perverse pleasure in that. Petty, I know, but a bruised ego takes what comfort it can.

"Is she capable of murder?" I asked.

"She couldn't strike the blow," Sir Richard said. "But when Charlotte wants something, she generally gets it."

"Her own brother?" Ian said, taking a healthy slug of whiskey. "Ye gods."

"To know him was to despise him," Sir Richard said. "Remember, it's one thing for a stranger or mere acquaintance to wrong you. But when the wrong comes from someone close, it hurts even more."

"What about the Bunches?" Kaz asked. "Weren't they put out when Charlotte was?"

"No, that happened some time before. There was a falling out of some sort between Elliot and them. I never learned what it was about, although I think they tried to mend fences with the man. Which reminds me," Sir Richard said, setting down his drink and opening a notebook. "I did make those inquiries about the British Union of Fascists. Alfred Bunch was a registered member. He resigned just before the war, as did a lot of them. Some were genuine and others simply wanted to erase their past."

"He may have been in the latter camp," I said. "He still has his membership pin."

"I won't ask how you know," Sir Richard said. "As for Chief Inspector Gwynne, the Home Office has him down as a sympathizer, never a member, but he clearly has fascist tendencies. Perhaps he never joined officially to protect his career."

"Which means his extremist views are known, but he is tolerated," Kaz said.

"Sadly, yes. He may be inclined to look the other way when it comes to party members like Bunch," Sir Richard said. "But I've also been told he is under great pressure to make an arrest. This affair is bad publicity for all concerned. It looks like Gwynne's career is a bit shaky. He was originally with the Metropolitan Police, then sent to Norfolk last year to help with the manpower shortage."

"From Scotland Yard to the fens of Norfolk? There couldn't have been much of a career to start with," Ian offered.

"I couldn't get any other information from my contact," Sir Richard said. "Perhaps it was because of Gwynne's association with the fascists. Or because he's simply not bright enough for

London, but his superiors thought he could keep up among us country folk."

"He sounds like the desperate type," Kaz said. "He may make an arrest quickly just for show, even though he knows there isn't sufficient evidence."

"You need to find the killer, Billy," Diana said. "Soon. I don't want my father to be the scapegoat."

Everyone's eyes were on me. I needed an idea.

"There will be a crowd at the funeral tomorrow," I said. "Perhaps the killer will be there. I'll drop a bombshell and see what happens."

"What bombshell?" Diana asked.

"I haven't thought that through well enough to explain," I said, struggling to buy time.

"Ah, there's a look I know well," Ian said. "The gawk-eyed face of a chap who's forgotten his lines!"

CHAPTER THIRTY

TREASURE. THAT'S ALL I thought about driving back to the Rose and Crown. Alfred and Mildred were snooping around for it. Cheatwood and Charlotte were turning drawers inside out looking for it. Dr. Bodkin had free rein at Marston Hall as well. What was he looking for as he wandered in and out of the rooms?

Was Stephen Elliot killed for treasure? Sure, greed is one of the main reasons for murder, right up there with love and passion. If you're going to kill for money, wouldn't it make sense to know how to get a hold of it? And if you can't, where's the motive?

Unless the motive is you don't want the victim to enjoy the treasure, or even life itself. Some might call that hate, when it's really passion. You have to care, in a really twisted fashion, about the victim in order to bash his brains in. I was beginning to think that Stephen Elliot had been killed in the heat of the moment, in a fit of anger. Anger at his position, perhaps? Or at the treasure that he was protecting and aiming to keep all for himself.

I pulled in behind the pub and parked. I sat in the jeep, working on that train of thought. It all derailed quickly. The whole sudden-fit-of-anger thing didn't mesh with the way the body had been disposed of. That was cool and methodical. One corpse, exit stage right, as Sir Richard had said. It didn't add up to the same person. No one could have known that the bomber would crash-land at the cliffs, but it drew an assortment of people to the scene, their arrivals staggered by the distance traveled. Somewhere in that mix, there'd been a confrontation. The blow was struck from behind, probably by a right-handed assailant, judging by the location of the fracture.

I got out of the jeep, trying to visualize the scene. I turned to walk to the front of the pub and imagine myself as Elliot at the cliffs, speaking to whomever he'd been with. Had it been a dismissive, cutting remark? He turned away, and then what? A rock or a piece of wood was picked up? One quick swing and there lies Stephen Elliot.

I'd run. If there were no witnesses, I'd get away as fast as possible and let the blame fall on the Germans, real or imagined. Why hang around and take the time to haul Elliot's body to the aircraft and get him inside?

It wasn't impossible for it to have happened that way, but in my experience, damn few murders are premeditated. Careful planning isn't a strong suit for the murdering kind. Passion doesn't plan. Passion lashes out. Unlike what happened here, on the ground where David Archer had died. I was certain he'd been followed here, probably to listen for what he had to say if he talked to me. People in the village had either given Archer a wide berth or taken whatever he'd said with a grain of salt, hearing no more than the rambling words of a man who spent his nights roaming about under the open sky. But a newcomer like me, interested in what he witnessed that night in May of '42, was likely to hear him out. Which had put his life in grave danger.

You don't understand.

His words haunted me, and all I could do was send up a promise that I'd do my best.

I went straight to my room, avoiding the pub. I didn't feel like sitting around wondering if a killer was eyeing me. Even as I washed up, I couldn't help but think about the differences and similarities between the two killings. Elliot's murder was unplanned but committed in a sudden frenzy.

Archer's was premeditated, in that his fate was sealed if he opened his mouth, but it was also a crime of opportunity. The sudden appearance of the V-1s in flight had drawn everyone outside in a state of confusion. It was a chance too good to miss, and the killer grabbed the perfect weapon to do the job.

Archer was a wary man, and it might have been hard to get the drop on him in normal circumstances, but the V-1 attack had drawn his eyes skyward in a last moment of awe.

The Germans had finally gotten him.

KAZ AND I had agreed to meet at eight o'clock this morning. We still had to go through the motions of searching the attic, otherwise it might have raised Cheatwood's suspicions after I'd insisted on it. I spit shined my boots, polished my brass buttons, and donned my Class A uniform, ready to send off David Archer in whatever style I could manage. When I arrived at Marston Hall, Kaz had already picked up the key, and we hoofed it up to the top floor to check things out in what daylight the attic's small windows allowed in.

"The only good thing about hiding in the dark is you didn't notice all the cobwebs and mouse droppings," Kaz said as he opened a chest of drawers and gingerly poked through the contents. "This isn't really necessary, is it?"

"Probably not, although we should make it look real in case Cheatwood pays us a visit," I said. "Make a mess."

"That will be easy." Kaz scattered clothing that looked like it had been packed away since the last war. I noticed the newspaper sheet that had fallen to the floor last night. It was a tattered, brittle page from the *Lynn News* in June of 1924. There were a few articles about crops, repairs to a drainage ditch, and tide tables for the Wash, seven days' worth. I spotted the chest where Cheatwood had found the newspapers and dug out the pile, flipping through the yellowed pages.

It was quite a collection.

"Look at this," I said. "They're all articles about the tides, marshlands, and drainage along the Wash shoreline. Some from the late 1800s, going right up to 1935, as far as I can see."

"Perhaps Elliot's book was about the Wash," Kaz suggested with little enthusiasm. "You said Cheatwood took some documents, but he evidently saw no value in these."

"You're right. This must have something to do with his research," I said. "Why else would he collect these clippings? When we're done with the funeral and your interrogation, why don't you keep searching the library? See if there's any connection that makes sense."

"What will you do?"

"I'm going to be dropping some hints about buried treasure at the funeral," I said. "I'll see where that gets me. Specifically, I want to talk to Dr. Bodkin. He's been spotted a few times wandering through Marston Hall, and I'd like to know if it was all strictly business."

"You mentioned the German prisoner who spoke with Archer said the doctor had been on his watch list," Kaz said.

"Yes. Maybe he was just another visitor Archer was keeping track of," I said. "Or maybe not. I was focused on Bodkin because of the bad blood between him and Sir Richard. Once that was explained away, I lost track of him, but perhaps that was a mistake."

"Were it not for the killing of David Archer, I would gladly leave this place behind," Kaz said. "Angelika could heal as well in London."

"The peace and quiet is probably good for her," I said. "Remember, V-2s are still hitting the city."

"Excellent point," Kaz said. "But I shall leave this attic behind, immediately. Let's have some of that excellent American coffee before we leave for the churchyard."

"I like the way you think, Kaz. On our way, let's drop off these newspapers in the library. I have a feeling they might come in handy."

"In what way?" Kaz asked as we descended the stairs.

"Bait," I said. "These newspaper clippings undoubtedly hold the clues as to the location of the treasure. Or at least that's what I'll let drop at the right time. I can't wait to watch Charlotte's face when she realizes Cheatwood overlooked them."

"Intriguing," Kaz said as we approached the library. "It may also lead them to peruse the papers they did take. Perhaps they could be caught at that."

"Yeah, I'd like to see what they find," I said, unlocking the library door. We left the newsprint and went outside, making for the American mess. I glanced at my watch and saw we had plenty of time for some hot joe. As I looked up, I saw Oberst Hansen headed our way. I told Kaz I'd catch up. I wanted to ask Hansen again about Dr. Bodkin, and I knew Kaz would prefer the company of a coffee cup to a German officer.

"Good morning, Colonel," I said, offering Hansen a salute. It was a military courtesy, and he wasn't the worst Fritz I'd ever run into.

"Captain Boyle." He returned the salute in standard military style. "I understand Herr Archer's funeral is today. I wish I could attend, but they say it is not possible."

"I will tell the vicar," I said. "He was a good friend of Archer's."

"Tanner, yes? Herr Archer mentioned him. He enjoyed his company," Hansen said. "I have seen him here a few times, visiting sick prisoners."

"David Archer wasn't keeping track of Father Tanner, was he?"

"Oh no. Just the people I mentioned to you," Hansen said, his voice almost a whisper.

"Dr. Bodkin was on his list," I said. "Have you ever noticed him poking around?"

"Poking? What does that mean?"

"Searching. Looking for something," I said. "In places where he had no business."

"Ah. To poke, *ja*? I did see him once in the library. The one down-stairs, not Elliot's library. The books are available to us, and I was reading one day when I saw the doctor. He was looking through each book, turning the pages. I thought it odd, but I simply kept reading. I did not want to get him in trouble. Or myself."

"Colonel Cheatwood wouldn't like it?"

"I heard he had done the same, soon after the death of Elliot. Strange, *ja*?"

"Yes, it is," I said, trying to add this puzzle piece to the mix. This was the first indication of Bodkin actively searching for something. "What about Alfred and Mildred Bunch? Did you ever see them in either library?"

"No. I do not recall seeing Mildred in the Hall. Once I saw her wait in the truck, but perhaps she did go in," Hansen said.

"But you said Archer was keeping track of them," I said, recalling our last conversation.

"Excuse me, Captain. The language makes it difficult. I know of Alfred's wife, Mildred. Herr Archer was talking about Alfred and his helpers," Hansen said.

"What helpers? I don't think he has anyone working for him," I said, then went on to describe Alfred's cousin Nigel.

"Yes, that is the man. Scars on his neck. The last war, perhaps?"

"Gas," I said. "What did the other man look like?"

"Younger than the cousin, I think." Hansen frowned as he worked to dredge up the memory. "Light brown hair brushed back, clean shaven, with a long, thin nose. I recall he was well dressed. For a farmer, that is."

"That's very helpful," I said.

"Does it help you to find the killer of Herr Archer?"

"If it does, I'll let you know," I said.

Inside the mess, I grabbed a cup of coffee and gave Kaz a quick rundown on what Hansen had told me.

"I don't think we had heard of Nigel being here, and certainly not this sandy-haired fellow," Kaz said. "Any idea who he is?"

"None, but I think I should pass that on to Gwynne," I said. "I'm sure he'll be at the funeral. Then I'll talk to Bodkin about what he was doing in the library."

"If he was searching for treasure, we can rule out jewels or gold coins," Kaz said. "Stock certificates, bonds, or a legal document, perhaps? Something thin enough to not be noticed between the covers. We went through every volume in Elliot's library and found nothing more than a bookmark."

"I wonder how many people have flipped through those pages." I gulped down my coffee. "Seems like half of Slewford has tromped through the place. Let's go."

Outside, I buttoned up my trench coat as the wind kicked up a few stray raindrops and swirled leaves around our feet. Most funerals are best under bright skies. David Archer's seemed to be leaning toward dark and muddy, as if the heavens knew what suited him.

During the short ride to the churchyard, the skies opened and let loose with a downpour, which eased up as we parked along the road. Father Tanner, an umbrella held over his head, stood outside the church entrance, waiting to receive the body. People clad in their best black funeral suits stood about, their faces hidden by hats, veils, and black umbrellas. A hearse pulled up in front of the vicar and six pallbearers took hold of the coffin.

I recognized Brian from the Rose and Crown. Behind him was Dr. Bodkin, then two others I'd seen in the village, both older men. The last two were in uniform, perhaps on loan from Marston Hall. There weren't many men of Archer's age left in Slewford. Most had died in his terrible war. The young men were off serving in this new terrible war, leaving a shortage of villagers who had known the man to carry him to his grave.

Father Tanner led the procession to the gravesite. As people followed the coffin, it was easier to see who was there. The full contingent from Seaton Manor was present, with Sir Richard looking impressive in his Royal Navy uniform. Captain

Carmichael was at his side, his upturned collar hardly masking the glances he shot around at the unfamiliar faces. Mrs. Rutledge walked with Angelika and Agnes as Diana brought up the rear guard. We exchanged glances, and I gave a nod of understanding to her defensive position.

Chief Inspector Gwynne, along with his constable, hung back, watching the crowd. Colonel Cheatwood held an umbrella over Charlotte Mothersole. Major Hudson walked along with Lieutenant Haycock and two others in British Army khaki. Alfred Bunch proceeded with Mildred on his arm, light rain dripping off their hats. Two other couples followed, as a group of older ladies lagged behind, most of them likely widows. In a small town, a funeral was as much a social event as a time for mourning. I don't know how many of these folks had passed the time of day with Archer, but here they were.

The pallbearers placed the casket next to the freshly dug grave. The ground was soaked from the rain, and stones and dirt crumbled at the edge and cascaded into the muddy water six feet below. It seemed as if David Archer were impatient to settle into this, his last entrenchment.

From inside the church, the organ played a slow, mournful tune. We stood close to the wall next to an oak tree, its dead leaves soggy underfoot, but arranged ourselves around the coffin as Father Tanner closed his umbrella, letting the soft rain fall on him like a benediction. He led the group in prayer, the murmured responses coming like a strange chant in a language I couldn't quite make out. It was a different service than I was used to, and I found it hard to follow as I considered that David's killer might be praying over him at this very moment.

Father Tanner closed his prayer book, shut his eyes, and held out one hand over the grave.

And in this mountain shall the Lord of hosts make unto all people a feast of fat things, a feast of wines on the lees, of fat things full of marrow. And he will destroy in this mountain the face of the covering cast over all people, and the veil that is spread over all nations. He will swallow up death in victory; and the Lord God will wipe away tears from off all faces. And it shall be said in that day, lo, this is our God; we have waited for him, we will be glad and rejoice in his salvation.

The vicar lowered his hand and nodded to the gravediggers who had been standing to the side. They lifted the coffin by its straps and lowered it slowly into the brown, wet earth.

"That wisdom from Isaiah was my prayer, not only for David, but for all of us. For the day when the cloud of sorrow shall be lifted from our faces, and we will see victory and peace," Father Tanner said, looking out over the gathering. "There is also a line from Psalm 34 that I share with friends and family of the bereaved, which I hope gives them some comfort. This psalm is attributed to King David, who told us, 'The Lord is nigh unto them that are of a broken heart; and saveth such as be of a contrite spirit.'

"He meant that God is close to those with broken hearts and who are crushed in spirit. This applies to no one here. There is no family left of David's. There are no comrades from the war, no lifelong friends. So, there is no one who needs that comfort more than he, no one whose spirit has been crushed as his was. Not a single soul in this village has had their heart cleaved as terribly as David Archer's. I hope each of us can look at how we treated our brother over the years and that it reflects well upon us. Peace be with you."

The benediction of peace had been given to us all, but I was sure as Father Tanner turned away that he had a more severe Old Testament wish for one person in this village.

CHAPTER THIRTY-ONE

BRIAN ANNOUNCED THERE would be sandwiches and pints at the pub, courtesy of an anonymous friend. That put everyone in a jolly mood, as did the clearing sky and sliver of sun that struck the stained-glass window over Archer's grave. The crowd moved off slowly, having time before the eleven o'clock opening.

I stayed, watching as shovelfuls of dirt settled over Archer's coffin.

"Strange, isn't it?" Diana said, linking her arm in mine.

"What is?"

"The feeling after a burial. After the weight of earth has been cast into the grave," she said. "For a moment, it seems so permanent. Then the memories are still there, aren't they?"

"Always," I said, glancing up and spotting Kaz at the far side of the graveyard, his head bowed. "I haven't visited Daphne in a while myself."

"Leave Piotr be," Diana said. "I think Father Tanner's psalm struck home. He'll never be over Daphne, I think, no matter who else he meets in this life. Will you wait for him, though? I should get back to Agnes."

"Sure." I gave her hand a squeeze.

"Oh, and Big Mike arrived just as we left," she said, heading down the walk. "He'd been driving for hours and was exhausted. Mrs. Rutledge nearly fainted when she saw all the food he'd brought."

I felt better knowing the big guy was in town. As I strolled through the churchyard, waiting for Kaz, I saw Ian coming out of the church.

"I'm afraid the padre won't be joining us for refreshments," he said. "I have the feeling he's none too happy with many of his parishioners, not even counting the one who killed his pal."

"People don't always want to hear the truth," I said. "It's easier to make believe everything is fine. In a week or so, they'll all be talking about the kind things they did for Archer."

"And in another week, they'll even believe it," Ian said. "Listen, I wasn't aware you knew Daphne and that the baron and she were close. Diana told me the bare bones of the story. Terribly sorry."

"Thanks. She and Kaz were made for each other," I said.

"Daphne was a terrific gal. I can wait here, if you want to get to the pub and do your detecting, Billy. Once the sandwiches are gone, you may lose your chance," he said.

That made sense, and I wanted to chat with Dr. Bodkin before he went off on a call. By the time I caught up with the mourners, the pub was just opening. Wet coats were hung on pegs as a warm fire worked to take the damp chill from the air. Brian was already at work pulling pints, and Dorothy set out trays of sandwiches, both cheese and sausage.

"Quite the turnout," Cheatwood said, guiding Charlotte to a chair by the fire. "I'm glad we could be there. Find anything in your search of the attic, Captain?"

"As a matter of fact, we did," I said, lowering my voice. "And it was surprising. I'll fill you in later. I don't want word to get around."

"What _ever_ did you find in _my_ attic, Captain?" Charlotte asked. I put my finger to pursed lips and moved on. The chatter in the room was rising as people shook off the funeral gloom and enjoyed the free food and drink. I could only imagine the look she was giving Cheatwood.

I managed to get within reach of a cheese sandwich and munched slowly as I threaded my way through the crowd to Dr. Bodkin, who was headed into the snug with a plate in hand. Then I spotted Ian and Kaz entering the pub. By the look on Kaz's face, he was glad to have someone to share memories of Daphne with. Angelika went to embrace him, and I scanned the room for Agnes, only to find her right behind me, holding two pints.

"Hello, Billy," she said. "I'm just going to sit with the doctor for a while. I've been too busy these days to speak much with him."

"I wanted to say hello myself," I said, blocking for her as we maneuvered to Bodkin's table. Not a drop was spilled.

"Thank you, my dear," Bodkin said as Agnes set down the glasses and took her seat. "Captain, I am glad you could attend the service this morning. The poor man deserved a military presence, not that he ever thought much of the army."

"That goes for a lot of us," I said.

"It was the generals he didn't like," Agnes said. "All those senseless orders to attack for a few yards of muddy ground. Madness, the way he described it."

"Are you any closer to a suspect in either killing?" Bodkin said, taking a careful sip. "If I may ask?"

"I think the two murders are connected," I said. "Although I still can't put my finger on why Elliot's body was placed inside that aircraft."

"Is that important?" Agnes asked, taking a healthy drink.

"It was to somebody," I said. "It's up to me to figure out who and why. But we did stumble across something this morning that might be useful." I stopped to take a bite of my sandwich, watching for a reaction.

"At Marston Hall?" Bodkin asked.

"Yes. How'd you know?" I said.

"Well, it seems to be the center of your attentions," he said. "What did you find?"

"Just some papers in the attic," I said. "I really shouldn't say anything more."

"Of course, I understand," Bodkin said, his eyes flitting quickly to Agnes. Was that a look of relief? She lowered her gaze and lifted the glass again, hiding her expression.

"Are you there often, Doctor? I've been told they don't have their own physician," I said.

"They have two very good medics who deal with minor issues," Bodkin said. "But they do call me in if anything serious arises. Thankfully, the worst was a case of appendicitis, about a year ago."

"You also check up on Colonel Cheatwood, right?" I asked.

"Yes, I monitor him for any changes," Bodkin said. "He suffered a life-threatening wound in the war, as you know. Sometimes he comes to my surgery and sometimes I visit Marston Hall."

"So you know your way around the place?" I asked, finishing off my sandwich. "Have you ever noticed anything unusual?"

"It is an extremely unusual facility, Captain Boyle," he said. "High-ranking Germans walking about freely, and German refugees in uniform. Not a run-of-the-mill military installation, is it?"

"No, it isn't. But taking that into account, have you ever seen anything out of the ordinary? Spotted anyone rifling through desks, searching the place?"

"Do you mean searching for what you've just found, Billy?" Agnes asked, throwing me off my pace with a good question.

"I'm not sure," I said. "One of the prisoners said he saw a man flipping through pages in the downstairs library."

"I once used a fiver as a bookmark and never saw it again," Bodkin said. "Perhaps your chap did the same."

"Well, I'm sure he had a very good reason," I said. "I'll leave you two alone to catch up."

I left the snug. Bodkin had played it cool, but I had the sense he and Agnes were holding back. I hadn't wanted to question him too directly with Agnes sitting right there. That would have to wait. Had Agnes accompanied him on a trip to Marston Hall? It was plausible, given she was a nurse and worked with him. I needed to follow up on that, but not right now, as Chief Inspector Gwynne was bearing down on me with Constable Parker in tow.

"So, what have you been up to, Captain Boyle?" Gwynne said as Parker stood to his side, eyeing the pints lined up on the bar and practically licking his lips. "You're not keeping anything from me, are you?"

"Kaz and I have been rummaging for clues around Marston Hall," I said. "We made a promising discovery this morning. I'll let you know how it pans out."

"You damn well should tell me right now." Gwynne put his hands on his hips and leaned into my face.

"We simply didn't have time to study the papers we found before leaving for the funeral," I said. "We're heading back there now."

"I think I'll do the same," Gwynne said. "Just to see if what you've got has any importance."

"Oh, I think it does," I said in a voice just loud enough to carry. "By the way, Constable Parker, you're a local man. Do you know a friend of Alfred Bunch's, a fellow with light brown hair? A lot of it, brushed back, and a long, thin nose? He might work for Bunch on occasion."

"I'm not sure, Captain, that's not much of a description," Parker said, glancing to Gwynne as if for inspiration.

"Who told you about this man?" Gwynne demanded.

"A prisoner at Marston Hall. He said he'd seen a man fitting that description go in with Bunch on several occasions. He assumed he worked for Bunch, but I never heard of him having an assistant," I said. "Archer was watching them from outside the fence."

"Was he now?" Gwynne said, rubbing his chin. "You haven't seen this man yourself then?"

"No. Maybe we should ask Colonel Cheatwood," I said. "He's the one who contracts with Bunch for meat deliveries."

"Never you mind about that. We'll look into it. Right, Constable? All in good time, eh?" Gwynne didn't even give Parker time to say *Sure, boss*, before he led him toward the door, whispering in his ear. The chief inspector had played down the importance of my mystery man, but from how they'd reacted, it was someone they knew of and were interested in.

Alfred was across the room, draining his pint. I thought about asking him about his sandy-haired pal but held back. I didn't think much of Gwynne's investigative skills, but something told me to leave it alone for now. I'd come here to stir the pot, and if nobody picked up on my heavy hints in a crowded bar flowing with free beer, then I wasn't a decent judge of small-town gossip. As Alfred set down his empty glass, his eyes held my gaze, a mix of anger and fear playing across knitted eyebrows. Looked like the story had spread to at least one person.

I turned away from Alfred's stare and almost bumped into Diana.

"Here," she said, handing me a pint that she'd started on. "Spreading rumors is thirsty work. Mrs. Rutledge told me she'd heard you found a bag of gold coins."

"Thanks," I said, lightening the glass. "I think my work here is done."

"Just in time, old chap," Ian said, appearing from behind and shrugging his coat onto his shoulders. "We have an appointment."

"Right you are," I said. I asked Ian to drive Kaz to Marston Hall and said I'd be close behind. Then I invited Diana to walk with me to the churchyard. As soon as she was done checking discreetly on Agnes, we headed out the door.

"She's in the snug with Angelika and Mrs. Rutledge," Diana said as we strolled arm in arm. "As good as two constables."

"I'm sorry I hadn't thought to visit Daphne's grave before this," I said.

"That's the thing about the dead, Billy. They're always there. In the churchyard or in your memory," she said. "They're quite patient."

At the church, the vicar was raking the area around Archer's grave, tidying up after the gravediggers had filled it in.

"You're not going to the pub, Father Tanner?" I asked.

"No, I'm not in the mood for the frivolity that follows an internment," he said. "It's good for some, but I prefer to leave this as nice as I can. We'll have the marker set in soon. Your friend was quite generous, I must say. Good day to you both."

Daphne's grave was close to her mother's in the family plot, as if the two of them were huddled together, waiting for the others to join them beneath the large granite stone that proclaimed this Seaton territory.

"She died much too early." Diana sighed, studying Eveline Seaton's birth and death dates. "The older I get, the younger my mother seems. Daphne will forever be that gorgeous young woman dining at the Dorchester as bombs rain down on London. Some days I don't feel sad at all. No infirmities, no heartbreak, no dull everyday life for Daphne. She shall always be magnificent."

"June twenty-second, 1942," I said, not needing to ask about the other days. "It seems so long ago."

"No, it was so long ago when Daphne and I would run along these paths after church as children, never giving a thought to grief or loss," she said, grasping my hand. "Now I can't even imagine how we never saw it."

We stood for a while, fingers intertwined, leaning into each other.

Father Tanner's rake scratched against the earth, grating against rocks as he worked to smooth out the ground settling over his friend. The faint scraping noises echoed against the stone church wall as we walked back. The padre was working at a way to leave David Archer to rest in peace while finding little enough himself.

CHAPTER THIRTY-TWO

MAJOR GUSTAVE HALM sat at the table in the interrogation room, trying to look calm. Ian and I sat against the back wall, under orders not to speak unless Hank or Oskar gave us the go-ahead. Right now, Hank was seated across from Halm, snapping at him in German and stabbing at a map with his finger.

Halm shook his head and calmly recited his name, rank, and what must have been a serial number. He was holding up well, considering he'd been captured only a few days ago. He sported a bandage around his left hand, along with a torn and mud-stained uniform. Hank had told us that normally a POW would be given fresh clothing and have his uniform laundered. All part of the service. But the plan was to keep Halm uncomfortable and guessing as to his fate.

Kaz was being held in reserve, and it was too soon to tell if he'd be needed.

Hank slammed the palm of his hand on the table, the stream of his German rising in volume and ferocity, which I knew to be the signal for Oskar's entrance. Halm was startled, his eyes wide as he glanced between Hank and Oskar, trying to determine whether this new man was more or less of a threat.

Oskar spoke in soothing tones, addressing his patter to Hank, as if calming him down. He patted him on the shoulder. Hank shook it off, stood, and went toe to toe with Oskar before stalking out, cursing all the way.

Oskar sat, shaking his head and offering what sounded like apologies. He set down a stack of files, took the map, folded it, and put it aside. This was the part where he let Halm think he was getting off easy. Oskar began with questions that Halm answered with his name, rank, and serial number, over and over.

Oskar shrugged and smiled as if he understood. Then he extracted a sheet from one of his files. I could see, printed at the top of the sheet, Halm's name and unit, the 256th Infantry Division. Hank had explained that Halm's division had fought in Poland and on the Russian front but was so badly mauled that it had been pulled out and was currently fighting in the Netherlands with greatly reduced numbers. Halm was one of the few experienced officers left in his unit, and he'd been put to work organizing minefields along the Scheldt. We'd taken most of the south bank of the river—a wide estuary leading to the major port of Antwerp—which was also occupied by the Allies. Without the north bank in friendly hands, there was no way for ships to bring in supplies to Antwerp. And our forces needed supplies.

Halm knew that, of course, and appeared to be growing in his confidence to get through this questioning.

Oskar leaned forward, whispering to Halm, seeming to plead with him. Oskar had told us that he used various techniques at this point, ranging from displaying a depth of knowledge about a prisoner's unit and commanding officers to practically begging for some tidbit to pass on to his own boss to avoid getting into trouble. Whatever he tried, Halm was obstinate.

Oskar stood, unfolded the map, and pushed it toward Halm.

"*Hier?*" he asked, pointing to a section of South Beveland, the peninsula that made up a good chunk of the northern coastline. "*Hier? Hier?*"

Halm didn't even bother responding. He gave a slight shake of the head each time, not even looking at the map. Oskar finally quit, throwing up his arms and saying something that sounded a lot like *I warned you.*

Oskar opened the door and ushered in Kaz. Oskar made a big deal of showing Kaz the paperwork about Halm's military career, going into detail about the 256th Division's role in the invasion of Poland and later in the fight as they retreated from Russia into eastern Poland. Kaz looked grim, and I knew it wasn't an act at all. It would have been far fetched for any German officer who fought back and forth across Poland not to have innocent blood on his hands.

"Are you prepared to accept the transfer of this prisoner, Lieutenant?" Oskar asked.

"Yes, on behalf of the Polish Armed Forces, I do," Kaz said, staring at Halm the whole time. He then repeated it in German.

"*Die Polen?*" Halm gasped, his gaze darting to the POLAND shoulder patch on Kaz's uniform. "*Nein!*"

Oskar then launched into what I knew to be an explanation about an agreement among the Allies for the Poles to take over one of the POW camps. Of course, the Poles were most interested in interrogating prisoners who might have been involved in war crimes within their nation. Since Major Halm had no interest in providing any information, as was his right, he would be transferred to a different military authority. Which was our right.

"*Nein, bitte!*" Halm pleaded, grabbing for the map and smoothing it out. Even if he'd never laid a hand on a single Pole, he knew that being a prisoner of Polish forces would be singularly unpleasant. There were scores to be settled.

"Major Halm!" Oskar snapped, then delivered the bad news. It was too late; Halm's transfer had been accepted. Oskar opened an envelope and shook out a manila tag on a string and hung it around Halm's neck. A large red *P*, for Poland, was scrawled on it. Then came the paperwork. Forms for Halm to fill out, notifying his next of kin about his transfer.

Halm began to weep.

That was Ian's cue.

"Excuse me, Lieutenant," Ian said. "It seems Major Halm is having second thoughts. Would you allow him the chance to provide what we need? You haven't signed anything official yet, have you?"

"No, I have not," Kaz said, looking at Halm with a sneer of disgust. "But we wish to talk with this man further." Halm was squinting at the two of them, as if that might help him understand what they were saying, although it seemed clear he knew his fate hung in the balance.

"Lieutenant Kazimierz, if you allow the questioning to continue, we will set aside the matter of the transfer," Oskar said. "If Major Halm provides useful military information, he will be sent to a POW camp in Canada. If not, you may take him away with our compliments."

"Kanada?" Halm asked. Canada was the holy grail for German POWs. Some of the camps in the States were in the Deep South, where heat and humidity reigned. Canada, with its snowy winters and green forests, reminded Germans of home.

"Very well," Kaz agreed, the reluctance in his voice palpable as he stepped aside.

"Excellent!" Ian said, approaching the table with a glance at Oskar, who gestured for him to proceed. "Ah, Canada, a lovely part of the Commonwealth. You'll like it there, Major Halm."

"Kanada," Halm repeated, a bit unsure of what was happening.

"All you have to do is mark up this map with the minefields you've so expertly placed," Ian said, producing a pencil, which he laid on the table as Oskar translated. "Then on to Canada, eh?"

"*Ja*, Kanada!" Halm said, grasping what the deal was. He leaned over the map, running his finger along roads and the low-lying coastline. Muttering incomprehensible German to himself, he began to draw crosshatched sections he labeled *Minen*. He worked for about ten minutes, finally surveying the map and putting the pencil down.

"Let's see what we have," Ian said. "It looks like the major has been quite busy."

"Are you satisfied, Captain?" Oskar asked as Ian leaned over the map, checking each quadrant.

"I'm satisfied this is complete rubbish," Ian said. "Look here, man, there's a canal that cuts across the peninsula. He's drawn the minefield on what would be their side of the canal. You'd have to be an idiot to place mines there. You want them forward of the obstacle, not behind it. This section along the coast, the Germans flooded it themselves not a week ago. Tell him he's a fraud and that I doubt he knows what a mine looks like. Then give him to our Polish friends."

Oskar translated, showing Halm the locations Ian mentioned.

Now Halm really broke down. He sobbed as Oskar called for a guard to take him away. Halm wailed as Kaz signed his name to a piece of paper. Halm grabbed Oskar's hand, begging for mercy, or at least that's what it sounded like.

"Will you allow one more chance?" Oskar asked Kaz. "The major begs your forgiveness. He says he foolishly thought the captain would not notice and it was his duty to try."

"Tell him I agree," Kaz said. "But only if you keep him here until his information is verified. If he lies again, I will be back."

"*Bitte, bitte,*" Halm said, nearly hysterical.

"Tell him the terms," Ian said. Oskar did, and this time Halm sounded genuine. Ian withdrew a pen from his pocket and gave it to Halm, who began to efficiently draw in the minefields. It probably took him longer to conjure up the false locations.

Finally, we had a finished map. Ian pronounced it satisfactory, and at Oskar's order, the guard led away a thoroughly defeated Halm.

"Makes sense," Ian said. "Clever work on old Halm's part. Some of these minefields are obvious, and we would've had at them in any case. But others would have caught us quite unawares. Marvelous work, Sergeant."

"Once I saw he'd been in Poland, I knew this scheme would work," Oskar said with a grin.

"He almost pulled one over on us, didn't he?" I said.

"But he failed," Kaz said. "Although if we didn't have our own expert on mine clearance here, it could have worked."

"And Major Halm would have been on his way to the glories of Canada," I said. "Exit stage right."

"Pardon me?" Oskar said.

"Deception," I said. "Look at those minefields he drew in pencil. If we'd accepted those, there would have been hell to pay for the advancing troops."

"You're right," Ian said, studying the contours of the land. "We only have so many flail tanks. We would have been clearing empty ground, while our chaps moved into the heavily mined areas."

"Well, he didn't get away with it, sirs," Oskar said. "Please excuse me, I have a new arrival to greet."

"You're not just talking about Halm and the minefields, are you?" Kaz asked after Oskar left.

"No. It's the parallel. Halm almost got his trip to Canada and at the same time sent our boys into a trap," I said.

"What is the parallel exactly?" Ian asked.

"I think on the night Elliot was killed, someone saw their chance to pull off a deception after he'd been murdered," I said.

"Like Halm seizing the opportunity to send us into the minefields," Ian said.

"Yes. Although they've done a better job of it," I said. "They may just get to Canada themselves."

CHAPTER THIRTY-THREE

"BILLY, I THINK we have been operating under a faulty theory," Kaz said as the three of us left the interrogation room.

"Which one? I can think of several," I said. "Beginning with Elliot's murderer being the person who stuffed him into that bomber. Or Archer's killer being the same as either of those two." There was too much that didn't make sense about this case, especially if you were trying to see events as part of a common thread. If I could tease apart this tangled web of assumptions, the truth just might emerge.

"No, not those," Kaz said. "We've assumed that whatever we are searching for—along with half of Slewford, it appears—is still here."

"What else could you search for then?" Ian asked.

"The hiding place," I answered, seeing where Kaz was going.

"The empty hiding place, you mean," Ian said. "What's that get you?"

"It can still tell us something," Kaz said. "Who had access to the location, both for hiding and retrieving the object, for instance. The size and shape of the thing as well."

"Dear me, I'm glad all I have to contend with is Jerry and his minefields," Ian said. "Now, I need to get a message off to head-quarters and let them know the information has been secured. I'll see you back at Seaton Manor. Remember—tonight, the play's the thing!"

"He's in a good mood," I said, watching Ian hurry down the hall.

"As he should be," Kaz said. "He's accomplished his mission. Let's get on with ours."

"Right. Let's go light a fire under Cheatwood," I said. "Then you can go back to the scavenger hunt at the library, and I'll visit Dr. Bodkin. I couldn't press him at the pub, not with Agnes present."

We walked upstairs, and I spotted Lieutenant Haycock and the pallbearers in British khaki coming in. The reception must have broken up, or the free beer had run out. I knocked at Cheatwood's door and entered. Across the room, I saw his face change from mild irritation to wide-eyed interest before settling into a neutral gaze. Hardly a poker face.

"Gentlemen, what news do you have?" Cheatwood said, rising to greet us and gesturing grandly to the chairs in front of his desk.

"It was gratifying to see such a nice turnout at the funeral service, don't you think?" Kaz said as he took a seat, crossed his legs, and shook out the crease in his trousers. I appreciated that he was keeping Cheatwood off balance to give me time to read the man. I looked at the glint in the colonel's eyes and heard the enthusiasm in his voice; he didn't strike me as a guy who was overly worried about what we might have found. Which meant it wasn't anything that would put him in a bad light. It might even be in his interest for us to lay hands on it before anyone else. Anyone who might not return it to the rightful owner, that is.

"Yes. The man deserved it, after all he'd been through." Cheatwood fidgeted in his chair, bursting to ask us again what we'd found, but he was smart enough to not look too eager.

"Did you know about his notebook?" I asked.

"Notebook? Of course not, I really didn't know the man," he said.

"Well, you do know that he watched Marston Hall, right?" I

said. "He kept track of who visited here and how long they stayed. He kept notes, and they're missing. They were probably taken by the person who killed him."

"I saw him hanging about, certainly," Cheatwood said, letting his impatience show. "What the devil does that have to do with me? Simply report on what you've found within my facility, if you will."

"Marston Hall is *mine*," Charlotte Mothersole announced, throwing the door open. "Anything you find is *my* property, Captain. Please remember that."

"Do come in, Charlotte," Cheatwood said, his timing off by a couple of beats as she advanced into the room.

"Please, have a seat." Kaz rose and offered his chair to Charlotte. "We were just about to tell Colonel Cheatwood of our discovery. Weren't we, Billy?"

"I'm not sure," I said, drawing things out. "This is an official investigation. I'm aware Mrs. Mothersole holds the title to this establishment, but I don't know if I'm authorized to brief her."

"Do you have ownership, Mrs. Mothersole?" Kaz asked. "Officially, I mean."

"There hasn't been time, has there, Baron? It's been only a few days since Elliot was found. At first, I was too distraught to even think about it, wasn't I, Graham?" At this, Cheatwood dutifully nodded. "I am to see a solicitor tomorrow, as a matter of fact. A lot of paperwork, I expect. Surely you don't need forms and legal documents to tell us what you've found? We're both interested parties, for quite separate reasons, of course." Cheatwood winced at that one. Was Charlotte cutting him loose now that she thought we'd uncovered what she was after?

"I guess not," I said. "You're not going to be too surprised anyway. You both have been looking, haven't you?"

"I have searched for some family possessions that were stored away, to be sure," Charlotte said. "Remember, I did live here once."

"Yes, of course," Kaz said. "Until you were forced out by the government. You're lucky Stephen intervened and obtained permission for you to stay in Marston Cottage."

"He was a good brother," Charlotte said, tilting her head back as if to put distance between her lips and the lie. Sir Richard had told us Elliot had done no such thing.

"Good god, man, what did you find?" Cheatwood said, slamming a hand on the desk.

"Tides. It all has to do with tides in the Wash, doesn't it?" I said. "Stephen almost had it figured out, didn't he? Or had he reached a conclusion before he was killed?"

"What are you suggesting?" Cheatwood shouted. "I had nothing to do with his death."

"Oh, Graham, do be quiet and calm down," Charlotte said. "Do you know the precise location, Captain?"

"Not exactly, no," I said with as much confidence as I could muster.

"Then we have little to discuss," she said, not taking the bait. "Graham, I walked here, and suddenly I feel very fatigued."

Cheatwood agreed to drive her back to the cottage, if only to get away from us, but I doubted it would be an enjoyable ride. Charlotte was a cool customer, but he was wilting under the pressure. I needed to get him away from her, and I wondered if Gwynne could be convinced to bring him in for questioning.

As we left Cheatwood's office, I checked my watch. There was plenty of time for Kaz to work on the library while I went to see Bodkin. But before we could go our separate ways, the main door to Marston Hall flung open and slammed against the wall.

"You'd best come," Diana said, her voice trembling. "Agnes has gone missing."

"What?" I said, hearing the words but having a hard time letting them in. "Never mind, let's go."

We piled into the jeep, which spit gravel as I hit the

accelerator. Kaz barely had time to vault into the rear seat. "Tell us," I said.

"She was in the snug, talking with Dr. Bodkin for quite some time," Diana said. "As I was getting ready to leave, I saw her with Lieutenant Haycock for a moment. She seemed quite worked up. I went to tell her I was leaving, and she told me she had an errand to run and would find a way back to Seaton Manor. I told her I'd take her wherever she wanted after I dropped the others off at home. I went to speak to Father, and when I turned around, she was gone. Father took the others to look for her, and I begged a ride here with Major Hudson to find you."

"How is Angelika?" Kaz asked, leaning forward from the back seat as we waited for the gate to be raised.

"She's fine, searching with Father, walking the shops in Slewford. Mrs. Rutledge stayed at the Rose and Crown in case she returns," Diana said. "It might be nothing more than a misunderstanding, but I thought I should tell you, should it turn out to be something else."

"Where was Alfred Bunch while this happened?" I asked. I hit the gas when the gate opened, then slowed as a truck came the other way on the narrow lane.

"He was still in the pub," Diana said. "Otherwise, I'd be frantic."

"Stop the jeep." Kaz clapped me on the shoulder.

"Why?" I asked as I braked.

"Haycock," Kaz said. "Perhaps the errand was romantic. You go ahead, but I'll speak with him and join you soon."

"Okay," I said, raising an eyebrow in Diana's direction as Kaz jogged back to Marston Hall. "Worth a shot, I guess."

"Agnes has never said a word about Lieutenant Haycock," Diana said. "She's a very quiet, levelheaded girl, but something got into her at the pub. This doesn't make sense."

"Are you saying she's not the type for romance?" I said, turning onto the main road to Slewford.

"I don't know, Billy. She was fine, right up until you left," she said. "That's when she began to look nervous."

"You mean right after I started the rumor about what we'd found," I said.

"*You* said it. I didn't. Drive to Dr. Bodkin's surgery first. He might know where she went. Or maybe she's there. They're very close, you know. Then go to Agnes's cottage—it's a little farther down the road."

We drove by the pub first. Mrs. Rutledge stood outside and shook her head, signaling no sign of Agnes. On the other side of the street, Sir Richard and Angelika were headed into the greengrocers. Diana pointed me toward Bodkin's, and I pulled in next to his automobile. Diana stayed near the jeep to keep an eye out for any sign of Agnes.

"Just a moment, Captain," Dr. Bodkin said as I entered his waiting room. He was escorting an older woman out of his office. I recognized her as one of the ladies from the funeral. I held the door as she exited and thanked the doctor for his time.

"It happens after a burial," Bodkin said after I shut the door. "Aches and pains suddenly materialize. A reminder of mortality, I think. Now, what can I do for you?"

"You can tell me where Agnes is, if you know," I said.

"What's happened?"

"No one knows," I said. "She left the Rose and Crown, and no one has any idea where she went. Did she say anything to you?"

"That's unlike her," Dr. Bodkin said, sitting himself down on a wooden bench. "Especially as she's caring for Angelika."

"Angelika is out looking for her," I said. "We're all beginning to get worried. Tell me, is she involved with Lieutenant Haycock at all?"

"Involved? I doubt it," he said. "They do know each other; they've spoken when she's assisted me at Marston Hall. Why do you ask?"

"She was talking with him before she left," I said. "Maybe she wanted a ride? To Marston Hall or somewhere more private? Talk to me, Doctor."

"Agnes did become distraught after you told us of your discovery," he said. "I told her it could mean anything."

"Why would it matter to her?"

"It's a very complicated story, Captain," Bodkin said.

"I know about Virginia Day Sallow," I said. "Agnes's mother, isn't she? Is that what the story's about?"

"It involves what happened to her mother, yes," Bodkin said. "But that isn't the whole story, and it's not my tale to tell. You'll have to ask Agnes."

"Where is she?" I said, growing impatient with Bodkin's evasiveness.

"I suspect she's in Elliot's library at Marston Hall," the doctor said. "It's where she goes when the world weighs heavily on her."

CHAPTER THIRTY-FOUR

"WHY?" DIANA SAID as I drove back through Slewford. "Why would she go to Marston Hall at all? How could she even get into the library? Are you sure you believe Dr. Bodkin?"

"There's something there she wants," I said. "I wish I knew what it was. As for Bodkin, you know the man. Do you think he'd lie?"

"Anyone will lie for what they feel is the right reason," Diana said. "To protect others. To protect themselves. But Dr. Bodkin? No, I don't think he'd lie about Agnes, at least not to her detriment. He's been close to her since she was born."

"He's holding back," I said. "They were both there the night the bomber crashed, remember?"

"Good Lord, Billy, you don't think the girl killed her own father? That's absurd," she said.

"I agree, but it's not absurd that they both witnessed something that they're afraid of or unwilling to talk about," I said. "Maybe she's searching for evidence or proof at Marston Hall."

"Seems like everyone is. I'm getting sick of the place myself. Let's hope we find her there safe and sound," Diana said.

I sped up, eager to get through this latest crisis and learn what I could about Agnes's sudden change of mood. I'd wanted to shake things up, but not at her expense.

Though why give her a special break? I knew she'd gone through a lot during the Blitz and had been on shaky ground for a while, but did that exclude her from suspicion? Agnes Day was a nice young girl who'd had a tough life. People I cared about liked her. In my experience, nice young girls did all sorts of bad things, for reasons both understandable and indecipherable. The fact that she was helping Angelika and was a guest at Seaton Manor shouldn't have influenced me.

But it had.

At the gate, I asked the sentry if Lieutenant Haycock had driven back with a woman.

"Couldn't say, Captain. The funeral party went out in a Morris. The lieutenant was in the passenger seat, but I can't swear as to who was in the back," he said as he raised the gate. The Morris was a British Army lorry with a canvas-covered cargo bed. I hoped they kept better track of who was leaving this place than who was coming in.

Inside, we made it upstairs without running into Cheatwood or anyone who might wonder what Diana was doing here. The door to the library was unlocked. I saw Agnes as soon as I opened it. She was curled up in one of the leather armchairs, clutching a blanket to her face. Next to her sat Lieutenant Haycock, who jumped at our sudden entrance. Agnes didn't move.

"I found her in the other room," Kaz said in a soft voice, leaning against the wall and looking up from the book he'd been reading. "She was going through the armoire and the boxes of Elliot's belongings."

"Agnes?" Diana said, kneeling next to her. "Are you all right?"

Agnes didn't answer, only turned her head away from Diana and stifled a sob. I tapped Haycock on the shoulder and nodded in the direction of the library.

"Explain yourself," I said once we'd moved out of the sitting room.

"Agnes asked for a ride," he said. "I didn't see the harm."

"This is a POW facility, not a hotel," I said. "Do you bring other civilians here?"

"No, of course not, but Agnes needs to come here occasionally. It calms her," Haycock said, keeping his voice down and glancing back to the sitting room. I could hear Diana talking in low, soothing tones, but I had no idea if Agnes was responding.

"And that's your job? To bring her to a nice private place and calm her down?" I asked, stepping closer to Haycock.

"No, no, it's not like that," he said, shaking his head and looking at the floor.

"She was alone when I arrived," Kaz said. "I went to fetch the lieutenant when I saw the state she was in. His presence did help to relax her."

"Listen, I don't know why, but there are times she needs a visit here. She looks through Elliot's stuff. What's the harm in that? There's some connection with her mother, but that's all she's ever told me," Haycock said. "Don't worry, there's no Germans allowed on this floor. It's safe."

"Who else knows about her visits?" Kaz asked. Haycock shook his head.

"I'm the one who lets her in here. Sorry I didn't mention it, but I saw no reason," Haycock said. He'd avoided naming anyone else, but I was sure a few others must have noticed her.

"When did this start?" I asked, feeling a familiar irritation at people who think they know better in a murder investigation.

"A short while after she came back from London," Haycock said. "She went through a lot in the Blitz, you know." He leaned on the library table, sighed, and brushed back his dark hair. He looked like a schoolboy about to take his punishment.

"We know," Kaz said. "Dr. Bodkin told us of her experiences and her return to Slewford. To rest and recover."

"Yes, that's how I met her. First, when she came here to assist the doctor, then once at the Rose and Crown," Haycock said. "You see, both my parents were killed in the Blitz. Coventry."

"I'm sorry," I said. Coventry had been hit hard by the Luft-waffe.

"Yes, well, it gave us a bit of shared misery, didn't it? So one day when she returned with Dr. Bodkin, she asked to see the library," Haycock said. "The doctor explained it had to do with memories of her mother and that it would be helpful to her. It sounded harmless enough, so I let her in."

"And you ended up giving her a key," I said.

"Yes. We're always finding keys stashed away in this place. I found one early on that worked for the library and gave it to her. I'd taken a look in there on my own and read a few of the books, no one the wiser," Haycock said. "But I never took a thing, I swear."

Cocking his head in the direction of the sitting room, Kaz asked, "Has she ever been like this?"

"I found her weeping once when I came to check on her," he said. "She wouldn't say why. Always kept mum about what was bothering her, but she seemed better for being here. Almost cheerful."

"You care for her," Kaz said.

"I do. But there's something wrong, and it has to do with this house, this damned monstrosity," Haycock said. "She's not well because of it, I'm sure."

"Is that why you want a transfer?" I asked.

"I want that transfer for the reasons I gave you," he said. "Also so I don't have to watch her suffer, because there is not a thing I can do to help her."

"Okay," I said. "Let's just keep this between ourselves for now. Your men—the ones in the truck—they won't snitch, will they?"

"The men like Agnes," Haycock said. "She's always been kind to everyone here. You'll take her back, won't you?" A young, pretty, vulnerable woman. Of course the men adored her and looked the other way.

"Yes," Kaz said. "She'll be in very good hands."

I watched as Haycock approached Agnes, who looked a bit more responsive. He took her hand, and she held it in both of hers and smiled. He told her he'd see her soon. As he opened the door, she managed a faint goodbye.

"Agnes, are you up to speaking with us?" Diana said, still curled up on the floor at Agnes's feet. "We were all so worried. We didn't know where you were."

"I'm sorry," Agnes said, her words escaping in a gasp. "I don't know what came over me."

"How did you get in? Do you have a key?" Diana asked.

"Here," Agnes said, withdrawing a chain she wore around her neck. It held an old iron key. She let it drop back under her blouse, close to her heart.

"Did you find what you were looking for?" Diana asked.

"Have you?" Agnes said, looking straight at me.

"I don't know if we're looking for the same thing," I said. "But I don't think I have."

"Keep looking," Agnes said, then shuddered. "I'm chilled."

With that, she lapsed back into silence, her eyes fixed on the cold fireplace as she drew the blanket tightly across her chest. She'd come back from wherever she'd been for a moment, but there was no use pushing things right now. I'd seen plenty of people fake going silent and plenty of others in a state of shock. Agnes wasn't faking, but neither had she experienced anything today, as far as I could tell, to put her in this state. She was holding secrets inside, and they were eating away at her, sending her deep into her own private world. One day, she might not emerge from it.

It was this damn house. It drew her in for whatever twisted reason but still gave her some sort of comfort, even as it drained her. She was emotionally spent and wouldn't be able to tell us anything for a while, even if she wanted to.

And I was pretty certain she didn't want to.

"Let's go home," Diana said, standing to take Agnes by the hands. "Angelika is waiting. She'll be glad to see you."

"She needs you," Kaz said.

Agnes looked at him, and his words seemed to register. She nodded and gripped Diana's hands, standing and letting the blanket fall to the floor. She shuffled to the door, glanced at the room, and released a heavy sigh.

"Can you walk?" Diana asked. "We don't want to attract attention, do we?"

"I'm fine," Agnes said, taking a deep breath and standing straight. "I can walk."

We left the library, and as I turned my key in the lock, the metallic noise echoed loudly in the hallway. Agnes looked back, startled at the sound, or perhaps she was simply nervous at reentering the real world from wherever she'd been.

We took the stairs to the rear entrance, avoiding the main hall where Cheatwood and Hudson had their offices. Diana helped Agnes into the back seat where the canvas top shielded her from view. As I started the jeep and backed out, I could see Agnes looking at Marston Hall, her lips trembling as if she might cry. I drove to the gate and slowed as the sentry opened it for us to pass, thankfully without asking any questions.

"We'll be at Seaton Manor soon," Kaz said, looking back at Agnes and smiling. She murmured a quiet response, and I picked up speed, happy to leave Marston Hall behind. As we passed the turnoff to Tower Hill and the cliffs, I heard Agnes begin to weep.

I glanced back, and Diana had her arm around her, pulling her close.

"I can't," Agnes moaned. "I can't."

I knew better than to ask.

CHAPTER THIRTY-FIVE

WE DROVE AROUND Slewford until we spotted Sir Richard and Angelika near the village post office. Angelika cried out in joy when she spotted Agnes. Tears welled in her eyes as she approached the jeep, her expression a jumble of confusion and relief.

At Angelika's insistence, Kaz gave up his seat so his sister could drive with us. She sat facing Agnes, one arm outstretched to hold her hand. While Kaz and Sir Richard hoofed it back to the Rose and Crown where Mrs. Rutledge stood sentry, I drove to Seaton Manor wondering how long it would take Agnes to recover from whatever spell she was under, and not just for her sake. Angelika was doing well, but she still needed help, and Agnes had just the right mix of skill and personality to keep her on track with her recovery. Angelika's healing—from not only her surgeries but also her time in Ravensbrück as well as occupied Poland—would be helped by a friend close to her own age. Not every nurse could provide that.

Unfortunately, I was still determined to view her as a suspect. For what crime, exactly, I was unsure.

We pulled into Seaton Manor, where Big Mike was waiting at the door. Angelika helped Agnes out of the jeep, and they linked arms as they strode to the entrance. Agnes ran a hand across her eyes and advanced with a smile. Maybe she was putting on a good front, or perhaps she felt better simply being away from Marston Hall. Seaton Manor was definitely a more welcoming place.

"You must be Big Mike," Angelika said, taking him by the hand. "Piotr talks of you all the time."

"Miss Kazimierz, you look great," Big Mike beamed. "I thought you might be laid up."

"No, and thanks for that are due to my friend and nurse, Agnes Day," she said, introducing them.

"There have been stories told about you, Sergeant," Agnes said. "Mrs. Rutledge feared for her larder for a time, but she told us you brought many delicacies."

They kept up the chatter as we went inside. Diana gave me a look of relief, but I kept an eye on Agnes. She seemed cheery, though there was a brittleness in her movements as her eyes flitted from one person to another. For all I knew, she was working at hitting the brakes on a full-fledged collapse.

"It's been a trying day," Diana said. "Why don't we take Agnes upstairs for a rest while you boys catch up? Father is on his way with Kaz and Mrs. Rutledge."

"Sure," Big Mike said, in a way that conveyed he'd picked up on the underlying tension. "We'll just wait for them, you go ahead."

"Oh, I do need a rest," Angelika said. "That was a lot of standing, was it not? Should I do some stretches, Agnes?"

Agnes agreed, and Diana accompanied the two of them up the staircase, just as Ian showed up at the door, briefcase in hand.

"First Sergeant Mike Miecznikowski, this is Captain Ian Carmichael. Friend of the family," I said.

"Big Mike, isn't it? Diana mentioned you'd be coming. Jolly good to meet you," Ian said. "I take it you're associated with the baron and this cutthroat?"

"You've got the cast of characters right, Captain," Big Mike said as they shook hands. "Are you on leave as well?"

"Business and pleasure, as they say. I depart early ack emma to rejoin my unit. I've sent the message off to my HQ, and I leave tomorrow with these maps," Ian said. "I'll pack them away, then you can tell me what you got yourself up to this afternoon."

A few minutes later, the three of us gathered in Sir Richard's library and helped ourselves to his whiskey. I brought them up to date on Agnes's disappearing act and my worries about her condition.

"Sir Richard gave me the basic rundown this morning," Big Mike said. "He's a suspect, and you think Agnes might be in danger if she's really Stephen Elliot's daughter. But what's up with her scooting out to Marston Hall?"

"Well, I forgot to mention I'd started a rumor that Kaz and I had just discovered evidence there," I said.

"The pub was abuzz with it in seconds," Ian said. "Worked like a charm, not that it seemed to help much, far as I could tell."

"You're right about that," I said. "Alfred Bunch took it pretty much in stride. Colonel Cheatwood wasn't all that excited about it either, and Charlotte saw right through my bluff."

"She's the dame who's Elliot's sister? The one doin' the horizontal foxtrot with the CO of Marston Hall?" Big Mike said.

"Exactly," I said as I heard the front door open.

"You summarize things nicely, Sergeant." Ian raised his glass to Big Mike. "Colorful."

"Helps me keep the list of suspects straight," he said, gulping his drink.

Sir Richard came in a few minutes later and reported that the evening meal would be catch-as-catch-can. Mrs. Rutledge had treated herself to a pint at the reception, then had been given a brandy to calm herself during the search for Agnes. Not used to drink while the sun was still up, she'd gone to bed after checking on Agnes.

Then Kaz strolled in and said that he'd been upstairs and that Agnes was behaving quite normally and running Angelika through a series of exercises.

"Mrs. Rutledge says there is ham in the larder and plenty of cheese and pickles," Diana said, joining us. "She tried to rally, but I told her to stay put since we needed to eat fairly soon. So a simple meal is best."

"The play," I said, explaining it to Big Mike.

"We'll watch the place, right, Sir Richard?" Big Mike said.

"Indeed, we will," he said. "Once Mrs. Rutledge is well rested, an intruder wouldn't stand a chance."

"Are you sure?" I asked him.

"My friend, whom I haven't seen in years, is appearing in a play in King's Lynn," Diana said, hands on her hips. "In case you don't recall, Billy, I'm on leave even if you aren't. So unless there's another murder or the Germans parachute into Slewford, you are taking me to the theater tonight."

"We shall be fine," Sir Richard said. "Mrs. Rutledge can handle a shotgun nicely, and I have my service revolver. Plus, I'm sure Big Mike arrived with sufficient firepower to guard the rations he brought us."

"Canned peaches, Billy," Big Mike said. "You know how valuable they are. Not to mention coffee and bacon."

"Don't let the local constabulary see any of that, Big Mike," Kaz said. "They'll think you're running with the black market."

"Well, I haven't been arrested yet," Sir Richard said. "But you never know when Chief Inspector Gwynne may come calling. By the way, Billy, I had Brian at the Rose and Crown pack up your belongings. I'm tired of this charade with Gwynne. You're my guest, and by god, you'll stay under my roof if you want. I'm beginning to think Gwynne is more bark than bite, but if you prefer otherwise, Brian is saving your room."

"I'd be much happier here, thanks," I said. "If anyone presses the point, I can truthfully say I see no connection between you and either crime."

"Good," Sir Richard said. "That will let the real villain know you're getting closer."

"That reminds me," I said. "You had Bunch's and Gwynne's connections to the British Union of Fascists checked out. Maybe we should look into Stephen Elliot. Was he political? If Bunch was part of the fascist crowd, he may have had a beef with his boss over it."

"I don't recall hearing anything about Elliot's politics," Diana said. "Though it's possible that he and Alfred argued over it. I have a hard time envisioning Stephen caring enough about people to be anti-fascist, but he could have been an enthusiastic fascist himself."

"What, then Alfred Bunch, already a member of the BUF, decides this one fellow who pays his salary is too mean-hearted of a fascist?" Ian said. "Hardly makes sense, does it?"

"You're lucky you're the man with free theater tickets, Ian," Diana said. "I'm going to get ready."

"And I'll make the call about Elliot," Sir Richard said. "The rest of you see about getting food on the table and shut the door on your way out."

A FEW HOURS later, I was in the back seat of Ian's staff car, with Diana by my side. She'd traded funeral duds for a fancy green dress, glossy red lipstick, and an upswept hairdo that suited her perfectly. I'd shined my shoes.

"Agnes seemed much better, didn't she?" Kaz asked from the passenger's seat.

"Almost back to normal," Diana said. "She was embarrassed, to be sure. I think it really was an uncontrollable urge to get close to her father."

"Subconscious, then," Ian said, slowing to turn onto King Street and looking for the theater. "You said you couldn't be certain Elliot was the father, although circumstantial evidence does point to it. I'd say her desire to be ensconced in the library is proof that she believes it to be true, at the very least."

"You're getting the hang of this detecting business, Ian," Diana said.

"It's hard on the gray cells, I must say. Don't know how that Poirot chap does it all day," Ian said. "I'll be glad to get back to tearing through minefields myself. Ah, there it is."

Ian pulled over near the King's Lynn Operatic and Dramatic Society, where a banner announcing KING JOHN in bold letters was draped across the front of the dark brick building, above a massive set of wooden doors. We were early, so there was plenty of time to go backstage and visit Maggie. We found her already in costume, wearing a colorful blue-and-gold gown that looked a bit worn up close. She and Diana embraced and told each other how wonderful they looked. Ian got a friendly peck on the cheek, and Diana introduced Kaz and me.

"Oh, so this is your dashing suitor," Maggie said. "And a real baron! We've got loads onstage, but it'll be nice to know there's an authentic one in the audience. Sorry, boys, but I've got to finish my makeup. Why don't you take your seats and let Diana and me gossip?"

We did. On our way, I asked Ian if he'd ever had a role in a Shakespearean play.

"No, except for student productions at the Royal Academy of Dramatic Art, which hardly count," he said. "My professional debut was in London, just before the war broke out. I played a robot, believe it or not."

"I am sure you will graduate to playing actual people when you return to the stage," Kaz said.

"*If* I do," Ian said with a laugh. "All that make-believe seems pointless at times, but I'm not sure what else I'm good for. Clearing minefields can take a chap only so far in civilian life, after all."

"You must know this play," I said. "Can you give me a quick rundown? It helps to get into the flow if I know a bit at the start." I'd always enjoyed Shakespeare, thanks to Sister Edith and how she'd presented his works. We'd had a couple of class trips and saw *Hamlet* and *Much Ado About Nothing*, both of which I liked. It'd always taken me a few minutes to settle into the rhythm of the archaic language, but as soon as that happened, a whole new world had opened to my young mind.

Ian laid out the basics.

King John of England was fighting with King Philip of France. Philip thought John's nephew Arthur was the rightful king, probably because he'd be easier to control since he was a child. Maggie was playing Constance, Arthur's mother.

"Wait a second," I said. "This is King John, as in Robin Hood. Richard the Lionheart's brother. A bad guy, right?"

"So the history books say. Around here, King John is still popular. They've got a statue of him somewhere," Ian said. "But the sentiment is not widely shared. There's never been another King John, which tells you something."

He went on. Richard the Lionheart's illegitimate son pops up at King John's court, is recognized and is knighted. Then there comes a battle, which neither side wins. Finally, someone suggests a wedding as a way out of the fighting—it would have been a smashing idea before hundreds of men were slaughtered. John and Philip agree, and John's niece is wed to Phillip's son. Constance and Arthur lose out, but he's given a noble title and a pat on the head. Peace is restored, but not for long. John still wants little Arthur dead, and the war heats up again.

"The French invade, and things don't go well for most of the characters," Ian said. "I won't spoil the end for you, though."

"King John died not far from here, I believe," Kaz said.

"Yes, north of here, Newark-on-Trent, after passing through and leaving his mark on King's Lynn," Ian said as Diana joined us.

"Maggie's leaving early in the morning as well," she said. "But it was nice to see her again. Thank you, Ian."

"You're welcome, my dear," he said. "I can't wait to see her performance."

"She's so disappointed that she dies offstage," Diana whispered.

"Of course she is! Any decent actor wants the chance to die with panache. Awfully hard to do from the wings."

The house lights dimmed, and I sat back, glad to know the gist of what was coming. It reminded me of what had happened back in Boston. I'd been in high school at the time, but I'd eaten up every story my dad told me about his job as a homicide detective. There'd been a big Jewish gang in Boston run by Charlie Solomon. When he died—of too many bullets in the men's room of the Cotton Club—his relatives and associates went to war over his kingdom of crime. Some things don't ever change.

Charlie's cousin Moe Abramowitz offered to merge with Eddie Cohen, who'd worked for Charlie, and rub out the rest of the competition. That worked for a while, but then Eddie turned up dead of a heroin overdose. No one seriously thought Eddie was an addict, but everyone admired how smart it was to come up with that trick instead of the usual couple of slugs. It'd taken the heat off Moe for a while, and by the time anyone suspected it had been done at his order, no one wanted to say it out loud. Last I heard, Moe had died of a heart attack and his younger brother was in charge. Nice, the way they'd been able to keep the family business intact. All it took was a couple of murders and a lot of muscle. Old Will Shakespeare would have loved it.

The play got underway, and I could see that King John owed a lot to his mother, Queen Eleanor, and that she was no friend of Constance and her son Arthur, who are backed by the French. John prepares for war, but first he must act as a judge. The brothers Robert and Philip both claim their father's inheritance, which is in dispute since Philip, although older, is illegitimate. Based on family resemblance, it comes out that Philip's father is the deceased King Richard, John's brother. In exchange for Philip renouncing his claim, John knights him, proclaiming he is now to be known as Sir Richard.

At the end of the scene, everyone departs except the newly knighted Sir Richard, who delights in his new name and fortune. *For new-made honor doth forget men's names.*

Like Virginia Day dropping her mother's last name, Sallow, making what new-made honor for herself she could.

The rest of the play was pretty much a downward spiral for King John. He ordered Arthur to be executed—and to have his eyes plucked out as well—but his henchman, Hubert, relented and let the boy live. As Arthur attempted an escape, he fell from the castle wall and died. That was when Maggie expired, regrettably not on stage. John's nobles fell away as they held him responsible for the boy's death, until the valiant Sir Richard was one of the few still by his side. John ended up poisoned, and Sir Richard came up smelling like a rose as he pledged loyalty to Prince Henry, John's son and heir. Sir Richard closed the last act with a rousing speech, and the crowd roared its approval as these lines were uttered: "This England never did, and never shall, lie at the proud foot of a conqueror."

When the standing ovation ended, we trooped backstage to say goodbye to Maggie. As we did, I thought about how Moe Abramowitz had finagled things, making sure his cousin's business stayed intact. The distraction with the drugs, that was nice. Mobsters usually went in for the more violent approach, not that sticking a needle into a guy's vein was exactly genteel.

Eddie Cohen, exit stage right.

"Well done, Maggie!" Ian said once we found her. "You were a terrific Constance."

"I'm so glad we got to see you perform, Maggie," Diana said, grasping her hand. "I'm sure you're destined for great things."

"Oh, thank you both," Maggie said, her blush evident even under the heavy makeup. She beckoned a cast member to join us. "And speaking of great things, meet George, our own King John."

Maggie introduced us and we all gave George a round of

well-dones. He was an older gent, his makeup hiding the lines around his eyes, and his wig darker than the gray hairs sticking out beneath it.

"Thank you all," George said, grinning. "It's great fun to play such a cad. But I do feel sorry for him at the end, every performance. Poisoned by a monk! What a lowly way to go."

"Is that how he actually died?" I asked.

"No, it was even worse," George said. "Dysentery. Right after he lost the crown jewels in the Wash. Not the best last days for a monarch, eh?"

"What?" Kaz and I said at the same time.

"A fortune, they say. Taken by the inrushing tide," George said. "Never been found. I did a lot of reading up on old King John for this part, and he always did have the worst luck. Say, are you chaps all right?"

"Old Hubert had it right, didn't he?" Ian said, reciting the lines from when he spared Arthur:

Well, see to live. I will not touch thine eye
For all the treasure that thine uncle owes.

CHAPTER THIRTY-SIX

"YOU DIDN'T SEE any reference to the crown jewels in Elliot's library?" Diana asked as we drove through the darkness, back to Seaton Manor. "Didn't he have a lot of books about the Wash and King John?"

"Yes, he did," Kaz said. "But our first efforts were to find something hidden in the library. We opened every book, but to search, not read. The same goes for his files, which we examined. He had reports and manuscripts, but I have not had time to peruse them."

"I found an emerald at the Bunches' house," I said. "I thought it was an old family heirloom. It could have been stolen from Elliot."

"Treasure," Ian said, his hands gripping the wheel as he drove slowly down the country lane. The blackout wasn't as stringent for headlights as it had been, but the visibility was still limited. "Real treasure. It's hard to believe."

"Well, now we know Cheatwood and Charlotte may have been speaking literally," Kaz said. "I need to study the materials in the library closely tomorrow. Do you think we should approach Alfred Bunch?"

"Not yet," I said. "They don't know I've seen it, and it might spook them. I think I will talk to Chief Inspector Gwynne about questioning Colonel Cheatwood. It's time to put real pressure on him."

"It's odd that Alfred had only that one gem," Ian said. "Was that worth killing over?"

"If Elliot had discovered where the crown jewels were lost, he likely wouldn't have found them all at once," Kaz said. "Perhaps Alfred absconded with his initial discovery, and they came to blows over that."

"Perhaps," Diana said, "but that doesn't explain how Elliot ended up in the bomber, does it?"

"No," I said, keeping the rest of my thoughts to myself. They weren't well formed enough to say out loud, and I wasn't sufficiently convinced of my evolving theory. Tomorrow we'd search the library in earnest. Having a clue as to what we were looking for was a big improvement.

IN THE MORNING, I found Mrs. Rutledge in the kitchen, no worse for wear after yesterday. The steaming cup of coffee she held in her hands might have had something to do with that.

"Coffee is in the dining room, Billy," she said. "I'll bring breakfast in a while. Sir Richard is busy talking back to the newspaper right now, so I'll give him some time to calm down. Better for the digestion. How was the play?"

"Very good," I said. "Maggie was delightful, and I learned a lot." More than I'd bargained for.

In the dining room, Sir Richard was mumbling as he turned the pages of the newspaper. Kaz sat across from him, flipping through the pages of the book about King John that Sir Richard had been reading. Kaz gave a small shrug as he reached for his coffee cup, letting me know he hadn't found anything yet about the crown jewels.

"Can you believe this claptrap?" Sir Richard demanded by way of greeting. "They've let that bastard Archibald Ramsay out of prison."

"What was he in for?" I said, pouring myself a cup from the silver coffee service.

"Treason!" Sir Richard said, slapping his hand on the newspaper spread out in front of him. "Ramsay was thrown in jail for his open support of fascism. He even found Mosley's British Union of Fascists too tame for his blood. As a member of Parliament, he gave a speech urging people to listen to the New British Broadcasting Service, a Nazi propaganda station in Germany. While we were at war, by god!"

"I recall he gave out the times and frequencies of the broadcasts from the floor of Parliament," Kaz said.

"He did. But it was only when he was caught working with a clerk from the American embassy who was also pro-Nazi that they threw him in Brixton Prison," Sir Richard said. "The American had passed Ramsay confidential communications between Churchill and Roosevelt. The blighter was going to use them to try and sabotage the Lend-Lease program."

"He sounds like an out-and-out Nazi spy," I said, taking a seat and sipping my coffee. Disrupting the flow of war materials being shipped to Britain from America would be a coup for Berlin.

"Worse than. A traitor and an anti-Semite of the worst order. Hates the Jews and all foreigners as well. I don't know why anyone saw fit to let him see the light of day," Sir Richard said, jabbing his finger at the newsprint. "It says here that he was able to return to his seat in Parliament since it was never revoked. The first thing he did was try to bring forward a motion to reinstate the 1275 Statute of Jewry, a medieval law that required Jews to wear a yellow badge. Can you imagine?"

"He would be at home in the SS. Didn't he form his own party?" Kaz said.

"More of a secret society than a political party, but yes. He didn't like playing second fiddle to Mosley and was bent on more active measures than the BUF offered," Sir Richard said. "The Right Club, he called it. Composed of some highly placed members of British society, along with enough foot soldiers to do their bidding. Most of the funding came from Lord Tavistock, the fourth wealthiest man in Britain."

"Was he imprisoned as well?" I said.

"Perhaps you missed the part about his being the fourth richest man in the nation," Kaz said. "And the fact that he is a lord?"

"Got it," I said. "What was the Right Club planning?"

"Much of this was held back, out of fear of panicking the public," Sir Richard said. "So keep it to yourselves. Ramsay, in conjunction with Lord Tavistock and others, was planning a coup if the Germans invaded. They had General William Ironside, the former commander of the home defense forces, ready to take over as the head of the government. Not only that, but they planned to bring back the Duke of Windsor and install him as king."

"That's the guy who gave up the Crown to marry Wallis Simpson," I said.

"Correct. They would have put Edward VIII back on the throne, after overthrowing his brother King George VI," Sir Richard said. "Then we'd have a pro-Nazi king and a government that would do Germany's bidding. Gladly."

"It's unbelievable," I said, understanding why this had been kept from the public. It was a far cry from the notion that the country was united in the face of Nazi aggression. "Could they have pulled off a coup?"

"Personally, I doubt it," Sir Richard said. "But they'd gathered arms and explosives and had a cadre of men at the ready, by all accounts. Also, if an invasion had occurred, the military would've had its hands full, so it's hard to be certain. If the Germans knew of the Right Club's plans, they'd certainly have tried to provide support. When Ramsay was finally arrested, much of the weaponry was found. But not all."

"There is little they could accomplish now, Sir Richard," Kaz said. "What would be the point?"

"I hope you are correct, Baron. But when dealing with men such as these, it can be difficult to understand the depth of their beliefs and motivations. All that *Perish Judah* garbage must rot the brain," Sir Richard said, nearly spitting out the words.

"What's that?" I said, feeling there was something familiar about the phrase.

"It's their motto," Kaz said. "It means *Death to Jews*."

"Do they have a badge, like the BUF lightning bolt?" I asked. "An eagle clutching a snake?"

"Yes, by Jove, they do. With the initials PJ beneath for that vile phrase," Sir Richard said. "How do you know that?"

"Because I saw one at Alfred Bunch's house. Right next to his BUF badge. I had no idea what I was looking at," I said.

"That's odd," Sir Richard said. "My contact at the Home Office confirmed Bunch's association with the BUF, but he said nothing about the Right Club. I wonder how Alfred came to have it?"

"Perhaps the Home Office missed the connection," Kaz said.

"I shall place the call again," Sir Richard said. "Right now. This is damned odd."

"Can you ask about Stephen Elliot and the Right Club as well? I don't know if they found anything connecting him to the BUF, but if they missed Bunch's being in the Right Club, they could have done the same with Elliot." Sir Richard agreed, and I was left wondering if this was another dead end, or if it might point to a reason for Elliot's and Archer's murders. If there had been Right Club activity in the area, it certainly could have gotten violent.

"By the way," Kaz said, "Ian left an hour ago. He had a train to catch in London. He left his regards for you and wished us luck. He asked that we let him know how the investigation concludes, if it is not a state secret."

"Sorry I missed him. He's a good guy," I said.

"I agree. I hope he does return to the theater world after the war," Kaz said.

"You know, I'm still thinking about the play," I said to Kaz as I refilled my delicate china cup.

"I thought Maggie acquitted herself well, but I can't say it was all that memorable," Kaz said. "Except for George's revelation backstage."

"Yeah, it would answer the question of what everyone's looking for," I said. "Except now I'm wondering if the treasure is an arms cache. We had zilch for clues, and now we've got two big ones."

"But that's not all that you mean, is it?" Kaz pulled the newspaper closer to scan the article about Ramsay.

"No. I'm thinking about names and inheritances," I said, hearing footsteps in the hallway. Diana came in, quickly followed by Agnes. Big Mike and Angelika were a minute behind them, so we kept the breakfast chatter light. Sir Richard returned, offering no clue about the result of his telephone call.

After breakfast, Agnes suggested to Angelika that they take a walk when they finished with their stretching routine.

"I'll go with you," Big Mike said. "I'd like to see the country-side, and I need to walk off this breakfast." They agreed to leave in thirty minutes and to take the horse path behind the barn.

"Good choice, the views are lovely that way," Diana said. Not to mention there would be less of a chance to be spotted. Once the two young ladies went upstairs, Sir Richard motioned us to join him in his library. Diana shut the door once we were all inside and updated her father and Big Mike about King John's treasure.

"That is fascinating," Sir Richard said. "I do recall hearing that story when I was a child, now that you mention it. Do you think it has any bearing on this case?"

"What if Elliot found the crown jewels?" I said. "Any number of people might have tried to steal them."

"I doubt that," Sir Richard said. "I never heard of Stephen Elliot mucking about in the Wash looking for anything. How could he find a fortune sitting in Marston Hall? What would they do with such treasure anyway? Sell it to a pawnbroker?"

"A king's crown would hold a lot of jewels," I said. "I saw an emerald in the box where Alfred Bunch kept his fascist badges."

"Yes, but the crown jewels can mean a whole host of things that belonged to the monarch," Sir Richard said. "It might not even include the actual crown he wears on his head. And I've never heard of King John himself going under in the Wash."

"What would the treasure be then?" Big Mike asked.

"The royal belongings," Sir Richard said. "In those days, kings traveled often, making their lords and barons put them up for extended periods. He would have had everything necessary for court life. Robes, a scepter, bejeweled belts, goblets, all the things a king wouldn't trust to leave behind, especially with the French threatening invasion and the Scots revolting against him. It would have been everything he owned—an entire baggage train, well guarded."

"Let's set that aside for now," I said. "Kaz is going to spend time in Elliot's library today. Maybe there's some clue there."

"Next item," Sir Richard said, leaning forward in his chair. "I placed another call this morning to my Home Office contact. I asked him yesterday to look into any connection Stephen Elliot may have had with the British Union of Fascists. This morning, Billy indicated that he'd seen a badge worn only by members of the Right Club next to Alfred Bunch's BUF badge."

"Ramsay's group?" Diana asked.

"Yes, and he's been released from Brixton," Sir Richard said, giving Big Mike a quick rundown of what the Right Club members had been up to. "Since the Home Office had not known of Bunch's involvement, I wanted them to check Elliot for both groups as well." He sat back.

"What was the response?" Kaz asked.

"There was no response," Sir Richard said. "My contact has been transferred to another department. I was told that the information about Alfred Bunch being a member of the BUF was given to me in error, and I was to cease any communication on the matter."

"How dare they talk to you that way!" Diana said. "Fools, the lot of them."

"The gentleman I spoke with was no fool," Sir Richard said. "He knew how to give fair warning. This matter is obviously being handled at a high level."

"What do we do now?" Big Mike asked.

"You stick close to Agnes," I said. "We still don't know if she's in danger or not."

"I'll get my shoulder holster on and be ready for them," Big Mike said. "It shouldn't be a long walk. Even though Angelika seems to be doing well, it's still hard for her."

"Is that what Agnes says?" Kaz asked.

"It's what I say. I injured my leg a while ago, and it's still not one hundred percent. I can tell she's holding in the pain. She's a tough cookie, Kaz."

Pain. It was everywhere, and people had their own way of holding it in or letting it go. Not too long ago, I'd thought this case would come down to love or greed as the motivation. Now I saw a third possibility, and that was it. Pain.

"Okay, I'll bring Kaz to Marston Hall, then I'm going to drop in on Dr. Bodkin," I said. "I have a few more questions for him."

"I'll drive Piotr," Diana said. "I want to drop by and visit with Victoria."

"Who's that?" I said.

"Victoria Tillstone is the village's sub-postmistress," Diana said. "I haven't spoken to her in some time, but when we were looking for Agnes yesterday, I saw her in her shop. She works in a small general store; she also handles the mail."

"She once worked at Marston Hall," Sir Richard said.

"Victoria was the woman Stephen Elliot assaulted," Diana said. "I thought a woman-to-woman chat might be in order. You never know."

"Smart. There may be something about that day no one else remembers," I said, knowing that an attack such as she'd suffered would have burned events into her memory. "Then after I see Bodkin, I'll speak to Gwynne and suggest he bring in Cheatwood for an interview. He looks nervous enough already, maybe this will shake something loose."

"What do you want with Bodkin?" Sir Richard asked, affecting little concern.

"I'm not quite sure." I stood to leave. "I'll know it when I see it."

But I already knew it. I was hunting for the hidden headwaters of pain.

CHAPTER THIRTY-SEVEN

I WAITED OUTSIDE Bodkin's office until he was alone. I knocked and entered to find him packing his bag.

"Ah, Captain Boyle," he said. "I heard you found Agnes at Marston Hall. I trust she's well today?"

"She seems so," I said. "I need to talk with you about her."

"I am heading out on a call," he said. "Perhaps later today?"

"Is it an emergency?"

"The patient is not bleeding or in agony, if that's what you mean," he said. "Still, they are waiting for me."

"Then they can wait a little longer." I took a seat across from the doctor. "Sit down, please."

"Rather abrupt of you, Captain," Dr. Bodkin said, but he did sit down. "What's this in aid of?"

"You've known Agnes all her life, haven't you?"

"Of course. I saw Virginia when she was pregnant with Agnes, so even longer than her entire life, you might say."

"You've always felt protective of Agnes, right from the beginning then?" I said.

"Is there something wrong with that, Captain? I don't like the sound of this."

"I mean nothing untoward, Doctor. I can just see how you must have felt. Virginia dies in childbirth—"

"It was a very difficult birth. Virginia hemorrhaged severely."

"I don't mean to imply you were at fault, Dr. Bodkin. I can only imagine what that must have been like," I said.

"I had a woman from the village assisting me, but there was nothing either of us could do," he said, his expression softening. He took off his glasses and rubbed his eyes. "Virginia was able to hold her child for a moment before she went unconscious. Her last words were to ask me to look after Agnes. She died minutes later."

"Leaving you with the burden of deciding what to do with Agnes," I said.

"Yes. There was no one else, so I had no choice but to accept the obligation," Bodkin said. "Elliot refused to entertain the thought that the child Virginia carried was his. Even if he had, he was not the sort to make a decent father. Or man, for that matter."

"Did you ever speak to him about it?" I asked.

"Yes, I did, on one of the few occasions he attended Sunday services. He called Virginia a common harlot and had the gall to say he'd dismissed her for her offering sexual favors in return for a raise in salary," Bodkin said. "He warned me that if I pursued the matter or spoke to anyone else about it, he'd be sure to thoroughly ruin Virginia's reputation."

"More than he already had," I said.

"Right, but among country folk, there's not the same shame in being born on the wrong side of the sheets as there is in the city," Bodkin said. "Virginia could have dealt with that, but to be called a wanton hussy? That would have been too much, and Elliot knew it. He simply walked away from what he'd done and never seemed to care. Never asked after Agnes or expressed the slightest sorrow at Virginia's death."

"Who paid for Virginia's burial and headstone?"

"I did. I wanted Agnes to be able to visit her mother when she was older. I wanted Virginia to be remembered," he said.

"You found a childless couple to take in Agnes," I said. "Not too far away so you could keep an eye on her, but not too close to Stephen Elliot."

"You are correct. I thought it best to have her brought up nearby. As soon as she was old enough, I brought Agnes back, to visit Slewford. To help keep the memory of her mother alive. She called me Uncle John but soon outgrew that fiction."

"It was you who suggested she change her name, wasn't it?"

"You don't miss a thing, Captain Boyle, do you? Yes, when she was old enough to leave home, she wanted to live in Slewford. I suggested she use her mother's middle name as her surname. I saw no reason to reveal to Elliot that his daughter was close by. It was better that he remain ignorant."

"Not a bad choice of name, considering the circumstances," I said, remembering my Sundays spent as an altar boy and the priest's words.

Agnus Dei, qui tollis peccata mundi, dona nobis pacem.

Lamb of God, who takes away the sins of the world, grant us peace.

"She was as innocent as a sacrificial lamb, and I wanted to shield her as best I could," Bodkin said.

"No one knew, did they? Even Diana told me she thought Agnes's father had died and that she'd gone to live with relatives. But Virginia had no relatives, so how could Agnes?"

"Exactly. I told people Agnes had been taken to live with an aunt and uncle. No one had any reason to question it, and it simply became accepted," he said. "A rather normal thing, in these parts. But tell me, Captain, how does this help you with these horrible murders?"

Dr. Bodkin's question was a good one, but I wasn't ready to answer it yet. "Who's the local expert on architecture around here? The history of buildings and ruins, that sort of thing?"

"That would have been Elliot. I daresay much of his research material is still sealed up at Marston Hall," he said. "The vicar is working on a history of St. Paul's. It has a medieval foundation, I know that much. Ask Sir Richard as well. When we were boys, we explored Tower Hill hoping to find Roman ruins. Perhaps he's kept up his interest. Now you have me curious. What's this about?"

"Have you ever heard of King John losing his crown jewels in the Wash?" I asked.

"That would have been in the thirteenth century, wouldn't it? No, I haven't, but all those Plantagenets and Tudors hold little interest for me. Never could keep track of their wars and connivances," Bodkin said. "Our Windsors are fairly tame by comparison."

"Except for the Duke of Windsor and his American wife," I said.

"Yes, well, that was an embarrassment, wasn't it? But a fair stroke of luck, having that Nazi-lover abdicate. I'd say we owe Wallis Simpson our thanks for taking Edward off our hands. Now, Captain Boyle, kindly return to my question. What does all this have to do with the murders of Elliot and Archer?"

"Elliot was dead when you arrived, wasn't he?" I asked, relieved to hear no sympathy for the fascist-leaning Duke.

"Of course, man! That bomber was underwater and rolling around in the surf. What sort of a question is that?" There was a barely suppressed undercurrent of fear in Bodkin's response. He could have simply dismissed my question, but his last phrase hinted at a fear of what I might know or guess at.

"You and Agnes arrived, and there was no one else there. The bomber was in the water, and the two of you were alone. Do I have that right?"

"Yes, although the aircraft disappeared under the waves quickly. We'd seen the Bunches' delivery van turning into their drive, but there was no one else when we got to the cliffs. Colonel Cheatwood came soon thereafter, then others started arriving, Sir Richard among them."

"But for a time, it was just you two. And Stephen Elliot, dead," I said.

"You're leaving out the Germans inside that aircraft, Captain."

"Right, sorry. Not to mention the pilot," I said. "Did you see him stumbling around, injured?"

"If I had, I would have tended to him, as would have Agnes. As I said, there was no one there."

"Stephen Elliot was seen leaving Marston Hall in his automobile," I said. "Did you notice it?"

"I can't say, Captain. It was dark, and we were focused on looking for survivors. I remember staring at the great gouge in the earth the bomber had made. I easily could have missed one vehicle. Later, there were several, parked all around, but I couldn't have picked out Elliot's."

"You say you didn't see Elliot either?"

"Repeatedly, Captain. What are you implying, that I killed him? Good god, you don't think Agnes did, do you?"

"No, Doctor, I don't think either of you killed the man," I said, standing. "Thank you for putting up with my questions." There was a pencil on Bodkin's desk. I gave it a slight flick, and it fell off the edge.

I drove to the vicarage and found Father Tanner in his study. He didn't look any happier than he had at the funeral. I began to think the man had lost his only true friend in Slewford, but he perked up when I asked about his interest in medieval architecture.

"I'm no expert, Captain, but I have learned a few things researching the history of our church," he said. "How can I help you?"

"What structures in Slewford would have been here in the thirteenth century?"

"The foundation and parts of the nave here at St. Paul's, certainly," he said. "The church has been expanded and rebuilt over the years, but those sections are original. Marston Hall as well, I believe."

"It doesn't look that old," I said.

"No, it doesn't, but the foundation and much of the building is," Tanner said with a chuckle. "Those turrets were a Victorian affectation, constructed by Sir Jerome Marston in the last century. The center foundation and front are definitely late medieval. It could be the thirteenth century, but don't hold me to that. I do know the first major addition came during Elizabethan times, and that is the total extent of my knowledge."

"Thanks, Padre, that's a big help," I said. "By the way, how was Stephen Elliot related to Sir Jerome Marston?"

"I don't know exactly, but when he died with no issue, it was young Stephen Elliot who inherited as the closest living relative," he said. "I fail to see how any of this helps, but I wish you well, my son."

Outside, I saw Diana pull over and park her father's sedan next to the jeep. She waved for me to get in.

"How'd it go?" I asked as I settled into the passenger's seat. As soon as I looked Diana in the eye, I knew it wasn't good.

"Agnes was at the party," Diana said. "I didn't know. I never saw her."

"What do you mean?" I said, taking her hand in mine.

"After I tried to stop Elliot, and after Father pulled him off me, Victoria ran out of the room," she said. "I was so distraught I didn't think to follow her, and Father was so angry he insisted we leave."

"But Agnes did try to help," I guessed.

"She did. She found Victoria in a downstairs washroom and told her to lock the door. Then Agnes went to fetch Victoria's coat. Agnes was going to walk her home." Diana halted, took a deep breath, and continued. "When she didn't come right back, Victoria went to look for her. She said she was ready to run without her coat, but she didn't want to leave Agnes alone. Then she heard her scream."

"Elliot."

"Yes. Elliot. He had Agnes cornered. He was pawing at her, kissing her, telling her to be quiet, saying he needed a new maid and wanted to try her out," Diana said. "His hands were everywhere."

"Oh god. Poor Agnes," was all I could say.

"He finally stopped," Diana said. "Victoria said Agnes placed her hands on his cheeks and held his gaze, then whispered something Victoria couldn't hear. Elliot stumbled backward and ran away. Then Victoria and Agnes left, each vowing to keep quiet about what had happened."

"It wasn't their fault," I said, knowing it often didn't make much difference.

"Of course not," Diana said. "Agnes had to protect herself. From the shame and pity, if nothing else. It was her father trying to rape her, for god's sake. How could she live with it if everyone knew?"

"How could he?" I whispered, not to Diana, not even to myself. I wanted God himself to explain how people like that were allowed to walk His green earth. But I knew the answer.

Pain. It was everywhere. The longer it worked at people, the more broken they became.

CHAPTER THIRTY-EIGHT

I SAT IN silence with Diana, neither of us able to say another thing. What was the use? Words would never heal the hurt Agnes had endured. No wonder she'd become a nurse and worked under dangerous conditions during the Blitz and in North Africa. If her own wounds wouldn't heal, at least she could try to make others whole. Not unlike Diana, I thought, as I squeezed her hand, knowing that she'd had to test herself to see if she deserved to live after so many had died around her in the cold Channel waters off Dunkirk.

I looked at her face, cheeks damp with tears.

But I saw something else. Through the window, driving past us.

A battered blue Vauxhall truck.

A familiar face under a shock of thick brown hair, his long, thin nose in profile.

"Follow that truck," I said, shattering the pall of melancholy that had settled over us. "Not too close, so he won't spot me in this car."

She started the engine and pulled onto the road before she had any idea what I was talking about. Quick thinking and fast responses were part of her SOE training.

"Who is it?" she asked, shifting gears but keeping her speed down.

"I don't know his name, but he was seen with Bunch on several occasions, making deliveries to Marston Hall. Archer probably had him down in his notebook. When I described him to Gwynne yesterday, he acted like it didn't mean anything. But it did. It made him nervous," I said. "Tall guy, big head of brown hair combed back, and a narrow nose. Spiffy duds compared to most of the men around here."

"I don't think I've ever seen him," Diana said. "What should we do? Telephone the inspector?"

"I don't trust the man." I took off my garrison cap in case he checked us out in his rearview. "He's aligned with the BUF, even if it's unofficial. Maybe he never joined them because he's a fan of Ramsay and his Right Club." We kept behind the Vauxhall as it drove by the Rose and Crown, the post office, and then Dr. Bodkin's surgery. Ahead, the road divided, and he took the left fork. Diana slowed to a crawl.

"What are you doing?" I asked.

"That road is straight as an arrow for half a mile," she said. "If he's watching to see if he's being tailed, he'll spot us if we turn too soon." We rolled on for another ten seconds before she hit the accelerator, taking the left fork smoothly.

Nothing.

"He must've spotted us and sped up," I said. Off to the right was low-lying water thick with reeds and no place for a vehicle to turn in. The left side of the road was nothing more than a drainage ditch and a wall of tangled brush.

"There's a lane ahead," Diana said. "See the bridge over the ditch?"

"Think he turned in there?" It wasn't much of a bridge, just a few heavy planks, but I had no idea where else he might have gotten to.

"I'll drive by slowly. You look down the lane," she said.

"Okay." I opened my field jacket and placed my hand on the butt of my .38 revolver snug in its shoulder holster. We drew closer, and I could see the rough dirt track between the trees, then a round outline and a shadow. "Keep driving, don't slow down!"

Diana gave it a little gas—we cruised by like we were out for a Sunday drive. I forced myself to not turn and look.

"What did you see?" Diana asked me, her hands tight on the wheel.

"A sentry," I said. "I caught a glimpse of a bicycle behind a tree and saw a figure move behind it as we passed. The Vauxhall is down that lane, and whatever's in it is important enough to warrant a guard. Do you have any idea where that track leads?"

"I do," she said, glancing in the rearview mirror. "There's a deserted cottage at the end of the track. There was a fire about ten years ago, and the thatched roof went up. More to the point, it's not far from the Bunches' farm. That's just over the hill beyond the cottage. When we were riding, we passed close by."

"There were hills around Alfred's place," I said, remembering the layout. "Sheep were grazing on them."

"Yes. There's a hill between the farm and the cottage. It would be easy to transport anything right up to the end of the lane and then carry it to the farm," she said. "It's all hidden from view."

"This is worth a look," I said. "Can you drop me off somewhere along here?"

"I'll go with you," Diana said. The road curved, and as soon as we were out of the guard's line of sight, she pulled over and turned the sedan around.

"No, two people will attract attention," I said. "If any more of their crew shows up and spots an empty car, they'll know something's up. I'll get out here. I'll cut across to the cottage and check things out."

"All right," she said. "It's about a quarter mile down that lane, but it will be longer cross-country. Don't get lost."

"I won't," I said. "Drive back past the guard. Come back in an hour, and I'll be waiting here. Behind that fir." I pointed to a large tree.

"If you're not, I'll keep driving and return in ten minutes," she said. "In case they're watching. If you can't come this way, go around the Bunches' lamb farm, behind their house and barn. Eventually that will take you to the horse path. You could walk back to Seaton Manor if you had to."

"It's a beautiful day for a stroll," I said. "See you in an hour."

It wasn't all that beautiful, but I wanted to sound upbeat for Diana. The sky was filled with low clouds coming in from over the water. The sharp smell of rain was in the air, and the winds had kicked up. That last bit was good news, since the sound of swirling branches muffled the racket I was making as I worked my way through the undergrowth. The spindly trees and scattered bushes marked this as a pasture gone to seed, which was too bad. What I could really have used was a thick oak tree to climb to get a better sense of where I was headed.

I kept at it. After a few minutes, I brushed aside a low-hanging evergreen branch and nearly tumbled onto the lane. I heard the murmur of voices and melted back into the foliage, hoping I hadn't been spotted. I couldn't tell how close I was to the main road or the cottage, but I was close to the footsteps headed my way. Two men, one of them muttering.

"Aw, what's the use of standing guard, anyway? No one's been snooping about."

"Keep a sharp eye out and stay hidden. Any trouble, you pedal as fast as you can. No shooting, just blow the damn whistle. Understood?"

"Aye, Freddie, understood."

I caught a glimpse of Freddie through the branches. Now my thin-nosed friend had a name. I eased out into the lane and watched their backs as the two of them made for the road, likely to relieve the guy who'd been standing sentry. I kept to the shadows, moving sideways along the edge of the lane. As soon as I saw the rear of the Vauxhall, I darted back into the brush and cut a wide circle, coming up on the rear of the ruined cottage.

The place was a shambles, overgrown with vines and dying weeds. Someone had nailed up corrugated tin on the roof where it had burned away. I needed to see what they wanted to keep dry.

I squatted next to a wooden cart and listened, trying to separate the sounds of swishing branches from footsteps. There was nothing but the wind slicing through the trees. I didn't have much time, so I rose and stepped quickly to the back door. I drew my revolver and pressed the latch. The metal-on-metal sound was improbably loud, as was the creak of rusted hinges.

I winced at the noise as I entered, but it was quiet inside. The kitchen table was strewn with food scraps, and mouse droppings littered the floor. The bits of food were dry and moldy, but not that old; otherwise the animals that called this place home would have cleaned up. The front room was bare except for two wooden pallets.

Two empty wooden pallets.

This place was a staging area. Were they getting ready to use it, or had they already? I searched the corners of the room and spotted a thin, dark metal container, about the size of a cigar case.

I picked it up and heard a rattling sound. I knew what was inside, and it wasn't a cigar. It was a timing pencil, the kind used by the SOE as detonators. A Number Ten Delay Switch, according to the engraved label. I pocketed the detonator and left the case where I'd discovered it. I needed evidence, but I wanted to leave the room as I'd found it.

As I turned to leave via the kitchen, a distinct aroma wafted up at me. What was it, other than definitely out of place in this tumbledown house?

Almonds.

The smell of almonds and SOE detonators meant one thing. *Explosif Plastique*. Plastic explosive. Nobel 808, more properly.

It also meant it was time to get the hell out of here.

The scruff of boots on the road hurried me along, and I stepped as gingerly as I could through the kitchen and out the back door as I holstered my pistol. There was no chatter this time, nothing but the smell of cigarette smoke as the figure walked right by the Vauxhall and the cottage. Was it Freddie, heading to a rendezvous at the Bunches' place?

I slipped around to the lane, watching as a figure vanished between two saplings. I didn't see or hear anyone else. Maybe the other sentry had been picked up or gone home. I had no idea if these men were from around here or brought in by the BUF or the Right Club. It was time for answers, so I followed the guy heading up the hill toward Alfred and Mildred's.

I didn't need to keep him in sight. Once I went between the saplings, it was easy to stay on track. The path was well trodden, the soft ground showing traces of many footsteps made by men weighed down with whatever had been carried to the cottage.

I made it to the crest of the hill and crouched to take cover behind a fence post. On the other side, there was little in the way of trees or undergrowth, and I figured this was one of the fields where Alfred grazed his sheep. While it didn't offer much protection, it did provide a nice view of the farmhouse and barn below.

Alfred's delivery van was there, along with a large sedan. I could make out the guy I'd followed coming off the hill at a trot and tossing off a wave to someone. I strained to hear what he said and the response, so I almost didn't hear the twig snap behind me.

I turned and there was Freddie, as surprised to see me as I was him.

I reached for my pistol, but before I could get a hold of it, Freddie launched himself at me and sent me flying backward against the wire fence. I grabbed him by his jacket and took him with me, realizing in a flash that he didn't want to risk anyone hearing a gunshot.

I fell back when the wire sagged, and brought my knees up as I hit the ground, getting my boot heels planted against his belly. I extended my legs and launched him over my head, just like they'd taught me in basic training, shocked it worked against a real opponent.

I heard Freddie gasp as the air was knocked out of him. I went after him, giving him a solid smack on the jaw. I patted him down and took a Webley revolver from his waistband in case he decided shooting me was worthwhile after all.

"Freddie!"

The voice came from below.

"Freddie, where are you?"

Apparently, Freddie was expected.

I pulled him up by the collar and dragged him back to the top of the hill, telling him to keep his mouth shut. He groaned at me, which I hoped signaled cooperation. At the fence line, I stood behind him, one hand on his collar and the other jamming the barrel of his pistol into his neck.

"Tell them you'll be right there," I said. "Nice and loud. And quick."

I heard a grunt and felt a solid, hard hit to my head. My knees went out from under me, and the last thing I knew, Freddie turned on me with a solid right hook.

CHAPTER THIRTY-NINE

I WAS BEING dragged downhill. My head and jaw hurt, but all that was good news. It meant I hadn't been shot or bludgeoned to death on that hillside. Maybe good news was a bit of a stretch, since I had no idea what Freddie had in store for me. I decided to play possum, which wasn't really all that hard. Once we hit level ground, they dropped me, and I went facedown onto the hard-packed earth.

"Where the bloody hell did he come from?" Alfred demanded, his voice a meaty growl.

"Found him up on the hill," Freddie said. The other guy didn't correct him and take credit for my capture, which told me Freddie was likely in charge, a mean bastard, or both.

"Dead?" Alfred said, poking me with his boot.

"Out cold," Freddie said. "For now. Get him in the barn while we decide what to do."

"This isn't a good sign, Alfred." That was Mildred. "He must have suspected something. How'd he get by your lads, Freddie?"

"Must've come through the woods, I expect," Freddie said. "Didn't come down the lane, that's for certain. My boys have that covered."

"Shouldn't they go check the road then?" Mildred said. "Look for that jeep of his." It was sounding like Mildred had more smarts than any of them. Of course, what did I know? I'd been captured and was lying with my face in the dirt, making believe

I was knocked out. Hands grabbed my arms and pulled me toward the barn. I could hear Freddie and Alfred arguing, and I doubted it was about the best way to cook lamp chops.

The barn door opened, and I felt the impact as they tossed me against a wooden beam. I knew my shoulder holster was empty, but they hadn't searched me yet, and I still had the pencil detonator in my pocket. Not the most effective weapon, but if I was going to use it at all, it was time to wake up.

I groaned. I moaned.

"Get some rope, he's waking up," one guy said.

I rolled to my side and clutched my gut, giving a good impression of the dry heaves. I wouldn't be the first guy to lose his lunch after being smacked in the head, and it didn't seem to surprise my captors. There was some discussion about hurrying up with the rope, but neither man was rushing, not wanting to be sprayed with vomit. Outside, sheep *baa*-ed in the paddock, and the phrase *lambs to the slaughter* came to mind.

I got the detonator out of my jacket pocket. These things were activated by crimping the thin copper tube at one end, which crushed a glass tube and released acid, which in turn ate away at a metal wire. Pliers or stamping on it with your bootheel was recommended, but my options were limited. I stuck the end between two loosely fitting barn boards and pushed. The leverage did it, and I removed the brass safety strip and shoved the thing up my sleeve.

Now for the tricky part. I rolled over, shook my head as if trying to clear it, and looked at my captors. One was beefy. His nose had been broken a few times, and he didn't look like the friendly sort. The other was short and wiry, with a bad complexion.

"I need to speak to Freddie," I said. "Now."

"You ain't givin' orders, mate," one of them said, tossing a length of rope to his pal. "Truss him up."

"He'll be mighty angry," I said, rising on my knees as Shorty advanced on me with the rope.

"Shut up, or I'll get a bigger rock and hit you again," Shorty said, looking back at his buddy and laughing. I shook my arm and palmed the detonator.

"Listen!" I shouted, reaching for Shorty's worn corduroy jacket and then pulling him toward me. I didn't care about talking with Freddie, but I needed to act like I was frantic to. "It's important. I need to talk to Freddie." From my kneeling position, I got a good grip on the jacket right above the pockets. I let the detonator go as Shorty lashed out and kicked my arm.

"I'll cut you if you try that again," he said. "Sit down."

"Okay," I said as he wound the coarse rope around my chest and tied me to the beam.

"Watch him," Beefy said, handing Shorty my revolver. "If he causes trouble, shoot him in the knee."

"It will be my pleasure," Shorty said, pulling up a crate and sitting directly across from me. Beefy left, and Shorty grabbed a pitchfork from behind him. "Tell you what, Yank. First sign of trouble and I'll stick you with this. Probably won't kill you straightaway. Second sign, the kneecap goes."

"Which one?"

"What?"

"Which kneecap? Left or right?"

He considered it. "Let's see. The left, I suppose."

"Your left or my left?"

"Shut up, or I'll do both, how's that?"

"Sorry, just making conversation," I said. "Now, how about you untie me and give me my pistol, and I'll be on my way."

"I don't think so, Yank."

"It would be worth your while."

"No, it wouldn't. Freddie would not be happy."

"Okay." I only wanted to give him fair warning. Well, semi-fair, I guess. I couldn't really be sure, since these pencil detonators had settings ranging from ten minutes to twenty-four hours. I knew they were color-coded and that these were yellow, but I didn't know if that meant ten minutes, a day, or something in-between.

I did know it wasn't going to be pretty. The explosive in the detonator was composed of a pyrotechnic mix that ignited the main detonating charge. It wasn't a huge explosion, just enough to set off the Nobel 808 it was jammed into—a contained, hot burst. The way Shorty was sitting, it was going to do some damage to his left hip.

Serious damage.

"You with the BUF or the Right Club?" I asked. I couldn't see my watch, but I knew we were getting close to ten minutes.

"The BUF is all talk," he said over the sound of the bleating sheep. "Like you. So shut yer gob."

"What's the operation?" I asked. "You might as well explain it. I know they're planning to kill me."

"We're going to get rid of the damn darkies and foreigners that are flooding into Britain! You'll see. After the war, they'll all want to stay here. Why wouldn't they? But that'll be the end of white Britain, and the Right Club won't stand for it, you hear?"

"How the hell are you going to do that?"

"No more talk!" Shorty said, standing with the pitchfork clenched in one hand. It was a mistake.

A short, sharp *crack* sounded as a white flash blossomed from his jacket pocket, which was now at the top of his thigh. Near the femoral artery.

Shorty folded up, going fetal as he tried to understand what had happened. He pressed his hands against the terrible burning wound in his thigh as blood pumped furiously out between his fingers. He looked at me, uncomprehending, which was for the best. In thirty seconds, he was dead.

I pushed myself up on the beam, thankful that Shorty trusted the revolver more than his knot-tying skills to keep me in place. I managed to twist around, get my hands on the knot behind me, and get it undone. I stepped out of the tangle of rope and retrieved my revolver. As unpleasant as it was, I patted Shorty down until I found his knife. It might come in handy.

I had two options. I could go back over the hill, wait for Diana to cruise by, then go to the police, who might be working hand in glove with these bastards. Or I could make for the house and try to find out where the explosives were, sneak in the back door again and give a listen. It was a long shot, but if they'd already planted them, I had to know where.

Besides, I was mad. I didn't like getting hit in the head, and I sure didn't like getting punched out by Freddie. Maybe that clouded my judgment, but I knew he was likely the ringleader, and if I could settle my score with him, it might screw up whatever the Right Club was planning. It had to be something big if Shorty had been telling the truth about getting foreigners out of the country.

I eased the barn door open, watching for anybody at the windows of the house, about thirty yards away. The curtains were drawn. No one was in sight outside. I slipped out and shut the door. I took a deep breath and ran low to the back of the house, my boots sounding thunderous against the ground. Or maybe that was my heart beating like a bass drum.

At the kitchen door, I knelt and listened. The murmur of voices drifted out from inside, but it didn't sound close. I pressed the latch and led with my revolver, advancing into the kitchen until I could make out the words from the other room.

"We could leave him here, tied up tight," Alfred said.

"Might as well finish him. In for a penny, as they say." That was Freddie. What a charmer.

"Aye," Mildred chimed in. "Best to get it done. We've other matters to attend to. But don't let Nigel know—he's nervous enough already."

"The Yank said he had to speak with you. Said it was important." That was Beefy, relaying my message.

"All right, let's see what he's on about," Freddie said. "Then we'll take him for a walk and dig a nice hole."

I heard the door slam, and it sounded like Freddie and Beefy had left. Was it just Alfred and Mildred now, or was there someone else? I didn't have much time before Freddie opened the barn door. I began to back out of the kitchen carefully.

"Still one more package to deliver," Alfred said. "I'd best be going."

"Be careful, dear," Mildred said, as if he were doing nothing more than running an everyday errand. I doubted he was still delivering lamb during this operation. Speaking of running, it was time for me to skedaddle. Quietly. "I'll have tea ready."

I stopped, waiting for a clue about where Alfred was headed. A lot of people around here called dinner tea, which was different from teatime. It sounded like Alfred would be gone for hours, but he said nothing as he left.

Damn. I'd wasted time for nothing, and Freddie and Beefy were bound to be at the barn in seconds.

As I got to the rear entrance, Alfred started the van, which helped cover the sound of the latch. I stepped outside just as Freddy and Beefy reached the barn door.

That was my chance. I waited until they'd turned to enter the barn, then moved along the side of the house, making for the rear. I wasn't fast enough, or Freddie had excellent reaction time.

A shout, and then one shot slammed into the house near my head. I fired back, once, twice, and saw Beefy duck as Freddie took cover. I sprinted around the back and scrambled up the hill, making for the horse path and the route back to Seaton Manor. Shouts rose from the house, telling me that there were at least two others in there with Mildred.

I heard gunfire and dove to the ground, not certain if I'd been spotted or if they were firing blind. Bullets whizzed through the shrubbery, and I decided it was time to leave. A wild shot would do as much damage as an aimed one.

I went on my hands and knees, staying low as I worked to find the horse track. It took a few minutes, but I finally tumbled out onto it, only to see Beefy with a shotgun, swiveling around at the racket I'd made. He looked confused. I realized he'd been listening to an approaching sound, coming from a nearby curve in the path.

"Drop it!" I shouted, holding my revolver on him. He gaped at me and then looked in the other direction. "Drop it or I'll shoot."

He dropped it. At that moment, a man stepped out from the other side of the path, a surprise to both of us by the look on Beefy's face.

Chief Inspector Gwynne, his revolver drawn.

Both men looked at me, then toward the steady drumming sound coming close to the bend.

Beefy dove for his shotgun as Diana approached, riding Dante at a gallop. Before Beefy could raise his weapon, Diana barreled into him and sent him sprawling as she drew in the reins on Dante, who reared and skidded to a halt, raising a swirl of dust.

Gwynne grabbed the shotgun, and I turned my pistol on him.

"Put that down, you idiot," he said.

"And then you'll kill us both. No thanks," I said, watching Diana as she edged Dante closer to Gwynne, ready to nudge him in the same direction as Beefy.

"I'm not going to kill you, Boyle, even though you've thoroughly wrecked our surveillance. I'm Scotland Yard. Special Branch. I've been after this nest of vipers for months."

CHAPTER FORTY

"CORPORAL! CALL THEM in," Gwynne shouted. A British Army noncom emerged from the bushes carrying a walkie-talkie. He set down the backpack and pressed the receiver, issuing a rapid series of orders. Constable Parker was on his heels, gathering up the badly stunned Beefy.

"Special Branch?" I said, shocked at the revelation.

"You know about the lane leading to the cottage, over that hill?" Diana pointed from her perch on Dante, reacting a lot quicker than I did.

"Yes, but only since yesterday, when we spotted one bloke bicycling into the village for a pint," Gwynne said. "Didn't know where he came from until we followed him back. Unfortunately, the cottage had been cleaned out. A very large American sergeant has been driving past the lane for a while. Yours, I suppose?"

"Yes," I said as Parker handcuffed Beefy and led him away. "What's going on, exactly? I had you pegged for one of them. The Home Office confirmed it."

"Of course they did, and thank you. It was an unpleasant performance, but necessary in order to gain the confidence of some unsavory types."

"Lieutenant Haycock is on his way, sir," the corporal announced.

"Good. Now, I suggest we move back. We've an observation post up here," Gwynne said. "Even room for the gallant steed."

We followed Gwynne as he brushed past the undergrowth and went up the incline. Two men in civilian clothes were crouched in a grassy depression, one of them watching the house through binoculars. The corporal joined us, set down the radio, and checked his pistol.

Diana brought Dante farther back, tying the reins to a tree where he could graze.

"Thanks for coming to my rescue," I said. "I guess you figured I'd need to use the escape route."

"I know you, Billy," she said, grasping my hand. "Big Mike took the car, as you heard. Father agreed to watch over Agnes."

"Good. Now, Chief Inspector, if that is your real title, tell me what's happening," I said.

"Not my real title or name, not that it matters," he said. That sounded about right for Special Branch. They were Scotland Yard's elite unit, originally organized to investigate Irish rebels back in the last century. Now they specialized in infiltrating and stopping politically violent groups. "Anything happening down there?" Gwynne asked the fellow with the binoculars.

"Bit of a hornet's nest, sir," he said. "The woman and three others, far as I can tell."

"There's a body in the barn," I said. "Short guy, bad skin."

"That'd be Williams," Gwynne said. "Won't be missed."

"Who's Freddie?" I asked.

"Freddie Leese. Nephew of Arnold Leese, head of the Imperial Fascist League," Gwynne said. "Another group that thought Mosley's BUF was too soft on Jews, which tells you something. Arnold was recently released from prison on account of illness, and Freddie is doing his footwork for him. Tetched in the head, that one."

"You were going to rescue me, weren't you?" I asked him.

"I was weighing my options," Gwynne said. "If we'd swooped down on them and found no weapons, all our work would have been useless."

"You know about the detonators and the Nobel 808, don't you?"

"Yes, but what we don't know is where they have them stored and where they're going," Gwynne said. "It's obvious now that they used the cottage as a staging area, bringing it in from somewhere. Several locations, perhaps."

"There's none at the Bunches' house?" I asked.

"None. We've been in a few times when they're out," Gwynne said, checking his watch. "They are smart enough not to leave any evidence where they live. Ought to be time for Haycock to show up."

"Not Colonel Cheatwood?" I asked.

"No, I invited him to an interview," Gwynne said. "He's waiting at the station. I preferred a more competent officer. Haycock's bringing a dozen men. I have a team at the end of the lane to the cottage, and we're positioned up here to catch anyone fleeing. He'll go straight up the driveway."

"You have someone tailing Bunch?"

"Yes. He's still making regular deliveries, nothing untoward so far," Gwynne said.

"I heard Mildred tell him she'd have tea ready when he got back," I said. "That's dinner around here, so he's going to be gone several hours. He said he had the last package to deliver."

The radio squawked, and the corporal handed the receiver to Gwynne.

"Blast! Bunch has gone missing. He went into the Rose and Crown, made what looked like a regular delivery, then never came out," Gwynne said.

"Back door," I said. "Someone was waiting."

"Listen," Diana said as the sound of a truck's grinding gears echoed against the hillside. "Haycock."

"Steady on," Gwynne said, crouching lower. "Miss Seaton, you may wish to move back and see to your horse."

In response, Diana withdrew a .32 Colt automatic from her jacket and flicked the safety off. "Dante will be fine, thank you."

"You know how to use that thing, Miss?" asked the corporal.

"She knows," Gwynne said, a faint smile curling his mustache. In a moment, two trucks drove into the scene below, one braking near the barn and the other by the house. Soldiers spilled out and took cover, and Lieutenant Haycock shouted for anyone inside to come out.

Two shots rang out from the house, answered by a Bren gun spraying the windows. Pistol shots came from the barn and got the same response. It was a lot of firepower, and I hoped these Right Club guys hadn't hidden any heavy hardware close by.

More shots came from the house, and now everyone joined in to eliminate the threat. I kept my eye on the barn as smoke started to billow from the open door. Haycock ordered the firing to stop and charged the house with four men, kicking in the door and leading the way.

I didn't like the looks of that fire. The smoke was pouring out now, and the sheep in the paddock were bleating madly and huddling on the far side, away from the barn. Visibility was poor, and between the animals and the shouts from inside the house, it was impossible to tell what was happening.

"Freddie," I said. "That fire is a diversion."

"Come on, then," Gwynne said to me. He told the corporal to follow along and his two men to watch for anyone escaping this way. At the bottom of the hill, Gwynne yelled out, "Scotland Yard" a few times, good insurance against getting shot by a trigger-happy Tommy. He had the corporal with him, and the uniform was a clear signal as to which side they were on. At Gwynne's order, the corporal radioed for Big Mike to be escorted in.

"Haycock!" I said, spotting him coming out of the house. "Whoever was in that barn used the smoke screen to get away."

Haycock quickly ordered his men to circle around and search up the hill.

"Two dead inside," he said. "Mildred Bunch was in the basement. She's unhurt."

"Odds are she's going to play the innocent wife, forced into silence by her cruel husband," I said. "But I heard her loud and clear when she urged Alfred to kill me."

"We need to question her now," Gwynne said. "Bunch is in the wind, and he's likely carrying explosives."

"Nigel. She mentioned Nigel," I said. "She didn't want Alfred to tell Nigel that they'd killed me. Said he was too nervous already."

"Which means Alfred was going to see Nigel," Diana said. "That could have been who picked Alfred up at the pub."

"Or Alfred is being taken to Nigel. At Sandringham House," Gwynne said, his face furrowed with worry.

"There's an army unit on duty, isn't there?" I said.

"Only when the royal family is in residence," Gwynne said. "I don't know their schedule—that's kept confidential. The rest of the time, the local Home Guard patrols the grounds."

"But the staff would be told," I said. "Nigel would know, even if he was informed only at the last minute. He's in the Home Guard as well."

"Then using the cottage as a staging area makes sense," Diana said. "They could be ready to move it at a moment's notice. Doesn't Alfred deliver meat to the staff?"

"He does," Gwynne said. "He could have been bringing blocks of plastic explosive with each trip. This last delivery could be the detonators."

"I'd bet they're the twenty-four-hour type," I said. "And that the royals are arriving tomorrow. Shorty told me they wanted to get rid of the foreigners and dark-skinned types once the war was over. Maybe this is the start of a bombing campaign with that as the goal."

"Or an attempt to bring the Duke of Windsor back. Who knows with these people," Diana said.

"Haycock!" Gwynne shouted. "Any luck?"

"No, sir," Haycock said, running up to report. "But there were some planks kicked out. He definitely lit that fire and got away. Should we fan out and go after him?"

"No. He's too smart to be wandering through the woods. Send someone to bring my men down from up there," he said. "Turn the Bunch woman over to them—they'll know what to do. Leave one lorry here and have the men conduct a thorough search. You and the others will come with me."

"Where to, sir?"

"Sandringham House," Gwynne said. "Who knows, you may get to meet royalty."

"Diana," I said. "Can you ride back and get word to Kaz? I'll head to Sandringham with Big Mike as soon as he shows up."

"We'll follow you," she said.

"In the jeep this time, not on horseback," I said, just as Big Mike pulled up in the sedan with a grim-faced detective at his side.

"It was fun riding to your rescue," she said. "But I can do the same in the jeep."

"What's going on?" Big Mike demanded. "This plainclothes copper won't tell me a thing."

"I'll fill you in on the way," I said, wondering how we were ever going to find the explosives if they'd already been planted in that massive building.

"Captain Boyle, if you are inviting Lieutenant Kazimierz to join us, please tell him Special Branch would be honored to have the assistance of the Polish Armed Forces," Gwynne said. "Now, on to Sandringham, and God Save the King!"

CHAPTER FORTY-ONE

"So WE'RE AFTER a plumber who has the keys to seventy-eight bathrooms in some damn mansion with a couple hundred bedrooms? Seems like we should call ahead and have security evacuate the joint," Big Mike said.

"That would only alert Alfred and Nigel," I said. "I don't want to let them get away. It was probably Alfred who killed David Archer, and I want him to pay for that."

"You sure about that?" Big Mike said as he sped up. Haycock's truck was behind us.

"I think David Archer was killed because he spotted Freddie Leese with Alfred on several occasions," I said, explaining about Freddie's fascist uncle. "I didn't see Freddie at the pub the night David was murdered, but I bet Freddie forced Alfred to silence Archer. Alfred was probably willing enough, but not Nigel. He's the weak link."

"Wait, didn't you tell me Archer was keeping track of who came and went at Marston Hall?" Big Mike said.

"Yep. Which means there may be treasure hidden at Marston Hall, but there were also explosives," I said. "Alfred's deliveries provided cover for moving them out of Marston Hall and then on to Sandringham House."

"Jesus," Big Mike said. "Alfred and his pals must have stockpiled that stuff before the war."

"Right. They were hoping for a German invasion that would

bring British fascists to power," I said. "Now their goal after the war is to get rid of anyone who isn't a white Englishman."

"Meaning it's fine for Indian troops and others from a dozen nations to fight and die to help Great Britain win, but they don't want them as neighbors in peacetime."

"Poles, Jamaicans, Indians, Czechs, the Right Club wants them all gone, and it looks like they're ready to set off a few well-placed charges to underscore their point," I said.

"Fanatics," Big Mike muttered. "Listen, I get why we can't alert anyone at Sandringham House, but Gwynne must have notified Scotland Yard, right?"

"I hope so," I said. "If my hunch about the royals showing up tomorrow is right, then the Royal Horse Guards may be on duty already."

But this time there was no armored car parked across the straightaway that ran under arched trees. We drove on, into open space, until we came to that huge brickwork mansion—four stories of limestone trim shimmering in the sun.

"You gotta be kidding me," Big Mike said, craning his neck to look at the entire building. I told him to pull around back as Haycock's truck braked by the main entrance. We went into the kitchen where I'd last seen Nigel. A woman with an apron and wispy gray hair done up in a scarf was peeling potatoes. That had been dug up by a princess.

"Hello," I said. "I'm looking for Nigel Fernsby. I met him in Slewford, and he said I should stop by."

"Oh, he did, did he? We don't encourage casual visitors, Captain," she said. "You've just missed him anyway. He went off with his cousin. To the pub in Dersingham be my guess."

"Alfred," I said, spotting the package wrapped in butcher paper behind her.

"Yes, Alfred. What a nice man, and his prices so reasonable."

"I'll bet you cook up a fine lamb roast, ma'am," Big Mike said, walking over to the counter and lifting the package, giving me a confirming nod that it was indeed meat. "I wish we were staying for dinner, but we promised Nigel we'd come see him. Sorry if it's not allowed."

"You'd best move along, both of you," she said with a kindly smile, the result of Big Mike's compliment. "You don't want to be here when the Horse Guards show up. They're all business, that lot."

"We'd better hurry then," I said.

She glanced at a clock on the wall. "You've got about thirty minutes. So off with you."

Out front, we found Gwynne in earnest conversation with a man in a dark three-piece suit, the same guy who'd been working on ledgers in the office when I was last here. He didn't look happy.

"I don't know why they're gone, I tell you," he said. "The Home Guard should still be here."

"There's half an hour until the Royal Horse Guards arrive," I said.

"So this chap tells me, and that the Home Guard stood down an hour ago," Gwynne said. "Orders, most likely forged. Scotland Yard is trying to get in touch with the Horse Guards. Hopefully that will spur them on to get here ahead of schedule, and with a bomb disposal unit."

"There isn't time to search this place," Big Mike said, gesturing with his hand at the expanse looming above us.

"We can help," Three-Piece said, looking a little confused. "We've dozens of staff on duty."

"You need to evacuate those people, and now," Gwynne said. "I'll have men search each floor and post a guard at the entrance."

"But why?" Three-Piece said.

"I told you. There's a chance a bomb was planted," Gwynne said. He'd downplayed it, probably not wanting to panic the poor guy.

"I understand, but why here?"

"This is Sandringham House, that's why!" Gwynne shouted, then caught himself. "Wait, what do you mean?"

"The royals haven't stepped foot inside here since war was declared," he said. "They use Appleton House. No one is supposed to know."

"Nigel said there are cottages on the grounds," I said, remembering how he'd bragged about his responsibilities.

"Where, man?" Gwynne said, shaking Three-Piece by the shoulder. He spat out the directions, and Gwynne ordered two men to guard the entrance to the main house and two others to patrol inside while the radioman corporal set up in the foyer. Haycock and the remaining two men were to follow us in five minutes and cover the exits from Appleton House.

"We need these guys alive," I said to Haycock. "Fire only if you have to."

"Hurry!" Gwynne said as the three of us piled into the sedan and drove down a curving drive. We took a right at the stables and pulled over as soon as the cottage was in sight. Some cottage.

It was huge, two stories topped by ornate gables. Solid-red brick covered in ivy. I put it at about twenty rooms, minimum.

"If it's just the two of them, they may be busy," Big Mike said, turning off the ignition. We were about fifty yards from the place, with a decent view of the front door and side of the building. Which meant Alfred could be staring right at us. "You gotta figure the plastic explosive was hidden and now they need to get to it with the detonators. Might take some work."

"Do you have any idea what weapons they may have?" I asked Gwynne as we got out of the automobile and quietly shut the doors.

"Other than revolvers? No, but we did have a report that the local arms cache included several Thompson submachines, courtesy of your Lend-Lease," Gwynne said. "They were stolen in 1941 and never recovered. The Right Club was suspected." We moved into the wooded area along the road, stopping at the edge of the tree line.

"Did Alfred buy your bit as a BUF sympathizer?" I asked Gwynne as we knelt and peered through the branches.

"Yes, I'm sure he did," Gwynne said. "But I never pressed the point since I didn't want him suspicious. We talked about people we knew in common, all of whom are still incarcerated. He responded well to anything I said about Jews. I took your Polish friend's name in vain quite often, and he enjoyed that."

"Can't wait to meet this guy," Big Mike said. "Would he believe you were with the Right Club?"

"No, I doubt it. They run a tight ship," Gwynne said. "But I did mention how ineffectual Mosley had been. Alfred called him a tool of the Jews, and we had a laugh about that. I do see where you're going, and I must say, it might work."

"Or you might get shot dead," I said.

"I think Alfred will give me the benefit of the doubt," he said. "And I don't see Nigel as a threat. It sounds like I'm off to warn my fascist comrade that the cavalry is on its way."

"Hang on," Big Mike said. "You see that round tower on the right, by the door? It's got no windows." There was a stout two-story tower with crenellated stonework at the top, the kind of architectural decoration the English liked to add to their country estates.

"We could make a run for it. If they're watching, we'd have a better chance than you strolling up there," I said to Gwynne. "And if they don't spot us, we'll be in position to move in once they open the door for you."

"If I wanted to stand watch, I'd be up on that tower," Gwynne said, squinting as he studied the layout. "No sign of them, so I'd say you have a good chance. Soon as you're in place, I'll walk up and shout for Alfred."

"You up for a sprint?" I asked Big Mike.

"Race you," he said, jumping up and taking the lead. I

followed, pumping my legs as fast as I could and making for the tower wall. Big Mike slowed into a lumbering gait. Still, he made it to the wall before me, going to his knees, glancing up, and watching for any sign of a guard above. Nothing.

I went low, hugging the wall and looking around the back of the cottage. A conservatory jutted out about halfway down, looking out over sloping gardens. Peaceful. Unlike the feel of blood pounding in my head.

No one to be seen. I went back to Big Mike and gave Gwynne the nod. I knelt just out of sight of the door, about six feet away, with Big Mike looming over me.

"Oi! Bunch!" Gwynne bellowed, his arms held out at his side. "Don't shoot. It's me, Roland Gwynne!"

Even through the brickwork, I heard boots coming down the staircase inside. Fast. It wasn't a stealthy approach, and that meant they weren't coming out shooting. I hoped. I holstered my revolver and took Shorty's knife out of my pocket.

"What are you doing here?" Nigel asked. "Alfred's working." Nigel's voice quavered. He had a bad case of the nerves, and he wasn't hiding it well.

"I've come to warn him," Gwynne said. "Scotland Yard raided his farm. They'll be here soon. I'm one of you, mate."

"That's what Alfred said, but I don't know," Nigel said.

I heard Nigel move back. I couldn't let him slam the door on Gwynne. I bolted to the open door. Gwynne was standing to the side, leaving me a clear path to grab Nigel. I flung my arm around his neck and held the knife against his cheek.

"Quiet," I whispered. Nigel's eyes went wide as I walked him outside and Gwynne checked for weapons. "Where's Alfred?"

"Upstairs," Nigel croaked. "Putting the floorboards back. They made me do it."

"Shut up," Gwynne said, producing a set of handcuffs and securing Nigel's hands behind his back. "Is he setting the detonators?"

"It's done," Nigel said, breaking into a sob.

"Nigel!" Alfred bellowed from upstairs. "You all right?"

"Let's go," Gwynne said, grasping Nigel's arm and shoving him into the foyer. "Tell him you're fine, then leave it to me." Inside, it was dark and gloomy, the heavy wooden paneling deadening what little light shone through the closed curtains.

"Yes, it's Chief Inspector Gwynne. He came to warn us," Nigel said, the words catching in his throat.

"Bunch! You've got to get out. Scotland Yard is coming. Hurry!"

A submachine gun blast from the upstairs hallway lit up the room; the muzzle flash like a bolt of lightning in the darkness. I dove past Nigel's body as it fell onto Gwynne, and made for cover beneath the balustraded walkway above. I blinked rapidly, trying to vanquish the white light burned into them.

Two shots came from the doorway, Big Mike blasting away at the shooter. I saw Big Mike run in and grab Gwynne by the collar, pulling him out from under Nigel's shattered body. I darted out, firing two quick shots upstairs, hoping to at least distract the shooter. I heard footsteps and moved against the wall, shielding myself from view.

I didn't like the odds much. A .38 revolver wasn't much of a match for a Tommy gun. I trusted that Big Mike was covering the front door and that Haycock would be arriving soon. Meantime, I needed to get the drop on Alfred.

I moved into the next room through an arched entryway. A table and chairs for twenty. A mirror above the fireplace on the wall opposite. Ten feet down on this wall, another open archway. I caught a glimpse in the mirror: the reflection of a figure moving toward me. I almost raised my pistol and fired, then stopped myself, still trying to focus my eyes through the swirling spots.

He hadn't seen me, or rather, my reflection.

I raised my revolver and aimed, straight at the mirror. Nothing. I thumped my boot lightly against the wall, drawing his attention.

He let loose with the Thompson, shattering glass as the sound reverberated in the enclosed space. I dove forward toward the opening and rolled, bringing up my arm and firing once, then again, at the shadowy figure holding the gun.

I stood, advancing to the body, pistol at the ready, the air thick with gun smoke.

I'd missed with one shot, but the other had hit Alfred in the chest. He wheezed as blood bubbled out of his nostrils. I kicked the Thompson away and knelt by his side.

"Where are the explosives?" I asked. "Help us. There's a bomb disposal unit coming. The royal family has been warned. Do the right thing, Alfred. For Mildred's sake."

"Go to hell." He gasped, spitting blood.

"Why kill Nigel? He didn't want any part of this, did he?"

"Nigel," Alfred managed before his last breath left him with a stunned look on his face.

"Billy?" Big Mike hollered.

"In here," I said, picking up the Thompson. "How's Gwynne?"

"Took one in the arm, but he'll be okay," Big Mike said. "Haycock has a medic bandaging him up right now. Looks like the bomb squad will have to find the charges the hard way."

"Yeah. Alfred told me to go to hell when I asked him to help us," I said.

"Well, he killed his cousin and tried to blow up the king and queen, so that's not surprising. Let's get out of here. The Horse Guards will be here soon," Big Mike said.

Outside, a medic was wrapping Gwynne's arm as he sat in the cab of the truck parked on the lawn.

"Pull it tight, lad, I'm not done here yet," Gwynne told the medic, who obliged with another round of bandaging.

"Through and through," Big Mike said. "Best way to take a .45 slug if you have to."

"All clear inside?" Gwynne asked, wincing as he tried to move his arm.

"Alfred's dead. He didn't have much to say," I told him. "Looks like it's up to the bomb squad now."

"He was a brute to kill his own cousin like that," Gwynne said. "I never stood a chance of seeing him in that dark hallway."

Haycock's men were carrying out the bodies as Kaz and Diana drove up in the jeep, halting next to us.

"Your radioman said the Royal Horse Guards are five minutes out, Chief Inspector," Kaz said, surveying Gwynne's bandaged arm. "That must hurt."

Diana stood in the jeep, shielding her eyes from the sun, looking up at the tower.

A thump in the grass and a green Plasticine bundle bounced ten feet from us.

Diana drew her pistol and snapped off several rounds at the turret, startling everyone into action.

"Bomb!" she yelled.

Nobel 808, with a yellow color-coded detonator. The ten-minute variety.

Freddie Leese looked down at us with a mad grin, then vanished.

CHAPTER FORTY-TWO

BIG MIKE WENT for the bomb like a linebacker scooping up a fumble. He grasped it in one of his big mitts and threw it high and far into the gardens between the woods and the house. Before it hit, I was off, making for the cottage in hopes of spotting Freddie before he got outside and disappeared into the forested landscape.

An explosion cracked the air. The bomb went off harmlessly, unless you counted the rosebushes.

Kaz was a few paces behind me. "Cover the door!" I shouted to him. "Go right," I then told Haycock, who was gaining on Kaz.

I planned on going left, hoping to spot Freddie vaulting out a window. Diana was on my heels, and I knew better than to tell her which way to go, so I sped up, making the turn at the corner before skidding to a halt and kneeling. I held out my revolver, scanning the windows and the rear door adjacent to the conservatory. Nothing.

I felt Diana's hand on my shoulder.

"Watch our six," I whispered, and she turned to keep an eye on the windows behind us. Freddie could pop out and surprise us from any one of them.

Another explosion boomed on the other side of the conservatory, not far from us. It was smaller but still powerful enough to shatter a lot of glass.

"A diversion," Diana whispered. "That was meant to drive us to cover. I hope Haycock's all right."

"Here comes Freddie," I said, watching a shadow flit through the conservancy. The snout of a Thompson emerged from the door at the far end of the glass-enclosed structure. A single shot sounded from the other side of the conservancy, suggesting that the lieutenant was still standing. The Thompson vanished, and a quick *rat-a-tat-tat* burst was sent in Haycock's direction, giving me half a chance.

"Cover me," I said, knowing that Diana's small pistol wasn't accurate at this range, but it might make Freddie duck. I launched myself, beelining for the open conservatory door, hoping that Freddie would be too busy watching for Haycock to notice my sprint.

But Freddie knew time was short and that he had to get away. I was ten yards out when the Thompson showed itself again as the door was cautiously opened. I sped up, lengthening my stride, then slammed into the door before Freddie had both feet out. He screamed and pushed back, trying to get the muzzle of his weapon pointed at me, but I held tight, keeping him pinned in place and hoping someone on my side would show up and break this stalemate.

I heard Diana coming up behind me. Freddie squeezed off a few rounds that didn't come close to either of us. There was no angle for Diana to get off a shot, what with me pressed against the door and Freddie's finger still on the trigger.

"I'll kill you!" Freddie's voice was a ragged curse. "Get out of the way!"

A shot sounded from within the conservatory. Freddie grunted, and his hold on the Thompson loosened. I let go of the door and grabbed his weapon, yanking it away as he slipped to the ground, clutching his leg.

"Bastard!" he yelled, looking up at Kaz who held his smoking Webley aimed at Freddie's head.

"Polish bastard to you," Kaz said.

"Get me out of here!" Freddie screamed, pulling himself out of the doorway.

"Bomb!" I shouted, grabbing Freddie by the collar and dragging him onto the lawn. Kaz got a hold of Freddie as well, and we made it to a set of stone stairs leading down to the garden. Diana yelled the warning again, telling everyone to get away from the conservatory.

"When?" I demanded of Freddie, who was back to moaning while he clasped the wound on his thigh.

The *boom* of another explosion sent shards of glass flying. I covered Diana with my arms as debris rained down on us, while Freddie laughed like a maniac. I brushed myself off and saw that the front of the conservancy had been blown away. Freddie must've been hoping we'd pursue him through it.

He hadn't shielded his face as the glass came down, and blood welled up from the shards impaled in his forehead.

"Too bad it didn't get a few of you," Freddie said, blinking away the blood seeping into an eye. "I need a doctor."

Diana rose to signal Haycock and Big Mike.

"There's one on the way," I told him, glancing at Kaz, who still had his Webley at the ready. "You shot Nigel, didn't you? Not Alfred."

"Alfred was weak," Freddie said, his skin turning white. He was about to go into shock, and I needed to keep him talking.

"You can't be in your business," I said.

"No. It had to be done. All of it," he said. "I felt bad about Archer, but he'd seen too much. Wasn't much of a life for him anyway, was it?"

"I understand," I said, trying to soothe him. "Help's on the way. Listen, there's a bomb squad coming too. Just decent Englishmen, your own people. How about you make it easy on them and tell us where the explosives are hidden? It's all over."

"No, it isn't. There's more of us ... and more weapons," Freddie said. "We'll have another go, don't you worry."

"I wouldn't count on the weapons cache at Marston Hall," Kaz said.

"What d'ya mean?" Freddie snarled.

"We have it all," Kaz said. "The Nobel 808, the detonators, the Colt automatic pistols, and more Thompsons. The treasure of Marston Hall."

"Stretcher-bearers are on their way," Big Mike announced as he stood over Freddie. "This ain't your day, kid. I bet your Uncle Arnold is going to be real sore you screwed up."

"He'll even be madder when we announce you informed, Freddie," I said, winking at Kaz.

"I'm not talking," Freddie said through gritted teeth.

"But you already did," Kaz said. "How else would we know where to find the weapons? People have been searching Marston Hall for years and never found them. Of course it was you."

"No one likes a snitch," I said. "Especially not in prison, which is where you're headed."

"You can't," he cried, with all the anguish of someone who knew with certainty we would.

"Just tell us where the bombs are," I said. "If you're square with us, we won't say a thing. Hold out, and your change of heart will be announced to the newspapers. That's a death warrant for you."

"Master bedroom, under the center floorboards," Freddie gasped out. "And the downstairs sitting room. That's it."

"Good, Freddie," I said, stepping aside for the medic and stretcher-bearers.

"How'd you find the cache?" he said, wincing as the medic checked his leg wound.

"Oh, I didn't actually find it," Kaz said. "Sorry for the confusion. I did find a list of what was hidden, though. Based on the small number of you here and the size of this house, I conjectured there was still more of everything at Marston Hall. I see I was correct."

Freddie gave out another gasp of pain, and whether it was

from Kaz's revelation or the medic probing his wound was anyone's guess. I sure didn't give a damn.

"Sounds like you had a good day at Marston Hall," I said to
Kaz as we left Freddie to be bandaged and bound.

"Well, *I* wasn't rescued by a lovely vision on horseback, but it
was an interesting morning nonetheless," Kaz said. "I'll tell you
all about it on the way back."

"Nice routine you ran on Freddie," Big Mike said. "Maybe it'd
work on Mildred. She doesn't know her husband is toes up."

"Why not try?" Kaz said. "We might learn the actual location
of the arms cache."

"And the treasure?" I asked.

"Ah, the treasure," Kaz said. "Still a mystery, but I learned a
good deal about Stephen Elliot's findings. He spent years
researching the lost crown jewels, most of the time trying to
calculate tides and water flow to find where the treasure might
have gotten to."

"Wait, he left a record of the weapons he'd hidden for the
Right Club but nothing about the treasure?" Diana said. "Does
that mean he never found it?"

"I think it means he feared for his life," Kaz said. "He had
second thoughts about the Right Club and what they were planning in case of an invasion by the Nazis. He wanted out."

"How do you know?" Diana asked as we stopped to watch the
arrival of the Royal Horse Guards.

"He left a letter," Kaz said, patting his jacket pocket. "It is
likely what Alfred and Mildred were hunting for. It contained
the list I mentioned, and several names associated with the
plot, including the Bunches. He'd likely threatened them with
it. It was unfinished, but there was enough information to
send people to the gallows. It is pure conjecture on my part,
but he could have been writing it the very night the bomber
crashed."

"He put it away and left to investigate," I said, waving over

Sergeant Bromley, who was standing with Gwynne, "then ran into Alfred, who suspected what he was up to."

"Or perhaps Elliot admitted it," Kaz said. "Our only hope of knowing is to convince Mildred to tell us the truth."

"Trickery is our only chance," Big Mike said as Sergeant Bromley headed to us. I gave the sergeant the location of the explosives and warned him about the ten-minute detonators Freddie had used.

"Does trouble follow you, Captain, or did you chase it here?" Bromley asked, surveying the damage to the conservatory and garden.

"Believe it or not, Sarge, this is how I'm spending my leave," I said.

"Right, Captain," Bromley said. "Seeing the local sights, were you? And just happened to thwart a bomb plot against the royal family?"

"Bit of a busman's holiday," Kaz said.

"You lot better move out before the brass shows up," Bromley said, glancing back at the line of vehicles making their arrival. "They'll be all over the place soon as we sound the all clear. You've saved us from a disaster, so who am I to keep you from what's left of your leave?"

"How much time do we have left, Billy?" Diana asked as we walked back to her car.

"Not much," I said. "Maybe we should get away from here and spend a couple of quiet nights in London. Just us and a few V-2s."

"Sounds absolutely peaceful," Diana said. "Now go have your chat with Mrs. Bunch."

CHAPTER FORTY-THREE

WE HAD A powwow with Chief Inspector Gwynne back at the King's Lynn police station. With his bandaged arm in a sling, he read Elliot's letter, smoothing out the pages carefully with his good hand and nodding in approval. Each of the two pages had been folded several times to fit in the hiding place.

"It seems as though Stephen Elliot redeemed himself at the last possible moment," Gwynne said, pocketing the sheets. "This is dated the twentieth of May 1942. The day the bomber went down."

"But too late," I said. "He was probably killed over his reluctance to continue with the plot."

"Perhaps not too late to do some good," Kaz said. "It caused his death, but without that event, there would have been no investigation when the aircraft was discovered."

"True enough," Gwynne said. "But that doesn't answer why his body was found inside the bomber, does it?"

It didn't, and I kept what thoughts I had about that to myself. I did ask Gwynne if he was up to interrogating Mildred. He'd lost blood, and his white bandage showed traces of red seeping through. He waved off the idea of waiting and insisted on interviewing Mildred Bunch as soon as possible, which was the smart move. As far as she knew, the explosives hadn't been discovered. That gave her the chance to pin everything on Alfred, but only if she did so prior to detonation. She was cunning enough to know that if a royal residence was blown up, anyone connected to the plot would be imprisoned.

"I'm afraid you and Alfred are going to have to change places, so to speak," Gwynne said as he settled into his office chair, cradling his wounded arm.

"If Billy is dead, then there are no witnesses to Mildred's active role in the plot," Kaz said.

"Indeed," Gwynne said. "There are the two men we captured at the farm, but she knows they might say anything to save their skins. It's the testimony of a US Army investigator she'd fear."

"Why does Alfred need to be alive?" I asked, not enjoying my act as a dead man after almost getting the part for real.

"I don't want her distracted by any actual grief she may feel," Gwynne said. "She can justify selling Alfred out since he'd serve time or visit the gallows in any case. He might even be glad she could betray him to save herself. But if she's distraught and blaming us for her husband's death, it could all go off the rails."

"Okay, makes sense," I said. "My bet is that she'll play the bewildered spouse, too frightened of her husband to disobey him." After overhearing Mildred at her home, I was beginning to think she was the more brutal of the pair.

"Mildred also may have reason to think she could get away with it," Kaz said. "Since we found no trace of the explosives at the farm, she could claim ignorance of what was hidden in that ruined cottage."

"True," Gwynne said. "But this letter you found clearly implicates her and Alfred by name. Even though it's unsigned, I am certain we can match the handwriting to a sample of Elliot's. What I want from her are the names of other conspirators. I won't let on I have this letter until she's signed a statement to us giving information about them."

"Seeing as how I'm deceased, and we know Mildred will get her backup if a foreigner sits in, we might as well get to Marston Hall. If you don't need us, that is," I said. The last thing I wanted to do was get caught up in police paperwork. The less involved we were, the better.

"You were never here," Gwynne said. "Do you think you can find where the rest of the weapons are hidden?"

"When I stumbled across where Elliot had hidden his letter, I discovered some materials that might be helpful," Kaz said. "But then Diana came to fetch me, and we went to the Bunches' farm straightaway."

"Where was the letter?" Gwynne asked.

"Concealed in a desk drawer," Kaz said. "Which gave me an idea. We shall let you know if it bears fruit."

"How'd you find that false bottom?" I asked Kaz as we drove to Marston Hall. The sun was setting, lighting the sky with reds and golds.

"It was a false side, actually. I had emptied all the drawers in Elliot's desk and gone through everything," he said. "I took each drawer and checked for false bottoms, but none were apparent. Then I noticed both sides of the center drawer were thicker than the others. After pressing and pushing every which way, one side finally opened. The unfinished letter was folded into a slight cavity."

"You said something about that giving you an idea," I said.

"The file cabinet contained architectural drawings of Marston Hall," Kaz said. "Some of them quite old and others showing additions and restoration work done over the years. I'd like to consult them more carefully."

Kaz didn't say anything more than that. He was onto something, but his research had been interrupted by the inconvenience of a bomb plot against the royal family. I knew he was itching to get back to the library and finish his work, so I didn't bother him with a lot of questions. I had unformed ideas to work on myself.

Once we arrived, Kaz took the stairs two at a time, making

for the library. I'd forgotten entirely about Colonel Cheatwood and had no idea if he was still cooling his heels at the police station or if Gwynne had cut him loose. Curious, I headed for his office, only to pass a British Army motorcycle courier on his way out.

Inside, Lieutenant Haycock and Major Hudson were leafing through a file, looking surprised. I knocked on the open door and asked if Cheatwood was in.

"He's been relieved of command, Captain," Haycock said, gaping in shock. "We just received the news. The colonel is facing a court-martial for conduct unbecoming an officer and a gentleman."

"That covers a wide range of offenses in the British Army," Major Hudson said. "You have any idea what this is about, Captain Boyle?"

"Oh no," Haycock moaned before I could respond. "I've been promoted."

"That's good news. You deserve it," I said.

"Thank you, but my captaincy is for the command of the British section at Marston Hall," Haycock said. "Now I'll never get to the front. Sorry, Major, no offense intended."

"Don't worry," Hudson said, tamping down a grin. "And congratulations."

"Listen, Haycock," I said. "Here are two pieces of advice. First, keep Charlotte Mothersole at a distance. Second, if you do get to the front lines, stay low. Both are in your best interest."

"You think she had anything to do with Cheatwood's dismissal?" Hudson asked.

"Maybe. What I do know for sure is that while Cheatwood played up his connection with security at Sandringham House, the Royal Horse Guards had no idea about him. I think he was promoting his own importance to stay in command here in order to search for loot Elliot might have stashed away," I said. Not to mention promoting a relationship he had little true interest in.

Cheatwood was a cad, and his affair with Mrs. Mothersole wouldn't go over well with his commanding officer, especially if the widow herself had made a complaint. Maybe she'd seen through Cheatwood's game, or perhaps she simply no longer saw the need for a partner to search through Marston Hall with. After all, she could wait until the war was over and search at her leisure.

Right?

Upstairs in the library, Kaz had papers laid out on a table. Plans and drawings of Marston Hall, some on yellowed paper, showing a much smaller building. Others highlighted the design of an addition, while the newest—from the last century—showed the added turrets and other Victorian design elements.

"First, let me show you this." Kaz set down a large leather-bound book on Elliot's desk. He opened the thick volume to the title page. "It's all here."

Roger of Wendover's Flowers of History: Comprising the History of England from the Descent of the Saxons to A.D. 1235.

"Flowers of history?" I asked.

"A bit florid, but it is a contemporary account of King John's rule. Written in the thirteenth century, but this edition was published in the nineteenth. It gives an account of what was lost in the Wash when the king's baggage train tried to cross it."

"I've seen the Wash in a storm," I said. "I have to wonder why they didn't go around."

"As you can see by the old maps Elliot has, the Wash was much larger in those days. Over the centuries, land has been reclaimed for farming and grazing. John was waging war against rebel barons and laying siege to their castles. He did not have the luxury of a slow, roundabout journey. He had to get north, and quickly."

As Kaz explained it, Wendover's book described how guides were used to take travelers across the Wash at low tide. Even then, the wet sands were treacherous and there were deep streams that had to be forded. No one knew exactly what happened, but the possibility of heavy fog was mentioned, and that the baggage train, which comprised three thousand men guarding the king's household goods, became trapped in the mud and wet sand. The sudden incoming tide apparently hit them hard, based on the lines Kaz read from the book.

"He lost all his carts, wagons, and baggage horses, together with his money, costly vessels, and everything which he had a particular regard for; the land opened in the middle of the water and caused whirlpools which sucked in every thing, as well as men and horses, so that no one escaped to tell the king of the misfortune."

Then came the list of valuables thought to be carried in the baggage train.

One hundred and forty-three cups, fourteen goblets, fourteen dishes, forty belts, fifty-two rings and pendants, four shrines, two gold crosses, three gold combs, a gold vessel ornamented with pearls, the king's coronation robe, a gold scepter, a necklace set with diamonds surrounded by rubies and emeralds, and a crown set with precious stones.

"Now that's a treasure," I said. "So where is it?"

"By now, probably gone, spread by tides and streams, buried under mud, or deep under land reclaimed by later generations," Kaz said. "There could be the odd item working its way up through the muck, but there is little evidence of that."

"So what's everyone searching for?"

"Ah," Kaz said, raising a finger. "Excellent question. I found a bookmarked page in a historical journal. It tells of a local baron, Robert Tiptoft, who in the next century came into great wealth. It was rumored he found the king's treasure, or some part of it. Or perhaps his grandfather had and kept it hidden."

"Where does that get us?" I asked.

"It tells us why there is no evidence of Stephen Elliot searching the local waterways for the treasure," Kaz said. "Because he was looking for it right here. He might have started his research trying to determine where the treasure was in the Wash, but I believe he gave that up to search Marston Hall."

"In the library?" I said, feeling a little thickheaded.

"No, here," Kaz said, stabbing his finger at the old plans. "Somewhere in the original foundation. See? The building dates from the early thirteenth century."

"Right after the treasure was lost," I said.

"Yes. The Crown would have wanted its property back. An unscrupulous lord might have hidden it. And look here, the addition that was made in the fifteenth century enlarged the rooms off the original foundation. That is what gave me the idea."

"I'm having a hard time keeping up, Kaz. What idea?"

"Sorry. I am too excited to explain properly." He grabbed another historical journal, this one from the turn of the century. "See here? In the fourteenth century, Marston Hall was owned by Philip Howard, a member of one of the most prominent Catholic families in England."

"Yeah, I see, but I don't get it," I said.

"Queen Elizabeth outlawed Catholicism in the sixteenth century. Priests and the practice of Roman Catholicism were banned under pain of death," Kaz said, looking at me and hoping I'd smarten up.

"Priest holes!" I finally shouted, remembering some lesson the nuns had taught us. "Catholic families would hide priests, right?"

"Exactly. Many Catholics pretended to convert to the Church of England but would secretly hold masses and shelter traveling priests. A dangerous business, one that required a well-constructed hiding place."

"The vicar told me Marston Hall had its first addition built during the reign of Queen Elizabeth," I said. "They may have built the priest hole then."

"Yes," Kaz said, his eyes glinting with excitement. "Based on these plans and papers, I'd say Elliot had been searching for the priest hole for years, hoping he would find treasure hidden there. Whatever he uncovered, it became the perfect hiding place for a weapons cache."

"How do we know where to look?"

"Right here." Kaz stabbed a finger at the yellowed scroll. "Where the addition abutted the original foundation. It would have been the most obvious location from a builder's perspective."

"But they didn't build these things in obvious locations, did they?"

"Of course not, and they also had to be constructed in secrecy," Kaz said. "The Howard family would not have wanted anyone from the village to see what they were doing. Working at the rear of their existing foundation would have shielded them from scrutiny. The problem will be finding the access point."

A few minutes later, we were in the basement. It was extensive, with whitewashed walls and concrete floors. We found a thick wooden door with iron hinges and went through into another world. We had to stoop as we switched on flashlights and explored the empty, dark space. The foundation was bare rock, and the floor was hard-packed dirt that gave off an odor of decay and mold.

"Here, on either side of the door," Kaz said, his flashlight beam dancing on the brick wall. "Somewhere."

The wall was old brick, red and dusty. Two wooden support beams on each side of the door were set into the brick, with a massive beam running across the top of them. The wood grain matched the door, and it all seemed centuries old.

"How do we find anything?" I asked, pressing my fingers against the brick and getting nothing but a reddish stain for my troubles.

"Any secret door would be extraordinarily well hidden," Kaz said. "There were priests who specialized in building them, as well as agents of the Crown whose job it was to find them. But we have an advantage the queen's men did not possess."

"What?" I asked, once again a step behind Kaz.

"Elliot and Bunch must have felt fairly secure in their choice of hiding place," he said, his light slowly playing over the surface. "But they came and went a number of times, using the door far more often than the original owners ever did."

"So they would have disturbed something," I said, moving to the other side of the door and searching for a section of brickwork that looked different, or maybe an exposed seam. After ten minutes of careful eyeballing, nothing.

Kaz came up empty as well. We went back out into the full basement and confirmed the walls lined up. No hidden chamber, or at least no sign of the space for one.

"This has to be the place," Kaz muttered to himself as we ducked back into the old cellar. "Perhaps the outer foundation."

No dice. The wall consisted of large pieces of solid stone fitted together by a stonemason who knew his job.

"The dirt floor?" I suggested, although it made little sense. There was no sign of excavation, certainly not in this century. Even so, I searched the ground for any hint of disturbance. My flashlight stopped at the base of the brick wall, near the rightmost erect wooden column, which was perpendicular to the dirt floor.

"What is it?" Kaz asked, bringing his own light to bear.

"Is that a heel print?" I pointed to a faint crescent-moon shape in the dirt. It was so close to the brick that there wouldn't have been room for a full footprint.

"Yes, I think it is," Kaz said. "They neglected to cover their tracks." He set his heel in the space and pressed his foot against the bricks. Nothing.

"More pressure," I said. "These things can't be too delicate, or they'd be easily found."

"All right," Kaz grunted, leaning forward as he pressed his foot harder.

A *clunk* came from within the wall. We looked at each other, waiting for something to happen. I leaned in to listen for another sound, my hand resting on the wood.

It was loose.

I pressed the upper part of the column. It gave way slightly, then bounced back, nearly smacking me in the head.

"My god, it's on a swivel," Kaz said as the column stopped with the top about a foot out from the wall. As Kaz shined his light, I reached up, grasped a chain hooked to the beam, and traced it back. It hung on a hook, and as soon as I worked it free, we were able to lower the top of the beam toward the ground.

"Brilliant," Kaz said as he cast his light into the narrow opening, which was a foot wide at best. He slid through, and I followed, going sideways. The chamber opened up as we turned right, revealing a space about eight feet long and four feet wide. Along one wall, a couple of tarpaulins were draped over what had been hidden away. We pulled at the canvas and were rewarded with the gleam of treasure, or at least what the Right Club would consider precious.

Blocks of Noble 808. Boxes of pencil detonators. A dozen Thompson submachine guns. Colt .45 automatic pistols. Plenty of ammo. Folded neatly on top of the pile were two flags. One was the red-and-blue banner of the British Union of Fascists. The other, red as well, sported the black swastika.

"This could have done a lot of damage," Kaz said.

"It already has," I said as I threw the Nazi flag to the floor. "It's gotten people who live in a democracy to embrace and fight for fascism."

"People who don't know the value of what they have," Kaz said. "I don't see any treasure, do you?"

"Treason, but no treasure."

I dashed upstairs to call Chief Inspector Gwynne, who sounded exhausted. He perked up right away when I told him what we'd found, and said he'd leave immediately. Then we asked Captain Haycock to organize the removal of the weapons, which entailed demonstrating how to work the swivel beam in case anyone got closed inside. I stood back, watching Haycock and his men open and close it a few times.

"This all came to you when you found the false side in the desk drawer?" I said to Kaz.

"Well, I had seen the article about the priest holes, but I didn't make the connection until that hidden space in the drawer revealed itself. Very cleverly constructed," he said. "Which is what brought the priest holes to mind."

"What was hidden in the compartment on the other side?"

"The other side? Oh, dear me," Kaz said, slapping his cheek with his hand. "Diana had burst in, and we left in a blazing rush. I never looked."

"You're forgiven," I said as we trotted upstairs to check. "There was a lot going on today."

In the library, Kaz showed me how to access the secret side panel in the middle drawer.

"You press down, like so," he said, and the panel opened on small brass hinges, revealing a narrow cavity, same as the one that had contained Elliot's confession. This side held a single sheet, and the first thing that I saw when I unfolded it was the date.

May 20, 1942. The day the bomber crashed.

The second thing I saw was to whom it was addressed, and as I read, the answer of how Elliot's body got into the bomber blossomed, fully formed, in my mind.

CHAPTER FORTY-FOUR

I FOUND GWYNNE and asked him to come to Seaton Manor in the morning at ten o'clock. I told him about the letter, but I didn't show it to him. It wasn't anything I wanted to introduce as evidence. As a member of Scotland Yard's Special Branch, his priority was rolling up the Right Club members linked to the bomb plot, and he'd accomplished that.

Mildred had cooperated, playing the browbeaten wife card. She'd signed a statement, and afterward, when Gwynne had shown her Elliot's letter implicating her, she shrieked and fainted away. She hadn't said a word since, but Gwynne thought she was faking. Time and a head doctor would tell. We were both too exhausted for much more, and Gwynne promised to lay it all out in the morning.

By the time Kaz and I got back to Seaton Manor, everyone was asleep. Mrs. Rutledge had left a plate of sandwiches and a bottle of whiskey on the kitchen table for us. We ate in silence, the only sound the clinking of crystal.

I fell asleep easily but awoke once from a dream about being lost in dark underground rooms, my heart beating in panic even as I told myself it was only a dream. Sometimes, when you're trapped, the only thing that matters is a way out. That's what happened back in May of 1942, and in the morning light, it was all going to come out.

■ ■ ■

SIR RICHARD WAS up early. I told him about Gwynne's visit at ten and that I had a favor to ask. Dr. Bodkin needed to be here, and I knew Sir Richard wasn't keen on having the man in his house. I thought it was time for Sir Richard to get over it, though I didn't put it that way. I told him he'd understand why in a few hours, but that it was important. He agreed more readily than I'd expected, and even volunteered to call Bodkin himself as soon as the sun was a bit higher above the horizon.

Diana came downstairs soon after and found me in the dining room, working on my second cup of coffee.

"Fancy a stroll?" I asked.

"All the way to the barn," she said. "You can help me with the horses."

"Something important happening?" Diana asked as we walked outside, glancing at my Class A uniform.

"The occasion called for it," I said, and told her about Gwynne's upcoming visit. "We found the weapons at Marston Hall—in a priest hole that Elliot had discovered years ago. We also found a letter hidden in his desk."

As we brought hay to each stall, I told her what Elliot had written.

"My god, Billy. Did you have any idea?"

"The play got me thinking, with all that plotting about name changes, succession, and family lines," I said. "But I never saw this coming, not by a long shot."

"Who would have?" she said, and as we finished with the morning meal of grass and hay, I gave Dante a rub.

"Thanks," I said, "for coming to my rescue."

"Are you talking to me or my horse?" Diana said.

I gave her a wink and let her wonder.

THE CLOCK IN the foyer finally chimed ten as people gathered in the sitting room. Sir Richard had announced Gwynne's upcoming visit at breakfast, and curiosity drew everyone together quickly. Angelika and Agnes sat on the couch, with Big Mike standing by. Diana sat next to her father, and Kaz perched on a chair in the corner, watching everyone. I hadn't filled in Big Mike, since it wasn't a tale I wanted to tell too many times.

Mrs. Rutledge went to answer the knock at the door, and I could hear the surprise in her voice as she greeted Dr. Bodkin along with Chief Inspector Gwynne.

"Is Sir Richard expecting you, Doctor?" I heard her say.

"I am," Sir Richard said in a loud voice as he rose from his chair. "Chief Inspector, Doctor, welcome."

Gwynne took the empty chair by the door, and there was an audible gasp or two as Bodkin offered his hand to Sir Richard. Then a sigh of relief when he took it and gave a nod of acknowledgment.

"Well, well," Mrs. Rutledge muttered as Bodkin sat next to Agnes on the couch.

"Please," Gwynne said to Mrs. Rutledge, noticing he'd taken the last seat. "I shan't be long."

"You have news, Chief Inspector?" Sir Richard said once everybody was settled.

"I do," Gwynne said, clasping his hands behind his back. "With the able assistance of Miss Seaton, Baron Kazimierz, Captain Boyle, and First Sergeant Miecznikowski, we were able to thwart a plot to blow up a cottage at Sandringham House while the royal family was in residence. Normally, this would not be an event we at Special Branch would discuss openly. But seeing as you've all heard one account or another by now, I thought I would do you the courtesy of informing you as to the outcome. With the understanding, of course, that this information must never be revealed. Aid and comfort to the enemy is not what we wish to offer, is it?"

"Not at all, and I can vouch for the silence of all those under my roof," Sir Richard said as we all agreed.

"Of that I have no doubt. As you know, Alfred Bunch and his cousin Nigel Fernsby were both killed as we attempted to apprehend them. Mildred Bunch is implicated as well, and based on her testimony, we are picking up other conspirators this very day," Gwynne said.

"What about David Archer?" Sir Richard asked. "Was his death connected to all this?"

"Yes. Mr. Archer had seen a man with Alfred several times, one Freddie Leese."

"Leese?" Sir Richard said, picking up on the name.

"Nephew of Arnold Leese, head of the Imperial Fascist League," Gwynne said, "recently out of prison and already at work for the cause. We have Freddie, but he's not talking. In any case, Mildred said Freddie pressured Alfred into killing David Archer before Archer spotted Freddie again. Freddie was worried that Archer was working with Special Branch. Alfred tried to explain the situation, according to Mildred anyway, but Freddie was adamant. So Alfred used the cover of those V-2s sailing overhead to murder the poor soul."

"David Archer tried to tell me," I said. "He said I didn't understand."

"Right," Gwynne said. "He may even have seen the explosives being transferred for all we know. Alfred overheard Archer's words to you that night in the pub and decided to do the deed right then, before Archer managed to explain himself."

"They could have let him live," Sir Richard said. "People paid him no mind, and he wasn't the most coherent chap, even at his best."

"What about Stephen Elliot?" Diana asked, doing a good job of not looking at anyone in the room.

"Ah, well. It's thanks to Mr. Elliot that we had documentation of the Bunches' role and a list of what was stored in the weapons cache. Apparently, Elliot had been associated with the Right Club early on and offered a hiding place within Marston Hall for the arms and bombs. A priest hole, according to the baron, who did fine work discovering it," Gwynne said. "We have a letter dated the same day as the crash of that bomber, in which Elliot disavowed himself of the plot and listed everything hidden at Marston Hall. It was never finished, and I conclude that he was interrupted in the writing of it by the crash. He went out to see it, only to have the misfortune of encountering Mildred and Alfred Bunch."

"You know this, I trust, from Mildred," Sir Richard said. "But why should she have confessed anything?"

"She laid it all at the feet of her husband," Gwynne said. "Not yet having been apprised of his demise. She said Alfred knew Elliot was no longer enthusiastic and had demanded that the weapons be moved into his safekeeping at Marston Hall. There was an argument, blows were exchanged, and Elliot fell back, striking his head."

"Did she say what happened to the pilot?" I asked.

"Yes," Gwynne said. "The German was dazed and on his knees, having crawled out of the aircraft. Elliot was helping him when Alfred and Mildred arrived. As soon as Alfred killed Elliot, he told Mildred they couldn't leave a witness. He bashed in the pilot's head with a rock and rolled him over the cliff and into the Wash."

"Enemy or not, the man was a prisoner and should have been treated as such," Sir Richard said. "Elliot was in the right on that, at least."

"What about the emerald Billy found at the Bunches' place?" Big Mike asked. "Was that from King John's treasure?"

"No. That was actually peridot, a family hand-me-down and a lesser gem," Gwynne said. "When you seek treasure, it can be easy to see only what you expect." He had me there.

"But Elliot was looking for treasure all along, wasn't he?" Sir Richard asked.

"As far as we can tell. When he first started, he focused on the Wash. Then he concluded some of it was hidden in the old foundation of Marston Hall," Gwynne said. "He did discover the priest hole in his search, but Mildred says it was empty. I take her at her word, since at that time she and Alfred worked and lived at Marston Hall. If she knew of any treasure, returning it to the Crown might help to reduce her sentence."

Plenty of people had been searching for treasure at Marston Hall, but they'd all been looking for something different.

"Chief Inspector, I hear we won't be seeing Colonel Cheatwood around any longer," I said.

"The colonel has been relieved of his command. A complaint about impropriety, as I understand it," Gwynne said. "I think that covers everything, and now I must go. I can say that as of today, the murder investigations of David Archer and Stephen Elliot are officially closed, by order of the Norfolk Constabulary and Scotland Yard. Again, please keep everything in confidence. Good day to you all."

As Gwynne made his way outside, a murmur ran through the room.

"But what about Elliot's body turning up in the bomber?" Angelika asked. "Did I miss something?"

"Maybe Alfred put it there," Agnes offered, smoothing down her skirt.

"No, Alfred didn't put it there," I said, standing and taking Gwynne's spot by the door. It gave me an excellent view of everyone's faces as well as blocking the exit.

"Who did then?" Big Mike asked. "And why?"

"Dr. Bodkin, you took an interest in Agnes's life the day she was born, didn't you?" I stated.

"Of course I did," Bodkin said. He sat up straight and rubbed his chin, seeming to organize his thoughts before going on. "I told you, her mother asked me with her dying breath to do so. How could I refuse? Even if I had wished to."

"Her mother, Virginia Day Sallow," I said. "Why did you drop your last name, Agnes?"

"I did it when I was older and moved back here," she said, her brow wrinkled in confusion. "I didn't want gossip trailing me. It felt like a way to be close to my mother while hiding my connection to that man."

"Stephen Elliot, the man who never acknowledged he'd violated your mother. Who fired her once she was with child. Who never acknowledged you," I said.

"What is the point of this, Captain?" Bodkin said. "Everyone in Slewford knows what kind of man he was." His face flushed red with anger, then his hand shook for a moment.

"I have the same question, Billy," Sir Richard said. "What is your purpose? The inspector said the case was closed."

"It is, and I'm glad of that, but we still need to clear up a few things," I said. "Agnes, you never told us you went to the party at Marston Hall. The party where Diana was attacked."

"Good god, man," Bodkin said. "Stop."

"You helped Victoria, the serving girl that Elliot first went after," I said. "You went to get her coat for her, and you were going to walk her home. But then Elliot found you. A young girl, alone."

"I don't want to talk about it," Agnes said, burying her face in her hands. "Please."

"Victoria told us the story," I said, "of how you got Elliot to stop pawing you. You put your hands on his face and said something. What was it?"

Agnes said nothing at first. Then her hands slipped from her face, and she gave me a steady stare.

"That I was his daughter," Agnes whispered. "His and Virginia Sallow's. He didn't know. How could he?"

"Blighter," Sir Richard muttered.

"He had been, definitely," I said. "But he changed after that, Agnes, didn't he?"

"He did," she said, leaning her head on Bodkin's shoulder as she wept. "He really did."

"Agnes, how did he change?" Angelika asked, moving closer and taking Agnes by the hand. "I have heard only bad things. Was there something decent we do not know?"

"Please, tell them," Agnes said to Bodkin. "Please."

"I will, my dear," Bodkin said, sitting up straight as Angelika put her arm around Agnes. "Elliot came to me, knowing I was the one person in Slewford who knew the truth about Agnes. He'd refuted paternity all his life, but he admitted that when Agnes confronted him during the attack, he knew without a doubt that it was true and part of him had always known it."

"He could no longer deny it," Agnes said, her voice barely a murmur.

"Right," Bodkin continued. "He was devastated by what he'd done. I had never seen the man take responsibility for anything in his life, but the attack on Agnes had finally registered as something terrible. 'A stain on his very soul' was how he put it."

"Is that why he joined the service?" Sir Richard asked.

"That was one consequence," Bodkin said. "He was over the age for conscription, so it was done voluntarily."

"Tell us about the other consequence," I said. Bodkin stared at me, wondering how I knew or if I was fishing.

"He wrote out a will," Bodkin said. "Passing on Marston Hall to his daughter. But there was a stipulation."

"I could never say anything about the attack," Agnes said, shaking herself awake. "If anyone ever brought it up and I failed to deny it, the will was null and void."

"Damned odd will," Big Mike said.

"I didn't want any part of it at first," Agnes said. "But Dr. Bodkin said it was my birthright and that I deserved it."

"The stipulation was a sign of his shame," Bodkin said. "I can't say I approved, but I understood."

"You both saw the will?" I asked, wondering if somehow we'd made it forfeit by forcing this conversation.

"He showed it to me," Bodkin said. "Agnes was still too shaken to be in his presence, regardless of the change in his nature. Elliot said he was going to send it to his solicitor within a few days, along with some other legal documents. He vanished the next day. Afterward, I contacted the solicitor, but he said he'd received no will from Stephen Elliot."

"Was there provision for his sister?" I asked.

"Yes. Mrs. Mothersole was to receive a cash settlement and the cottage in which she now lives," Bodkin said.

"Billy, I am glad to hear of Elliot's change of heart. Truly, I am," Sir Richard said. "But where does this get us? Do you know the whereabouts of the will?"

"No. And that was the problem you faced on the night of the twentieth of May, wasn't it?" I said, looking at Agnes and Dr. Bodkin.

"What?" Bodkin said, his jaw slack, his eyes blinking in fear.

"As far as I can determine, you and Agnes, who was acting as your nurse, arrived at the crash scene right after Alfred and Mildred left," I said. "Tell us what you found."

"It was horrible," Agnes said, looking to Bodkin, who nodded for her to proceed. "We found him—my father—dead on the ground. Dr. Bodkin realized the will had likely not been sent. And it was not with him."

"Leaving Stephen Elliot intestate, for all practicable purposes," I said. "Without a will naming Agnes as his beneficiary, or any document acknowledging her as his daughter, his nearest living relative would inherit. Do I have that right under English law?"

"Precisely," Sir Richard said. "You're not implying that Charlotte was involved, are you?"

"Not at all," I said. "She probably had no idea. But the two of you came up with a plan. Agnes was about to lose any chance of inheriting. Charlotte, as his sister, would be the only person to go through his personal effects. There was no way to be certain how she would react. Perhaps you didn't trust her to keep the will."

"Holy cow," Big Mike said, connecting the dots. "You wanted time to look for it, to delay any inheritance."

"It was all my idea," Bodkin said. "Elliot was already dead, and the flames would soon overwhelm the aircraft. The fire in the engine had been smothered somewhat by the earth that had been thrown up during the crash landing, but it was still lively enough to spread. We had only moments, and I realized that if Elliot disappeared, we would have time to search for the will. Even if Agnes had to wait years for her father to be declared dead, Marston Hall would still be hers, and I would have fulfilled my pledge to her mother."

"I agreed . . . and helped," Agnes said, her voice remarkably calm. "I consigned my father to the fire."

"I'm sorry you had to go through that," I said, kneeling in front of Agnes. "It was dangerous too. The plane went over the edge right after that, didn't it?"

"It did," Bodkin said, patting Agnes's hand. "Right after we climbed down off it. The flames never got to Elliot, but the tide carried the plane into the Wash. Ironic, isn't it? That Stephen Elliot should end up there after all his searching for the king's treasure."

"Are you going to go to the police with this?" Sir Richard demanded in a tone that told me he wanted these sleeping dogs to dream on in peace.

"No. You heard the chief inspector. The case is closed. All I'm going to do is give this to Agnes." I withdrew the letter from my pocket and handed it to her. "Gwynne mentioned a document your father was writing the night the bomber crashed, the one about what the Right Club was planning. My guess is that document, along with the will, was what he originally planned to send to his solicitor. But this letter was even more important to him. Read it."

Agnes unfolded the sheet and began to read. At first her eyes widened, then her lower lip trembled, followed by a gulping sob that quickly overwhelmed her.

"My father," she said, tears streaming down her cheeks. "My father."

"When the time came, he was a man trying to undo his wrongs," I said.

Agnes clutched the letter to her heart, a smile finally emerging through the glistening tears. She didn't want to read the letter out loud, but she gave it to Dr. Bodkin and asked him to convey the gist of it.

"He wrote that he has just burned the will," Bodkin began. "He was so used to manipulating people that he thought he had to force Agnes to not reveal what had happened. He'd grown uncomfortable with that and realized it was unworthy of him to place any stipulation on Agnes. In this letter, he openly acknowledges her as his daughter by Virginia Sallow. He asks that she provide for Charlotte in whatever way she sees fit, since he trusts in Agnes's decency and judgment more than his own. He goes on to say he has other wrongs to right."

"And that he cares for me," Agnes said, her voice quavering with emotion. "My father loved me, if only at the end."

"He was ready to go to the authorities about the activities of the Right Club," I said. "Which is what got him killed." He'd had a change of heart, too late in life for my liking, but if it gave Agnes comfort, I was ready to let her have it.

"One thing you should know," Kaz said, "is that if his body had not reappeared as it did, this investigation never would have been launched, and his wish to reveal the plot would not have been realized. Nor would we have found this letter. It is as if he came back to finish what he'd started."

"What a strange world we live in," Bodkin said. "Sir Richard, what is your opinion on the legality of this letter?"

"Is it signed?" Sir Richard asked. Bodkin said it was. "Then, as Stephen Elliot died intestate, according to the law, his closest relative is his daughter, legitimate or otherwise. Therefore Agnes Day inherits Marston Hall."

■ ■ ■

THERE WAS A subdued celebration at lunch. Reliving the events of that night in 1942 had to have been tough on Agnes, and Dr. Bodkin as well. I'd apologized earlier for bringing it out as I did, but I'd known it was better for both if they told the story themselves. Now it was out in the open to a group of people they could depend on for support when Agnes claimed her birthright.

Dr. Bodkin was welcomed to the table. Diana was sitting next to her father but stood and beckoned Dr. Bodkin to take her chair. As he took his seat, both men looked away awkwardly. The first glass of wine smoothed out any embarrassment, and soon they were talking like chums.

"Old grudges are the best grudges," I whispered to Diana. "There's so much more to catch up on."

"Catching up," Kaz said from across the table, "is something the two of you need to do now that this affair is concluded. I've called the Dorchester, and my suite will be at your disposal for whatever leave is left to us. I shall remain here and spend more time with Angelika."

"Thanks, Kaz," I said. "That sounds perfect. How about it, Diana?"

"My bags are already packed," she said, raising her glass to Kaz. "I'm ready for London. Who knows? We may all be back here for Christmas."

Home for Christmas. How many soldiers, sailors, and airmen were having that same thought right now? The Germans were on the run, retreating everywhere.

"Here's to a happy New Year," I said, and raised my glass. It was already empty. Bad luck, if you believed in that sort of thing.

HISTORICAL NOTE

THE RITCHIE BOYS were part of a Military Intelligence Service project to interrogate German prisoners of war. Over 15,200 servicemen were trained for these duties at Camp Ritchie in Maryland, with that name becoming synonymous with the specialized, and classified, program. About 2,200 of the Ritchie Boys were German or Austrian Jews, many of whom came to the United States as children, often without their parents. As natural-born German speakers, their expertise in the language and understanding of German behavior made them highly valued and effective interrogators. Ritchie Boys worked at every level, from frontline units to headquarters and POW centers such as the fictional Marston Hall. A postwar intelligence study attributed 60 percent of actionable intelligence in the European theater to the Ritchie Boys, and their job was not without danger. In the opening days of the Battle of the Bulge, Kurt Jacobs and Murray Zappler, Ritchie Boys attached to the 106th Infantry Division, were captured when their unit was overrun. One of the former German prisoners identified the two men to his commander as "Jews from Berlin." The commander had them shot on the spot. That Nazi officer was himself apprehended and executed after a court-martial in 1945.

Fans of Dorothy L. Sayers and her Lord Peter Wimsey mysteries may recognize Captain Ian Carmichael as the actor who portrayed the aristocratic sleuth in *Masterpiece Theatre*. Carmichael did serve in the Royal Armoured Corps with the 22nd Dragoons as an officer in charge of mine-clearing tanks. He did lose a fingertip to a tank hatch, explaining his penchant for being photographed with one hand in his pocket. It is my invention, but one consistent with the historical record, that Captain Carmichael consulted with the Ritchie Boys to gain intelligence for an advance in Holland. While he was not of the aristocratic class, his father being an optician, his speech, as I wrote it, does sound a bit like Lord Peter at times. I took this from his delightful autobiography, *Will the Real Ian Carmichael*, which is written in a breezy and witty tone. Perhaps it was an affectation he developed over the years, but it fit him so well that I tried to be true to it. Besides, it was great fun.

Less amusing was the story of the British Union of Fascists, the Right Club, and the Imperial League of Fascists. Oswald Mosley's BUF is the most well-known, with over fifty thousand members at its height. As the war neared, Mosley became even more extreme and anti-Semitic. Mosley and over seven hundred other fascists were jailed in 1940.

The Right Club was organized as a home for those who found the BUF to be too mild in their stance on Jews. Its leader, Archibald Ramsay, introduced the 1275 Statute of Jewry to the House of Commons as soon as he was released from prison. Arnold Leese (along with his fictional nephew, Freddie), also dissatisfied with the BUF and wishing to push his own brand of virulent anti-Semitism, formed the Imperial Fascist League. All of these extreme right-wing groups favored the Duke of Windsor (the former King Edward VIII), who was a Nazi sympathizer. Historians generally agree that Hitler would have reinstated Edward as king had a German invasion of Great Britain been successful. Each of these groups plotted in one way or another to place themselves at the center of a Nazi puppet state, hoping for a German victory early in the war.

In Chapter Eleven, Billy recounts the story of a veteran of the

First World War in South Boston who walked with a constant high-stepping motion due to his traumatic experience on a sinking ship. That memory is based on the true story of Edward Mucci of Southington, Connecticut. He walked the streets of my hometown in exactly the same manner, never taking a normal step. Eddie's gait was due to having to step over hatchways as he scrambled to escape a sinking submarine during World War II. I was about twelve years old when I encountered him and saw the psychic wounds of war for the first time. I've never forgotten Eddie Mucci.

King John did lose the crown jewels crossing the Wash in 1216. By all accounts, the Wash in that century was extensive and treacherous, yet it was routinely crossed, with guides leading travelers across solid sandbars at low tide. But a baggage train guarded by three thousand men takes a long time to move through soft sand, and chroniclers agree that King John's troops were caught in an unusually heavy onrushing tide. The description from *Roger of Wendover's Flowers of History: Comprising the History of England from the Descent of the Saxons to A.D. 1235* is an accurate accounting of what Wendover listed, but not all historians are on the same page. Some claim that the list is correct, but that John did not take it all on that ill-fated trip. However, many items detailed there have never been seen again. Where is the treasure?

No one knows.

ACKNOWLEDGMENTS

ONCE AGAIN, I owe a debt of thanks (for many things) to my wife, Deborah Mandel, who has listened to every line of this book read aloud and has done a thorough job of reading and editing the first draft. She makes me look good. As do first readers Liza Mandel and Michael Gordon, who have provided meaningful feedback and are also superb typo hunters.

I am also lucky to work with the highly professional and supportive staff at Soho Press. They work their magic on everything from editing, book design, and publicity, and they do it with panache.

My agent, Paula Munier of Talcott Notch Literary Services, is the best guide I could ask for as we navigate the world of publishing to bring these stories to life.

I owe much to the intrepid booksellers at independent bookstores across the country. So much of the success of this series is due to their efforts. The same goes for you, dear reader, especially those of you who've been at Billy's side throughout this journey. You're why we're still here, and why there's more to come.

Thank you, all.